A POISONED MIND

NATASHA COOPER

SIMON & SCHUSTER

LONDON • NEW YORK • TORONTO • SYDNEY

First published in Great Britain by Simon & Schuster, 2008
A CBS COMPANY

1 3 5 7 9 10 8 6 4 2

Simon & Schuster UK Ltd
Africa House
64–78 Kingsway
London WC2B 6AH

www.simonsays.co.uk

Simon & Schuster Australia
Sydney

A CIP catalogue record for this book is available from the British Library

ISBN 978-0-7432-9547-5

Typeset by Rowland Phototypesetting Ltd, Bury St Edmunds, Suffolk
Printed and bound by CPI Mackays, Chatham

A POISONED MIND

Also by Natasha Cooper

CREEPING IVY
FAULT LINES
PREY TO ALL
OUT OF THE DARK
A PLACE OF SAFETY
KEEP ME ALIVE
GAGGED & BOUND
A GREATER EVIL

For
the Carters
with love

Acknowledgements

As always many friends and experts have helped me as I wrote this novel. They include Suzanne Baboneau, Mary Carter, Emma Dunford, Jane Gregory, Gerald and Alison Johnson, Gavin Parfitt and Libby Vernon.

Prologue

Angie Fortwell looked out at the most beautiful view in the British Isles and hated it. The land that sloped gently away from the grey stone farm buildings was hers, hers and John's, and she had once loved it more than anywhere else on earth.

Old oaks, toughened by centuries of battering rain and wind, led down towards the little lough, where the wild duck slept. Sometimes a flat silver sheet, the water was yeasty tonight as the wind lashed its surface. But the wool of the sheep lying nearer the house was too tightly curled to move. They looked like lumps of whitish fat dotted about under the trees. Over everything, the moon cast a spooky bluish glaze.

A hardness in the junction between the shivering trees and the sky suggested yet another frost. Who'd have thought it could be so cold in April, even in Northumberland? Indoors, the Aga helped, but only if you were actually leaning against it. Otherwise the high ceiling sucked all the warm air away, and chill from the stone-flagged floor reached right up through your shoes and socks.

Still, tonight Angie's hands were warm from the washing-up. She let them rest in the water, seeing even through the suds the calluses and cuts every farmer had. John's hands were the same; and she was pretty sure his heart had broken as long ago as hers. But they never talked about that sort of thing these days, just as they no longer looked for an escape from the disaster they'd made of their lives. In a weird way the piling-on of problems had formed a kind of glue between them, and the words they'd recited in the London church all those years ago had come true. For richer, for poorer; in sickness and in health; forsaking all other . . .

She said them aloud now, feeling warmth from the repetition as well as from the greasy water. The comfort spread through her until it almost touched the forbidden icy spaces in her mind. Soon he'd be back and they could eat their mutton stew and talk – or not – as the mood took them because there were no walkers booked in tonight.

Even though it was still early in the season, they'd had three separate couples already this week, including one pair who were obviously spying for the Inland Revenue.

They weren't the first investigators Angie had had nosing around, so she'd guessed what they were after as soon as they'd insisted on paying cash and been reluctant to sign her visitors' book. She'd taken enormous pleasure in making them wait while she'd slowly filled out the duplicate invoice form in front of them and insisted they record their full details in the visitors' book. How many times would she have to show the tax-gatherers she was keeping honest records of her pathetic little business? And how much of her hard-earned money were they wasting with these spiteful little traps?

That pair had been gone a couple of days and the last of the others had left this morning, so tonight she and John could have the house to themselves.

Where was he?

She pulled her left hand reluctantly from the hot water to look at her watch. Waterproof and expensive, it was a relic of her old life. Eight o'clock. He was never out this late, except during lambing, and that was over for this year. Maybe one of the sheep had got stuck somewhere inaccessible. Yes, that might be it. A cast sheep. No need to worry about that. And he had Schlep, the old collie, with him. He'd be all right with Schlep.

Or he could be in one of the buildings, working to repair a creaky machine, scraping off the rust one more time in the hope of finding sound metal underneath. But if so, he should have stopped by now. Fit though he was, he'd be fifty-six next month, and he'd been driving himself into the ground for twenty-five years. He needed rest.

Leaning forwards over the sink to peer through the window into the ghostly light, she longed to see his shambling figure, with the old leather-patched coat he always wore swinging around his lean body, Schlep at his side, coming home.

'Sod it!' she shouted, as she felt wet creeping up her front. Her untucked flannel shirt had somehow got itself into the sink and soaked up some of the water.

Pulling it out, she mangled it between her hands, watching the drips fall back into the sink. The Aga would dry it out in no time and there was a clean one of John's on the pulleys above it. She let the ropes run between her hands so she could reach the clean clothes, enjoying the slight burn, and soon had her own shirt unbuttoned.

An almighty crash ripped through the air, like a bomb or something. For an instant she stood there, with her hands on the buttons of her open shirt, trying to understand.

Another explosion. She looked towards the window over the sink and saw the blue light had yellowed, warmed up. It was flickering, too.

Without thinking, she hauled the pulleys back up out of the way, dragged the heavy stewpan off the hotplate and banged down the lid. Her stockinged feet were inside her gumboots a moment later and she was running towards the yellow sparking light. Only the cold on her tight midriff and the slapping sensation told her the wet shirt was still undone. Running, tripping over her boots, she fumbled for the buttons and their holes.

Her throat was burning and her nose filled with a vile, acrid smell. Now she knew what had happened, but not yet how bad it was.

A third crash bit into her eardrums before she was anywhere near the cypress-ringed enclave where the tanks were, but the spurting fountains of sparks that shot up above it were clearly visible, like some multimillionaire's firework display. She could hardly breathe and her heart felt as though a giant had it between his hands and was squeezing, twisting the life out of it just as she'd wrung the water out of her shirt.

Down now, over the edge of the dip where the tanks were, she stopped in front of a vision of hell, both hands over her mouth and nose in a hopeless pretence of keeping out the fumes. Whatever had made the tanks explode had set fire to the great Lawson cypresses they'd planted to disguise the hideous concrete enclosure. As she stood, paralysed, she saw the flames leaping from tree to tree and let her gaze follow. There was a pylon far too close to the furthest. Its dangerous cables festooned over the tip of the tree, almost touching the topmost fronds. Any minute now the fire would reach them too.

John. She forced herself to look away from the cables, searching through the shifting flames. The noise was like a hurricane mixed with the roaring of a cageful of aggressive animals. A gust of wind pushed the flames aside for a second and in the blazing, trembling, terrifying light she saw the two lumps on the ground. Bodies. John and Schlep. It had to be them. The flames came down again and they were hidden.

Even now she couldn't make herself move. Nothing could save them. But she had to get help. She couldn't deal with the fire and the poisons on her own. And someone had to shut down the electricity before the pylon and its cables burst into flames with the rest. A new huge gout of fire rolled towards her. She couldn't see through it and at last turned, lumbering back over the edge of the dip. Why hadn't she picked up her phone as she left the house? How could she have been so stupid as to put on these heavy great boots?

The toe of one caught in a tussock and she sprawled, face in the prickling mud, eyes spurting tears triggered by the chemicals. Her chest felt as though she was being pressed to death. Fighting the urge to give in, she kicked off her boots as she lay, then forced herself up. A drop fell on her face, then another. Thank God! Rain. That should help put out the fire. Ramming her arm across her face, she ran for the house, and the phone, and help.

Chapter 1

'The face of courage,' said the caption under a photograph that made Trish Maguire's teeth ache with sympathy.

Angela Fortwell's spare features were stripped of everything most middle-aged women used to disguise reality. There was no make-up or floppy fringe to soften the harshness of her cheekbones or the lines on her forehead, and no fake colour in the hair itself. She'd kept her own washed-out browny grey, and the ragged ends looked as though she'd cut them with sheep shears. Her eyes, deep set and very dark, looked out of the newspaper with an expression that said '*J'accuse*' more clearly than any headline.

Trish let herself reread the interview, skimming back through the woman's description of how she and her husband had decided over twenty-six years ago to abandon their City jobs for the satisfactions of sheep farming on the fringes of the Northumberland National Park. Some phrases stuck out: 'We wanted our children to breathe clean air and eat honest food. We couldn't have them growing up with all the scary greed we'd found in London.'

How cruel that such a wholesome ambition should have been punished with one disillusion after another, Trish thought.

Having successfully produced a son they called Adam while they were still in London, the Fortwells had never produced another child. The one they had grew up to resent them for what they'd given up. He'd departed at the age of eighteen and cut off all contact. The last line of the interview read: 'He didn't even write or phone when his father was killed. He could be dead, too, for all I know.'

And this was the woman Trish's head of chambers was about to trounce in court. The ache sharpened as she jammed her teeth even more tightly together.

In spite of the barristers' cab-rank rule, which stated that any suitably qualified member of the Bar who was free to take an offered case must do so, Trish wondered how Antony Shelley could bring himself to accept this one. Brilliant and cynical as he was, he'd trot out all the familiar answers if she ever put the question, so she wouldn't bother.

Instead, she contemplated the only task she had this morning and the various ways she might spin it out. She had taken silk earlier in the year, becoming a senior barrister with the grand title of Queen's Counsel, and her practice had suffered in the usual way.

Once you were a silk, you were much more expensive than you'd been as a junior, and you had to have a junior of your own on every case, adding even more to the costs for the client. Few of them would willingly take a risk on an untried QC, but until you'd done a few big cases, you couldn't prove yourself capable.

Trish was used to self-control these days, and to organising her thoughts to stop them destroying her peace. Counting her pleasures usually helped so she set about it now. The most childish was provided by the jealousy of her old rival in chambers, Robert Anstey, who was still a junior.

When the position of QC had been reinstated after a short interval and a great deal of protest, both of them had applied. Only she had succeeded and Robert still couldn't understand how anyone could possibly prefer her to him. After all, he was endowed with everything she lacked: masculinity, a comfortable upbringing amid rich legal connections, a posh voice, public-school education, and three glorious privileged years at Oxford.

She should also have found pleasure in her rare freedom, but that was harder to appreciate. For the first time in years she had unoccupied hours during the day. Once she would have been too busy ever to sit idly like this without having to pay later. Now she could put her feet on her desk and read the newspaper, look forward to a long lunch with Antony, and still know she'd be home in time to organise tea for David, the 14-year-old half-brother who lived with her, and probably for his alarming new schoolfriend too.

The thought of the friend made her swing her feet back to the floor and open her laptop, to look again at the draft of a letter she'd been writing to their head teacher. Several false starts had made her bless the laptop for saving her from all the screwed-up balls of rough paper she would once have chucked in the bin. Eventually she felt she'd achieved the right tone of stern reproof, without descending to insult – or not much insult – but she wanted to be quite sure before she printed and sent it off.

Dear Jeremy,

David has been bringing Jay Smith home for tea most days since the start of term, and we have now come to know each other well enough for him to tell me his place at Blackfriars is only temporary. It was clear he wouldn't be happy answering questions, so I may have some details wrong, but the impression he gave me is that one of the teachers at his old school was so frustrated by his combination of brains and refusal to work that he negotiated for Jay to be given a single term at Blackfriars to see how rich boys are educated, in the hope that it would make him focus on what he was throwing away. If this is true, I am shocked.

From the little Jay's said, I know he has a difficult background, and it's not hard to deduce from his attitude and the few anecdotes he's shared that he must often have been in trouble. He is clearly bright, has a great deal of charm, and has never put a foot wrong while I've been around. But I think the stress of knowing he will soon be sent back to what sounds like the worst of sink schools is undoing any good his time at Blackfriars might have achieved.

I seriously dislike the thought of any child being subjected to the torture of Tantalus, and that's more or less what you're doing to Jay. I believe that, having taken him on, you have a duty to keep him until he has had a chance to take his A levels. I feel so strongly about this that I am willing to share the cost. If you and the governors agree to keep him, I will pay half his fees for the next four years.

Yours ever, Trish Maguire

Even though her earnings had dropped after her recent promotion, she'd been stashing away more than enough over the past few years to cover all Jay's fees and never miss the money, but she was so angry with the way the school had behaved she was determined to make them pay a fair share.

Aware that rage often made her pompous, she went through the letter again and decided the torture of Tantalus was over the top.

What she actually wanted to say was: you've chosen to bring into the school a boy with so many problems he's like an unlit Molotov cocktail. Anything you do to make him angry will be like putting a match to it. If it were not for the fact that my beloved brother likes him and has more or less adopted him, I would leave you to deal with the inevitable disaster yourself. As it is, I can't.

She rewrote the letter in the simplest style, avoiding the torture of Tantalus and all hints of criticism, decided it would do and faxed it to the school. She was just checking her email in-box when Antony put his head round her door to summon her to lunch. This was his last working day of freedom before he had to go to court to defend Clean World Waste Management, whose exploding chemical tanks had killed Angela Fortwell's husband, and he wanted to make the most of it.

Trish nodded to him, clicked out of the email window, and reached behind her for the new jacket slung across the back of her chair. Its rich chestnut-coloured silk tweed did much more for her pale skin than the black and white she had to wear in court. Over the years, she'd learned to seize any opportunity to sport something brighter, however clearly it might advertise her brief-less status.

'Weird how that bull's-turd colour suits you,' Antony said as they emerged from chambers into the late autumn sun.

Ignoring him, she turned her face up to the warmth. This was one of those special London days, when the air tasted clean, the sun shone in a bright blue sky, and the trees still held on to some of their newly reddened leaves. The ones that had already fallen were neatly swept into piles awaiting collection.

Trish loved their smell. The spiciness might be the product of rot, but it always made her think of childhood firework parties, and roasting apples with the sugar slowly turning to caramel.

'If George were here,' Antony went on as they strolled towards his favourite restaurant, 'he'd be reciting Keats's "Ode to Autumn". "Season of mists and mellow fruitfulness" and all that.'

Trish shot a quick sideways glance at him. Whenever she'd seen him with her partner the two men had got on perfectly well, which was hardly surprising given that George was a successful London solicitor and they had a lot of friends in common, but Antony rarely passed up any opportunity to tease her about George's more stolid qualities.

'His taste's a bit less obvious than that,' she said, trying not to sound defensive. 'And it's not his fault anyway. It's the kind of British-Empire family he comes from. They brought him up to use poetry for all the feelings proper chaps aren't meant to have. *Other Men's Flowers* and all that.'

Antony laughed. 'You always rise to the bait, Trish, even now after – what? Ten years?'

'Not quite. But getting on that way.'

'How's it going?'

'Great,' she said, without explanation.

She'd passed through several stages with George, none of which she would choose to describe to anyone else and some of which had been pretty rough. Now they'd both regained their sense of humour, and they lived in a state of emotional comfort that still seemed extraordinary. They knew who they were and why they had come together in the first place. Trish also knew that, whatever happened, she could trust George. She hoped the same was true for him.

'What are you thinking about?' Antony asked, pushing open the door of the restaurant so that she could precede him.

'The menu,' she said and knew from his familiar snort that he didn't believe her for a second.

Angie was standing in the kitchen of Fran and Greg's first-floor flat in Kentish Town, gaping at the heaps of files they'd filled as they'd worked to prepare her case against the people responsible for John's death.

'What's the matter, love?' Fran said, tossing a swathe of silky red-blonde hair over her ample shoulder. 'You look like you've seen a ghost.'

Angie shook her head and rubbed a hand over her eyes, feeling the edge of an ancient callus snag on her eyelid. Next to Fran's magnificence, she felt dried-up and old.

'I just don't know what I've done to deserve all this,' she said, waving at the files before she remembered her ugly hands. She stuffed them in her pockets. 'Without you two, I'd be stuck up there on the farm, writing my useless letters to people who couldn't care less about John or the farm or me, and wondering whether I'd starve before the cancer got me.'

The temperature in the heart of the fireball had been high enough to destroy the carcinogenic benzene there, but plenty had been left on the fringes of the explosion to leach into the ground and poison the watercourses. And the rain that had seemed like a godsend at the time had actually made everything far worse, diluting the fire crew's foam and spreading the pollution far and wide.

Fran leaned over to give her a kiss. 'And without you, I'd still be handing out our leaflets in shopping centres, knowing hardly anyone would bother to read them or understand why companies like CWWM have to be stopped before they destroy the whole world with their filthy chemicals.'

'She's right, you know,' Greg said, pushing a stoneware mug towards Angie. 'If you hadn't been brave enough to risk everything by being a litigant in person, we'd never have got them into court.'

Angie nodded her thanks for the tea and he beamed before returning to the cooker to stir his pan of bean stew. Steam billowed out, scented with onions and herbs, which made her realise how hungry she was.

Enough to enjoy another compost heap of vegetables? she asked herself with a disloyal spurt of silent laughter.

'What's so funny?' Fran asked, sounding hurt enough to need an answer.

'I was just thinking how much John would have liked you.' These days Angie could usually say his name aloud without crying or feeling as though someone had her guts on a hook and was slowly pulling them out of her, but it had taken a long time. 'And yet how hard he'd have had to work to stop himself quarrelling with you.'

'Quarrelling? Why? He sounds like such a good man.'

'He was, and he'd have loved your generosity, and the way you care so much.' Angie enjoyed Fran's smile and hoped it would last. 'But he would have had difficulties with some of your principles.'

Greg stopped stirring and turned to look over his shoulder again. His brown eyes were oddly set, with one apparently higher than the other, which often made it hard to read his expression.

'Like what?' he said.

'He claimed that if everyone went back to eating meat we'd get our farm in profit again *and* save the planet.'

'I don't understand.' Greg's eyes looked as vulnerable as a new lamb's and his voice was puzzled. Angie wished she didn't have to spell it out.

'Well, one of the chief causes of global warning is methane. And you know how a diet of beans—'

Fran managed to laugh, but Greg didn't. Angie wondered if he was about to explain that cows produce more methane than any other living creature.

'Was money so very tight?' he said after a short tricky silence.

'It gave us nightmares for years.' Angie had lost all desire to laugh. 'That's why John cancelled all the insurance policies, which is why I *have* to win this case if I'm ever to get enough money to make the farm habitable again.'

'You will win,' Fran said, stroking Angie's bony wrist. 'And you'll get justice for John. When it's over no one will ever again be able to say his death was an accident.'

'I hope to God you're right.'

In the first terrible aftermath of the fire, Angie had assumed the police would charge the directors of CWWM with murder, or manslaughter at the very least. When she'd heard nothing from them, she'd written to everyone with any kind of power, from the local Chief Constable to the head of the Crown Prosecution Service, her MP and the Prime Minister, begging them to help. No one had done anything except tell her to wait until after the official investigation.

None of the lawyers she'd approached had been prepared to help either. All of them had wanted to know the results of the official inquiries before they decided whether to act for her without money up front. Legal Aid hadn't been available. She was too asset-rich to get that, which would have been funny if it hadn't been so cruel. The fire had made the farm and the land even less saleable than they'd been when she and John had first tried to find a buyer for the wreck of their broken dream.

Close to despair, she'd started to look up the friendlier of her old City contacts, most of whom were now chairing multinationals and quangos. Some had been sympathetic but none had seen a way to help. One had even written to criticise her 'vindictive attempt to pillory CWWM', adding:

> It really won't help to use emotive words like 'murder'. Whatever happened to the tanks, John was not murdered. Stick with reality and you'll do better.
>
> I know you, Angie. You let your temper ride you at the slightest possible opportunity. Give yourself a chance *this time* and ignore it. Wait for the official report, not least because you could get far more compensation then than if you push for a sum now.
>
> In case your financial situation is too parlous to wait, I'm enclosing a cheque to tide you over.

If he hadn't reminded her about the past consequences of her awful temper she might have seen the generosity in his cheque. As it was all she'd noticed was how patronisingly he'd phrased his letter. She'd torn up both and sent the pieces back, telling him charity was no good to her; she wanted justice.

Only the next day she'd had the first approach from Fran, offering both sympathy and the practical help of her small pressure group, Friends Against the Destruction of the Environment, which she'd explained was known as FADE. Angie could still remember how she'd leaned back against the cold Aga, reading and rereading Fran's letter, looking for the trick in it because by then she'd learned never to rely on anyone, except her best friend Polly Green.

But it had been genuine. Over the next months, Fran had become a real friend. Greg was kind too, although he didn't have Fran's lovely powerful warmth or her ability to laugh at all the right moments, and their flat had turned into far more of a home than the empty farmhouse with its agonising echoes of John.

Angie looked round the bright kitchen now, watching them work, occasionally turning to smile at her or say something easy and unimportant she could answer without thinking.

In the far-off days of her City career, when she and John had been high-spending young stars of corporate finance, she would have looked down on this Housing Association two-bedroom, first-floor flat in one of the grottier areas of Kentish Town. Now, with the laborious years stretching out behind her, she felt cradled in luxury at the very thought of the shabby refuge, with its hot water on demand, bus stop right outside the front door and tube station an easy walk away.

Chapter 2

'Stop looking like Oliver Cromwell,' Antony said as he poured a generous slug of garnet-coloured wine into Trish's glass. 'I know you disapprove of my extravagance, but I've been working like a dog on preparation for CWWM and I deserve my treat before we embark on the actual fight.'

'Sorry,' she said. 'I didn't mean to spoil it.'

She took a mouthful of wine and let its rich flavours distinguish themselves against her tongue. Writers who used words like tobacco and leather and chocolate to describe wine often irritated her, but with a complex, exciting mouthful like this, she could understand why they did it. Swallowing, she smiled.

'Delectable. And if I was frowning, it was nothing to do with the wine. I just can't stop thinking of that poor woman and everything she's been through. She's got nothing left. If you do your usual stuff, she won't even have the satisfaction of seeing CWWM beaten.'

Antony's lean face creased. His turquoise eyes glittered. She waited for the tease.

'I don't know how you've survived at the Bar this long,' he said. 'Caring for your clients to the point of derangement is bad enough; but to start fretting over the opposition . . .'

'Not being involved in this case means she's not *my* opposition.'

Antony was drinking as she spoke. Anyone watching his face would have thought there was something wrong with the wine.

'A Freudian slip,' he said. 'If you hadn't managed to get silk, you'd be my junior this time too, and I'd be a lot happier.'

Memories of all the cases they'd fought together and the fun they'd had, as well as the bitter desperate arguments, made her eyes go fuzzy. Had she been stupid to give up all that, and the pleasure involved in being the admired second-in-command to a brilliant and hugely successful man, for the dubious satisfactions of becoming a so-far unemployable QC?

'Robert's a fine lawyer,' he said, watching her with an unreadable expression in his eyes. 'And he's done a good job on the preparation; but he's not you. I've always felt more comfortable with you behind me than anyone else. And with a case like this we can't possibly win, I'd—' His eyelids fell, hiding whatever message they might have carried. 'I have to be glad you got silk – for you – but for myself I'm seriously pissed off.'

'That's like kicking a girl when she's down, you know. I've been wondering how I could have taken such a risk, whether I'll ever rebuild my practice.'

'Of course you will. Don't be a clot. Good: here's the grub, at last.'

The waiter put down their plates. On each was a plump partridge, sitting on its little cushion of cabbage, belly pork and chipolata. Thin aromatic gravy was offered in a silver sauceboat. This was exactly the kind of grand, old-fashioned, British food Antony enjoyed. Trish, who'd grown up on baked beans and mince, ate it only in his company.

She began to dismember the small bird, asking him as she did it why he didn't believe he could win the case for CWWM. He outlined his reasons with his usual incisiveness, making her wonder whether she would ever find this kind of satisfaction from working with anyone else.

By the time he'd paid the enormous bill and their coats had been retrieved from the waiters' cupboard, Trish felt like going home to sleep. It wasn't so much her small share of the wine as the quantity of food that made her feel flattened. The shock of cold air helped a bit as they emerged on to the pavement, and the brilliant sunshine made her blink herself back into full awareness.

'Shall we get a cab?' he said.

'I ought to walk. Otherwise I'll never shift the calories.'

'Women! OK.' He glanced at his watch. 'But it'll have to be briskish; I need to sort out a few things and get home by four. We're away this weekend.'

Her legs were almost as long as his and she had no trouble keeping up. They walked through Covent Garden, dodging all the street entertainers, shoppers and dawdling tourists, and made their way through the Aldwych to the Strand.

'Hey, Trish!' came a confident female voice just as they were stepping on to the zebra crossing that would take them down into the Temple. She turned, recognised an old friend and stopped to talk.

'Great to see you, Anna. How've you been? And what are you doing here? Not another legal film?'

'Absolutely. And this is a real corker with huge implications. It's an environmental case. We—'

The air was suddenly filled with the stench of burning rubber. A simultaneous mechanical shriek was chased by a human scream, tinkling glass, and then a silence more sinister than all the rest. Only a few seconds could have passed, but Trish felt as though her whole life was unreeling at one thousandth of its normal speed. She turned away from Anna to face the crossing again.

A motorbike lay with its front wheel still spinning as a stocky figure in leathers and huge beetle-like helmet limped forward. Thrown a little way from the bike lay a figure wearing Antony's clothes, with blood spurting from his leg in a bright scarlet arc. The blood was the only thing about his crumpled body that moved. Trish watched the small crowd pressing towards him. A young black man detached himself and bent over the body.

'Don't touch him,' she yelled, her ever-ready imagination drawing pictures of broken vertebrae pulled out of alignment, torturing pain and lifelong paralysis.

She was on her knees beside Antony an instant later, ancient, half-remembered instructions from school first-aid lessons stuttering in her brain.

'We've got to stop the bleeding,' said the young man, who'd been leaning over him. 'It's all I was going to do.'

'Great. You're right. Can you hold his leg, just above where it's coming from? Both thumbs hard down on the leg without pulling at the joint? Oh, have you got a scarf or something? Belt? Tie?'

'No.'

She couldn't waste any time waiting for the rest of the gawpers to come to their senses, so she ripped off her coat.

Too thick to tear or twist. The silk tweed of the jacket was no better. But her shirt would do. Thin striped poplin, it would make a bandage. Not absorbent, but better than nothing. Half the buttons sprang off as she wrenched it away from her body. She twisted it into a rope. The cold puckered the skin of her small breasts, but she couldn't think about that now. Her helper's strong black hands had reduced the bleeding to a trickle.

Moving with terrified care, she slid her shirt-rope under Antony's leg, trying not to joggle the rest of his body. At last she had enough cloth to use and drew both ends up and round his thigh. She twisted them as tightly as she could but knew it wasn't enough.

More memories trickled back and she tied a knot, then grabbed a tough biro from her bag and used it to turn her improvised bandage tighter and tighter, praying the plastic casing wouldn't crack before it had done its work. At last, she could turn it no further, looked at the young man and said:

'I think it's safe to take your hands away.'

She'd forgotten about breathing and couldn't understand why she felt so light-headed. Then as he removed his thumbs she saw the tourniquet was holding and let out the pent-up breath in a single gust.

'Yeah! It works.' His tense face split in a triumphant smile.

The crowd started to clap. Trish ignored them, knowing there was more to be done and scuffled through her bag again. There were no other pens and she didn't carry anything useful like a lipstick. A shadow fell between her and the sun and a woman with an American accent said:

'Use this.'

Squinting upwards, she saw a small gold cylinder being held out, took it, uncapped it and scrawled a large scarlet T on Antony's forehead, checked the time and added that: 2.55. Now no paramedic or doctor would miss the tourniquet or leave it on too long.

'And you might care to borrow my jacket,' said the owner of the lipstick.

Trish put a hand to her thin chest, looked down and realised that she was squatting, half-naked in the middle of the street right outside the Royal Courts of Justice. Thank God she'd put on a reasonably respectable bra this morning.

'Oh, shit!' she said, grabbing the chestnut jacket she'd flung off, and the thicker, darker overcoat. 'It's OK actually. I've got my own here. Thank you very much.'

A siren in the distance made her look up. The crowd hadn't been as useless as she feared. Someone had done the sensible thing and called for an ambulance. She tried to stand and found she couldn't get up. The young black man came to her side. With the American woman on the other, he helped Trish to her feet.

'Thank you both so much.'

'Trish, I don't . . . I couldn't . . . You were so quick,' said Anna Grayling, at last coming to join her.

'It's fine. I—' Trish wiped her hand across her forehead. It came away sweaty. Red, too. She must have just smeared Antony's blood all over her face.

The ambulance pulled up, and blessedly knowledgeable people took over all responsibility for him. Trish turned away from Anna to tell them what had happened and who she was, aware all the time of the biker, now sitting on the kerb with his head in his hands and his helmet by his side. Two uniformed police officers strode towards him. Trish clutched her overcoat more tightly around her and looked back at Anna.

'It's OK,' she said, recognising her friend's impatient need to be elsewhere. 'I know you're busy. Don't hang about. I'll go with him in the ambulance.'

Anna looked embarrassed but relieved as she backed obediently away. Trish peered around her, searching the crowd for the young man who'd helped her with the tourniquet. She wanted to thank him, but when she found him she lost all sense of what she wanted to say and just took his bloody hands and looked up into his face, letting the coat flap.

''s OK,' he said. 'You did great.'

'What's your name? And your address. I know he'll want—'

'No worries. They want me now. See you later.' He walked towards the beckoning police. Trish felt something hard in her hand, she glanced down and saw the gold lipstick case with its mashed red stick. Its owner was standing close by, smiling with amazing benevolence.

'I'm sorry,' Trish said. 'I think it's ruined.'

'That's fine. It was in a good cause.'

'You must let me pay for it.'

'Don't be silly. My small contribution to saving your friend. You did very well.'

Trish felt idiotic tears heating her eyeballs and looked away.

'You did everything anyone could,' the American woman said with deliberation, before adding more lightly: 'But if you are going with him, you should go now.'

Trish gestured to the paramedic who was standing by the open back door of the ambulance. He nodded. She put out her hand. The American was wearing stiff beige suede gloves. Ignoring the blood and mess, she squeezed Trish's hand between both of hers.

'If he lives,' she said, deliberate all over again, 'it'll be because you were here. He's lucky. Stay with him now.'

'I will. Thank you.'

A moment later, Trish was pulling herself up into the ambulance. She smelled disinfectant and was surprised by the dim light and the machinery all round, with its dials and tubes, and the heaviness of the door the paramedic pulled shut on the three of them. Antony's neck was immobilised in a yellow plastic contraption, and he was lying unconscious under a thin red blanket, strapped to a stretcher. Red to hide the blood?

The ambulance swayed as the driver set off. The atmosphere felt strange: official, yet intimate. The paramedic sitting opposite Trish pulled out a clipboard and in a professionally kind voice she recognised from all sorts of other carers, he asked for Antony's name and details.

'He's Antony Shelley QC, head of chambers at 1 Plough Court. He lives in Holland Park.' Her mind began to work again, but jerkily. 'Someone should tell his wife. She's Liz, Elizabeth Shelley. I've got her phone number here.'

'Does she know he's with you?' A hint of curiosity in his voice sharpened her dazed mind even more.

'Of course. I'm a member of his chambers,' she said, at last buttoning her long dark overcoat over her goose-pimpled skin. 'Can I use my phone in here?'

'If it's important.'

She phoned Liz, told her what had happened, heard her gasp and choke back a cry. Trish had to break off her attempt at reassurance to check which hospital was going to receive Antony. Then she phoned Steve, the head clerk at Plough Court to tell him what had happened, assuring him that she'd stay with Antony until Liz got there. At last she could lie back against the fake leather of the banquette and close her eyes, cradling one aching hand in the other.

She could still feel the squeeze of the beige suede gloves and hear the comforting American voice:

'If he lives, it'll be because you were here. He's lucky.'

If, she said to herself, feeling her stiff lips move. If, if, if, if, if, if . . .

Chapter 3

Trish's sleep had been disturbed by menacing dreams and restless legs and once or twice by George's snoring. But it was the ringing phone that woke her properly just before eight on Saturday morning.

As she reached for the receiver, she looked in the opposite direction to see George still asleep with his mouth open

'Hello?' she said quietly, cupping her hand around the receiver to keep the sound from waking him.

'Trish! You don't sound very alert this morning.'

'Antony?' Her dreams had all been of his funeral or wheelchairs and day-long operations. To hear his voice, even slurred like this, made her shiver. Odd that relief could make you feel so wobbly. '*Antony*! Fantastic to hear you. Listen, hang on while I go downstairs to the other phone.'

She replaced the receiver as quietly as possible and slid out from under the duvet. Her dressing gown was in the wash, so she pattered downstairs in nothing but the long T-shirt she wore instead of a nightdress. Its hem barely covered the top of her thighs, but there was no one to see, and she didn't want to waste time.

'Antony,' she said in a more normal voice, sitting down at

her long tidy desk. 'This is just . . . brilliant. How are you feeling?'

'Never mind that. I need you here. You're taking over the CWWM case, and you'll have a lot of work.'

'I can't. I—'

'Trish, I've got a broken neck, ripped artery and concussion, so not much patience. You need a big case. I need someone I trust to—'

'But that poor woman.'

'Don't be sentimental. If you're not here in half an hour, I'll never forgive you.'

A buzz that sounded like a dying bee told her he'd cut her off. The leather of the chair felt horrible under her bare thighs. Her feet were freezing and her long toes looked as bony as a chicken's claws when she glanced down, trying to decide what to do. A loud tick from the kitchen clock marked out the seconds with a remorselessness that matched Antony's.

'Who was that?' George said from above and behind her.

She looked round to see him standing at the top of the spiral staircase, wearing a bath towel like a Roman toga. His dressing gown was in the wash too.

'Antony. Awful injuries, but his mind's as sharp as ever. He wants me to step into the CWWM case.'

George's face, so much less pudgy these days than when she'd first known him, lit up like a beacon.

'But I can't. You know what that woman's been through. How can I think about making money from her misery?'

'Don't be so wet. Or so bloody arrogant!'

Trish flinched. She'd heard his deep voice velvety with affection, springy with laughter and cold with anger often enough; she'd never known it sound as contemptuous as this.

'It's not your job to comfort the whole world. If you turn this down, you'll infuriate the man who's done more to help your career than anyone else; you'll give your clerk every reason to stop trying to get you work; and you'll make *me* exceedingly angry. Whatever you may think about what's-her-name, Angela Fortwell, your job is to represent your clients and put their case as well as it possibly can be put. There's no moral dilemma here, Trish.'

Still she didn't get up.

'This is make or break time. Start moving. I'll get your clothes together while you shower.'

He didn't wait for an answer, just hauled his great towel more tightly over his left shoulder and tramped off.

Trish made herself walk towards the foot of the stairs, feeling contrary ideas jerk forward and back in her brain. He's right. They're both right. And it's not just the unhappy Mrs Fortwell I'm worried about. What if I lose? Antony was sure he would and no one would have thought the worse of him. But if I screw up, everyone'll say it's my fault. George thinks I'm arrogant. I'm not: I'm scared. I owe Antony too much to let him down. But there's David too. And Jay. If I go to work now, I can't let him—

David's voice stopped her and she stood with one bare foot on the bottom stair, looking at him over her shoulder. His dark hair, much thicker than hers, was tousled around his white face, and his black eyes were soft with sleepiness. Already he topped her five feet ten, and his old red pyjama trousers hung a good four inches above his huge feet.

'What's going on?' he said.

'Hi, David. Sorry we woke you. I've got to go to work –

which means, I'm afraid, that you'll have to put Jay off today.'

'*Why?*' David scratched his head and scowled at her from under his ruffled fringe.

'I don't want him here without either me or George, and George is going to Twickenham. We can sort out another weekend for Jay and do something extra special with him to make up.'

'You let Sam be here when you're not. Just because Jay's family's not rich like Sam's, you think he'll nick something. It's not fair, Trish.'

This was too important to ignore, in spite of George's voice from upstairs calling, 'Trish! Hurry up, for God's sake.'

'David, I'll explain what I mean about Jay when I can. It's not that I think he's going to steal our stuff. Honestly. But it's true I don't think it's . . . safe for him to be here with only you. As soon as I've got time, I'll talk it all through with you. But right now, I've got to go.'

'You never have time.' He turned away and launched a heavy kick at the back of the black sofa. 'Not for anything. It's not *fair*.'

'David, grow up!' George was halfway down the stairs again. 'And don't worry, Trish, Jay can come today as planned. I'll be here.'

'But it's one of the Autumn Internationals,' David said, bemused. 'Us v. New Zealand. You always go to Twickenham for that.'

'Doesn't matter. Trish has to go to work. And Jay has to come here. So I'll see to it.'

David's tense frown eased into his best smile and he almost danced back into his own room, the bright pyjamas flapping around his long thin frame.

'Come on, Trish. I've called a taxi for you. It'll be here in eight minutes. So you'd better hurry up.'

'Why, George? It won't hurt David to do without Jay's company today and rugby matches like this are your biggest pleasure.'

He shrugged. 'David could easily cope with a mild disappointment; I'm not so sure about Jay. Giving him a day here is more important than going to the rugger. Don't stop to argue. You haven't time.'

Antony's eyes were closed when Trish arrived, wearing the tight black jeans and coral sweater George had picked out for her. She was glad to have a moment to quieten her banging heart and deal with the shock she felt at the sight of the man in the bed.

He had a contraption like a cross between a cage and a steel crown screwed into his head and reaching down over his shoulders, presumably to keep his neck from moving. His right leg was heavily bandaged and there was a long scrape down one side of his face, red and crusting at the edges. The thin white tabs stuck across it didn't seem strong enough to hold it together.

She bent sideways to let her briefcase down on to the floor as quietly as she could. It was heavy with a laptop and dictating machine, as well as pens and paper. There was a chair about five yards away. She walked silently in her sagging leather boots to collect it.

'Knew you wouldn't let me down,' he said. She almost dropped the chair.

'I thought you were asleep.'

'Your scent woke me.'

'Not wearing any. There wasn't time.'

His short laugh made her relax a little more. 'Must be yesterday's shampoo then, or maybe just you. Now listen carefully because I haven't the strength to say it twice; don't argue; don't protest. OK?'

'All right. But before you start, why not ask for an adjournment? You'd get one with no problem for something like this.'

'CWWM don't want to wait.' A faint version of his old wicked smile tweaked at his features. 'And I want you to have the chance. Don't fight me.'

'OK.'

'Robert's on his way to chambers. Help you prepare. But listen, Trish: the judge'll bend over backwards to help Angie Fortwell. Don't sneer or make it hard for her.'

'I won't.'

'She'll use the rule in Rylands v. Fletcher. CWWM have a strict liability over the escape of dangerous chemicals. You've got to mitigate the damages. Contributory negligence. Maybe *volenti*. Don't forget—'

Antony seemed to be growing paler, and he was scarily breathless, as though his lungs or heart had been damaged along with all the rest. Watching him, Trish wasn't even tempted to remind him that, although it was twenty years since she'd qualified, she knew all about strict liability tort in general and Rylands v. Fletcher in particular.

He choked and his eyes watered, but he fought his weakness to add: 'Big implications here, Trish. The world produces filthy waste that kills. Companies like CWWM contain it.'

'Most of the time,' she said with a dryness that made him blink.

'Don't. They mustn't be ruined by frivolous litigation.'

If his face hadn't contorted in pain, she might have said what she thought about his calling Angela Fortwell's suit frivolous. Her husband had been killed by the explosion in CWWM's tanks. There was nothing frivolous about wanting punishment for that.

Antony was fighting for control of his body. His muscles were rigid, the cords in his neck stuck out like high relief decorations, and sweat poured off his skin.

'You'll need to get a grip on how the filters worked.' The slurring in his voice was worse, but he battled on. 'And the way the tanks breathed, and . . . Sod it! I can't. Robert'll tell you. Go now.' His right arm twitched, as though he wanted to gesture but couldn't.

Was he paralysed?

'Don't let me down, Trish. Or yourself.'

His arm turned slightly so that his hand was lying palm upwards. She put hers on to it and felt his fingers move. Relief acted on her like heat on a lump of wax, taking all the stiffness out of her muscles.

'I'll do my best, Antony. Don't worry. Save your strength.'

She could see what it had cost him to keep his mind on his work and wondered just how much pain he was managing.

'Are you—?'

'I'll be fine. Go now. Trust yourself, Trish.'

She watched his eyelids close again. A squeak behind her warned of a nurse's arrival and she gestured towards the door. The nurse nodded and waited there until Trish joined her.

'How long will he have that thing screwed to his head and neck?'

'Two or three weeks probably. Maybe more. He hates it.'

'I'm not surprised. How much damage is there?'

'His neck is broken, but the people who stopped his arterial bleed had the sense not to move him, so he should make a good recovery.'

'No paralysis, then?'

'He'll need physio, of course, and it'll be a slow process, but provided there are no complications and no infections, he should be all right. The doctors think he could be able to use a wheelchair by the week after next.'

'Thanks. Don't let him go too long without painkillers, will you?'

Seeing the nurse's surprise, Trish thought about explaining how long she'd known him and how much she cared. Then she remembered Robert in chambers, and the speed with which she'd have to educate herself about the storage of explosive chemical waste and farming, as well as the bundle of documents in the case. She said goodbye and ran for the street.

Chapter 4

'It's coming, Ange,' Greg said, 'but you're still not showing the authority you'll need.'

Angie rubbed her eyes and pushed her hands through her ragged hair, trying not to show any of her feelings. She'd never expected Greg to be leading these role-playing sessions. As the founder of FADE, Fran had always been the boss till now. But here was lanky Greg sitting behind the kitchen table, pretending to be the doctor who'd been the first on the scene after the explosion had allowed carcinogenic reformulated benzene to spill out on to her land.

'Let's start again,' Greg said. 'OK? Ready? You first, asking if my name is Barry Jenkins.'

Tempted to shout, you bloody well know it is, she smiled a little, nodded in as dignified a way as she could and asked the question.

'What I don't understand,' she added before she could stop herself, 'is why we have to go through this pantomime. We've sent in our skeleton argument and so have they. We've disclosed all our evidence and the witness statements and everything. So why do we have to have this theatrical Q&A in court at all?'

'It's the way they do it, Angie love,' said Fran, looking

over one shoulder and twisting her long straight hair into a rope to get it out of the way.

The reddish blonde colour suited her. With her big square shoulders and strong-featured face, it made her look like a Viking warrior-princess. Angie thought it all wrong that such a powerful woman should be cooking today's vegetable stew.

'Greg's taken me to sit in on lots of trials now, and we do know what we're doing. I promise you that.'

'I know,' Angie said, regretting the spurt of temper. Why was it that her ever-present rage kept popping up to bite the wrong people? 'I'm sorry. It just seems such a stupid waste of time. Not stupid of *you*; the system. No wonder it's so expensive no normal person can afford to go to law.'

'You're telling me,' Greg said, smiling at last. 'Come on, let's get to it, then we can have lunch and a drink. The new apple wine is just about ready now and tasting seriously good.'

'Great,' she said faintly, pining for an absolutely enormous gin and tonic of the kind she hadn't drunk in years.

'Cheer up. You'll be fine, Ange. I only want to make sure that when that bastard Shelley starts challenging your witnesses in cross-examination and rubbishing your evidence, you won't get angry and forget what really happened. These blokes can twist anything they hear and make you confirm the way they see it before you've realised what they're doing.'

Trish watched Robert as he led her through the story of what had happened at the Fortwells' farm. Most of her mind was taken up with what she heard, but she wasn't quite disciplined enough to avoid surprise that he was being so straightforward, so generous with his information.

As she'd already said to Antony, most cases like this would have been adjourned if the leader were taken to hospital at the last minute. If, for some reason, the judge wouldn't allow it, a junior with as many years' experience as Robert could have expected to take over himself. In his place she'd have been pretty resentful.

When they broke for a cup of coffee and a recap just after noon, she said as much. He stopped stirring chocolate dust into the top of his cappuccino with his forefinger, licked the foam off it, and said:

'I might want to kill you for it, Trish, but with Antony, Steve and the client all agitating for you to lead me, I'm stuck. Being stuck, it makes sense to do everything I can to help you do the best job of which you're capable. It's my reputation too.'

She wanted to find a way to thank him without sounding either doubtful or pompous.

'It's like when you're climbing,' he said, surprising her even more. He leaned back in his chair, crossing one dark-green corduroy leg over the other and revealing bright-yellow socks. 'You have to choose a leader and then support him all the way, never questioning his orders or putting forward alternative ideas. If you do either, you risk damaging his confidence, making him doubt, and if that happens you're likely to end up at the bottom of a crevasse with him and the rest of the team. Dead.'

'I didn't know you climbed.'

'I don't any more. There isn't time to keep fit enough. But I did a bit of snow-and-ice stuff in the Alps with my father and brothers before I went up to Oxford. Taught me a lot about life. Now, back to work. Have you grasped the principle of the activated charcoal filters?'

'I think so. The principle and the various risks. What I don't understand is how enough oxygen could have got into the tanks at the Fortwells' to feed the fire.'

She pulled forward one of the drawings that showed the design of the tanks with all the safety features demanded by the regulations governing the Control of Major Accident Hazards, apparently known in the trade as COMAH.

In the old days she might have expected a sneer about her lack of scientific education. Not this morning. Robert merely put a clean, unsucked finger on the relevant bit of the drawing and gave a potted lecture about the way the storage tanks responded to the external temperature.

'It's as though they're breathing, you see, Trish; breathing out as they warm up during the day and in again when they cool down at night. The exhalations are smelly and loaded with toxic particles that are known to increase the risk of leukaemia, so something has to be done about them.'

'The activated charcoal,' she said, to prove she had been listening properly and had understood the drawings laid out in front of her.

'Exactly. The emissions are drawn across the activated charcoal, and that adsorbs . . . you will get that right in court, won't you, Trish? It's *ad*sorbs, not *ab*sorbs.'

'I've got that.' She smiled, working as hard as he was to bury their old rivalry.

'Good. Now, because activated charcoal gets hot, and has even been known to ignite as a system like this breathes in at night, these particular tanks were fitted with a special venting system so they could inhale through quite separate valves, which wouldn't allow fresh air – with all its dangerous oxygen – to be drawn over the carbon and turn it red hot. D'you understand so far?'

'Yup.'

'The valves had worked perfectly well for the three years the tanks had been there,' Robert went on, 'so there was clearly nothing wrong with the fundamental design or operation of the system.'

'So what do you think did go wrong? Could the valve have been blocked?'

'That's the obvious thing,' he said, with the approving nod of a teacher relieved at the first sign of a dim student's intelligence. 'The one real danger in fact, because however well designed a protective cage around the air inlet might be, there's always the risk of, say, a glue-like pad of wet leaves being blown against it and getting stuck and blocking the inflow.'

'Which is why CWWM paid John Fortwell this regular salary to make visual checks?'

'Precisely. If not leaves, there could, I suppose, have been a kamikaze bird that dive-bombed the cage and somehow got stuck. You'll see the list of possible hazards from the expert-witness statement. Not that anything removes CWWM's strict liability.'

'No,' Trish said, making herself smile. 'I know all about that.'

'Of course you do.' Robert's smile was as forced as hers. 'It's hard sometimes to get out of the habit of explaining things to pupils.'

If this is the way you keep supporting the leader, she thought, maybe it's a good thing you don't go snow-and-ice climbing any more.

'And there's no evidence of whatever the blockage could have been,' she said aloud, 'because—?'

'Because everything was devoured in the explosion and subsequent fireball. Along with all the fire-protection devices, sprinklers and so on.'

'And we don't know exactly where John Fortwell died, do we? If it was on the land CWWM leased from him and occupied, i.e. their land, not his own, my memory of Read v. Lyons suggests the strict liability of Rylands v. Fletcher wouldn't apply to his death.'

'Right.' This time Robert looked surprised, as though he hadn't expected her to remember any of the relevant cases. She didn't tell him she'd spent the taxi journey from the hospital, looking them up on the Internet. Lots of people were reluctant to use wireless access because of security fears, but there were times when it was too useful to ignore. This had definitely been one of them.

Rylands v. Fletcher was the name of a nineteenth-century case, which had established the rule that if you had a dangerous thing on your land and it escaped, you were liable for any damage it did, even if you hadn't been negligent. The thing could be an animal, a gas, a chemical, even water. Read v. Lyons was a much later case, which clarified the rule a bit and meant that if someone came on to your land and was damaged by the dangerous thing there, you might get away with it.

'Although,' Robert added, 'if CWWM had been negligent over the design or maintenance of the tanks, then they would be liable for that, too, wherever the victim was when he died.'

'Naturally,' Trish said, writing notes as a way of pinning the information into her brain. 'I'm getting there. Angie Fortwell says CWWM have a strict liability for the escape of a dangerous thing, which killed her husband on *his* land – not theirs – and contaminated that land, making it impossible for her either to continue to farm it or to sell it, thus leaving her incapable of earning a living and prey to continuous anxiety about her own health.'

'Very good, Trish.'

'And we say he was on CWWM's land when he died, the body merely being thrown in the explosion on to his own field, and that the balance of probabilities is that he failed to complete the checks for which he was paid, thus mitigating CWWM's liability by contributory negligence. I can see why Antony didn't think it's winnable.'

'So can I. Chemical waste is an emotive issue. Angie Fortwell's going to be a touching advocate for her dead husband. And what were CWWM doing putting their tanks of filthy benzene on a working farm only just outside a national park anyway?'

'They've got to go somewhere,' Trish said, at last finding some much-needed indignation on behalf of her clients.

'Tell that to FADE.'

'Who?'

'The environmental pressure group that's behind Angie Fortwell. I doubt if she'd have known where to begin as a litigant in person without them.'

'Who are they?'

'Bunch of whiny North London vegetarians,' Robert said, at his most unpleasantly dismissive. 'You know, the earnest sentimental sort, who feed sweet furry foxes in their gardens because they look like Basil Brush or something out of a baby's ickle-wickle picture book.'

Trish didn't have the strength to tackle his prejudices and quickly reverted to the facts of the case.

'CWWM must have had planning permission,' she said. 'Presumably an isolated chunk of countryside is thought to be safer than somewhere like an industrial estate. Imagine if this explosion had happened in the middle of a city.'

He surprised her with another approving nod. 'Precisely. And don't forget, if the judge doesn't accept our defence of mitigation and CWWM have to pay big damages, they may decide to shut down other smallish tank sites all over the country – and perhaps abroad as well – and then where will the chemical waste go? Less scrupulous companies may shunt it off to the third world, where there aren't such strict laws, or bury it or dump it in quarries or out at sea. Wildlife will die. People will die. Children and the elderly especially.'

'Pity we can't use that argument in court,' Trish said, noticing the way Robert was playing to her well-known sympathy for vulnerable victims.

'True. But don't forget: they briefed John Fortwell on what he was going to be storing for them and on all the dangers – their letters to that effect are in the bundle – and no one forced him to take their money.'

'Just as no one forced Doctor Faustus to take the Devil's deal,' Trish said almost to herself. 'OK. Thanks, Robert. I think I'm clear on the basics, so I can stop spoiling your weekend and get to work on my own now.'

'Sure?' He glanced at the clock on the wall. 'I'll still make lunch if you really don't mind.'

'I'm happy. Leave me your mobile number, though, so that if I get stuck—'

He pointed once more to the top sheet of his notes. She saw the numbers of his mobile and land line, as well as the number of his lunch hosts' house.

'Great. I hope I won't have to bother you. See you in court on Monday morning.'

'Good luck, Trish. Don't forget to eat and sleep.'

Greg turned on the television while they ate. The butternut squash and tomato stew was aromatic with spices and very filling. Angie admitted to herself that she had had a bellyful of mutton from the exhausted sheep she'd killed over the years.

The international news was over and the weather forecast had begun. It was heaven not to have to listen to it. Here in Kentish Town it didn't matter if there was rain or frost to come.

A perfectly dressed and groomed young woman appeared on the screen to give the local London news. Now this did matter: if there were to be a tube or bus strike on Monday, they'd have to borrow bicycles to get to court, and it would be hard to get the documents there without some kind of trailer. Could they afford a taxi?

Angie tried to stop worrying. Greg and Fran knew their way about London as well as the courts and the legal system. They would take the lead. All she had to concentrate on was asking the right questions with enough confidence to stand up to Antony Shelley.

'Antony Shelley, a senior barrister, was run over by a motorcycle on a pedestrian crossing outside the Royal Courts of Justice yesterday afternoon,' said the news reader in icily distinct syllables no one could ignore. 'His condition is said to be serious but stable.'

The three of them looked at each other. After so many weeks of hating the very idea her adversary, Angie thought this sounded as though the Fates must be on her side at last.

Not that she'd wanted him to be hurt, of course. Or not much. But it was hard not to take it as a sign.

'Does it mean the case will be postponed?' she asked, trying not to let herself feel hopeful. She'd waited for this for so long it seemed mad not to want to get on with it. But as the day came closer, she was getting more and more afraid.

Greg shrugged. 'Adjourned, not postponed, Ange. You must get the terminology right. Probably. We'll have to find out. I've got all CWWM's solicitor's phone numbers. He must be answering one of them, even on a Saturday.'

He pushed himself up from the table, a trail of bright orange squash caught in his beard.

'Whiskers, Greg,' Fran said, twinkling at Angie as she added: 'It's always happening and I've sworn I'll always tell him. Too awful to go out looking like that.'

He picked the fibres out of his beard and washed them down the sink. As he slopped out of the kitchen in his ill-fitting sandals, Angie said:

'If it's not adjourned, d'you really think we've got a chance?'

Fran took Angie's disfigured hand and held it firmly. The head of the long blue-and-green snake tattoo that spiralled up Fran's right arm showed beneath the raggy cuff of her yellow sweater.

'I do,' she said, meeting Angie's twitchy gaze with steady confidence. 'Honestly. Greg and I wouldn't have gone this far with you if we didn't.'

'Because they could take the farm,' Angie said, 'couldn't they? If we lose and they get awarded costs.'

'In the very worst case, yes: you could lose it, love. It's true. I've never hidden that from you, have I?'

Angie shook her head. 'Somehow you don't see things so clearly at the start. Not when you're on fire with rage. Now—'

She clamped her lips together, staring at the chipped worktop, which still held the curling bright-orange peel from the squash. It wouldn't be fair to Fran to collapse on her, but Angie had to explain.

'We worked so hard for so long to keep the land in good heart, the thought of throwing it away on fees for CWWM's sodding lawyers is—'

'I know.' Fran slid her hand up under Angie's sleeve and held her forearm in a strong grip. 'It's why we have to fight. They killed John. And they polluted your place, maybe for decades. You've a *right* to damages. Lots of damages.'

'But if we don't win and I have to give up the farm, I risk living on charity for the rest of my life.'

'It's benefit, Angie.' The warmth in Fran's face had gone and she removed her hand. Her expression was scarily hostile. 'Not charity.'

Angie could just imagine John's harsh voice telling her that was a matter of opinion. She buried the thought and said: 'I know. Of course I do. I'm sorry. It's just that I've always paid my way. I don't mean—'

'You get used to it,' Fran said, still not smiling but looking a bit less warlike. 'And it means you can do useful stuff like we do fighting with FADE. You could join us full time, if you wanted. We'd love to have you.'

Angie put her hand across her mouth, holding in everything she couldn't – didn't want to – say and tried to make her eyes offer the gratitude that was becoming harder to feel as her fears sharpened their teeth.

*

David was walking behind George and Jay because the pavement was so narrow here. And they were all laden with clumsy carrier bags from Borough Market. The two back views made him laugh. George, more than six feet tall, had big broad shoulders inside his Hackett's jacket and was a bit like a giant redwood, while Jay was barely five feet three and looked extremely weedy in his tight white T-shirt and jeans. He was shivering with cold, too, which was his own fault because he'd insisted on leaving his hoodie behind when George said he couldn't wear it up.

'Why d'you bovver with all this crap,' he said suddenly, 'when you could just get a burger and chips already hot?'

David winced. Food was George's most important thing, almost like a fetish. Criticising it was like the worst insult.

For once George laughed, shifting two of his bags from one hand to the other. He had the heaviest of all.

'Because burgers taste vile compared with the best well-hung fillet steak,' he said. 'Besides I like cooking. It's so different from my work it makes me relax.'

Jay looked over his shoulder at David with an expression on his round face that said: 'Mad or what?'

David tried not to laugh.

'You mean,' said Jay in a voice that suggested he was making a huge effort to understand someone from outer space, 'like a kind of hobby?'

'That's right,' George said, pausing at the crossing while a lorry thundered past, then leading the way to the opposite pavement. 'And there's no need to sound so snotty. It's a much more useful hobby than nicking things.'

David clenched his hands so tightly around the thin plastic of his carriers that they felt like knives digging into his fingers. If George was hard to tease safely, Jay was impossible. There was a scary silence. Jay lagged so he was nearly as far behind George as David himself. Then he speeded up again.

'You wouldn't say that if you wasn't so old and clumsy. You'd be out lickin' the belly with the best of us if you could. *I* see you looking at them lobsters and wanting to stuff one up your shirt when the bloke told you how much they was.'

'Ouch,' George said with a laugh. 'What a horrible boy you are.'

'You did, though, didn' you?' This time when Jay looked over his shoulder at David, his face was full of glee. 'Admit it. Go on.'

'I admit I did have an extraordinary moment of idiotic temptation, which I had absolutely no difficulty whatsoever in resisting because I am an honest bloke with a will of steel.'

'Yeah, and a mouth like a fucking dictionary.'

'Don't swear. And speed up or we'll be late for tea.'

David followed them feeling really happy. No one else saw the things in George that Jay could see, or talked about them like this. It made life at home more interesting than usual. And a lot less lonely.

By nine o'clock that evening, Trish knew she'd read as much as she could absorb without a real break.

'*Ad*sorb,' she said aloud in Robert's languid patrician accent. 'Not *ab*sorb, Trish.'

She realised she was light-headed with overconcentration and lack of fresh air. Only one other member of chambers was still at work, so she looked into his room to warn him she was off and would leave him to lock up.

'How's it going? You're taking over Antony's stinks case, aren't you?'

'Going OK, I think, although I could've done with a bit longer to get my head round the welding of tank seams, fire protection systems, the dangers of reformulated benzene and so on.'

'You'll be fine,' he said. 'We're all rooting for you, you know.'

Touched, she waved her thanks and stumped downstairs, feeling the hardness of the stone steps through her boots, and painfully aware of tight muscles she'd been clenching all day as she hung over her desk and twisted her legs around the central pillar of her chair. For once she looked forward to the lavish dinner she knew George would have cooked to welcome her back.

In the murk at the foot of the stairs a pale rectangle lay on the front-door mat. Bending down, she saw it was an envelope with her name and address typed under a heavily underlined 'Strictly private and confidential'.

Worried, she ripped it open as she left the building and set off towards Blackfriars Bridge and home. She'd walked the route so often she didn't need to look where she was going, and there was just enough light from the streetlamps to read the handwritten letter from David's head teacher.

Dear Trish,

Many thanks for your generous offer to pay some of Jay's fees. We may take you up on it in due course, but we have yet to see any signs that he could guarantee the self-discipline and effort necessary to justify our taking him into the school on a long-term basis. He knows he still has to prove himself.

I think it only fair to warn you of some of the things he's done in the past before you commit yourself. You see, it's not just theft and antisocial behaviour – you might expect that. There's arson, too. He did a year in secure accommodation for setting fire to his old school. And his behaviour was even worse before he reached the age of criminal responsibility; when he was three, he was seen to do some quite serious damage to his baby sister – hands round her throat, squeezing; a few years later he set light to his mother's clothes when she was lying insensible with drink in the kitchen. There was a stepfather at that stage. Later on, Jay was several times found to be carrying a knife into lessons.

It is, of course, a risk to have taken him into Blackfriars, but so far we have seen signs that he may have outgrown such behaviour, and he is searched each morning and evening – something he very much dislikes but accepts. There have been no knives. We are in close touch with his social worker, who is relatively optimistic. But what we now need is hard, i.e. written, evidence of the brains we as well as you have discerned in him, and some proof that he is prepared to apply them.

I'll keep you in touch with details of his progress and of our deliberations.

Thank you, once again, for your most generous offer.

Yours ever, Jeremy

PS I have absolute confidence in your discretion and good sense, Trish, so I know I don't have to ask you not to pass any of this on to David.

'So why did you?' she muttered, pausing at the crossing for the traffic lights to change. She folded the letter and slipped it back into its envelope, before carefully tucking it into her handbag. It had better go into the safe in her bedroom for complete security, she thought. Not that David ever went through her handbag, but she couldn't leave something like this anywhere accessible to Jay.

What a relief to know he wouldn't be there tonight! Quite apart from needing some peace after a day of cramming her brain with chemistry, she wanted time to get rid of the mental pictures of Jay's drunken mother lying at his mercy on the kitchen floor.

Trish had reached the foot of the iron staircase that led up to her flat. She knew the big airy loft still felt soulless to George, just as his cosy Fulham house stifled her, which was why they'd kept both. He spent most weekends in Southwark with her and David and sometimes week nights too. But he liked to be able to retreat to his much-loved cottagey refuge sometimes.

She no longer fretted over the eccentricity of running two expensive places within a few miles of each other. They could afford it these days and their relationship worked so much better than many of their friends' marriages that they were both reluctant to take any risks with it.

In the end they'd probably pool their resources and buy somewhere in a more conventional area of London than this dark narrow street of redundant warehouses and industrial buildings. But the time hadn't come yet.

Still, she wouldn't have minded changing the approach to her eyrie. The iron staircase, more like a fire escape than anything else, seemed much steeper than usual and the thought of getting herself up it was daunting. She hadn't been this tired for years. It must be a result of the lax way she'd lived over the months since taking silk. Once she'd been able to work all night and still skip up these stairs for a bath and breakfast before turning round to go straight into court.

She'd soon be back in training, she told herself, as she set one foot on the first step and pushed herself up off the ground. All her muscles shrieked in protest. A foretaste of middle age. She made sure she didn't cling to the handrail or actually pull herself up.

Wafts of delicious smells surrounded her when she eventually reached the front door. Inside, firelight flickered on the high walls. David was stretched out on one of the black sofas near the great open fireplace, wearing his navy towelling dressing gown over the red pyjamas, reading, with the earpieces of his iPod firmly stuck in his ears. He must have decided to have his shower before eating, to compensate for her late return.

Conscience-stricken at the thought of keeping him hungry, she could still smile at the sight of his hairy legs and envy him his lifetime's freedom from waxing and razoring. Maybe one day genetic engineering – or even evolution – would result in perfectly hairless female bodies.

Yes, she thought, and maybe there'll be self-cleaning houses too and no-calorie clotted cream.

She closed the front door and double locked it, kicking off her slouchy boots and draping her coat over the back of a chair. She couldn't face another climb to put them away in her bedroom yet. The sounds of an earnest arts discussion on Radio 4 issued from the kitchen until the voices were suddenly muted.

'That you, Trish?' called George.

'Safe and sound. What's cooking? It smells great.'

'Sauce for the fillet steaks: mush, dried mush, butter, wine, garlic and a soupçon of thyme. We went to Borough Market today and loaded up. Now you're back I'll cook the steaks.'

'At last!' said David, pulling out his iPod with a theatrical sigh.

He looked up at Trish and gave her the wary smile that was reserved for days when he felt he ought to apologise for something but didn't want to lower himself by putting it into words.

She ruffled his shaggy hair and bent down to kiss his head. To her distress he winced, as though she'd actually hurt him, then shuddered:

'Ugh, Trish! I'm not a baby.'

'I know,' she said, feeling better. 'But I need comfort after the kind of day I've had while you've been swanning about having fun. Borough Market indeed! I suppose you ate lots of those fab sandwiches.'

'Course we did.'

'How did Jay take to it?' She was careful to avoid any suggestion of a comment.

'I'm not sure,' David said, looking self-conscious. 'He doesn't understand food the way George thinks about it.' He cheered up. 'But he liked the sandwiches.'

'Good. What did you do then?' Trish lowered herself on to the opposite sofa, closing her eyes and letting the clanging information in her brain settle a little. 'I'm not going to sleep; I'm listening.'

She heard him laugh, a low, spluttering sound that was new. 'Homework. He can't do it at his flat because they're all always making a noise and there isn't any space, so we did it here, while George watched the match upstairs. Then we played Scrabble for a bit.'

Back to Scrabble, Trish thought sleepily, noticing that David's chatter had stopped.

He and George had moved on to chess as their preferred battleground, but you can't play chess with three.

'And the wretched Jay was showing signs of beating me hollow,' George called into the silence, 'when it got so late I thought I'd better run him home, so we'll never know if I'd have pulled back. Steaks'll be ready in about half a second, so if anybody's going to wash—'

Trish's eyelids flew open and she exchanged an open-mouthed glance of wildly exaggerated horror with David, before they both dashed for their respective bathrooms. Of all the things that set off George's tight-lipped irritation, letting his freshly cooked food get cold was just about the worst.

David was back first, and Trish hurried down the spiral stairs as she saw George bringing the third plate to the table.

'Just in time,' she said, flinging herself into her chair.

'You're mad, Trish. You could have done yourself a serious mischief pounding down the stairs like that. I'd rather the food got cold than you broke your neck.'

'Are you *sure*?' she said, making David laugh and George pretend to cuff her around the head.

She was home. It was time to let facts and fears about leukaemia-inducing benzene and blazing tanks sink to the very bottom of her mind.

The steaks were perfect, soft to the teeth, but much better flavoured than any mass-produced supermarket meat, and the sauce George had invented intensified the taste rather than masking it. There was a baked potato with butter for David, while the adults made do with an austere dressing-less green salad. George had struggled to lose weight a couple of years ago and was determined not to regain it. Trish carried no spare flesh, but disliked feeling full and was usually happy to keep her fat and carbohydrate intake as low as his.

Afterwards, while she stacked the dishwasher and George put his feet up with the day's newspaper, David took himself to bed. House rules allowed him to read for as long as he liked on Saturday nights, but he had to be in bed by ten-thirty. So far, Trish hadn't had any trouble with him, but she wasn't sanguine enough to believe it would never come. Exposure to drugs, binge drinking, sex, fights and worse hovered just out of sight in the inevitable future, but she wasn't going to waste time worrying until she had cause.

By the time she'd scoured the grill and saucepans and cleaned the kitchen surfaces, George was asleep on the sofa. She carefully pulled apart the glowing embers in the fire-place, dragged the mesh safety curtain across it, and went to have her shower. She'd wake him later and get him upstairs to bed.

When she emerged, the back of her dark hair damp and her whole long body glowing with heat, she saw him sitting in the spoon-backed chair in the corner of the bedroom, wearing nothing but striped pyjama trousers, cutting his toenails. There was only the smallest bulge of flesh under the lowest ribs and a little mottling of his upper arms.

'So romantic,' she said, unwinding the red towel that was doing temporary duty as a dressing gown and draping it over the radiator. Today's extra-large T-shirt was new, a present from David, with great red letters across the chest, saying: 'World Beater'. She pulled it over her head.

George looked up from his task, one ankle balanced on the other knee, like a classical statue.

'About as romantic as your negligée.'

Trish squinted down at the slogan and laughed with him.

'What really happened over the Scrabble, George?'

He put down the scissors and laid a neat piece of big toe nail beside them. 'I wondered whether you'd picked it up. There was a bit of a spat. David was already doing well when he bunged the x down on a triple he could use in both directions to make ox and ax and therefore got fifty points, which put him right out of Jay's reach. Jay lost it. He started swearing in the filthiest language I've ever heard – really gross – then grabbed the board and cracked it down on David's head before I could stop him, scattering tiles everywhere.'

'Oh, shit.' The actual assault didn't sound at all serious, but Jay's overreaction to an ordinary bit of frustration was exactly what Trish had always feared.

If David *had* been on his own with him and retaliated, anything could have happened. Thank God for George's generosity in giving up his afternoon at Twickenham.

'I thought it best to take it casually,' he said, 'so I asked David to clear up while I drove Jay home. And I said I'd pick him up again tomorrow at ten.'

'Why this enthusiasm for the wretched Jay's company?' Trish disliked her reluctance to have him here quite as much as the proof that she'd been right to be cautious in the first place.

'I feel sorry for him, I suppose.' George went back to his nails. 'And I like the fact he's not a wimp. With a drunk for a mother, no father, brutal elder brother, he could easily be a victim. But he isn't; he fights back.'

Trish stared at his bent head, and at the capable fingers shaving more and more off his toenails.

'He certainly does,' she said, knowing she sounded as dry as the most stick-in-the-mud kind of judge. She took the head teacher's letter out of her bag. 'You ought to read this.'

He took the letter in silence, tilting it towards the light. 'Doesn't surprise me too much. And he's never shown signs of that sort of thing here. All he did was whack David over the head with the Scrabble board. There've been times when I wouldn't have minded doing it myself.' Pausing, he looked up at her worried face and added: 'Come on, Trish; it was hardly life-threatening.'

'No.' She shuffled through all the things she wanted to say, then abandoned them. 'Coming to bed?'

'Soon.' He bent back to his task of reducing his toenails to the smallest possible size.

What was he not telling her? She knew him well enough to be sure there was something; but she also knew asking too many questions too soon would act on him like a hermetic seal. If she could be patient, she'd get it in the end, whatever it was.

Chapter 5

Angie raised herself on one elbow so she could smooth the deep ridges in the sheet beneath her body. Her eyes burned and the blood thumped hard enough in her head to make it ache.

She wished she'd never challenged Fran, never suggested living on benefit was in any way wrong, or that it was FADE's fault she was facing destitution. Somehow she'd have to explain that whatever happened in the case she wasn't going to start dishing out blame. The whole thing was her own responsibility and, whatever her terrors and regrets, she was genuinely grateful to Fran and Greg. Still. And to the other FADE volunteers who'd given up their time to research old cases as well as all the latest scientific reports about groundwater contamination, and the way benzene particles could increase the risk of all kinds of cancer, and everything else she was going to have to quote in court.

The sheet was smooth again. She made herself lie flat on her back and pulled the light hollow-fibre duvet up over her shoulders, closing her puffy eyelids.

Could she do it? Could she keep all the facts in her head when the other side started to interrupt and question and accuse her of misunderstanding the legal system or bringing in evidence that wasn't allowed or generally showing herself to be ignorant and amateurish?

Years ago she'd felt like this during takeovers. Her back ached and she turned on her side. In those days, she'd been one of the youngest on the bank's team and merely had to scurry about doing what she was told. It hadn't stopped her worrying, though, or hating everything about the life and most of her imperviously confident rivals.

All the squash she'd eaten had given her dreadful wind. Trying to laugh away her angst, she thought of the old-fashioned shepherd's remedy she'd seen in the film of *Far from the Madding Crowd*. If she'd been a ewe, someone could have jammed a spike into her stomach to let out the gas. She pulled down one of the pillows and hugged it against herself. That was better.

You couldn't see the moonlight here in Kentish Town, only the yellow glare of the streetlamps, and the elongated triangles of light that swept across the ceiling every time a car turned into the street.

John would still be alive if they hadn't left London twenty-six years ago. Adam might not have abandoned them. She might have had a proper family instead of having to make do with Fran and Greg.

A rumbling sound was clearly audible through the wall, then a series of softer, almost tearing whispers as though someone was pulling bedclothes and plumping pillows. Air clonked in pipes, probably from the flat next door. She hadn't felt as hemmed in by other people since she'd been a child at boarding school, and she longed for the isolation of the farm.

'You're never happy anywhere,' she muttered to herself.

Lonely at home, fretted by lack of freedom in London, too cold or too hot, furiously angry with the rest of the world, she was horrified by her own failings. 'Get a grip, for heaven's sake, and if you can't rest, take a pill.'

If sleep was this hard now, with the whole of Sunday to come, what on earth would tomorrow night be like? She'd better save the pill till then.

Trish was at her desk in chambers by half-past six on Sunday morning, with two huge cardboard cups of extra strong coffee in front of her and two giant chocolate-chip cookies to give her energy. She thought she deserved the extra carbs for all the work she'd be doing today.

Her first task was to check her memory, scribbling notes of the main facts she'd learned yesterday. Only when she was sure she'd got the chemistry right, and the basic design of the tanks and all their safety features, did she put those documents to one side and embark on learning about life as it had been lived on the Fortwells' farm.

The most obvious thing was how hard it had been. The intensity of their struggle rose from the formally worded documents like a smell. They'd earned no more than ten thousand pounds from the sheep in each of the last five years, which was a lot less than she'd be earning for this one case. It certainly wasn't much to feed and clothe two adults, as well as run the necessary tractors and Land Rover and maintain their ancient buildings. Fees from bed-and-breakfasters added another fifteen hundred pounds in the better years. The surprisingly generous ground rent and salary CWWM paid them for the tank enclave made all the difference. With it, they could manage; without it, they would have been sunk.

As Trish scrutinised the financial statement Angie had provided to support her claim, she thought back to the interview she'd read with all the details of the careers the Fortwells had abandoned more than a quarter of a century ago. She and George had plenty of friends working in the City who were all earning six-figure salaries with even bigger bonuses. If the Fortwells had stayed . . .

'Don't go there,' Trish said aloud.

If she were to act in Antony's stead for the next two or three weeks, she couldn't allow her brain to be distracted with sympathy. She broke off a large piece of chocolate-chip cookie, dipped it briefly in the coffee, and chewed as she read the draft he'd left for his opening speech.

The facts were fine and the inferences, too, but the style was all wrong. If she tried to learn this by heart to spout tomorrow, it would sound artificial, unconvincing. She picked up her pen to create her own version.

Angie was sitting at the kitchen table, rereading CWWM's witness statements for the twentieth time, trying to drill their lying hints so deep into her mind that she would be able to ask the right questions, however cleverly they tried to twist the true facts. She felt a large, gentle hand on the back of her head.

'Time to knock off, Angie,' Fran said, stroking her rough hair. 'You know it all now. You need to relax. We've asked some friends round for a party to cheer you up.'

'I can't. I mean, it's really kind of you; I just don't feel like socialising.' She closed her eyes. How could anyone who knew what she was going through expect her to be polite to a bunch of strangers at a moment like this?

'There's method in it,' Greg said from behind Fran.

Angie looked round over her shoulder and past Fran's wide hips to see Greg carrying an armful of two-litre bottles of wine. At least it's the real thing, she noted, instead of that disgusting apple stuff. She smiled at him to make up for the silent ingratitude. He didn't notice because he was lining up his old-fashioned corkscrew for an assault on the bottles.

'You need to have a kind of line between all this prep and real life; otherwise you'll go mad,' Fran said. D'you feel up to helping make some eats? I've got some dips to go with carrots and cucumber and celery. They'll need cutting up into sticks. OK?'

'Sure.' Angie pushed the hair away from her eyes and smiled properly. 'I can do that. Peeled as well?'

'Don't bother with peeling,' Fran said. 'Such a waste of good fibre.'

They all laughed. Angie realised they were trying to cheer her up and tried to join in. It was the least she could do after all their efforts on her behalf. And they might be right: she had got herself into a rut of manic rereading and self-doubt. This unwanted party would provide distraction, if nothing else.

While she surreptitiously pulled the strings from the celery and cut off the most discoloured of the carrot skins, Fran tidied up the files and carted them out to the narrow hallway, where a small trolley waited.

'So who's coming?' Angie asked as she breathed in the sweetness of the carrots.

'Mainly members of FADE,' Greg said, scratching one bulbous nostril. He bent down to pull a recalcitrant plastic cork from the third huge bottle.

Looking at his narrow shoulders and squidgy biceps,

Angie thought he'd have done better with the sort of corkscrew that had arms to act as levers.

'Ouf. That's better. And a few neighbours. You'll like them. There are some bags of breadsticks in the cupboard; you can put them in glasses and dot them about the room.'

Angie did everything she was told, then retreated to the spare room to try to make herself look less like a downtrodden ghost. She'd found a neat black suit that didn't cost too much in one of the West End's Oxfam shops. Its label would have impressed her even in the old days, and it was more or less the right size. But it had to be kept for court, hanging on the back of the bedroom door safely shrouded in plastic. Apart from that, she hadn't any clothes except jeans or the last few pairs of John's corduroy trousers.

She did her best, picking the least shabby pair of black cords and adding a white T-shirt. The effect was fairly bleak, though, so she stuck her head round the kitchen door and asked Fran if she had any kind of bright scarf to spare.

'Of course. Hang on a sec.'

Only moments later, Fran emerged from her room with a handful of old Indian silk scarves. They were very soft, and age had thinned them almost to transparency, but they were still beautiful. One was red with gold lozenges on it; another deep green and blue, like the snake tattoo on her arm. There were purple, yellow and orange: more colour than Angie had seen anywhere but a shop window for years and years. She picked the red-and-gold one, added the yellow, and twisted them together, threading the result through the belt loops in her cords.

'Hey, Angie! You look great.' As she spoke, Fran bowed, which made her straight red-blonde hair swing like a waterfall.

Fran looked more than great, Angie thought; magnificent really, in a long gipsy skirt of purple cotton and a tight black velvet jacket threaded with silver. She was wearing make-up, too: lots of kohl around her eyes and some smoky pink lipstick. She gave Angie a box of matches.

'Will you light the joss sticks?'

Angie was soon inhaling the scents from a sand-filled bowl holding several different sorts of incense stick and remembering wild university parties that had smelled just like this.

What would she think now if she met the girl she'd been, with the long ungovernable hair, anarchic humour and tiny skirts? She wasn't sure, but she could easily see how the girl would pity the dried-up, bad-tempered old ratbag she'd become, and that was awful.

Luckily there was no time to think. The front-door bell rang and Greg went to answer it, bringing back the first batch of guests. Three were women who worked for FADE. Angie had met them several times now and they shook hands in a friendly enough way, although they obviously couldn't be bothered to talk to her. They were off to the far end of the room in no time to enjoy what was obviously a riveting gossip.

The fourth guest was a stranger: a tall man with thick greying hair and an aura of money and confidence that set him apart from the rest.

'This is Ben,' Greg said. 'He lives round the corner and wanted to come and wish you luck in court.'

'That's kind,' she said, shaking his hand. 'Are you involved with FADE, too?'

'Absolutely not.' Ben's voice was much grander than any of the others, whose accents varied from Fran's tight north

London twang and Greg's looser, all-purpose Estuary to the soft Irish lilt of the prettiest of the women. 'Not my kind of thing. Although of course I admire what they do.'

'Have a drink, Ben.' Greg held up one of the bottles.

'Better not. I'm driving. Water would be great, if you've got some.'

While Greg went off to fetch it, Angie lifted her own glass. The thin red wine was sour but distinctly better than the peculiar home-made version of the previous few days.

'I also admire your courage,' Ben said. 'It's not easy to be a litigant in person. How are you feeling about the case?'

'Terrified,' she said and thought again of the girl she'd been, who would never have admitted any of her innumerable fears.

Most of them had been about being a failure or not popular enough. Or being found out. The people she'd called her friends had been so pleased with themselves and so contemptuous of everyone else she'd felt sure they'd turn on her if they knew what she was really like. Maybe there was something to be said for middle age after all. Even if it did shrivel you up and make you angrier with every passing year, at least it took away the need to pretend to be something you weren't.

Ben laughed as though she'd been joking, but she was fairly sure he knew she hadn't. She waited for him to say something else. In the silence beween them, she heard the three women chattering excitedly about someone else who'd just fallen in love. Ben grimaced in their direction, but he didn't say anything, so Angie had to spin out the conversation herself.

'But I do feel a bit better than when I thought I was

going to be facing Antony Shelley. Ever since we had some preliminary discussions about the actual ownership of the land where the tanks were, I've had nightmares about him. Now the other side's solicitor have told us about this woman who's taking his place, I feel better. She *has* to be an improvement.'

'Trish Maguire won't be any kind of walkover,' Ben said, now watching her with a beadiness she found unnerving. She'd seen job interviewers look at her like this, and spies for the Inland Revenue.

'D'you know her?' she asked to distract him from whichever of her failings he was trying to assess.

'Not personally. But I know all about her: wrong side of the tracks made good. Some people can't stick her; others think she's a bit of hero. She's very tough in court, however gentle she may seem outside.'

Angie put a hand against her chest, feeling her heartbeat speed up. 'Don't. Please. I'm scared enough as it is.'

'You should be fine, so long as you stick to the point,' he said with a slight doubt in his drawly voice, as though he didn't have half as much confidence in her as he had in himself. 'You must press the other side all the time on all their weak arguments and *always* address the judge with respect. Whatever else you let slip, never lose hold of that. Respect for the bench is essential.'

Angie had never enjoyed being told what to do, even in the old uncertain days, even by people she knew well.

'You sound as though you know a lot about it,' she said coldly, glad to see more guests arriving. As soon as she'd found a way to get rid of this one, she'd find somebody less arrogant.

'Don't forget you'll have Greg with you,' he said, ignoring

her comment, 'dealing with your papers and reminding you of anything you may have forgotten, so—'

'Not Fran?' Angie was so shocked she didn't even notice she'd interrupted him. Her hand suddenly felt slippery on the thick glass.

'Didn't Greg tell you? I warned him that the combination of you and Fran could look too female. The courts are still a traditional sort of place, and you don't want your case imprinted on the judge's mind as a bit of girly froth. If you have a bloke with you, you'll avoid that. I must go in a minute, but I'll send Fran over with another drink for you. Give me your glass.'

She handed it over obediently and watched him cross the room to Fran, saying something that made her laugh and blow him a kiss. Then he moved on to Greg, who left the little knot of people he'd been entertaining to talk privately to Ben. They had their heads together and it looked as though Ben was asking for something. Greg shook his head and Ben appeared disappointed but almost deferential, which seemed odd.

Someone behind Angie was telling a joke, which aroused gales of laughter and made her feel excluded from everything. What was she was doing with all these cheerful people, who all knew each other so well and treated her as a cross between a museum exhibit and an inadequate entry for an agricultural show? Ben stuck out his hand and Greg shook it, then opened the door and ushered him out.

'Here, love,' Fran said, bringing a full glass of wine. Angie grabbed her opportunity.

'Who is Ben?'

'Just a neighbour.' Fran looked worried. 'Why?'

'He seemed to know an awful lot about me and my case.'

'Greg found out that he's a lawyer, so we started to ask him things whenever we got stuck. You don't mind, do you?'

Angie rubbed her forehead, wishing she'd grown out of paranoia as well as the need to hide her fears.

'I suppose not. I was just shocked when he casually told me you wouldn't be sitting with me in court, as though I ought to know. When did you decide?'

'Only this evening, love.' Fran smoothed Angie's hair back from her forehead. 'When Greg phoned Ben to invite him to the party at the last minute and they were chatting about the case, Ben pointed out how it might look if you and I were sitting together in front of the judge. Greg and I talked it over – you were changing at the time, I think – and decided he was probably right.'

'Angie! Remember me?' The bright attractive American voice came as a welcome distraction.

She turned away from Fran, to see the plump smiling young man who'd done the preliminary research into the dangers of benzene.

'Hi, Marty,' she said, kissing him. 'Lovely to see you! You know, your notes are the clearest anybody provided. You must be a proper scientist.'

'I haven't done any seriously since school,' he said, thrusting a plate of crudités at her. 'Have some of these. Keep up your strength for tomorrow.'

Chapter 6

Trish prepared as methodically as she always did before court. Her dark hair was blown dry to the flat neatness that would make her wig sit well, and her make-up was discreet. Her black suit was as well pressed as her gown, and her bands were crisply starched. She had the whole case mapped in her mind and could see several different routes to take if Angie Fortwell's cross-examination enticed any of her witnesses away from the line she'd planned for them.

When facing other barristers you'd know more or less what they were going to say. You did sometimes get surprises, but usually you'd worked out every possible argument so you could counter any one of them. With an amateur, a litigant in person, you were on much wobblier ground.

'Feeling OK?' Robert said as he came into her room to collect her.

'Absolutely fine.' She resisted the temptation to brush the shoulders of her jacket or tweak her hair. 'Have you got the documents?'

'My pupil's already gone ahead with two trolleys. Let's go.'

Trish slowly got to her feet, testing her reactions. She'd expected to be nervous and was glad to notice nothing out of the ordinary. You needed some apprehension to get the adrenaline flowing and keep your mind sharp.

She stepped out beside Robert, feeling her ribs expand with every breath she took. He knew better than to talk or offer advice just before a court appearance, and she was grateful for that.

Angie waited by the security guards as Greg fed their bags of documents through the scanner. They rattled towards her over the narrow metal rollers and she hauled them off one by one. Her black suit felt odd: tight around her stomach and yet much less heavy than her usual clothes. She felt exposed, too, with her legs out of trousers for the first time in years.

Greg, who hadn't bothered to dress up for court and was wearing his usual saggy jeans and sweater, followed the bags. There were no embarrassing bleeps or hold-ups. He was waved through and they made their way to Court 14.

The building was intimidatingly churchy, with high gothic arches in the main hall and a floor of inlaid coloured marble. But the court itself was a plain room, not nearly as large as the exterior suggested, with a slightly shabby red carpet, cream-painted walls and mid-brown wooden furniture. In a way it was a bit like a meeting room for hire in a not-very-expensive hotel.

Greg showed her where to sit and explained who else would be in the room with them. Most of yesterday's resentment had been overtaken by gratitude. Without him and Fran, she'd have found it hard to get this far, and, if she had, she'd have been fainting with the anxiety by now.

The double doors from the corridor burst open and a small party fluttered in, with their black gowns streaming out behind them. They looked frighteningly clean. And rich.

Angie felt her hands brushing down her lapels and forced herself to stop. Unlike Greg's jeans, her clothes were perfectly clean, and she'd never suffered from dandruff. There was no need to feel at such a disadvantage, even if she didn't have a wig and gown like theirs. The first was a tall thin woman with glossy black hair, who must be Trish Maguire. Her face was pale but not entirely natural.

Looking closely as she approached, Angie saw she'd shaped her eyebrows with a dark-brown pencil and smoothed them over with something, maybe hair gel, and she'd lengthened her lashes with mascara. There was a faint apricot coloured stain over her cheekbones and her lips were a little richer than seemed likely to be their natural colour. From far away she wouldn't look made-up, just defined in a way Angie had failed to achieve. Women barristers were probably taught to do this when they had their first lessons in advocacy.

'Good morning,' she said in a voice that made sense of Ben Givens's comment about the wrong side of the tracks. There was none of his pomposity and it wouldn't have sounded out of place anywhere. 'You must be Mrs Fortwell. I'm Trish Maguire. How do you do?'

Angie's knees felt insecure, as though they might give way and dump her on the floor. The other woman's gentle dark eyes held all the compassion she'd longed for since John's death and not found anywhere. Angie tried to think of something to say as they shook hands.

A moment later the kindness might never have existed. Maguire's expression retreated into cool formality and she turned her back to talk to the men who'd come in with her. One was about her own age, even taller, broad-shouldered, and very good looking in a smooth kind of way. The other, much younger, was a bustly little fellow with freckles and an engaging grin.

He busied himself opening his document cases and laying papers and folders out in what was obviously a preordained pattern, while the elder stared at Angie with all the arrogance she'd expected from the lot of them.

She couldn't bear it, so she introduced Greg as a way of shifting his disdain from herself. He gave his name as Robert Anstey and didn't bother to shake hands.

The next few minutes were like being blindfolded and whirled round and round in a cement-mixer. People came and went and said things Angie couldn't hear or understand. There was a roaring in her ears. Only Greg's hand on her wrist kept her together. He explained the significance of each new arrival until a door behind the judge's throne opened and an usher brought in the judge, a tall man with a calm and empty face, wearing robes not all that different from the barristers'.

Everybody stood until Mr Justice Flambard had lowered himself to the bench, then they all sat.

'No, no,' Greg whispered. 'You stand now, Ange. And you begin. Remember?'

She remembered all right; she just wasn't sure she could do it. The words should be easy enough to say. She fumbled about in her mind for the sense of outrage, for the idea of justice denied, for John. This was her one chance to establish the truth about his murder.

He'd been the best of men, she reminded herself: honest, hard-working, faithful, kind. So kind. And he'd been rubbed out of life by the very people who were paying Trish Maguire a fortune to fight her now.

A faint sensation of something that might be courage made Angie raise her chin. She looked at the judge, who peered at her over his half-moon glasses, and smiled encouragingly, nodding to get her started.

Trish listened to the laboured formalities and wished she could lean over and advise Angie to soften her neck muscles, which would help her vocal cords relax. Her voice sounded as though she was being strangled, and it was clear she was more or less holding her breath as she gabbled her way to the end of each sentence. She'd lose concentration if she went on like this, and the wear and tear on both her mind and body would be tremendous.

'And so my husband was killed, My Lord,' she said at the end of her opening speech, 'and the farm to which we gave over twenty years of our lives was contaminated, all because of the dangerously polluting chemicals the defendants allowed to escape from their land on to ours.'

Trish waited until the judge had finished writing his notes, then rose and in an easy persuasive voice outlined the ways in which she proposed to defend her clients. She chose much less formal language than Angie and felt herself entirely at home. Reaching the end of her speech, she smiled first at the judge, then at her opponent and sat down again, ignoring Robert's whispered congratulations.

She watched Angie lick her narrow lips and heard her breathe heavily. The judge completed his notes, then nodded to her. Her unsuitably dressed friend had dropped the papers he'd been holding out to her and muttered 'sorry'. She bent down and was raising her head at just the moment he reached for them. They banged their skulls together and Angie gasped. For a moment she stood, ignoring the notes as she rubbed her head and wiped the back of her bony hand across her eyes.

'Ange, pull yourself together.'

The snap in the man's hissing voice would have made Trish want to hit him, but it seemed to help Angie, who took the notes, turned back to the judge and called her first witness.

He was a doctor, the local GP, who had been the first on the scene after her desperate calls to the emergency services. He had seen the blaze from his house ten miles away and phoned 999 himself. The operator told him the fire had already been reported and the electricity shut down. With the ambulance likely to take about forty minutes to reach the farm, he was asked to go straight there. Trish thought of the statement she'd read over the weekend.

There hadn't been anything the doctor could do for John Fortwell, but he was able to deal with Angie's shock and advise her about minimising the likely risks to her current and future health from the fumes. He'd also been able to describe the scene in his statement with a vividness untainted by the kind of understandable hysteria Angie herself must still feel.

She asked him to give his name and address to the court and confirm that the statement was his own and that he stood by it. The words she used weren't precisely the ones Trish expected, but they were near enough. She rose for her cross-examination, met the judge's gaze and was impressed that he showed absolutely no sign of fellow-feeling or amusement at Angie's throttled formality.

'Doctor Jenkins, in your statement you have given

evidence about the claimant's mental and physical condition after the explosion and fire at her property, Low Topps; did you know anything about her state of health before that night?'

'Yes. She had several times come to consult me in the months leading up the explosion, and so I had given her various checks. Her general health was excellent then.'

'In which case, what were the symptoms that had led her to consult you?'

'She was suffering hot flushes and sleeplessness. She wanted to discuss the possibility of taking HRT.'

'Were there any psychological symptoms associated with the condition?'

He seemed to hesitate for a moment, then looked towards the judge to give an uncomfortable-sounding answer: '*She* did not mention any psychological symptoms, My Lord, nor did she show any signs of them in my surgery.'

Trish considered his hesitation, and the emphasis he'd given to the pronoun he'd used, then she said: 'Nevertheless, Doctor Jenkins, did you have any reason to suspect such symptoms?'

This time the pause was longer. The judge looked over the top of his glasses first at Trish, then at the witness, and reminded him that he had to answer.

'Her husband had come to see me twice, once in the week before her last appointment and once after it, to ask me to prescribe anti-depressants for her. I told him I couldn't do so unless she consulted me about depression and reported symptoms consonant with the condition.'

'What did he say then?'

Trish could feel Robert tensing behind her and ignored it. She knew what she was doing.

'He gave me a list of her symptoms as he had observed them.'

'Which were?'

'Sleeplessness, which, as I said, she later ascribed to the hot flushes; anxiety; lack of concentration and lack of appetite.'

Trish glanced at Angie Fortwell and saw an expression of outrage, which gave her exactly what she wanted.

'Did you believe him?'

She felt a tug on her gown, nodded briefly to the judge and turned to glare at Robert, who was holding out a small piece of paper. He looked so anxious she took it and opened it to read: 'Not part of Antony's plan. Where are you going with this? Fatal to ask questions not knowing answers.'

Hiding a smile at the reminder of one of the first rules any baby barrister learned, Trish looked at the witness once more.

'Did you believe him, Doctor?' she said again.

'Not entirely.'

'Why not?'

'Because Angela Fortwell was entirely capable of consulting me if she had those feelings, and she had never mentioned them.'

'To what extent do you believe he could have been describing his own feelings?' Trish was careful not to let her voice betray how much she cared what his answer would be.

'I have to say quite a great extent. It definitely did seem the likeliest explanation for his coming to see me.' The doctor's reluctance was as clear as the apology in his expression. He no longer looked at Angie Fortwell.

Trish paused for a moment, then smiled at him. 'Would it

be true to say that among the commonest symptoms of depression are forgetfulness, an inability to complete planned tasks, lying about the consequences of that, and . . .' She paused for emphasis: 'And suicidal thoughts?'

'It would.'

'Did Mr Fortwell mention those, either in connection with his wife or with himself?'

'No.' Doctor Jenkins was firm. 'Absolutely not. Never.'

'And did he make any further appointments to return to your surgery?'

'He did make one more, which he failed to keep. When my receptionist phoned him, he said he had forgotten.'

'What inference did you make then?'

The doctor glared at Trish, then looked more politely towards the judge: 'That he had forgotten.'

The judge didn't bother to hide a smile.

'Thank you, doctor.' Having got exactly what she wanted, Trish sat and left him to be re-examined by Angie Fortwell.

She had just risen to her feet for her next stint when the judge said he thought this would be a good moment to adjourn, inviting them all to return to court at two o'clock. Angie looked puzzled, then made to sit down again. The bearded man with the worryingly loose red lips shook his head and stood up beside her, pulling down the cuffs of his hand-knitted sludge-green jersey.

The judge also got to his feet, everyone else followed suit and bowed. He left by the door behind the bench and the others collected their bags. Trish overheard Angie muttering, but couldn't distinguish any words.

She felt Robert twitching her gown and turned her head, leaning back to hear him hiss:

'If you were my pupil, I'd take you behind the nearest bike sheds and give you the thrashing of your life. What did you think you were doing just then?'

Trish giggled. Robert's exaggeration was too absurd to take seriously. She couldn't even remind him that he ought to have a bit more faith in her experience – and at least fake some respect for his leader. Still laughing, she straightened up and found herself only inches from Angie Fortwell, whose weather-beaten face looked even more accusing than it had done in the newspaper.

'It's just a game to you, isn't it?' A film of tears looked like an extra lens plastered over each eyeball. 'You think it's *funny*.'

Trish sobered at once.

'How can you?' Angie stopped to take a deep breath. 'If you had any idea of the kind of man my husband was—' A few tears fell. She had to breathe in again, across a sobbing exhalation, and nearly choked. She clutched her hands around her stomach as though to hold in unbearable pain.

The scruffy man with her tugged at her elbow, trying to make her stand up straight. At last Angie swallowed hard and stopped hugging her stomach.

'You shouldn't be *able* to laugh,' she said. 'There are people involved here, *real* people in *real* pain. It's not so funny when you think of it like that, is it?'

'You and I can't discuss the progress of the case.' Trish tried to ignore all the sympathy that was making her feel so queasy.

Angie coughed with a harsh sound that must have rasped her already tight throat.

'You're trying to suggest he killed himself. But he didn't.'

Her voice was rising. 'He'd never have done that. He was murdered by your clients. And you're an evil bi—'

The man grabbed her, turning her and pulling her against him. He had one hand on the back of her head, holding it hard against his shoulder. Trish thought he was more interested in keeping Angie quiet than in providing comfort.

You shouldn't mistrust someone just because he had an uncontrolled beard and inappropriate clothes, or even because he'd snapped at a woman *in extremis* and wouldn't let her speak. But there was something about him that set Trish's teeth on edge.

She left them to it.

'Not bad,' Robert murmured into her ear as they pushed their way through the crowd of angry spectators. 'At least you didn't join in. But you're dicing with danger, you know. Getting an illegitimate guesstimate of the deceased's mental state was never part of Antony's plan. And it doesn't fit with the skeleton argument, so you're likely to piss off the judge. And—'

'Robert.' Trish paused until he'd wheeled round to look at her. 'Remember the climbing analogy?'

'Of course.'

'If you don't shut up, I will cut the rope and let you drop into the crevasse and die. This is my case now and we do it my way. OK?'

Watching his face made her think the lunch hour they were about to share might be a little tense.

The first lesson after lunch was chemistry. David dreaded it. In the old days all science lessons were just boring and difficult. Now it was different. He'd been given Jay as his partner in experiments instead of Sam, who'd been moved up into the A stream this term, so he had to spend the whole double period watching to make sure Jay didn't do anything dangerous.

At first, he and Sam had barely noticed the new boy, except for laughing privately about his awful spots and the short kind of round haircut with the weird fringe. Then Mr Watson, the science teacher, had asked David if he'd help look after Jay while he found his feet. David probably would have said yes anyway, because you didn't say no to Mr Watson unless you had a seriously good reason. But it was the way Mr Watson looked at Jay that made David really want to help.

Trish used to do it to him when he first came to live with her. She'd looked scared all the time, as if he might do something awful, but sugary and sympathetic too, which made for a really creepy mixture. And she'd watched everything he did in a way grown-ups didn't usually unless they were doctors. Peering at him, checking everything he did and didn't say, or do, or eat, or read, till he had nothing left of his own at all. He'd wanted to shout and scream and throw things. But of course he couldn't.

Jay could, though. In most places David felt like cheering him on. But it was different in the labs. The stuff there was dangerous. Even thinking about what a spray of acid could do to someone's face made him feel ill.

'Come on, Dave.' Jay whacked him on the back. 'Cheer up. Watson can't lay a finger on you even if you haven't done your homework. An' if he shouts too much you can just tip over the Bunsen burner and set his trousers on fire, innit.'

David shuddered, pretending he was pretending. Jay gave him a look as clear as anything Trish ever did.

'It's a joke, mate,' he said. 'You're meant to laugh.'

'Hee hee.'

Angie spent the first part of the afternoon demolishing Trish's attempt to establish the fact of John's depression, and she did it with unexpected neatness and apparently no emotion whatsoever. Trish was relieved she'd got herself together so quickly but more than a little surprised.

At last the doctor was allowed to go and Angie's next witness was called: an estate agent specialising in the sale and purchase of farms like hers.

Trish listened to his account of why it would now be impossible to sell the farm, and asked her questions to establish that few such properties were selling in this particular area of the north-east of England. It was all textbook stuff and it took no particular skill. Even Hal, the pupil, would have managed all right, and Robert could have done it standing on his head. She reminded herself to hold on to her patience the next time he criticised her handling of the case.

He was still sulking as they left court, and the short walk back to chambers with the documents was conducted more or less in silence. Hal looked uncomfortable so Trish suggested Robert should let him go home as soon as he'd seen to the stowing of the files in her room.

'What about me? D'you need me straight away?' Robert said. 'Or have I time to nip over to the hospital to see Antony? I can't think what Liz is doing leaving him at the mercy of the NHS instead of moving him somewhere more civilised.'

'You get great care in the NHS,' Trish said mildly.

'That's as may be, but there's better company in any

private hospital. Knowing him, he'll be dead bored and in dire need of decent conversation.'

'Fine,' she said, not having the energy to waste on his snobbery. 'See you later. Give him my love, won't you?'

As soon as Robert had gone, Trish felt released into a much bigger space. Now she could follow her own ideas wherever they took her, without being pulled up or questioned by anyone.

What she wanted first was more information about Angie's bossy bearded friend. Somewhere there should be reports provided by the firm of enquiry agents retained by CWWM. They'd spent several weeks following all the members of FADE, in an attempt to find something that could be used to discredit the organisation.

Here was the file. There were far too many individual reports to read in detail. Trish went straight to the conclusion:

'We are satisfied they're harmless do-gooders, acting out of genuinely held beliefs about protection of the environment. All the volunteers who have been researching aspects of the case have other, legitimate, jobs or are legally living on benefit.'

Antony's scribble in the margin made her smile: 'Tiresome, isn't it?'

Trish should have known he'd have considered every possible way of getting his clients off the hook. Still, she wasn't giving up yet and scuffled in the mountains of paper to find the photographs and individual biographies that had been supplied with the report.

There were about thirty pictures. Most had been snatched in streets, banks, shops, pubs and libraries. Angie Fortwell appeared in one or two, but Trish recognised Greg Waverly in all of them.

She'd met a few environmental protesters with friends over the years, and none of them had struck her as being like him. They'd all been either products of well-organised pressure groups, who'd understood spin and presentation and would never have appeared in court in a ravelled jersey and grubby jeans, or else savagely angry individuals whose private demons would have been too urgent to keep them involved in tedious complex litigation.

She turned to the biographical notes and skimmed through Waverly's. They showed he'd been living on benefits after an organic food-supply business had failed. His bankruptcy had been discharged two years ago, and he'd moved in with Frances Showring eight months after that, when he'd also become a paid-up member of FADE. There'd been rumours that he'd set up the food business with profits made in the dotcom boom but the investigators hadn't gone that far back. All they'd been asked to establish was whether he had any hidden assets now. None had been found. The collapse of his company had wiped him out financially.

Was he so humiliated by his failure that he'd looked for a way of publicly beating a much more successful company?

CWWM was active right across the world and had delivered record profits for its shareholders in almost every one of the last twenty years. What could be better for a despised bankrupt than triumphing over them in the Royal Courts of Justice, while still looking as though he lived under a hedge?

A voice disturbed Trish an hour later, saying: 'What on earth are you doing *now*?'

She looked up to find her eyes blurred with all the close peering she'd been doing. Blinking to focus better, she saw Robert in the doorway.

'Sorry,' she said, as she rubbed her sore head. 'I didn't hear you come in. How was Antony?'

'Shocked by the way you're going with the case.'

'I didn't mean that. I meant how was *he*? In pain? Weak? Confused?'

'I told you: shocked.' Robert pulled off his coat and flung it over one of the chairs that stood near the wall under the regimented bookshelves. 'And what's all this chaos? What are you looking for now?'

Trish pushed the hair out of her face, reminded herself yet again of how Robert must be feeling about her elevation and bit down on everything she wanted to say to him. After a moment's hard effort, she smiled.

'I was looking at the FADE biographies when I stumbled on something else. '

'Oh, yes?' said Robert in a voice that meant: what are you going to waste my time with now?

'I think the other side are hiding something.'

'What on earth d'you mean?' No one could have sounded wearier at that moment than Robert. He dropped into a chair and began to unlace his shoes. 'You don't mind, do you? I've got a blister on my heel. Sodding new shoes. Handmade, too, and bloody expensive.'

Trish's eyebrows met as she frowned. A moment later, she ducked down behind her desk to pull open the bottom drawer, where she kept spare tights, needle and thread and a rudimentary first-aid kit.

'Here's some plaster. And scissors.'

He looked up from the nasty red mess above his wrinkled sock. At last his face eased out of the snootiness she'd always hated. 'Thanks, Mummy.'

Trish felt her jaw muscles relax. 'I've even got an antiseptic wipe, if you'd like it.'

'I think I can manage without.' He applied the dressing, pulled his sock up and his trouser leg down. 'I'm myself again. *What* d'you think Angie Fortwell's hiding.'

'Not sure yet. But think of the change in her over lunch. Remember how she was by the door of the court . . . crying, hurt, angry and hating us.'

'Hating you, certainly. OK, I'll give you that.'

'Then this afternoon, as she unpicked what I'd got the doctor to say, point by point, she could have been a pro. It was all so . . . cool. Effective. Quite different. I think she – or more likely the unsavoury Greg – must have reported to someone by phone, who told them what to do.'

'Aren't you being a bit snobbish here, Trish?'

She had to laugh. Robert of all people to accuse her of that!

'I mean it, Trish. Angie Fortwell's an intelligent woman, even if she has spent the last couple of decades tilling the earth. She must be more than capable of reading a few student law books and working out what she's got to do to spike your guns.'

'Maybe.' Trish checked her memory again and was determined to push Robert to see things her way. 'But look at these.'

She slid three of the photographs towards him and pointed to a tall man standing on the edge of the crowd in one. He was dressed in a long dark overcoat that looked smoothly expensive, and a hat, and he was turned away from the camera. Almost nothing could be seen of his face or head except a suggestion of full greying hair between the hat brim and the coat collar. His shoulders and back were straight. Everything about him was different from the comfortably slouching FADE supporters in their jeans and beanies and sweatshirts.

'There's the same figure somewhere in each of these shots,' Trish said. 'But the investigators haven't identified him once.'

'What makes you think he's anything to do with FADE?' Robert was back into his preferred mode of patrician disdain. 'Or that it's even the same person in each photograph?'

'I've been measuring him against the others, and I think it's him each time. Given that these three photographs were taken on quite different dates and in quite different places, that's too much of a coincidence. So I want you to phone the solicitors first thing tomorrow to get the investigators to find out who he is.'

'Trish, for God's sake.' Robert sighed in exasperation and she wondered how his many girlfriends had put up with him since his marriage collapsed. 'Even if it were possible at this juncture, what would it tell us?'

'If someone's behind Angie and FADE, we need to know who he is. And why he's involved.'

'Is there any reason someone shouldn't give them a spot of pro-bono legal advice?'

'Absolutely not,' Trish said, wishing she didn't have to spend the evening arguing as well as the working day. 'So there'd be no need for this kind of secrecy.'

'Perhaps not, but—'

'Before you go,' she said, not prepared to waste any more

of her own time, 'have you ever seen anything in the documents that identifies the bed-and-breakfasters who stayed at the Fortwells' farm?'

'Can't remember.'

'Check it out, please.' The crispness of her voice made him look at her with a new expression. Could it be respect? Or impatience like her own? 'And can you bring me all the stuff about the tank design again? I need to have another go at it.'

'Trish—'

'Get on with it.'

Much later she walked back across Blackfriars Bridge. She was halfway over before she realised that all the tiredness she'd felt at the weekend had gone. With her brain properly engaged, adrenaline fizzing through her body, she was herself again. There was a huge moon tonight, hanging over the black water of the Thames and making her think of a book she'd had as a very young child: something about a character seeing the moon in a bucket of water and trying to get it out.

She must have been three or four, she thought, and unable to read for herself. So it would have been in the time of ordinary family life, before her father dumped her and her mother. In those days he would come back from the insurance office where he worked to read her bed-time stories and let her play with his cufflinks. She used to lie back on her single pillow, smelling the dinner her mother was cooking downstairs, and listen to his voice reading from one of the small thin hardback books from her collection. Most evenings, he embellished the text as only he could. Smiling at the memory, she felt almost as though she could hear his voice, very Irish as it still was when he was telling stories:

'And to be sure, Trish-my-dear, aren't we all chasing for the moon and pouring it down the drain at the selfsame time?'

Had she made it up, or had he really said something like that? She ought to phone him as soon as this case was over and make an effort to see him. She'd got over her rage about what he'd done to her long ago, but she still couldn't forgive the way he'd ignored David's existence after the break-up with his mother, Jeannie.

Trish had known nothing about either of them until six years ago, when Jeannie had sent David to her for sanctuary. Jeannie was being terrorised by a crime family against whom she'd given evidence. Later, after her death, David had had nowhere else to go, and Trish had adopted him.

Thinking about that terrifying time, she rounded the corner of her street and climbed the iron staircase as quietly as possible. If you caught your toe at the wrong place on the treads, you could set up a vibrating clang that would wake anyone in the flat.

Inside, she double-locked the door, laid her keys in the bowl with the barest chink and turned to climb up to bed, only to see a line of light under David's door. Frowning, she held up her wrist to see from the faintly illuminated figures of her watch that it was past one o'clock.

She pushed open his door to see that he'd fallen asleep as he read. He was lying flat on his back with the book just touching his chin. With her hand on the switch of his bedside light, she looked down at his sleeping face and winced. His eyelids were red and swollen and there were sticky streaks under them.

Never once in their life together had she seen him cry. Even in the early days when he must have lived every hour in loneliness and terror, he had never broken down in front of her. Occasionally, when George had shouted at him before they'd sorted out how to work round each other, he'd been a bit sniffly, but that was all. Could she wake George now to find out what had happened?

When she pushed open the door of her own bedroom, she looked down at George's face and saw all the customary strain smoothed out by sleep. He was lying on his back, with one arm crooked above his head and the duvet pushed down to waist level. She touched his cheek, which made him turn towards her in his sleep and move his face against her hand, more trusting and vulnerable than he'd ever allow himself to be in the daytime. She couldn't disturb him now.

Chapter 7

Antony's sleeping face was very thin inside the cage that was keeping his neck vertebrae together while they healed, and his skin looked like fine white modelling clay. Trish wound the strap of her shoulder bag round and round her fingers, wishing she hadn't allowed herself to be so angry when she read the message he'd left for her at chambers on Wednesday morning.

Her feelings couldn't hurt him, but they had shaken her. The thought of Robert scurrying over here to the hospital at the end of each day's proceedings and revving up Antony's anxieties about how she was performing made her feel like a giant turtle being gawped at as it went endlessly back and forth in a tiny tank instead of ranging the seas in freedom.

'He's not likely to wake,' said a passing nurse. 'The pain was so bad we had to give him a pretty big dose of morphine. D'you want to leave a message for him?'

Trish scuffled in her bag for a pen and accepted a piece of scrap paper from the nurse. After a moment's thought, she wrote:

Antony, I came flying to answer your summons, but you were out of it and not expected to wake in the

> foreseeable future. (It's nearly 8.30 and visiting will end in a few minutes.) Don't worry. Whatever Robert has told you, I'm in control of my material – and of the case. Forget about it and concentrate on letting your bones knit. Must get back to work. I'll come back when it's all over. Love Trish.

She folded the paper in half and left it on his table, tucked between the two narrow glass vases that held rare-looking orchids, asking the nurse to tell him where it was. It seemed safer to leave it there than to risk losing it amid all the forms and charts at the reception desk.

As if I didn't have enough to worry about without chambers politics, she thought as she walked out of the quiet, dimly lit ward.

The most important thing was making space to talk to David and find out what Monday's tears were about.

She switched her phone back on as soon as she'd left the hospital's main doors and felt it buzz to alert her to her voicemails. There was the expected clutch from Steve, her clerk, and Robert, but there was one from David, too.

'Hi. It's me. George says you want to talk to me. We've had supper; he's put yours in the oven. He's working upstairs and I'm about to go on the computer. So if you want me, can you ring soon?'

Ah, David, she thought: so practical.

She rang him and apologised for interrupting, adding: 'I just wanted to say how sorry I am that work's overtaken me. I've been to the hospital to talk to Antony Shelley and now I'm free for a bit. I thought I might come home. We could talk while I eat. But if you're stuck into the computer, I—'

'OK,' he said casually, as though he didn't mind either way. She remembered the morning he'd kicked the sofa and complained that she never had time. It seemed astonishing to think it was only four days ago. 'Whatever. I'll be here.'

'Great.'

She hailed a passing taxi and was deposited at the foot of the iron staircase only ten minutes later.

George had laid her a place at the table, with a clean napkin and a highly polished wine glass. A bottle of Chilean Merlot, with about a glass and a half left in it, stood in front of her place.

'That was quick,' David said.

She waited for him to offer to fetch her food from the oven, as he would have done a couple of years ago. Nothing came, so she went to the kitchen and helped herself to a plateful of sausage and lentil stew from the dish in the oven.

When she came back, she put it down and had a good look at David's face. There were no signs of tears today and she couldn't feel any tension when she ruffled his head. He didn't wince this time, either, which suggested the bruise left by Jay's assault with the Scrabble board had healed.

'You'd better eat or it'll get cold.'

Trish picked up her fork and took a mouthful. As made by any ordinarily careless cook like herself, this stew could have been claggy with fat and stodgy too. But George had used all-meat sausages from his favourite butcher in Borough Market and the finest of Puy lentils, a good dose of the Merlot and careful seasoning. The result was a rich, earthy, yet subtle-tasting mouthful of comfort.

'Did Jay like it?' she asked as she swallowed.

David's face barely altered, but she was watching carefully enough to see the faint quiver of his nostrils and a tiny clenching in the corners of his eyes. His newly protuberant Adam's apple moved too, as though he was trying to swallow something unpalatable. He turned away and took a real apple from the bowl, biting into it, which meant his voice was barely audible as he said:

'He didn't come today.'

'I thought he was always going to come now to do his homework.'

'Not any more.' He swallowed too much apple at once and choked. It could've been the spasm in his larynx that made his eyes water.

Trish looked away, so that he would not think she was prying, and said in the kind of casual voice he so often used, 'D'you want to say why? Or should I just ignore it and talk about . . . oh, I don't know: ballet?'

'Ballet.' In spite of loving *Billy Elliot*, he sounded disgusted enough to reassure her. 'No, thanks.'

But he couldn't find a way to tell her, so she had to go on with her questions.

'Did you have a fight?'

'Not exactly.'

'So someone said something. Was it you?'

He was staring down at the half-eaten apple in his hand, so all she could see was hair. That shifted like a curtain as he shook his head.

'I hate him already,' Trish said lightly.

'You mustn't. It's . . . pro'ly my fault.' He was picking the pips out of the exposed core and arranging them at the edge of his plate as he'd done when he first came here to the flat.

'I doubt that, David.' How much should she say? 'It often feels easier to blame ourselves for things people we care about do to us; but, you know, in a way it doesn't do them any more favours than it does us. Sorry; that's getting a bit complicated.'

'Yeah, but I know what you mean.'

Now he was looking at her again, and his black eyes were lighting up with interest. Had she known in the beginning how easily he would come to share her curiosity about the mysteries of human behaviour, she would have been a lot less worried about taking him on. But even at her most anxious, she'd never had the feeling she had with Jay all the time: that he was dangerous and anything might trigger disaster.

'Blaming him means all sorts of trouble, so I didn't,' David said. 'But the things he said was . . . were, I mean—'

'You don't have to tell me if you don't want to.'

He rearranged the apple pips for a long time. Then, still without looking at her, said: 'I do. It's just it's hard. He was angry because I'd tried to stop him getting into trouble at school, and he said he wasn't surprised my mother was . . . was killed, if she was anything like me because I'm a fucking waste of space and no use to anyone and I stink.'

She longed to take him in her arms and knew she couldn't. At fourteen and taller than her, he was way beyond that kind of simple consolation.

'Taking the silliest bit first: you do *not* stink. OK, David?'

He shot a shy smile at her.

'And your mother was killed because she was the very opposite of a waste of space. The few people who are allowed to know anything about her know she died because she'd had the courage to give evidence against the most brutal kind of villain.'

Should she go on? His bottom lip was already tucked

between his teeth and they must be biting hard because there was no colour in the surrounding flesh.

'You know why Jay said it, don't you?'

David didn't look away, but he shook his head.

'Because he's jealous. His own mother drinks too much and behaves so weirdly he can never rely on her. Not to protect him or to be the kind of person he could look up to. He must be very angry with her. Your mother was different. She was a hero and she did everything she could to keep you safe. Never forget that.'

There was no choking to explain away these few tears that were slipping out of his eyes. He sniffed.

'You'd better get yourself a bit of kitchen paper, David,' she said with all the tenderness she'd have loved to express physically.

She gave him a minute or two of privacy, then carried her dirty dishes out to the kitchen.

'Don't do anything with these. I'll wash them up later, but I really ought to go back to chambers soon, unless you need—'

'I'm OK.' He didn't smile.

'Will you tell George for me? And say I thought the sausages were great.'

'Don't you want to see him?' He sounded amazed.

'Not now. I only wanted to see you.' She risked kissing his forehead and didn't wait for a response.

His voice caught her on the threshold and held her back.

'Trish.'

'Yes?'

'After he said it . . . Jay, I mean. Afterwards, I—'

'Yes?'

'I hit him. Twice. His lip kind-of burst. There was a lot of blood. He ran off.'

Angie was walking off her feelings. Trish Maguire had been vile all day in court; even worse than she'd been on the first two days. These streets couldn't give Angie the freedom of the hills, and tonight all she could see was the peeling paint and the narrowness of the grey-and-cream façades instead of the cosiness they'd once suggested, but at least she didn't have to talk to anyone. She could let her hatred of Maguire's insinuating questions sink down into the nastiest muck at the bottom of her mind, and with luck she'd soon be able to stop feeling as though Greg was her jailer.

Having him beside her all day was more and more difficult. This afternoon, she'd wanted to slap his hand away when he held out yet another document she didn't need. And his ghastly beard was really getting to her.

Do stop it, she told herself, well able to understand that none of it was Greg's fault, that he was merely the convenient symbol of everything she couldn't let herself feel about the case. About John. About herself and her horrible temper.

As she walked, she tried to find some of the old earthy humour that had kept her going through many bad times. When that failed she fought for the sense of Greg and Fran as her friends, as the only people other than Polly who were keeping her from drowning in loneliness and rage.

But it was hard. Even as she'd been leaving court, Greg hadn't been able to let her alone. 'Have you got your phone, Ange? What if you get lost, Ange? Better come home with us, Ange. We can eat and then all go for a walk together, if you want exercise; you're not used to London streets; it's not safe; wait, Ange.' And the overall unspoken message beating through everything else: you're our property now. You're answerable to us; you have to stay within our reach.

She'd wanted to stop feeling excluded for most of her life, but she'd had no idea how inclusion would suffocate her. The only way to get out of his grip had been to accept his mobile phone. She'd stuffed it in the pocket of her suit jacket, saying, 'And don't *you* phone *me* unless you want me to jack in the whole case and go home.'

Already regretting the outburst, she'd strode away and heard Fran's blessedly sensible voice: 'Leave her alone, Greg. She'll be fine. She just needs some space. What are we going to eat tonight?'

I don't care because *I'm* not having another bloody vegetable stew, Angie thought, looking around for a burger bar, where she could indulge herself with the kind of food Greg would most detest. I really will need a spike driven through my abdomen if this sodding flatulence gets any worse.

A large wet drop hit her right eye and she wiped her finger across it, expecting to see bird shit. But it was only rain; heavy though. Within minutes her whole scalp was wet and rain trickled through her hair and down her neck. She turned up her face to the cold fresh wetness of it, hoping to feel as though the worst of her ingratitude could be washed away.

Walking on, she trod on a loose paving stone and felt a spray of sticky fluid up the back of her calf. Looking down, she saw it was dirty as well as wet and her pleasure in the rain dwindled. A flash, followed by a gut-churning crack of thunder took her back to the night of John's death and she knew she had to get to shelter fast.

The thickness of the rainfall made it hard to see more than a few feet ahead of her, and the reflected headlights from the oncoming cars didn't help, but eventually she identified a swinging pub sign on her side of the road. That would do. Whatever it was like, it would be better than staying out in this deluge.

She pushed open the door to find herself in the kind of place she thought no longer existed in a city. A long bar of scarred wood took up half the room. The rest was filled with a row of equally battered tables with benches behind and small, unpadded stools in front. There were no gaming machines, no posters, and very little decoration.

'Yes, miss?' said the elderly man behind the bar.

'Could I have—?' Angie broke off, looking at the equally ancient bottles ranged on shelves behind his white head. 'Oh, maybe, some ginger wine.'

'To warm you up. Good idea on a night like this.' He grinned, revealing several gaps in his teeth. 'Drop of whisky in it?'

'Why not? Have you got anything to eat?'

'Ham sandwich any good to you? My wife can make you one.'

'Perfect. Thanks.' She took her drink to a table in the far corner and looked around.

Her few fellow-drinkers were all men and all well past sixty. One must have come in just after her because he was wet, too, and hadn't got a drink yet. The other five looked as though they'd been here for hours; two sat together but they weren't talking, and the others were solitary: all reading their papers or making notes. Reckoning up the odds? Or doing the latest puzzles? She couldn't decide. And it didn't exactly matter.

The whisky mac tasted surprisingly good, the sweetness of the ginger nicely spiked with spirit. She had no idea where she was and felt an extraordinary liberation. If she didn't know, then no one else did, so none of them could get at her.

Something buzzed at her side. For a second she thought there must be a live wire somewhere within the plastered wall, or maybe the bench. Moments later, she realised the vibration had to be coming from Greg's phone in her pocket.

She pulled it out, hating him all over again. Why couldn't he leave her alone?

At last, she remembered he could only get to her if she answered, so she put the phone back in her pocket. When the buzzing stopped she let her head flop forwards as she tried to mop the worst of the rain from the back of her neck with an old tissue she'd found under the phone in her pocket.

It buzzed again. Again she ignored it. But he wouldn't stop calling, and once the other drinkers started to stare at her every time the insistent noise started up again, she knew she'd have to do something.

The phone wasn't like her own brick-heavy old-fashioned one and she couldn't work out how to turn it off. None of the obvious buttons worked and the noise just went on, getting louder. At last she found the right button and stopped the buzzing dead.

'Ham sandwich?' called a woman from the internal doorway at the back of the pub. 'Who ordered a ham sandwich?'

Angie raised her hand and the woman, who was dressed in the kind of flowered apron that buttoned at the back and hadn't been seen anywhere else since the early 1960s, put down a large plate with a doorstep sandwich. It had been cut into quarters and was flanked by damp-looking lettuce and slices of beetroot that were already leaking purple juice into the bottom slice of bread. Angie paid, smiled her thanks and rescued the sandwich from the beetroot juice.

The ham tasted like real meat and the bread not at all bad. She'd expected limp, steam-baked slices. Chewing hard through the dense crust, she realised that most of what had made her feel so weak had been hunger. Another mouthful of whisky mac and she'd be fine.

The depth of the bread meant she couldn't eat too fast and there was still nearly a third of the sandwich to go when the pub doors opened and another man came in. Were there no women up here in the wilds of north London?

The man removed his damp raincoat and shook the drips off it, turning to look around as he did so. She recognised Ben Givens from the party and lowered her head, hoping he wouldn't clock her.

He walked straight to the bar to order a pint. While it was being pulled, he turned casually and leaned back against the bar, surveying the other drinkers. When the barman put the full tankard on the bar, Ben pointed to Angie and, with a quite exaggerated leer, said: 'And give me another of whatever the lady's drinking.'

The barman looked across at Angie, as though asking permission. Not at all sure what was going on, she shrugged, then nodded because it seemed easier than risking a scene. Moments later Ben brought both drinks to her table.

'Mind if I join you?' he said in a voice she didn't quite recognise.

'If you want.'

He hooked a stool forward with his right foot and sat down, leaning his elbows on the table, which meant he could more or less cover his mouth without being obvious.

'You're a long way from home,' he said. 'What's happened?'

'Nothing,' she said. 'I just needed time on my own. D'you want a sandwich? This is quite good.'

He shook his head. 'I'll be eating later. What happened in court? Did Maguire rough you up?'

'She's vile, you know. It gets worse every day. She's obsessed with proving John did it deliberately – bunged up the filters to make the tanks explode, as a way of committing suicide.'

Ben laughed openly, but the sound didn't convince her; nor did the apparent ease with which he leaned back on his stool.

'I doubt it. She's never been a fool, and only a fool would run a defence like that. She's trying to distract you while she's going after something else. Tell me exactly what happened, what she asked your witness and what he replied.'

'Why the hell should I?' Angie's aggression shocked her as much as it surprised Ben. He patted her knobbly hand in an avuncular kind of way and she wrenched it away.

'Is he annoying you, Miss?' said the barman, coming out from behind his bar with a cloth in his hand.

For a second she was tempted to say yes, then dreaded the fallout that might follow and the inevitable fight with Greg. She shook her head. The barman's creased face hardened and gave her a look that more or less told her she deserved anything that was coming to her if she let herself be pushed around by a stranger.

'Why?' she said again, loudly enough to make everyone else see that she could take care of herself. All the old men in the pub looked up. She could tell most of them disapproved of the noise.

'So I can give you some relevant sympathy,' Ben said much more quietly, lifting his glass and smiling at her over the top of it. 'I rather thought you needed it.'

'I don't need anything, except for this bloody case to be over. I wish I'd never started it, and quite frankly I've been wondering what I could do to persuade CWWM to settle. Almost anything would be better than letting the judge ruin me with costs and damages when Maguire wins for them.'

Ben put down his drink and spent some time examining his nails as though deciding what to say. Then he looked up with an expression that scared her.

'It's too late to back out now.' There wasn't a single scrap of sympathy left in his voice. 'You've come too far and taken too much from Fran and Greg.'

'Is that why you're here? To keep me on the straight and narrow? Were you following me?' She saw from his slight withdrawal that he must have been, and added with far more aggression than she usually allowed herself, 'How dare you? What's *your* interest in my case?'

'Friendship,' he said quickly. 'I told you: I admire what FADE do for absolutely no reward. You stand to get a lot of money if you win, but Fran and Greg? Even if the decision goes the right way, all they'll get is the satisfaction of seeing a polluter punished and a beautiful part of England restored to health.'

Angie wouldn't have thought anyone could make her feel worse until now.

'Come on,' he said a little more kindly. 'Finish that sandwich and I'll take you back to them.'

He hustled her out of the pub and unlocked the doors of a top-of-the-range BMW. As she slid into the passenger seat, the rich woody scent of the leather made her think of the car John had had when they'd first met.

They'd hardly ever had time to do any of the usual things a couple on the edge of a relationship would do: no candle-lit dinners, no romantic weekends wandering through beautiful beechwoods before coming home to eat gourmet food and quaff champagne. But there had been journeys in his car. Most of their closest moments had been spent sitting side by side, on their way to client meetings, talking their way into love. They'd known all about each other before they'd made love the first time, and neither of them had ever had to pretend to be more successful or glamorous than they were.

Turning her head to the side as though she wanted to look out of the window, she wiped her eyes with the cuff of her coat sleeve.

'Angie, I'm . . . Bugger!' A phone rang with a proper old-fashioned ring, not the sneaky buzz of the one Greg had lent her. 'That'll be Greg. Could you answer and let him know I've found the lost sheep and am bringing her home? The phone's there in the box by the gear lever.'

Hating him, Angie let it ring.

Chapter 8

'Message from Mr Shelley.'

Trish looked up from her desk on Friday morning to see Steve peering round her door. His expression was cheerful enough to keep her from worrying.

'He said your note got lost yesterday, but one of the cleaners just gave it to him, and he wants me to tell you—' He fished in his pocket. 'I thought I'd better write it down to get it right. He says: "Tell her I didn't summon her for a wigging. Just wanted to see her. I promise not to be asleep next time she's got a minute to come over. But she'd better phone the ward first so they can keep me awake. Chin chin."'

The absurdity of 'chin chin' as a farewell made her smile, but it was the meat of the message that gave her the real lift. 'Thanks, Steve.'

'How's it going?'

'Not too badly. They finished their case yesterday. Now it's our turn. So I need to keep focused.'

'Right you are. Good luck.'

'Aren't you supposed to say "break a leg" or something?' she said as she went back to her papers and reached for another yellow Post-it to mark a particular piece of evidence.

'"Superstition is the religion of feeble minds."'

'I never knew your hero was interested in superstition,' she said, still concentrating on her work. 'Or religion.'

'Hero? What hero?'

'Churchill. I can't remember ever hearing you quote anything about superstition before.'

'I've moved on, see.' Steve sounded strange enough to make her glance up again and meet his shifty gaze. He smirked. 'Or rather back. It's Burke now. He said even more useful things than Mr Churchill.'

'Lucky old you.' Trish's mind was already back with her evidence, and she didn't even notice Steve walk out of her room.

Robert had calmed down as he'd watched the last couple of days' cross-examination and, although he still wanted a turn on his feet, he'd stopped giving her warning notes whenever he thought she was straying. He'd even made a few jokes of his own about checking the climbing ropes and ensuring she had enough carabiners and pitons in her kit.

The door crashed open and he erupted into the room, waving a clutch of paper.

'What on earth has happened?'

'I've got to hand it to you, Trish: you've got a splendidly devious mind.'

'Aha! The mystery man. Have they found him?'

'Absolutely.' He dropped into the better of the two visitors' chairs and shoved the piece of paper across her desk.

A short printed report was clipped to a selection of black and white prints of the interior of the most depressing kind of unreconstructed pub. The first showed Angie Fortwell, looking as though she was halfway through an operation without anaesthetic, ignoring the wine glass between her hands. A man was sitting opposite her with his back to the camera.

Trish shuffled through the prints until she came to one that showed him full-face emerging from the pub.

'Who is he?'

'Don't you recognise him?'

'I'm not sure. It *is* him, though, isn't it? The bulk and the shoulders are right. And I think I've seen that Burberry in one of the original shots.' She reached down to the bottom drawer of her desk, where she had the first set of surveillance photographs. 'Yes. It is. Look: here and here. Who is he?'

'Benjamin Givens.'

'Givens? Why do I know that name? *Givens*? You mean the barrister?'

'That's it. You're a clever baggage, you know, when you put your mind to it. I've been looking through all the investigators' reports and I think you're right that he did deliberately evade the watchers. Which means you may also be right about his involvement with FADE.'

'When were these taken?'

'Wednesday night. You wanted the dogs put back on Angie and her confrères. They were picked up outside the RCJ on Wednesday evening. And the people following her found this. They made the identification yesterday.'

'I wonder what was so important that he came out of hiding,' Trish said, half to herself.

'No time to argue about it now. We'll be late if we don't get moving. I've sent Hal on ahead with the documents. Have you had enough coffee?'

'What? Oh, lord yes. Plenty. Let's go.'

But she found it hard to put down the photograph and even harder to stop her mind crunching through the possibilities thrown up by the identification of Ben Givens. Was he really giving pro-bono help because he cared about the protection of the environment? Or was someone paying him?

Probably not. Accepting secret payments for legal advice could get him disbarred if anyone found out. But if he wasn't being paid, why the secrecy?

David was standing outside the head's office, waiting to be called in. He hadn't done anything wrong, so he was cross. Everyone could see him here, and they'd all think he was in trouble. It wasn't fair. And he had work to do. At last his form teacher came out of the head's room and jerked his head back.

'You can go in, David.'

He slouched forwards to show what he thought about it all and found himself looking around Mr Black's room like a tourist. He'd never been in it before and was surprised to see how like Trish's chambers it was. There were the same white-painted bookshelves all along one wall and a desk just as big as hers, but not as messy.

'Now, David,' said the head, stroking his heavy chin and looking out from under his hairy eyebrows, 'what's all this I've been hearing about Jay and your trainers?'

'Nothing. Why?'

'It's not nothing. Jay has been seen wearing a pair of trainers, box fresh and just like your new ones. You have been seen wearing the old worn-out ones. It doesn't take a genius to make the connection.' He waited a moment or two but David didn't volunteer anything. 'I don't want to go running to your sister without having the full story.'

'I give them to him.'

'Gave, David; gave, as you very well know. Why did you give them to him?'

'He hasn't got any. And his family hasn't got any money to buy them for him.'

'That's true, but it's not enough of an explanation. Why now?'

David shrugged and said he didn't know. The pattern on the carpet was interesting, all geometric with lozenges and octagons. He started to count the different shapes in the way he'd learned when he was young and people were telling him things he didn't want to hear.

'David, pay attention!'

He went on counting.

'You're not in any trouble. I just need to be sure that Jay hasn't been putting pressure on you to give him expensive things that belong to you.'

'Course not.' He looked up, having arrived at eight for the number of different patterns. 'I told you I *gave* them to him.'

'Why?'

'Because I wanted him to have them.'

'Is your sister happy about it?'

'She doesn't know yet. She's busy at the moment. She's got a big case. But I'll tell her soon.'

'That's not good enough, David. I've been teaching boys of your age for twenty-five years now, and I know when there's more to a story than they're telling me. Things haven't been right between you and Jay all week. Now here he is wearing your best trainers. What's going on?'

'Nothing.' Now he was counting the lines of different lengths. There were patterns there too.

'I'm going to have to send a note to your sister to alert her to what's going on.'

'Don't do that.' There were three sorts of short lines and six longer ones. They could probably be subdivided even more. 'She's busy.'

'You leave me no alternative. I'm too worried to let this go.'

He went back to counting the shapes. He could've missed one the first time.

'David?'

'Oh, OK. I'll tell her tomorrow or Sunday, when she's not working all the time.'

'Good. Make sure you actually do it. You'd better get going now. You've got English next, haven't you?'

'Yes.' Which was good. He liked English.

'Right. Well, don't go giving Jay anything else. If I see any sign of him in possession of anything that belongs to you, I'm phoning your sister's chambers right away, however busy she is.'

David didn't answer. There wasn't anything to say. He thought of the jeans Jay wanted. They were still hanging in the cupboard at home because David liked them too much to let them go. But if he had, he wouldn't be in this mess now: Jay wouldn't have worn the jeans at school, so no one would've known. Maybe he'd talk to George tonight and get him to sort Trish out. Maybe. It would depend what mood George was in when he got home.

Now Trish was so busy, George stayed in Southwark every night instead of only sometimes, and he was always there first, ready to cook supper. But he usually had a briefcase full of papers to work on afterwards and worrying about them could make him irritable and uncooperative. You always had to pick your moments with George, even when Jay was making him laugh.

When Trish got back to her room in chambers after the day's session, she recognised the head teacher's writing on the hand-delivered envelope at once. Her mind lurched. What had Jay made David do now? She longed to rip the letter open right away, but it would have to wait until she'd dealt with Robert and CWWM's solicitor, Fred Hoffman.

'I still don't understand, Trish,' he said in his agreeably relaxed voice.

She'd always liked him for his brains and his determination to cooperate whenever he could. He must have been in his mid-fifties and there were plenty of solicitors of his generation whose first reaction to any request was to explain why they couldn't provide what you wanted. Not Fred.

'Have a seat,' she said, waving towards the better of the visitors' armchairs and leaving Robert to the one with the broken spring.

'Run it past me again.' Unusually Fred was frowning, which made his eyebrows protrude and hang over his brown eyes like a gorilla's.

'Evidence from the surveillance photographs suggests Angie Fortwell is being secretly coached by Benjamin Givens,' she said, trying to banish the ludicrous image of Fred as a vast primate thundering through the damp Rwandan forest. 'There's no obvious reason for the secrecy so I need to know what he's up to.'

'How d'you suggest I find that out?' Fred's tone was sarcastic but even now he wasn't refusing to try.

'I've no idea, not being a detective,' she said, smiling. 'But you and CWWM employed plenty of those in the run-up to the case, and whoever you've got now produced these helpful photographs from Wednesday night. I have every faith in them – and in you, *dear* Fred.'

He produced a sharp, humourless crack of laughter, then drummed his broad fingers on the edge of her desk. 'Far be it from me to turn away a compliment from any silk, Trish, but I'm not sure how—'

'"Find the money,"' she quoted. 'Find out if there is any and, if so, follow it. There must be ways.'

'Probably none you could use in court.' The dark eyes lit with amusement, which made her think he must be fantasising about wicked schemes of burglary and intimidation.

'Maybe not. But there's still time to settle this thing. Just.' She put her elbows on the desk and leaned towards him.

He moved forwards too, hunching his broad shoulders, as though trying not to overwhelm her with his size.

'Look, Fred, what I most want is to avoid CWWM being forced to pay big damages and only later finding out that FADE and Angie Fortwell have been up to something illegal all along. With such an impoverished bunch, we'd never get the money back for CWWM even if we won on appeal. So it's pretty urgent.'

He leaned back and dug a hand in his pocket to extract a small leather folder with gold edges. He peeled one card away from the rest and wrote himself a note. Trish thought of her huge legal pads and wondered why anyone, but particularly a man as burly as Fred, would confine himself to such an affected, shopping-list kind of jotter.

'How long d'you think you'll take with our witnesses?' he said, looking up again.

'Not much more than a week.'

'But we could spin it out a bit,' Robert said from the sidelines. 'Quite legitimately.'

'"Quite" meaning partly,' said Trish with unusual dryness, 'rather than absolutely. What a useful word that is. Will you get it under way, Fred?'

'Will do. Now, d'you need me for anything else tonight? I've got to go to Heathrow to meet CWWM's managing director. He's on his way back from sorting out some disaster in the States and wants a first-hand report on how things are going here.'

'I'd heard they were having a run of bad luck, but I hadn't realised it extended across the Atlantic,' Robert said. 'What's been happening there?'

'Too complicated to go into now.' Fred kept checking his watch and was visibly itching to be off. Trish nodded to him.

'You get on, Fred. Robert and I can manage here. Thanks.'

He extracted himself from the deep chair with surprising ease for such a big man and ambled out. Trish and Robert worked their way through the other questions thrown up by the day's proceedings.

Only when Robert had eventually followed Fred out of the room could she at last pick up the head's letter. Trying to think of the worst it might contain, she tore open the envelope.

Dear Trish,

I'm sorry to trouble you when, as David tells me, you're in the middle of a large and important case, but

I'm worried about what is going on between him and Jay. Already Jay is having a deleterious effect on David's language and behaviour. I've never known your brother so obstinate, even obstructive, and his homework is slapdash in a way none of us has ever seen from him before.

This is of concern in itself.

Worse, however, is the discovery that he has just given Jay his new trainers. His motive may have been purely altruistic, as he claims, but I fear that Jay may be exerting undesirable pressure on David. If this is true, it needs to be dealt with before it escalates, as I'm sure you will agree.

I told David I wouldn't bother you with this while you're so busy, but I've decided it's too urgent to wait, so I do hope that you will be able to take the time to talk to him over the weekend. I would appreciate a discussion – by telephone if necessary.

I look forward to hearing from you.

Yours ever, Jeremy

Trish put down the letter, wondering what on earth to do about Jay. She still admired his courage, and his brains, and she wanted to help. But if he was going to make David miserable and screw up his time at school, she'd have to separate them. If Jeremy Black was right and the pressure on David did escalate . . .

'Shit!' she said aloud, trying to block out pictures of all sorts of horrors that might never happen.

'Really, Trish.' Robert's voice came from just outside the door. He pushed it open and she saw he was already kitted out in overcoat and scarf, with his briefcase in his hand. 'Aren't you too grand now to use language like that?'

'Sod off,' she said lightly and was relieved to hear him laugh. 'Have a good weekend. See you Monday.'

'Sure. Same to you.'

Hearing him run down the stone stairs and bang the front door behind him, she cleared her desk completely, locking up every scrap of paper. If Greg Waverly and FADE were as devious as she was beginning to believe, she didn't want to take any risks with her confidential documents.

As she walked home, she tried to put him and the case right out of her mind so she could concentrate on David.

Somehow she'd have to protect him from his own generous impulse to include Jay in everything he had and did. She owed George time, too. They'd had no more than a few minutes' sleepy chat for days, and he'd been carrying the whole domestic load for her.

Better eat first, she decided. I can talk to David after supper, see him safely in bed and reading, and then focus on George.

That would be easier if there weren't still a residue of the constraint she'd noticed on the evening he'd cut his toenails in her bedroom. He hadn't volunteered an explanation of what had been bothering him, and she hadn't had time to winkle it out of him.

Once again the iron staircase felt like Everest and she wished she could be somewhere else, anywhere, even arguing with Robert about the best way of dealing with CWWM's difficulties.

'Stop it,' she muttered, shoving her key into the front-door lock.

The door seemed extra stiff, as though the wood had swollen in all the rain that had emptied itself from the clouds in the last few days. She put her shoulder to it and pushed hard, only to feel it yield so fast she was propelled into the room by her own force.

'How very flattering!' George said, looking up from the newspaper. 'I knew you missed us, but not that much.'

'Hi,' she said, leaning over his shoulder and bending her head so she could kiss him under the chin, just where his skin was most sensitive. 'Good day?'

'Not bad.' He moved a little, like a cat stroking itself against a friendly body. Maybe she'd imagined the constraint. 'You?'

'We're making progress with the case, but I can't quite see my way through to a win or even satisfactorily limited damages.' She sighed in frustration. 'Still, it's the weekend now, and I'm not going to think about any of it tonight. What are your plans?'

'We're going to train in the pool tomorrow morning,' David said from the other sofa. 'Me and George. D'you want to come?'

'I'd only feel inadequate as I flap about like a water-boatman on the surface and you two do your otter thing slicing through the water. My time would be better used cooking some delicious kind of lunch so it's hot and ready when you get back.'

'Great,' David said with a smile that looked forced to her oversensitive eye. He lowered his lids, looking away. 'Can we have that chicken thing with the ciabatta and Parmesan crust top?'

She had to smile at his tact. He'd just picked the easiest of all the dishes George had taught her.

'Sure. D'you think Jay will like it?'

David dropped his book.

'I doubt if he'll be here this weekend,' George said, with a warning expression on his face. 'I'll get supper on the table now. Can you manage without a shower tonight? It's a bit late already.'

'I'll just wash my hands,' she said, letting her eyes put the question she couldn't ask aloud.

George very slightly shook his head and looked upwards. Long experience told her this meant the news would be better kept until they were upstairs in bed and out of David's earshot. A little reassured, because it was clear George already knew something, Trish asked David if she could use his bathroom to wash and so save time going upstairs.

'After all, mustn't keep George's food waiting,' she said, grinning.

David's answering smile was only the palest version of his usual one. She abandoned the attempt to get through to him and went to clean the London smuts off her hands.

'So what's been happening?' she asked when she and George were alone. 'I had a letter from Jeremy Black, telling me David's given Jay his best trainers and asking me to intervene, but I'd better have the full story before I try.'

'You know most of it then, and I wouldn't have thought there was anything you could do. Apparently Jay's wanted those trainers ever since he first saw them. At that stage David refused to hand them over. He changed his mind only after he beat Jay up the other day.'

Trish made an inarticulate protest. Before she could organise her ideas, George said:

'Didn't you hear about that? Jay's split lip and all the blood? David told me he'd confessed.'

'He did talk a bit about the fight, but he didn't say a word about feeling he had to give Jay a lavish present as a penance.'

'He was afraid you'd tell him to ask for them back and he wants me to make sure you don't.'

'I suppose I might have, although it's a bit unlikely. Why didn't he tell me himself?'

'What he said to me,' George said in a deliberately casual voice that worried her all over again, 'is that he didn't want to bother you when you're so fraught.'

You never have time, she quoted to herself in silence.

'Apparently when he apologised for losing his temper and drawing blood,' George went on, 'Jay just looked at him in a "yeah, yeah" kind of way that made it clear he didn't believe a word of it. David said he had to do something to *show* he wished he hadn't hit him. Hence the trainers.'

'Oh, bugger it all!' Trish said, sighing. 'For some idiotically naive reason, I thought we'd be able to help Jay without it costing anything but money. D'you think we ought to try to cool the friendship now?'

'David's tougher than you think,' George said, settling his wide shoulders against the pillows. 'And it's no bad thing for him to have to deal with rage and guilt and a bit of anxiety about someone else. Only children can get very self-absorbed, you know.'

'Yes, I do,' she said, quick amusement lightening her voice.

George patted her thigh. 'I didn't mean you.'

'I bet you did really.' She kissed him. 'So maybe I should ask the question that's been nagging at me for days: what is it about Jay that makes you talk as though we all owe him something?'

'He needs help,' he said quickly, as though he wanted to

stop her asking anything else. 'David had a rough enough start, but his day-to-day life was nothing to what Jay has to put up with all the time. If we can do something to mitigate it, I think we should. That's all.'

'How do you know what Jay goes through? Does he tell you? He's never given me any details.'

'It doesn't take much imagination to fill in the gaps,' George said.

Yellow light from the streetlamps leaked in at the edges of the blinds and lit up the few grey strands in the thick tufts of his brown hair. There was a strange half smile on his lips, which didn't look happy, or even familiar.

'And I admire the way he comes out fighting, instead of pretending everything's fine and fantasising about violence in silence as . . . as lots of people would.'

Trish opened her mouth to ask for more and he propped himself up on one elbow so he could trace her lips with the other hand, saying: 'Let's talk about something else.'

Next morning, Trish made herself lie in bed after George and David had left for the pool. Long experience had taught her that, although work was the only sure way of fighting off worry, there were also times when she had to slow herself down and make the effort to clear her mind of everything. Otherwise contradictory ideas could generate so much stress they acted on her brain like dirt in an engine's carburettor, making it cough and slow and eventually stop altogether.

George and David had already done the supermarket run on Friday evening, so the ingredients she would need for lunch were in the fridge. She had no need to hurry. Eventually, she put the newspaper on the floor and slid out of bed, to give herself the luxury of an extra-long, very hot shower.

All week she'd had tight knots in all the connections between her arms and shoulders, legs and groin, neck and trunk. As the hot water powered down on her, needling and soothing at the same time, they began to loosen and at last to untie.

Flexible again, and feeling as though her mind was more or less free of everything except trivialities, she turned off the water and wrapped a huge scarlet towel around her body. The towel was old, with much less pile than it had once had and edges already shredded. She ought to buy more and wondered whether she had grown out of the need for scarlet. Running through the more grown-up possibilities of colours like beige and mushroom, she decided she was still some way off that stage.

The idea of spending the whole day in a dressing gown was tempting, but impractical with everything she'd have to do in the kitchen, so she pulled on her softest, oldest jeans and layered three different tops over them, taking perverse pleasure in the clashing orange, pink and purple. With the central heating turned luxuriously high, she could leave her feet bare and pattered downstairs to make a start on the chopping.

Tears were still pouring down her face, even after the onions were safely in their pan, and she was running her hands and the large chef's knife under the cold tap in a vain attempt to clear the burning in her eyes. A loud knocking on the front door made her curse in terms that would probably have made Robert blench.

She dropped the huge knife in the sink, turned off the taps and the gas under the pan of sweating onions. Wiping her eyes on the back of her hand, she opened the door to see Jay Smith, with a baseball cap crammed low over his forehead and his hood up over it, staring at the floor.

'C'n I talk to Dave?' he said in a voice so deep and strangulated she could barely decode it.

'He's gone swimming. Was he expecting you?' she said, knowing he hadn't been.

Jay's bent head swayed from side to side. A thin trickle of blood oozed out from under his cap and spread down the side of his round face. His skin was the colour of oatmeal, much paler than usual, so his spots stood out even more clearly.

'You'd better come in. They'll be back in about half an hour. D'you want some juice? Or a cup of tea?'

'Yeah. OK. Tea. Three sugars.' His voice was a little easier to understand as he slowed it down, but nothing like as clear as it could be.

He slopped across the floor and she checked the trainers. These were old and very dirty. There was blood on them too, but darker, older. Only when she'd shut the door securely behind him, did Trish say, 'I'll put the kettle on, Jay. But tell me: are you hurt?'

'Nah.'

'There's blood on your face.'

'Fuckin' hell,' he said, wiping the back of his hand against it, then rubbing his hand up and down his jeans.

'Jay, what's happened.'

''s nothing.' He shook his head with such vigour that the blood flow increased. The more he tried to wipe it away, the faster it came. Soon there was blood all over his hand and the hood. He pushed it back. With the shadows gone, she saw the swelling in his lip, where David had hit him.

That didn't look nearly as bad as she'd feared, and it wasn't bleeding any longer.

'Jay, I need to do something about that cut. Will you take off your baseball cap?'

She saw he'd been crying and knew she mustn't comment. 'Look, I've got a first-aid kit here. Let's go into David's bathroom and I'll clean it up for you and put on a plaster. That way you won't drip blood everywhere.

When he took off his cap, she had to fight hard not to gasp. There was a growing bruise just above his temple and a pattern of dents, along with a slash that had not only broken the skin but gone quite deep. To her unaccustomed eye, it looked as though someone had given him a tremendous, back-handed blow with a hand that wore a heavy ring with several sharp edges. It was far too fresh to have been part of David's attack.

She pulled down the loo seat and its lid. 'Why don't you sit there, in the light, and I'll have a go. It looks nasty, but I think you'll be able to manage without a stitch. Look, I'm going to use antiseptic wipes, just to be sure the cuts are properly clean, and they will sting. OK?'

He nodded. The tears had stopped. She hoped she was doing the right thing in not taking him to hospital. As gently as possible, she tipped his head to one side and began to wipe the edges of the wound with the Dettol-soaked tissue.

'Who did this to you, Jay?'

'Me fuckin' bruvver of course.'

'Does he often hit you?' She tried to keep all expression out of her voice so that she didn't rev him up even more.

'Yeah. They call it "justified chastisement".'

'*What*?' All her good intentions disappeared in a rush of outrage on his behalf. 'Who does?'

'It's what my social worker said once when she was talking to Darren. He tells me to do stuff, 'n if I don't he hits me. Not always. But us'y.'

Trish was working out what to say next, how to express her absolute condemnation of Darren's violence without making life at home even harder for Jay.

'Today he telled me to watch Kimberley. My sister. 'n I was playing with David's PSP and I didn't see when she run off. So Darren hit me.'

Trish stopped what she was doing. She couldn't trust herself to be gentle enough while she was trying to work out the whole story.

'David's Play Station Portable? Did he give it to you?'

'He give me a lend of it. That's why I come this morning. When Darren hit me, it broke.' He looked up at her.

His blue-grey eyes were huge and worried beneath the unattractively short fringe. They looked honest, but that didn't mean anything.

'I had to tell him. Cos I haven't got no money to buy him another one. I was goin' to, like, say—' He let his head sink down again.

At last Trish could see something of what must be making David cling to the friendship. Jay wasn't just an exotic stranger with an occasional talent for wicked humour; he was generous-minded and brave. And he obviously cared about David. It would have been so easy to pretend someone had stolen the broken Play Station, but he'd come to confess.

She went back to cleaning the wound. There wasn't a sound from him as she worked, but he couldn't stop himself flinching when the pressure of her fingers hit the tenderest bits of his forehead. It took nearly five more minutes before she had his face clean and dry enough to fix on a large, waterproof plaster. He was lucky, she thought, that the blow had missed his temple.

'D'you feel dizzy?' she asked. 'Or sick?'

'Hungry,' he said with a shadow of his old gleeful grin.

'That's a good sign. But lunch won't be ready for another hour. D'you want to come and help me cook?'

He shrugged, perhaps not wanting to admit he didn't know anything about cookery, but he followed her out of the bathroom and past the fireplace to the kitchen.

'We're having a kind-of chicken-crumble thing,' she said, pointing to the glass square in the oven door, where the chicken was roasting so that she could tear the meat off the bones and add it to the sauce. 'Baked potatoes and broccoli. Then cheesecake. I should've made that yesterday, but I was too tired. I think it'll set in time.'

She assembled her modest ingredients and the quiche dish that would hold the finished pudding. As she started to bash a bagful of biscuits with the rolling pin, Jay said:

'What're you doing?'

'Making the base. When the biscuits are reduced to crumbs, they'll be bound together with melted butter and smoothed into the dish. It's instead of pastry. D'you want to do this bit while I do the butter?'

He accepted the rolling pin and went at it so vigorously he split the bag. Trish contained her laughter and found another bag. Later, she showed him how to smooth the sticky crumbs up the sides of the dish, then explained how the mixture of condensed milk and cream would be turned by the lemon juice into a cheese-like substance.

'I've never seen anything like that before,' he said, as he watched the thickened pale-yellow mixture flop out of the bowl. 'How d'you learn it?'

'From my mother,' Trish said, noticing that he was back to using standard English and glad of the opportunity to open real communication with him. 'She was a single mum, too. My dad ran away when I was seven, so I know a bit about—'

Jay looked at her with such clear disdain that she both rejoiced at his intelligence and quailed at her misjudgement.

'Yeah,' he said after an uncomfortable pause. 'But you didn't have no brothers, did you? Not like me 'n George.'

'George? George Who?'

'You know: *your* George.'

'He hasn't got any brothers,' Trish said, picking up a large broccoli tree to break into florets.

'*Course* he has. One anyway.' Jay's contempt for her lack of knowledge was as nothing to her own surprise. 'Henry. The one he won't have even at his own funeral.'

'Oh, him,' Trish said, as the only way of stopping this uncomfortable conversation. 'Can you lay the table for me while I deal with the veg? Oh, and you'd better put the cheesecake in the fridge. OK?'

He did as she asked but kept coming back to ask questions about the table laying, which seemed to be wholly new to him. Each time he interrupted her own silent questions: had George been exercising his imagination as a way of helping Jay talk about his experiences at home? Or did he really have a brother he hated so much he'd never said a word to her in all the years they'd had together? She knew about his two sisters and had met them often, but there'd never been any mention of a brother called Henry.

*

That evening when they'd taken Jay back to the estate and David was asleep, George was leafing through the newspapers for an article he wanted to keep.

'Jay told me something odd today,' she said, putting out a hand for the rejected sections so that she could stuff them in a recycling bag.

'Odder than usual?' George was clearly distracted by his search.

'He talked about someone called Henry; your brother?' Trish let her voice turn up at the end of the sentence to make it a question.

George kept his broad back to her.

'Hmm. It's somewhere, this piece about a money-laundering case that ended in the organised crime gang's murder of their cash-carrying stooge.'

'Try the business section,' she said without thinking.

'It's not there,' he snapped. 'Which is why I've already dumped that bit.'

'Sorry.' She let a moment pass, then tried again. 'And I felt a bit of a clot because it was obvious I'd never heard of Henry. Is he—?'

'Still alive?' George's voice was still clipped, almost harsh. 'As far as I know.'

He turned at last. His face looked held in, as though he was fighting to keep all possible clues out of his expression.

'He wasn't in fact half as bad as Jay's Darren clearly is, but he made my life a misery. I don't want to think about him. OK? Ah, thank God. It's here.'

The tearing sound of the newspaper being ripped between his big hands seemed horribly appropriate. Trish knew she had to keep her mouth shut this time.

Chapter 9

Angie woke in the night with an astonishing sense of well-being. For nearly a minute it held and she lay, listening to the cars' engines pause and rev as they changed down for the corner and watching the pattern of headlights sweep across the ceiling. Then she remembered: John was dead; not, as in the dream, powerful and in charge, driving them to where they needed to go, and making everything come right.

Nothing was going to come right now. However she reworked the evidence, it got worse. Nothing Trish Maguire had made her listen to since the first day had been as important as the revelation of John's depression.

She hadn't noticed it. She'd loved him; she'd believed the feeling between them was like superglue and felt it made all his irritability and the privations and anxieties bearable; but she hadn't noticed he was on the edge of despair. He hadn't even told her he'd been to the surgery.

What else had she missed? She still didn't believe Maguire's shitty insinuations about suicide. No farmer would need to create a toxic fire to kill himself. Not when he had guns and ropes and all sorts of ordinary, swallowable poisons to hand. And no sensible, responsible man would take a risk with something as dangerous as reformulated benzene.

But day after day Maguire's questions were making it sound as if the fire *had* to have been caused by blocked vents, and they were what John was paid to prevent. *Could* he have become so bogged down in misery that he'd lost all sense of responsibility?

Angie turned over again, bashing her pillow and thinking about Maguire's first expert witness, who'd given evidence on Friday, with that story about how John must have been in the tank enclosure when the explosion happened. Greg had long ago explained that, if the judge believed the story, it would give him a reason to cut their damages and so they had to make it sound incredible in her cross-examination. But she was beginning to wonder whether it could have been true.

Greg had given her a list of questions to put to the expert, and she hadn't really thought any of them through. Which was why she'd added one of her own: 'Was there any evidence of cypress bark or needles on the deceased's back?'

She'd assumed that would prove the explosion had happened when he was beyond the tank enclosure. But the expert had pointed out, in the tone of one explaining the obvious to a child, that it wouldn't make any difference; there were cypress trees all round the enclosure, so the traces could have come from any of them, whether he'd been inside or out. Of course he was right. She'd felt such a fool and Greg had been vociferously angry. Maguire had looked at her with pity, which was worse.

Then there'd come CWWM's contracts man, who'd explained to the court that he'd laid out for John precisely what risks they'd face if they had the tanks next to their land, and how important it was for him to monitor the filters every single day. If he'd done that, the man had said, there could never have been an explosion.

Why hadn't he checked? What had been going on in his mind? Why hadn't he talked to her about what he was feeling? Had he thought she wouldn't want to help him?

She closed her eyes, as though that could stop the thoughts and let her sleep. It didn't even block out the cars' headlights.

'Are you coming with us to collect Jay, Trish?' David called up the spiral stairs as she emerged from the shower on Sunday morning.

No one hearing his casual voice would suspect the constraint and misery that had been building up in him last week. Trish thought of the quickly changing expressions on his face yesterday when he'd found Jay in the flat on his return from swimming. First there'd been suspicion, then hope, then a kind of letting-go, followed at last by his best smile: happy and so confident it was almost cocky.

'We're off in five minutes,' David added. 'So you'd better hurry if you are coming.'

Trish was tempted to suggest he and George should go off without her while she wrote to the head teacher to warn him about what Jay suffered at Darren's hands. But she didn't want to look as though she was sulking after George's irritable response to her probing of his hidden life last night. She could always write her letter this evening and drop it in at the school on her way into chambers tomorrow.

'I'll come with you,' she called back, 'so long as you don't mind if I have wet hair.'

She moved quickly on to the bedroom to dress and was at the foot of the stairs before George had finished clearing breakfast. His smile was tighter than usual, but it was real. So long as she didn't say anything more about Henry for at least today, all should be well.

The three of them made for George's comfortable Volvo, which was parked in his favourite place under the nearest of the streetlights. He couldn't leave it here during working hours because of the residents' parking rules, but there was no problem in the evenings or at weekends.

'Southwark has changed,' he said, bleeping the locks open. 'When I started staying with you, I never came out without expecting to find broken windows or graffiti.'

'Considering the flat round the corner's up for sale for a million quid,' David said, shooting a prideful smile at Trish, 'I should think it has.'

But bits of the borough are the same as they always were, she thought, as George drove down towards Peckham and the miserable estate where Jay's family had their flat. Geographically it was almost next door, but it could have been in another country. It reminded Trish horribly of the place where David and his mother had lived for the first eighteen months of his life, after Paddy Maguire had abandoned them.

David's mother had been a teacher, who'd believed she could help her pupils only if she understood everything about their lives. Trish often wondered what she'd thought about that decision after she and her toddler son had seen the savage killing that had taken place on their doorstep.

She still hoped David had been too young at the time to have any real memories of what he had witnessed or of the estate where it had happened. He certainly seemed to have no problems with coming so close to it now, but he so rarely talked about his past she couldn't be sure.

As soon as George had parked, just under the sign that gave the estate's name and a map of the various tower blocks and rows of low-rise maisonettes, David was out of the car, shouting:

'I'll give him a call. Won't be long.'

He'd gone before Trish could remonstrate. She turned to George, who smiled again, looking as polite as a friendly stranger.

'D'you think we're mad?' she said.

'Probably. In what particular respect?'

'Letting David more or less revisit his own past like this.'

George had both hands on top of the steering wheel and leaned forwards so that his chin was resting on them as he stared out of the pristine windscreen.

'I don't know. Some people think it's necessary to go back and face the horror in order to heal, don't they?'

Trish was silent. This wasn't about David.

'And others,' he went on, sounding tougher, 'think it's safer to live in the present and avoid tearing oneself apart with memories of a time that can't be changed.'

'You're right. And—' She flinched as a heavy fist banged down on the outside of George's window. 'What the hell?'

A hooded figure was bending down, peering in. She couldn't see much of the face. The fist banged on the window again. She looked around for David and Jay. There was no sign of them.

George activated the central locking, then wound the window down a little way.

'Yes?' he said, at his most detached and authoritarian. He sounded almost as bad as Robert.

The hooded face came closer. Trish saw the man couldn't be much more than seventeen or eighteen, but he looked hostile enough to make her palms sweat. Beneath the hood, his head was shaved.

'You're the wanker messing about with me bruvver, ain't you?'

Trish looked at his hand and saw an ugly great ring with a hideous black stone set in rough-edged metal. She thought of the marks on Jay's forehead and lost most of her fear. 'Are you Darren Smith?'

'Yeah. And he's the wanker who keeps taking Jay and sending him back with money and presents. I know what you're up to. And I know how to pertect him. So you can fuck off now, the pair of you, fucking preverts.'

He moved away and took something from his pocket, shielding it with his other hand. Trish moved, but George put a hand on her thigh, holding her down, then unlocked the doors himself. As he stepped out, Darren fled, waving a spray can at them.

'Oh, bloody hell!'

'What is it?' Trish got out of the car and joined George. Along one pristine silver-grey side of the car were two and a half straggling red letters: N O N.

'I'm sorry,' he said. 'As soon as I've got you and the boys back at the flat, I'll take it to the garage and get this professionally cleaned off.'

'Sorry?' she said. 'Why?'

'Because however much I hate mindless yobs, I hate paedophiles even more, and that's what he's accusing me of. This was going to be "nonce" if I hadn't interrupted him.'

Trish touched his stubbly cheek. 'It's not a real accusation, George; just the kind of meaningless insult a violent stupid mindless bully like him would use. Good. Here are the boys.'

She waved to them, beckoning, and George ushered them into the car from her side so they wouldn't see the sprayed letters. He reached over to kiss her cheek as he settled himself back in the driving seat.

On Monday morning Trish collected a quadruple espresso on her way into chambers, banishing – or trying to banish – all memories of the emotionally charged adventures of the weekend. Her defence of CWWM had started well on Friday and she had plenty more to offer. Today it would be the turn of the head of the team that had designed the tanks, explaining the blueprints that formed part of the judge's bundle of documents.

Similar containers were in use all over the world and, so far, there had been no trouble with any of them, even the ones in places like India and South America, where they existed under much more severe climactic conditions than in the north-east of England. None of them had exploded. There was nothing in the design or materials to explain the fire at the Fortwells'.

Pushing open the door of chambers with her back because one hand was occupied with coffee and the other with her heavy briefcase, Trish heard her name and glanced up to see Fred Hoffman, so gloomy he looked even more like a gorilla than usual.

'Hi. D'you want to take this for me?' She handed over her tall cardboard cup and led the way to her room. 'What's happened?'

'Disappointing news, Trish. I thought you should have it in case you planned to start running any hares in court today.'

'Oh, yes?'

'I know why Ben Givens is involved with FADE.'

'OK. Hit me with it. Why?'

'He's been quietly giving money to several environmental campaigners since he won for GlobWasMan over a year ago.' Seeing her blank look, Fred added: 'I didn't remember the case either, but I'm told it was widely reported at the time.'

'I must have missed it. What's GlobWasMan?'

'Global Waste Management. They're much smaller than CWWM and they were more or less fighting to survive until Givens got them stonking libel damages. They grabbed their chance then and used the dosh to expand.'

'Successfully?'

'Absolutely. They're about to go public. Apparently the Pathfinder's just out and the City's looking at it quite favourably. Maybe we should all invest.'

'You can if you like, but I certainly won't,' Trish said with a spurt of amusement, 'having seen how hard it is to manage dangerous waste safely. Who libelled them?'

'A journalist called Robin Atkins accused them of polluting a water-treatment plant in East Anglia and bribing their way out of trouble.'

'And they sued? Bit over the top, wasn't it?'

'You'd have thought so, wouldn't you? Especially since there was evidence to show some money had left their bank without an obvious destination and a precisely similar sum without a clear source had found its way to someone on the local council.'

'But no actual proof that it was the same money?'

'Exactly. Even so, no one expected them to win, but Givens gave such an impassioned final speech about deliberate attempts to shut down a brave little company dealing with the kind of stuff we'd all prefer to ignore that the jury lost their heads. They awarded millions. Everybody was amazed, including Givens himself, I gather.'

'So why wasn't there an appeal?'

'Apparently the owners of Atkins's paper were so shaken by the verdict they thought it was safer to pay up than risk even more huge costs next time round.'

Trish thought of David and Jay and the trainers as she unpacked her briefcase.

'And you're suggesting Givens is helping FADE as a kind of penance, like planting a forest to compensate for your carbon footprint?' she said, looking up.

'That's the obvious way of looking at it.'

'But if the answer's as simple as that, why's he being so secretive?'

'That's easy, too.' Fred was looking sorry for her. 'What barrister would want it known he'd followed up a big win by funding his client's natural enemies? His clerk wouldn't be able to sell him to anyone.'

Trish felt her teeth grinding and knew she'd give herself a migraine if she didn't stop.

'Of course. Thanks, Fred.' She forced a smile. 'See you in court.'

'Sure.'

He was almost out of the door before she remembered what else she needed.

'Hang on a minute: did Robert ever ask if you had a list of all the bed-and-breakfasters who'd stayed at the Fortwells' farm in the weeks running up to the explosion?'

'No. What're you on now?'

'It's a bit of a wild card,' she said sweetly, burying her

fury that Robert had ignored her request, 'so I won't bother you with my thinking till I know more.'

'Give me a clue, Trish.'

'Third-party intervention is a defence against Rylands v. Fletcher,' she began, but he interrupted.

'Antony wasn't going to go for it.'

'I know.' She let herself smile properly and saw an answering warmth make him look really human. 'But it wasn't his first case as a silk. He could afford to ignore wild cards. I can't afford to ignore anything at all.'

Not even the tiniest marketing opportunity, she added to herself, glimpsing one in the distance. If GlobWasMan were going public, they'd probably have plenty of work for a silk who'd done well for another big chemical-waste company. Maybe she should send for the Pathfinder prospectus after all.

'I'll see what I can do,' Fred said.

As he shouldered his way out of the door, she levered the plastic lid off her coffee. He'd taken enough time to reduce it to a drinkable temperature, so she gulped it down, and felt her mind sparking more quickly as the caffeine tickled up her brain cells. She reread her outline for the morning's questions.

Soon every step in her argument was clear in her mind, as easy to see as a tower made of brightly coloured nursery building blocks. She'd be all right now. She collected her wig and gown and went to roust Robert out of his room.

George's car looked like itself again when Trish paused to check on her way home. In daylight there might be a faint shadow where the graffiti had been, but in the yellow brightness of the streetlamp there was nothing. The garage had done a good job.

Today there were none of the usual savoury smells wafting out of the front door and she paused with her key in her hand, suddenly worried. He always cooked something when he was here. And he'd promised to be around for David and Jay.

'George?' she said before she'd even got the door fully open.

'What is it?' His voice sounded reassuringly normal. 'Trish? You OK?'

He was lying on one of the black sofas, with a chunk of printout on his chest. His briefcase stood open beside him on the floor, next to a heavy tumbler that looked as though it had had whisky in it.

'I'm fine. Have you eaten? Shall I do something about supper?'

He looked at his watch. 'Good lord! It's nine o'clock. I had no idea. We'd better just have bread, cheese and salad. Sorry. I'll get going.'

'Don't worry. I'll deal with it. Has David had anything? Where is he?'

'Working on his computer. He had the usual disgustingly fatty toasted sandwich when he got in, so he won't be starving.'

'No Jay tonight?'

'The head got your note about his wound and – with some difficulty, I gather – organised for his social worker to collect him and take him home for a mediation session with Darren.'

I suppose that's something, Trish thought. But I can't imagine the skinhead we met on Sunday is going to be easy to change.

George deposited his heavy document on the floor and levered himself to a sitting position.

'Don't move,' she said. 'You look as though you've still got work to do. It's my turn to cook.'

'Sure? You're right: I do need to finish this before tomorrow.'

'I'm sure. I'll sort out something to eat and bring you a plateful here. D'you want more whisky?'

'Not yet. Thanks.'

He'd already retrieved his inch-thick printout and was reading again. She left him in peace and put her head round David's door to take his order for supper.

He looked almost as engrossed as George. She hoped he was dealing with his schoolwork on the computer, but she was afraid it was a game, or worse. Soon she'd have to talk to him about his teachers' anxiety over the way his friendship with Jay was affecting him, but she was too tired now to be sure of getting it right. She couldn't risk the delicate structure of trust and confidence she'd spent so long building between them.

'Hi, David,' she said. 'You hungry?'

He hit a key on the keyboard, shouting 'Yessssss!', then turned. His face was flushed and his black eyes shone.

'I'm always hungry.'

'Sandwich of some sort, or omelette?'

'If it's one of those thick ones with onions and stuff, omelette.'

No mention of 'please', she noticed and wondered whether that, too, was the result of Jay's influence. David was staring at her as though she'd suddenly come out in bumps. Then he understood.

'*Pwease*, Twish,' he said in a babyish voice loaded with such mockery she turned away without a comment.

Three minutes later she was working in the kitchen and wondering whether George's retreat behind the wall of work had anything to do with the questions she'd asked him about his brother, Henry.

She kept making connections with what he'd said about Jay, admiring the way he refused to be a victim. There'd been something about lots of people like him fantasising about violence in silence . . .

Were 'lots of people' a code for George himself?

Angie knew Fran and Greg were arguing and she was afraid it was about her. Their voices were never hushed like this unless they were embarrassed.

She sat in their spare room, looking at the two letters in her hand. Polly's would be a treat she'd keep until she went to bed. The other was the problem. She hadn't seen her son's writing for many years, but she'd have known it anywhere.

I can't take any more, she thought. If this is another attack I'll crack up completely.

Perhaps she should throw it away without reading it.

But what if it wasn't aggressive? What if offered support at last, or even a vaguely friendly overture?

She let her mind play around with the worst Adam could have written. That way, she'd have a kind of armour. But she found herself getting angry all over again as she argued with the imaginary figure she'd conjured up.

Groping among her long-buried memories, reaching for

something – anything – to make herself feel kinder, she recreated the picture of him as a tumbling, roly-poly, blond-haired boychild in red-and-white striped shorts stretched tight over his nappy. They'd played football, the two of them. At least, he'd kicked with one fat little leg as he stood unsteadily on the other, and she'd reached out for the ball to give it back for a repeat performance.

At last it seemed safe to slide one finger under the flap and rip open the envelope. The paper, or maybe it was the glue, was stiffer than she'd expected and she wrenched the finger hard enough to hurt.

'I'm getting soft,' she muttered, thinking of all the lambs she'd helped to birth and the hay bales she'd hauled around with these same hands. Or was it just that in those days she'd expected hands to hurt?

How would he start the letter after all these years? With some kind of endearment? Using her name?

Next door the angry whispering stopped and there was a loud clatter of pans. It would be time to eat soon and pretend to be serene and confident. She opened the letter and looked down. There was no salutation at all. It began abruptly:

> I'm sorry you feel I've abandoned you. That was never the intention. I felt I had no place in your world and you had no interest in mine. I was in the States when your interview was published, which is why I'm responding to it so late. A colleague here in Sussex has just shown it to me and asked if your Adam and I were any relation.
>
> If it would be of any help to you, I should be delighted to come up to London. Just let me know by phone or email. Adam

How stiff and formal was that? 'I should be delighted' was the kind of politeness you'd offer a total stranger.

And she didn't want him in court. Not while she had to concentrate on the evil machinations of Trish Maguire, whose first parade of gentleness and compassion had clearly been no more than a kind of softening-up process to disguise the traps she was planning to set.

'Angie? Supper!' Fran's voice sounded a little strained.

Angie refolded the letter and put it in her handbag. She would deal with it later, when she felt stronger.

Sodding beans! she thought as she walked into the kitchen and saw the steaming platefuls on the table. I'll explode.

The first forkful reminded her it wasn't the taste of these stews – or even their wind-inducing properties – that made her want to spit them out but the worthiness, the hint of sanctimony. Moments later a more charitable idea occurred to her: beans or squash cooked up in a dozen different ways were probably all they could afford. And they were housing and feeding her out of their limited income.

'There's still a bit of money left in my account,' she said. 'I'll write you a cheque for it all tomorrow. You shouldn't have to—'

Fran left her chair, moving with a lightness amazing in someone so solidly built, and put an arm around Angie's shoulders.

'We're glad to do it. And you need to keep whatever cash you've got, love, for life after the case.'

Angie couldn't speak for guilt and dependence, and for the longing to be free of both. She let her neck fold and laid her head against Fran's arm.

'Did the letter upset you, Angie?'

'What letter?' Her head returned to its usual position with a snap.

'The one from Brighton. Seeing the postmark, I . . . I hoped it might be from Adam.'

'It was, Fran. Chilly, but polite. Even supportive, in a way.'

'Fantastic!' Greg's smile made his beard jiggle as his cheek muscles bunched up.

Angie didn't respond. She thought there was something faked about his pleasure. She wondered what he and Fran had been arguing about.

'When's he coming?' Fran asked, pouring more filthy apple wine into Angie's glass.

'Not until I say I need him,' she said through lips stiffened as though with cold. 'And I don't think I can deal with him right now. It's too—'

Fran was looking at her with a concern that still seemed genuine. Angie let herself believe in it and told the truth.

'It's too important. If I say the wrong thing because I'm concentrating on the trial, I could lose him for ever.'

There was a long pause. Fran chewed her beans. Angie watched, fascinated by her powerful jaw and her perfect skin. Their peculiar diet was clearly healthy.

'What happened, Angie?'

'To make him go away, you mean?'

Fran nodded and the fall of reddish-gold hair slithered over her shoulder.

'He didn't like the farm.' Angie's eyes misted. 'And I suppose he grew out of wanting to be with John and me.'

'But—' said Greg, while Fran made an unsubtle hushing gesture before he could finish his protest or ask any more questions.

Angie wouldn't have answered. She'd never told anyone the whole story of what had happened to make Adam disappear, and she certainly wasn't going to offer it up to Greg.

He got up to fill himself a glass of water at the sink and let it overflow, soaking the cuffs of his jersey. The peculiarly nasty, almost meaty, smell of wet wool was so familiar from the ever-present washing that had hung from pulleys over the Aga at home that she was lost. Greg's voice faded as she thought of the night her life had gone so horribly wrong.

There were gumboots warming at the side of the Aga. Schlep waited obediently for the word that would allow him to bend his nose to his food.

Adam was there, standing in the doorway, waiting too. At last John gave the word and Schlep bounded forward to eat with all the hunger of a working dog fed only once a day.

'You like doing that, don't you?' Adam said in a voice colder than the flagged floor.

John raised his head. His eyes looked small in sockets swollen with wind and rain and rubbing. The lines that ran from the side of his nose to the bottom of his chin on either side of his mouth could have been drawn with thick black marker. His wrists were balanced on the table's edge with his bent hands pointing to the ceiling so that the blood could retreat and ease the pain and swelling in his fingers.

'What did you say?' There was no real expression in a voice hoarse with tiredness, but the menace was clear.

'You enjoy making Schlep wait to eat,' Adam said, talking with the glassy precision of someone addressing a foreigner. 'You're a psycho control freak. Here we all are,

Ma and me and Schlep, two paces behind you, making your world work, and still having to wait on your pleasure for anything *we* might need.'

'Adam! Don't be stupid.'

'It's true, Ma. Look at yourself. You were a high-flyer and he's turned you into an ugly worn-out drudge. Ruined your life. Well, he's not fucking ruining mine.'

'Adam,' Angie called out again, as he left the room. 'Adam, wait.'

'Leave him,' John said, not moving. His hands still stood up from the table's edge like misshapen trees guarding a gateway. 'He'll get over it and apologise. Or he won't. But it's his problem to deal with. He's too old to have you running after him to offer comfort.'

She looked down the length of the well-scrubbed table and wondered if you could ever mend a broken life. Somehow she must try. 'It was you I wanted comfort for. Not him.'

The left side of his mouth twisted a little. 'Oh, Angie, where would I be without you?'

'Angie! Angie! Are you all right?' Fran's voice was urgent enough to make her focus. 'You look all faint, love. You'd better put your head between your knees.'

Instead Angie looked up at Fran and hated herself for taking so much kindness without giving anything in return. She didn't have much to give, but honesty would be a start.

'Adam and John had a row one evening,' she said. 'Adam had attacked him for . . . Oh, nothing. It was pointless. Worse: cruel. So next morning, when Adam asked for a lift to the station, I told him I was too busy to take him. I hoped he'd apologise to John and life would become bearable again for all of us.

'Anyway, he stomped off and I went back to heating bottles for the lambs whose mothers had died. The Land Rover's engine sputtered a few minutes later and I rushed out. There he was, in our only means of transport, heading out of the farmyard. I got to the open gate ahead of him and stood in the way, so he had to stop.

'That was brave, Angie.'

'Or foolhardy.' Greg's voice had none of the admiration in Fran's. Angie ignored him.

'I waited and Adam eventually got out and came towards me, both hands stretched out, palms up. They were shaking, as though *he*'d been the victim.'

Angie picked up her fork again. She couldn't tell them quite how badly she'd lost her temper.

'Then what?' Fran said when the pause had gone on too long.

Angie heard echoes of some of the things she thought she might have said to Adam and hoped she hadn't.

'I more or less told him to grow up and learn how to behave like a human being. He . . . he yelled back at me.'

'Saying what?' Fran's voice was gentle, but far too interested for comfort.

Angie couldn't bear even to try to remember. She just shook her head, then found her voice again to finish the story so she could push it all to the back of her memory again:

'He got back into the Land Rover, slammed the door, revved the engine and drove straight at me. If I hadn't moved, I'd have been dogmeat. That's the last time I ever saw him.'

Her face was hot and she could feel the blood thudding in her veins, exactly as it had done that day.

She'd stormed about the yard for a full five minutes, stubbing her toes on the inside of her boots with almost every angry step. Then she'd gone indoors to phone Polly, who'd listened in silence to a highly edited version of what had happened, before offering not only her usual laconic sympathy but also practical help. She'd driven over to Low Topps at the end of her hard day and taken Angie to the station so she could pick up the Land Rover Adam had dumped there.

Hold on to the thought of Polly, Angie told herself, and you'll be able to keep going.

Polly had often called her 'pet' in the Northumbrian way, but it had never sounded sentimental. Anything but. Polly's sympathy had been the kind intended to stiffen the victim's sinews, not make her softer and needier than ever. Angie missed her horribly.

'It sounds,' Fran started, then stopped. For the first time Angie saw her blush.

'You can say it. I give you permission. Whatever it is, I can take it.'

'I just thought it sounded as if Adam had inherited your temper.' Fran's smile was carefully judged: kind and twinkly but edged with criticism.

It's not only the temper, Angie wanted to say. He got my paranoia, too.

But that was an admission she couldn't make to anyone now that John was dead. Oh, God, how she missed him!

'Not that I've ever seen you angry,' Fran said quickly. 'But you've talked about it quite often. Maybe Adam's been regretting everything he said and trying to find a way to come back all along and not known how. Couldn't that be why his letter's a bit cold . . . out of kind of shame, don't you think?'

Angie put down the fork again and took hold of Fran's big hand between both of hers.

'I think you are the most generous person I have ever met, and the best bridge-builder. But I don't think you have a clue what you're talking about.'

'You were pretty angry with me, weren't you, Trish?' Antony's voice was spookily normal as it issued from between the struts of his cage. 'That note you left last week could have sent me into a decline.'

'Sorry.' She barely brushed his hand, but he grabbed hers and gave it a good squeeze.

His grip felt infinitely stronger than the soft clasp he'd managed on his first day in here, when she'd been so afraid of long-term damage to his spine. Now he had a better colour than anyone else in the ward. If it hadn't been for the cage and the almost healed cut on his face, he'd have looked his usual self again.

'I thought—'

'You thought I was encouraging Robert to squeal on you. I know. How's it going, Trish?'

'Not too bad, but I still wish I wasn't up against Angie Fortwell.'

'Because you're agonised by her suffering?' Antony's smile was more benevolent than usual.

'Not exactly.' She hadn't analysed any of her feelings about this, let alone told anyone else, so the words came out unplanned: 'It's more what she represents. She could have been a power in the City by now.'

'So? It was her choice to throw it all up for sheep farming. All choices have consequences.'

'That's why I'm so twitchy.' Trish rubbed her head, letting herself understand the ideas that had been building up for days now.

The familiar squeak of a nurse's shoes was followed by a brisk question about the workings of someone's bowels. Trish glanced round and saw the man in the bed opposite Antony's blushing as he met her eyes. She quickly looked back at Antony.

'Angie Fortwell made one wrong decision and look at her now.'

'True. But so what?' he said, ignoring the nurse and her questions with an irritable scowl that told Trish how much he hated being in this place, powerless over everyone except his visitors.

'If you hadn't persuaded me to come back to the Bar after my sabbatical,' she said, feeling all the old gratitude, 'the same thing could've happened to me.'

'I doubt it. Whatever you'd chosen to do, it wouldn't have left you in a polluted mudpatch. Wherever you'd gone, you'd have ended up in a position to wear a suit that fits like a miracle and cost—' Antony broke off to examine her, his eyes making all the moves his neck and head could not. 'A thousand quid?'

'Not quite. Antony, forget my twitchiness. Tell me: did you never think the explosion in CWWM's tanks could have been sabotage, some kind of environmental terrorism?'

'It's a non-starter, Trish.' His tone was that of the head of chambers again, brisk and not prepared to waste any time. 'Even if someone did bugger about with the tanks, there's no way you'd get any evidence at this stage.'

'Although,' she said with a wistfulness that made his smile kinder, 'given it's a civil trial we'd need only to establish the balance of probabilities.'

'Forget it. Sabotage is a forlorn hope over which you'd break your heart and waste time you haven't got, *and* the client's money. Concentrate on mitigating the damages. That's all you need to do. But we shouldn't be talking about work. It makes me even more aware of this bloody cage.' He put both hands on the side struts and for a moment looked as though he was about to wrench them apart.

'Antony, don't—'

'Don't worry: I won't. In any case, I can't. They're absolutely unbendable.' He forced himself to relax, letting his arms fall by his sides and producing a grin like a corpse's rictus. 'So entertain me. How's the glamorous George?'

She manufactured a laugh at the adjective he'd chosen. The smell of disinfectant caught in her throat as she inhaled. Turning away from him to cough it clear, she caught the eye of a new visitor, an elderly woman in a tightly buttoned overcoat, sitting in silence beside the man with the bowel problem. What was their story? Why had the woman come if they had nothing to say to each other? Did it help the patient? Did it help her? Or was it just duty?

'Not a good topic, I see,' Antony said. 'David? No; not him either. So what *is* good in your life?'

'At the moment? The sight of you itching with boredom because it means you're mending and I don't have to let dark nightmares of fatal outcomes terrify me any longer.'

'Ah, Trish. My Trish.'

'Sabotage,' she repeated, ignoring the hand he was holding out to her. She pointed to the contraption holding his broken neck together. 'I don't know that it is such a non-starter. Have you never wondered whether someone could have wanted you off the case so CWWM had less chance of winning?'

His lean, lined face creased even more as his lips parted, and his eyes could have belonged to a big cat seeing a juicy wildebeest within easy reach.

'Your imagination is as entrancing as your idea of my importance. But you're quite mad, you know. Even if someone had wanted me off the case, they'd never have done it like this.'

'Why not?'

'Use your brain. One: you and I had been walking through the pedestrianised part of Covent Garden so we could hardly have been followed by a murderous biker. Two: no one's going to have an assassin waiting on the off-chance that I'm likely to be crossing the road outside the RCJ on a Friday when I'm not due to be in court. Three: the biker and I both misjudged it; I was almost across the zebra and even had one foot on the island so he was within his rights to gauge my speed as he did. It's just that I turned back to find out why you hadn't answered my question. There you were, still on the pavement, and there was I under his wheels. It's what they call an accident.'

'Right.'

'Now, that's enough of that. I told you: you're here to entertain me. Make me laugh.'

Every funny anecdote had been sucked out of her brain. She couldn't even remember the playground jokes that had once reduced David to heaving giggles.

'What happens to Angie if I win?'

'Don't be a baby. She's not your problem.'

'But she has no one, Antony. Imagine being absolutely alone.'

'Bollocks. She's got a successful grown-up son, hasn't she?'

'He's abandoned her.'

'Why?' A taunting note in Antony's voice made her look more closely at him. 'What did she do to *him*?'

'Why should she have done anything?' Even Trish could hear the outrage in her voice. 'Maybe it was his fault, whatever it was that went wrong.'

'Oh, come on! What's that mantra of yours, Trish? It's never the child's fault. I've often wondered at what age in your private world someone becomes an adult and loses that kind of get-out-of-jail-free pass. Can you tell me?'

Thinking of Jay's brutal brother, Darren, only three or four years older than Jay himself, she couldn't.

Back in chambers a couple of hours later, she dealt with the twenty or so emails that had built up during her absence, then reread her notes for the next day's evidence, wishing she hadn't let herself get so bound up in Angie Fortwell's problems. As Antony said, they were not her business. Just as it wasn't her business to find out what had really happened to trigger the tanks' explosion. All she had to do was make her client's case as irresistible to the judge as she possibly could.

But she couldn't stop herself thinking of sabotage and who might have had a motive. She was sure Angie Fortwell was innocent, and her husband too. No one who knew what he was doing would have blocked the vents and then risked his own life by going into the tank enclosure before they exploded. But the unconvincing Greg Waverly was a different matter.

Was there more to his involvement than helping Angie manage her case against CWWM? Could he have taken some kind of active role in blowing up the tanks? Would his loathing of CWWM and its global success have made him angry enough to do something so potentially dangerous to the environment he'd sworn to protect?

Trish had always thought most terrorism was driven by a need to hurt people who had something the terrorist desired so strongly he had to make himself believe he hated it. Maybe CWWM's efficiency in generating money from toxic chemicals had been too much for Greg Waverly to bear after he'd made such a cock-up of his own tiny, environmentally friendly, organic-food business.

And maybe she was complicating a perfectly simple case with absurdly dramatic speculation.

A beep from her screen told her another email was coming through, but it was only some spammer wanting to entice her into buying counterfeit watches. She deleted it without looking, then clicked on to Google. Antony was almost certainly right in telling her she'd be wasting time if she looked for evidence of sabotage, so she might as well clear all the speculation out of her mind by doing something useful instead. Like finding out about George's mysterious brother.

As she typed the name Henry Henton into the search box, she didn't know what she expected to see. There was hardly going to be an account of where in the family pecking order he came vis-à-vis George, or what he'd done to George, or what age they'd been at the time.

It wasn't hard to isolate the right Henry from all the other thousands of entries. He lived in Shropshire now and worked as a carpenter, specialising in making tables from old railway sleepers, disused pallets and other waste timber. He was divorced and had three sons. There was even a photograph of him, looking remarkably like George except for his thinner greyer hair and more ruddy complexion.

Parents, Trish thought, usually go grey younger than the childless. So maybe Antony's right and I've never faced up to the burden children can be. Maybe Angie Fortwell *was* the victim of her son, not the aggressor.

She substituted Angie's name for Henry's on the Google home page and began to click her way through the entries that appeared.

One website listing bed-and-breakfast operations in Northumberland still had details of the Fortwells' farm and the prices they charged, along with chatty recommendations from past visitors. No one had been allowed to stay there since the explosion nearly eighteen months ago. Why hadn't a note been added to the website to say the farmhouse was now closed? How out-of-date could the Internet be?

'Robert!' Trish shouted.

There was no answer. She ran down the corridor to his room. A strip of light underlined the door. She pushed it open.

'Robert!'

'He's gone,' said his red-headed pupil, pushing himself to his feet. 'Can I help?'

'Sure, Hal,' Trish said, surprised by the old-fashioned courtesy. 'If you're not too busy. What I need is someone to find out whether there are any blogs by ramblers who walked through the Fortwells' bit of Northumberland around the time of the explosion.'

Hal's round face didn't suit a frown: it was designed for

jokes or comfortable placidity. He looked as though he wanted to protest but wasn't sure it was allowed.

'Robert may have told you I think there's more to what happened than straightforward bad luck, or—'

'He did.'

'But there are no sources of evidence for the existence of any saboteurs like the ones we'd get in a city: no CCTV; no petrol station attendants; no passers-by. The only possibility is a rambler who might have seen something relevant and recorded it on a blog. There may be nothing anywhere, but I'd hate to miss it if there were.'

The unconvincing frown was back and he was fiddling with the pens on his desk.

'But Miss Maguire—'

'Trish. Please.'

'Isn't it a bit late for this kind of search? I mean the skeleton went in months ago; and we're halfway through the trial. Don't you think—?'

Trish reminded herself of the years when she'd had to stand up to the old prejudices of the Bar and prove she was as good as any of her male colleagues. Hal couldn't have been much more than a toddler then, so it wasn't his fault. But she needed him to do what she told him.

'I have to fight the case in the way I see fit,' she said, adding a smile to soften the impact, 'and I want to know who was walking around the area before and after the explosion. OK?'

He shoved a hand through his red hair as the blood rushed to his freckly cheeks. 'I'll see what I can find, although Robert's given me rather a lot of work, so—'

Her mobile rang in her pocket. 'Hang on a minute, Hal.' She put the phone to her ear and gave her name.

'Trish? Jeremy Black here.'

'Just a second, Jeremy.' She put a hand over the phone, smiled at Hal again and said: 'Do what you can for me. OK? Great. Thanks.'

Putting the phone back to her ear, she said: 'Jeremy. I'm here.'

'Good. I wanted a word with you. Have you a moment now?'

'Yes. What's happened?'

'Nothing in school, but I thought you should know that after you alerted me to the way Darren has been beating Jay, I talked to his social worker, Shelby Deedes.'

'Yes, I know. George told me.'

'It might be a good idea for you to meet her, too, so that you can understand what's going on.'

'Darren's physically abusing Jay,' Trish said. 'It's not hard to understand.'

'There are other views. According to Shelby, Darren is not all bad. In his own overphysical way he's trying to keep his family together.'

'He damaged Jay. If the blow had landed an inch or two to one side, he could have cracked his skull. Or ruined the sight in that eye.'

'Darren's only seventeen and, in the face of the mother's alcoholism and erratic behaviour, he is doing his best to care for Jay and their 11-year-old half-sister, Kimberley. He also has to manage the family's inadequate budget. When he sees Jay ignoring his share of the tasks and playing with the highly desirable, extremely expensive, hi-tech equipment David keeps giving Jay, he is – understandably – enraged.'

Trish didn't comment. She was trying to think of another way of showing David that generosity could be destructive, and that giving people things couldn't make up for the misery of their lives – or act as a kind of defensive earthwork to keep the same misery out of your own.

'You should know – and find a way to tell David – that Kimberley became involved in a potentially risky situation because Jay was distracted by the Play Station. According to the social worker, if Darren hadn't happened to see her agree to go off with a stranger to earn ten pounds, we could be looking at a rape or worse.'

I'm certainly not going to tell David that, Trish thought, noticing how formal Jeremy Black was being as he reported the social worker's threats. Did he dislike the drama, too?

'I'll talk to him again,' she said aloud. 'Thank you for letting me know. How much further have you and the governors got with my proposal about keeping Jay in the school?'

'At the moment, we're rather wishing we had never agreed even to this term's experiment. Having at last reached you, I must now get on. Please do what you can to stop David exacerbating the situation by handing over more desirable presents.'

'I'll try.'

Chapter 10

'What d'you want me to say, Trish?' David's voice was hard and his dark eyes looked very cold across the remains of their breakfast. 'That I promise I won't give Jay anything else, however much he wants it, or however much I want to show I'm sorry for something I've done – like when I hit him and made his mouth bleed? Is that it?'

'Yes,' she said, not avoiding his gaze. 'It sounds stingy, but yes. For the moment that is the message. I hope, when Jay gets more to used to us and school, and manages to sort out the gap between us and his home, it'll change. D'you see what I mean?'

He nodded, but he didn't look happy, and his mouth was pinched in disapproval.

'You'd better go or you'll be late for work,' he said. 'I'll ask Jay for my i-Pod back if that'll make you happy. And I *will* lock up; don't worry.'

How could she not worry?

Ten minutes later, hurrying across the bridge, she knew she was going to be late for her pre-court discussion with Robert, but it had been important to tackle David quickly. Had she been too formal, too infected by Jeremy Black's style? She'd wanted to keep the emotional temperature cool, but maybe she'd overdone it.

Too late now, she thought, wishing George hadn't gone home to Fulham last night. If he'd been at breakfast with them, he could have said something that would have stopped David looking at her like a hostile stranger.

Robert's expression was just as bad when she walked into her room in chambers and found him waiting there. She had never seen him angrier.

'What?' she said, unbuttoning her coat.

'I have just sent Hal home.' His voice bit. 'He was apparently here *all night*, searching for stuff on the Internet for you.'

'I didn't ask him to do that,' Trish said, dumping her case on the floor and pulling off her coat. 'I just asked him to look up some blogs for me when he had time.'

'Do I have to remind you that he is *my* pupil, and answerable to me? He claims he protested that doing your research would get in the way of what I'd already asked him to do, but you—'

'He did.' Trish arranged her coat on the hanger she kept on the back of the door.

'But you told him that didn't matter?'

'Robert, this is not a good morning to stand on your dignity or beat me up. We've got a bare hour before we have to be in court, and there are things I have to do. I'm sorry if I've offended you and I'll make it up to you – and Hal – later.' Her own anxieties rose up, mixed with her irritation at his lack of cooperation, and boiled over.

'And next time you're angry with me for asking your pupil to do something for me,' she said with a ferocity that made him blink with surprise, 'you might reflect on the fact that *you* never bothered to ask Fred Hoffman for the Fortwells' b & b accounts. I waited so long I had to do it myself in the end. Now I've got to work. I'll tell you when I'm ready to leave for court.'

She sat at her desk without looking at him again. He had a point, but she couldn't deal with it now. When there was time she'd apologise to Hal. She should have been clearer about how much she'd expected him to do.

'He insisted on emailing you the results of his search before he left.' Robert's voice was laden with all the old dislike. 'Looking like shit, I may say. Don't forget to use the product of his exhaustion. To ignore it would be the final insult to us both.'

Trish waited until he had gone before she let herself rub her eyes.

'All choices have consequences,' she quoted to herself. Then she flicked on her laptop and summoned up her emails.

Despite the fast broadband connection, Hal's took a while to download. He must have found something. As soon as she could she opened the email and read the first paragraph.

'Trish, there's a fair amount of rambling (in both senses of the word) bloggery devoted to that bit of Northumberland around the time of the explosion. I don't know whether any of it's useful. The urls are all listed below and I've cut and pasted anything that seemed remotely relevant. Including maps of the area. Hal.'

With a whole series of highly detailed maps, no wonder the thing had taken so long to come through. There wasn't time to read all the text now, so she merely pulled out the list of all the known members of FADE and searched Hal's documents for each one. None appeared. She filed the huge document and set about preparing herself for the day's proceedings.

'I can't go home, Dave.' Jay's voice wasn't usually anxious like this. 'Please let me come with you. I gotta work and if I go back Darren'll lay into me again. Please.'

'We're not allowed,' David said, trying to remember how Trish had said to him at breakfast that he wasn't responsible for Jay, however much he liked him and wanted to make his life better. 'My sister's in court and George has to work.'

Jay turned away. Then he looked over his shoulder. His face was sulky but his eyes were all scrunched up. David knew that meant he was thinking the whole world was against him again.

'Look,' David said, aware of the danger. 'Wait. I'll phone George and see if—'

'It's fine,' Jay said, sounding almost like Trish at her crossest.

'No, it isn't,' David said, using one of George's simplest but most effective answers when she was in a bad mood and trying to pretend she wasn't. 'Wait there. I'll phone.'

George's number was programmed into his phone, so it only took a minute to get through. David explained.

'I can't come back to the flat,' George said, sounding harassed but OK. 'I've got a client meeting. But you could bring Jay here and do your prep in one of the small meeting rooms. Hang on a sec and I'll check there's one free.'

David sent a hopeful look in Jay's direction and held up crossed fingers like in the old Lottery advertisements.

'David? All's well. There'll be a room free for you. I'll

probably be with the client when you get here, so just tell Charlie, the receptionist, who you are and she'll show you the way.'

'Thanks.' David knew he didn't have to say any more. George would see what he meant.

'And don't forget you're in someone else's office, will you? No racket or larking about. D'you want me to have a word with Jay myself?'

'Yes, please.' David handed the phone over to Jay and watched his face. It tightened up, but then he smiled and said:

'I can see you wanting to trash your brother's whole room when he pissed you off, but I can't see you doing it.' He laughed. 'Nah. I knew you wouldn't of. All right. I'll pretend I'm you then. Yeah. Right. Great. Cheers, mate.'

He gave the phone back to David.

'George?'

'That's all settled, David. Jay and I have a deal. I'll come and get you both, probably about half past six, and we'll go and eat. But if the client takes longer I'll be late. Bye now.'

'How far is it?' Jay said as David stowed the phone in the inner pocket of his blazer, tucking it down as carefully as George did with his wallet.

'Shouldn't take us more than fifteen minutes if we get going.'

'OK. So, what's your sister done?'

'What d'you mean, Jay?'

'You said she's in court. What's she done?'

David laughed, relief tickling him all over in the best kind of way. 'Nothing. She's a barrister. Didn't you know?'

Jay shook his head. 'If I'd known, I'd've—'

'What?'

'Doesn't matter.' A lorry crashed past them, throwing up fans of dirty spray from its enormous wheels. Jay moved sideways to get out of the muck, pushing David into a shop window. Luckily the glass didn't break.

'I had a brief once,' Jay said, 'but he wasn't like Trish. If I get nicked again, I'll have her. She'll see me right.'

David thought about telling him the difference between civil and criminal law, but couldn't think of a way of doing it that wouldn't sound superior, so he didn't, just led the way up New Bridge Street, into Fleet Street, up Chancery Lane, and so to George's offices.

It felt weird being shown into the meeting room, all pale grey and empty-looking, instead of into George's own office, which had some of his own stuff in it and was much more like a real person's room.

There was a water cooler in the corner here, and Jay dumped his bag on the grey table straight off and went to get himself a drink. David watched, worrying about what he might do with the water, and if he'd let the paper cup overflow. But he didn't. He just filled it and drank, then chucked the cup in the bin.

'D'you want some?'

'No. I'll only need to take a piss.' David unzipped his rucksack to get out his homework, hoping this would be one day when Jay wasn't too edgy to settle.

Jay roamed around the room, pulling all the knobs like a baby. Some of the cupboards opened, but there wasn't anything interesting in any of them, luckily. The blinds opened and shut on a kind of electrical system, but he only activated it five or six times. Then he grabbed his bag and undid it and pulled out his own books.

David didn't dare breathe too deep in case it set Jay off,

but he bent his head and tried to forget he wasn't alone. Trish had told him more than once that if you concentrated hard enough you could make even Piccadilly Circus feel like an empty room. Maybe he'd learn how one day.

Jay turned a page and picked up his pen. Then he started to write – and on the proper paper, not in the textbook or on the pale-grey tabletop.

'You're not responsible for Jay,' David said in his head, imitating Trish's voice as well as he could. If he said it often enough, it might come true.

But today was all right. Quite soon he let himself believe Jay really was working so he could start on his own essay.

The judge listened to Trish's witness with his usual courtesy, but she knew he was anxious to adjourn for the day. They were already half an hour later than usual, but Angie Fortwell had been dangerously vigorous with her cross-examination of the vet who had been testifying to John's forgetfulness and ever-increasing refusal to be on time for any appointment. Trish had had to do a certain amount of damage limitation.

She asked her last question of the livestock transporter, who had also found John impossible to deal with in the last months of his life, got a satisfactory answer, nodded to the judge and told her witness he could step down.

When the judge rose everyone stood in the approved fashion, even Greg, who occasionally flexed his radical muscles by refusing to conform. Which was odd, Trish thought, given how bossy he was whenever Angie got anything wrong.

'Well done, Trish,' Robert said quietly. 'That could have damaged us, but you pulled back beautifully.'

'Thank you,' she said, trying to hide her surprise. Was this genuine, or had Antony been giving him some lessons in silk-management over the phone? 'How's Hal?'

'Recovering,' he said. 'I shouldn't have lost my temper. Did his research produce anything?'

'Not yet.' She was reluctant to say more here. 'I'll show you what I'm after when we get back to chambers. If you deal with the trolley, I'll take those extra files.'

'Sure you can manage?'

She pulled two heavy box files under one arm, tucked her wig on top of them, and led the way out through the familiar small crowd of FADE supporters, while Angie and Greg were still tidying their papers. By now Trish recognised most of the faces, but this time there was a man who was completely strange to her, sitting a little apart from the rest.

He was about her height and had a sharply defined face with high cheekbones and deep eye sockets. If it hadn't been for his beautiful mouth, he would have looked forbidding. As it was, his expression was pretty severe. He must have felt her staring at him because he met her gaze with a challenge in his eyes. She smiled faintly and turned aside to speak to Robert.

Once they were back in the echoing halls, she asked him if he knew who the young man was.

'Not a clue. Are you off on another frolic like the Ben Givens one? That didn't get us very far.'

'Not this time.' She smiled to dispel the implied criticism. 'I was just curious. He was different from the usual bunch of FADE members, though there was something about his face I thought was familiar. I can't pin it down.'

*

Angie was looking at her son for the first time in eight years, while words tumbled through her mind: dangerous, unsayable, scarily needy words. Her head felt hollow, echoing, and her hands were shaking. She prayed for self-control.

'I had to come,' he said, and he didn't let his eyes drop. She wished eyes really were windows on to the mind – or the soul or whatever it was – then she'd have known what he was thinking. 'We need to talk.'

'Yes.' She turned to Greg, introduced the two of them, then said: 'Adam and I need some time. I'll come back to the flat later.'

He put a heavy hand on her shoulder. 'Fine, Ange. Take as long as you need. We'll see you for supper. And if Adam wants to come and eat with us, too, there'll be plenty.'

'Thank you,' he said with some coldness, perhaps interpreting his mother's unspoken feelings, 'but I'd like to take her out myself this evening.'

Greg hesitated, met Adam's eyes, and then nodded, as though he was giving permission.

'Whatever Ange wants. I'll take the files back and see you when I see you. Don't be too late: you need to mug up all the stuff Maguire's going to do to you tomorrow.'

Angie said nothing. When Greg had loped off, only dropping three bits of paper, which he then scooped up and crammed into his distended pockets, Adam looked at her again.

'Ange? When did you start calling yourself that?'

'I don't. It's Greg's speciality.'

'I see,' said Adam, sounding censorious. 'Like the way he orders you about. Don't you mind?'

She felt a smile tweaking the edges of her mouth and fought for gravity. But she couldn't do it and found herself laughing as no one should laugh in the august surroundings of the Royal Courts of Justice. Her nightmare of another bout of frenzied bad temper receded.

'What?' Adam said, just as an usher came over to them and said they had to leave.

She tucked a hand in the crook of his arm. 'I wasn't sure I could deal with everything you and I have to say to each other while still fighting this effing case, but you've done me good already. I have to say I *detest* being spoken to like that. And there isn't anyone else I could tell.'

He didn't smile, but he pulled her hand a little closer to his side. 'Where would you like to go? I'm buying.'

'It's a bit early for dinner.'

'I know. But we have to go somewhere: a bar? Hotel tea for scones and cream?'

'Let's go to a bar.'

He took her to Chez Gerard in Chancery Lane, where they found a quiet table and ordered a bottle of house wine.

'Still red?'

'Still red,' she said, looking idly at the menu. 'What a good place. We might even have a steak later if you can afford it. Since I came to London I've eaten enough veg to last my whole life.'

'Great. Whatever,' he said again, fiddling with a small pot of toothpicks. He opened his mouth as though to say something else, then shut it again.

'It's going to take us both a while to do the hard stuff,' she said, trying to get control of her longing. 'So why don't we stick with news first. How are you? What are you doing these days? Fill me in – as though I were a stranger.'

'That's just it.' He looked at her, less censorious but still wary. 'You *are* a stranger, but I know you absolutely. It's a weird feeling – sick-making in a way.'

She stiffened at the insult.

'You know, like ... Oh, sod it! I was an academic, supposed to be articulate. It's like a kind of vertigo. I don't know if the ground's solid beneath me any more, whether it's me or the world that's shifting.'

'You're safely sitting on a leather banquette in a three-quarters empty bar, with polished wood all around you and about to drink a glass of wine,' she said, feeling better for his explanation.

The waiter appeared with their bottle and glasses.

'Tell me about being an academic. Did you stick with Eng. Lit?'

'No.' Adam gulped the tasting sample of wine and nodded his approval. The waiter poured two full glasses and left them. 'After ... after a while, I realised I couldn't deal with all those washy, amorphous concepts and feelings. I wanted rigour and discipline and facts.'

He looked straight at her and she thought she could see shadows of the chubby toddler kicking his ball at her. She wondered what he saw and thought of the last time she'd faced her reflection in a mirror: dry patches of reddened skin on a face that was almost cadaverous; dark eyes sunk into sockets like bruises; and cracked lips with flaky patches.

'Facts are a lot less uncomfortable than ideas,' he added.

'I can believe that.' She forced a smile and tried to forget how awful she must look. 'So what did you pick? Maths? You were always rather good at sums.'

'Chemistry. Which turned out to be not such a good idea when the university axed the department.'

'Where are you now?' She pushed down the thought of all the years when he'd existed quite apart from her.

Once she'd known everything about him. Now he'd had years of experience, friends and probably lovers too, of which she hadn't been allowed to know anything. She understood what he meant about vertigo.

'I'm working in a commercial lab, but still publishing with an academic press.'

'That's great.' Smiling was an effort, but she had to do it. She was this unknown man's mother. 'But why chemistry? Although of course you did get a good chemistry A level, didn't you?'

'I'm surprised you remember,' he said with an unbelievably nasty tone in his voice, then he pulled back. 'Sorry. I didn't mean to do that. Getting up to speed after the subject switch was hard work. But it gave me my facts and I clung to them.' He put down his glass. 'They were all I had that was safe. Bugger it! I didn't mean to get into all this.'

'Nor did I, but here we are.' She wondered how far to go, whether the two of them were strong enough to deal with wherever their words and feelings took them, whether she might make the gap between them wider if she spoke clumsily now. In the end, she decided she had to try.

'Adam, I've gone over and over the things that happened that last morning and wished I'd kept my wretched mouth shut. But—'

Faced with him, seeing through his adult face to the beloved baby for whom she'd given up so much, she couldn't go on. Why should she take it all on herself?

'But you couldn't forgive me for what *I*'d said, so you couldn't see why you should apologise first,' he said, like an echo of her own thoughts.

'If I hadn't moved,' she said, not looking at him, 'would you have mown me down with my own Land Rover?'

'*Of course* not. How could you think that?'

There was enough passion in his voice to make her glance up again. More people had come into the restaurant but they were just a blur as she concentrated on her son's face.

'I felt the tyres practically graze my legs. It would take a saint to be the first to apologise after that, and I'm no saint.'

'No,' he said with such emphasis that she stiffened up all over again.

She looked around, hoping for any kind of distraction.

'But you were always a martyr,' he went on, 'wallowing in all that unnecessary misery. *Why* did you try to make me buy into it too? I'd rather have eaten sheep shit every day for a month than have my life devoured like yours was.'

She covered her face with both hands, propping her elbows on the table and pushing the wine aside.

'I don't want to do this,' she said from behind her hands.

His fingers closed about her wrists, amazingly strong for someone who had never picked up anything heavier than a book or a test tube, and pulled her hands away from her face.

'Look at me, M . . . No; I can't call you that again. Not yet anyway. Look at me.'

She'd fought harder enemies than this so she kept her eyes directed at the table's glossy surface.

'OK, don't look at me.' He dropped her wrists. 'But listen. We *should* do it. I came today, hoping to see signs that we might be able to. And you were you again in court; your voice was yours; your mind was operating at full throttle; you were back to being a real person, not a skivvy.'

He picked up his glass and swirled the wine around in it.

She watched him from under her lashes. He didn't drink. At last he looked up again.

'Which is why I thought I'd be able to talk to you. But now I realise you're still stuck.'

She rubbed one wrist with the other hand. His grip had been painful, but in a way it was a relief to have a physical hurt to manage.

'Stuck?'

'In denial. Pretending you didn't hate the fucking farm; pretending you didn't resent what he'd done to you, the way he'd gobbled your real self and spat out only the rubbish bits he was prepared to let you keep. Sticking with the fiction that you shared his tastes mattered more than anything else, didn't it?'

A familiar sensation surged up in her brain. Anger, hot and terrifying, like magma spouting from a volcano, destroying everything in its path. This time, she had to keep it in.

'It wasn't a fiction.'

'Oh, for Christ's sake stop lying. Anyone could see how much you hated it. It used to drive me mad. Didn't you ever wonder what all those lies did to me?'

Holding in her feelings, controlling the boiling, burning, poisonous words was getting harder.

'Presumably not,' he said and sipped his wine. Then he put down the glass and looked at her again. 'After all, you never cared about me.'

She clasped her hands on the tabletop. It was the only way she could stop herself reaching out to grab him by the neck and shake some sense into him.

'You were the most important thing in my whole life,

Adam,' she said when it was safe to speak. 'You *must* have known that.'

He gaped at her. She thought of the rest, the confession she might never be able to make: but I knew I'd have to let you go one day, so I had to make the rest of my life work. I *had* to pretend to like working on the farm if I was to keep John more or less happy. There was no other way of making our hellish existence bearable.

'How the hell could I have known?' His eyes were narrowing into accusing pinpoints she recognised from ancient photographs of herself in childhood. His voice was rising too, as he accused her. 'You never said anything kind or encouraging to me in my whole life. Not ever.'

'This is a joke,' she muttered, feeling the anger rising again in spite of everything she did to hold it down. 'A sick joke.'

Grabbing the wine glass, she took too big a swallow and choked. With her throat in spasm and her nose and eyes pouring with humiliating quantities of mucus, she had to run for the ladies.

By the time she got back, mopped and clean, the waiter had wiped the table and brought new nuts and olives. Adam had gone, leaving a wad of money on the table beside the half-empty bottle. In his absence, the money was like a slap.

A sentence in the middle of a long, waffly weblog by someone calling himself Peterthewalk caught Trish's drowsy attention and she whipped back into full wakefulness:

> Adam warned me off going to Low Topps farm, said the people there aren't half as welcoming as the ones in

another farm six miles to the west, within the national park. He knows the area well, so I believed him. And I had the best pork pie ever with the Greens at Manor Farm. Polly Green is just the best cook and breakfast was to die for. I ate double the other couple there – Sal and Chris – and had to have a little lie down before I set out, which means I was in a rush to get to my next stopping point before dark. So I cheated. I wasn't going to say so, but what's the point of a blog if you tell lies?

I came over the hill near Rushy Knowe and found a biggish road. I was tired and I'd run out of water, so I was scared of dehydrating before I got to the Handwells at Dark Edge Farm. Well a milk lorry came along and I stuck my thumb out. He gave me a lift and I made it to Dark Edge before Sal and Chris had eaten all the food. It wasn't as good as Polly Green's, but they were making up for missing out on some of her breakfast. They were a bit weird about where they'd been and how I couldn't have seen any trace of them all day. Then Sal blushed and said she'd got them lost. They'd hitched a lift too. I didn't feel such a fraud then. She said they were going to Low Topps next day, so I passed on what I'd heard from Adam.

In the morning I . . .

Trish's eyes were beginning to close again. Talk about parish pump gossip, she thought. How odd that something as hi-tech as the Internet should be encouraging this kind of garrulous sharing of unimportant information.

But the mention of Adam in the context of the Fortwells' farm was interesting. She woke herself up properly and made a note. Adam was hardly a rare first name, but the possibility of a useful coincidence sharpened her mind. She'd get Robert's permission to put Hal on to the blogger tomorrow and find out if he'd ever known Adam's surname.

'Ms Maguire?'

Her head shot up at the sound of the man's voice. Its owner was a perfect stranger, standing silhouetted against the brighter light in the corridor outside her room. It was good to hear sounds of other people walking, talking and working all over the building.

'Yes?'

'Don Bates.'

My client, the managing director of CWWM, she thought, as she stood up and held out her hand. 'We shouldn't really be meeting without—'

'It's fine. I'm only a few minutes ahead of Fred Hoffman. He'll be here any time now.'

'Good,' Trish said, trying to think of something she could say that wouldn't impinge on the case. 'How was your trip to the States? He said you'd been to sort out some problem.'

Bates moved away from the door, unbuttoning his cashmere overcoat as he did so. He flung it over the back of the better visitor's chair and Trish saw the superfine navy cloth was lined with heavy satin. His suit was just as impressive and, now she could see him clearly, so was his face: a craggy slab of well-shaped handsomeness with warmth in his smile and intelligence in his blue eyes. He kept them fixed on her with an intensity she found disturbing. Even when she looked away, she could feel his attention. When she glanced back, he was still staring at her.

'Did you manage to sort it?' she asked, as a way of defusing the tension.

'Not entirely. We're being targeted by a whole new

generation of eco-activists over in the States. It's a right bugger, and it's one reason why I don't want this case dragging on any longer than it has to. I have to stop the bad publicity fast. So, Ms Maguire—'

Trish held up one hand, like a traffic cop. 'We can't discuss it till Fred's with us.'

'He is,' said the solicitor, lumbering into her room. He grinned at her, panting from the doorway.

Trish relaxed. But Bates's gaze hadn't moved away from her. What was he looking for?

'Sit down, both of you,' she said. 'Would you like a drink? I've got some whisky.'

'No, thank you. What I want is an assessment from you of how we're doing. What are our chances?'

'Impossible to quantify for sure,' she said, picking up a pen. She always thought better when she could write notes. 'They never are, even at this stage. We're on fairly firm ground with the fact that John Fortwell was on your land when the explosion happened, so that will mitigate the damages. We're on absolutely solid rock with the fact that it was his job to keep the filters clear and he obviously hadn't, probably because he was suffering from depression, which means contributory negligence. But—'

'I don't like indecision,' he said, forgetting to smile but not to keep his attention on her. 'Tell me without shilly-shallying or protecting yourself.'

Trish suppressed her instinct to shrug. 'I can't help believing we should be looking at sabotage. To be fair, Antony told me to have nothing to do with the idea because there's no way we could prove it, but if you're after a way to silence bad publicity and environmental activists, I can't think of a better one.'

At last she was released from his obsessive stare. He turned to Fred. 'What do you think?'

'She's right on all counts,' he said, smiling out from under his heavy brows, like an old silverback approving a promising young member of his troop. 'Particularly the impossibility of getting any evidence of sabotage at this stage. Everything was burned in the fireball, so there are no fibres, fingerprints, DNA. Nothing.'

Bates was on his feet now and swinging his overcoat back over his shoulders.

'Now I know where I am. Don't mess about with sabotage. Waste of time and money. Stick with contributory negligence and get it done fast.'

'All right,' Trish said, feeling a rebellious bubble she had to hide.

'How is Angie?' he said, sounding still more abrupt.

'D'you know Mrs Fortwell?'

'The papers call her that. How's she doing as a litigant in person?'

'Astonishingly well,' Trish said with a dryness that made him smile. She wondered whether to tell him about Benjamin Givens and the secret help he was giving, then saw Fred Hoffman very slightly shaking his great head.

'Good. I can't be seen to be bullying fragile widows and orphans. Bad for the image. Glad to have met you. I'll try to come to court tomorrow. I must go now. Fred?'

Hoffman hadn't bothered to take off his coat, merely unbuttoned it, presumably having plenty of experience of his client's impatience. He waved in Trish's direction and hurried out.

She wondered whether Don Bates's use of Angela Fortwell's nickname had really come from nothing but reading the papers. But she'd had her orders: get the case finished as quickly as possible and don't look for evidence of third-party intervention.

Her screen was blank, saving power, until she moved and joggled it. The blog came back, pointlessly now. She put a finger on the delete button but couldn't make herself press it.

I want to *know*, she thought and heard a voice in her head that sounded remarkably like Antony's: don't be such a baby.

She filed the document and reached for her coat.

Passing the clerks' room, she looked towards the pigeonholes. There was something sticking out of hers so she made a detour to fetch it. The envelope had Hoffman's address printed on the top right-hand corner, and there was no stamp.

Intrigued, she opened it to find photocopied pages from Angie Fortwell's visitors' book. The note clipped to the top sheet was written in Hoffman's tangled scrawl. He must think she had all the time in the world to decipher the letters he'd jumbled up into an incomprehensible web of ink across the page. Eventually she made out the message:

'Trish, I think these lists and pages from the Fortwells' visitors' book are all we have. FH.'

She took the pile of paper back to her room, switched on the light again and fired up the computer, still wearing her coat.

The comments in the visitors' book were all much easier to read than Hoffman's note. One or two had been quoted in the visitors' blogs. Some were straightforward dryly worded advice to other walkers, warning of difficult weather or faults in guidebook descriptions of the hardness of chosen routes. Others were sentimentally lyrical about the landscape around the Fortwells' farm, the magnificent straightness of the old Roman road, the amazing survival of parts of Hadrian's Wall, and the charm of the kitchen where they'd eaten, or the deliciousness of the mutton stew.

That dish featured in several of the entries. Had Angie ever cooked anything else for her paying guests?

Most of the visitors had scribbled an address, sometimes only for email, after their entries. And a few had added details of their blogs. Trish compared them with Hal's list. There were two mentioned in the visitors' book that didn't appear on the list. She clicked on to the Internet, downloaded the relevant sections, and started to read.

One mentioned Peter, the discursive blogger who had met Adam and been warned off the Fortwells' farm. Another offered tips for all the best b & bs on the most obscure routes and referred to another farm to be avoided, where there was an uncontrollably savage dog. 'And you'd do well to bypass the witch at Bothwell's if you can; she turns off the heating at 6.30 p.m. and keeps the boiler so low only the first person gets even a warm bath.'

There was obviously a protective kind of family-feeling among the regular ramblers. Wide awake now, and looking for anything that could hint at some kind of disapproval of CWWM for their use of such amazing countryside to house their chemical-waste tanks, Trish read on and on. But she found nothing.

None of the bloggers so much as mentioned the tanks. And nowhere was there even the slightest mention of Greg Waverly or any dangerous waste or environmental protest or anything whatsoever that could have had even the remotest possible bearing on the case in hand.

Trish smiled. In her tiredness and frustration she was falling into the ways of the traditional silks she'd listened to in her earliest working years, who would allow their voices to swing with the rhythm of their dramatic sentences and add wholly unnecessary words and emphasis to perfectly ordinary questions. Now she was at it. Time to go home. She turned off the laptop once again and shuffled the papers into neat heaps.

Only then did she notice the schedule of Angie Fortwell's income from the bed-and-breakfasters at the back of the pile of visitors' book pages Fred had sent. Pinned to the schedule was a list of the names and addresses of everyone who had stayed the night, with a note beside each saying what they had paid and how. Just what Trish had wanted.

No sign of any Adam, she noticed, but the Chris and Sal mentioned in Peterthewalk's blog were there. They'd obviously ignored his repetition of the advice to avoid the Fortwells. Interestingly they were the only people in the whole list who had used cash, rather than cheque or credit card.

Forty-five pounds for two of them to stay the night and eat not only a full English breakfast but also a three-course dinner was pretty cheap, Trish thought. Even if the bulk of dinner was the mutton stew. But why use cash? The price of one night wasn't going to weigh anyone down, but if they'd used real money for a whole holiday they must have lugged around a wodge of notes and a tidy weight of coins. Why bother in these days of debit and credit cards?

She pushed the schedule through the photocopier, found a red pen and wrote on the top of the copy:

Hal, can you find out more about this couple for me? They stayed at the Fortwells three days before the explosion and were still in the area just after it. I'd like to know how long they spent in Northumberland in all, how they paid for the rest of their trip, and anything else you can find out, e.g. are they members of FADE?

Trish.

If Robert got to hear of this, his reaction would be fury, and she was tempted – just for a second – to ask Hal to keep the request to himself. But that would hardly be dignified, so she dropped the note on his desk, unfolded, and went home.

George greeted her with a sleepy smile as she crept into her bedroom.

'Sorry to wake you,' she whispered as though there were someone else she might disturb.

He pushed himself up and bunched the pillows behind him, blinking.

'I've missed you,' he said. 'It's worth being disturbed for a chance to chat. Have you eaten?'

'No. But the moment's passed.'

'What did you have for lunch?'

'Yoghurt, I think. Too long ago to be sure. Don't worry about it.'

'You get snappy if you don't eat properly for more than a day or two,' he said, now feeling around with his bare feet for his slippers. He pulled on his dressing gown. 'And I don't like that. I'll bring you up something. Have a shower and get comfortable. It's not that late. There's time to eat and talk and still get enough sleep.'

She blew him a kiss, feeling easier with him than at any time since the evening he'd been so tense that he'd cut his toenails to the barest stumps, and went to wash the day away under the hot shower.

Later, when they'd made love and she'd felt all the crumbs she'd spilled grinding into the skin of her back, he grabbed hold of her hand.

'I should've said something about Henry before I told Jay about him. I'm sorry.'

Trish leaned sideways to stroke his shoulder with her cheek. 'Don't worry about it. I was taken aback, but so what? It's your story to do what you want with.'

'I don't think about him these days. So there was no point telling you. But Jay needed to know because of the way Darren makes him feel.'

They'd turned out the lights a while ago, so she had only the faint yellow glow cast by the streetlamp outside and it wasn't enough tonight to show her anything helpful in his face. She lay back against the pillows and waited, with her hand still tightly held in his.

'I can understand why Henry did it,' George said into the dimness, sounding formal and detached, like the lawyer he was. 'A natural reaction to the appearance of an interloper. He'd been the only child for three years, then I appeared and – presumably – looked like grabbing all the attention, food, love, whatever. You could put it down to evolutionary psychology or sibling rivalry. I *can* understand, but I can't forgive. Not him; nor myself for letting it happen.'

'But—'

'Don't say it, Trish. You don't need to. It happened forty years ago and it's not relevant any more.'

'But what did he do?'

'Nothing much.' He turned his head a little so that he could smile at her in reassurance. 'This isn't a story of torture or anything like that. He just told me, and showed me in every possible way, that I was a—' Something clicked in his throat and he rolled his head back so that he was looking across at the far wall again. He took a moment longer, licked his lips, then brought out a single word: 'failure'.

She had heard the tiny catch in his voice, understood it as easily as the power of his understatement, and wanted to help. His grip on her hand was tight enough to warn her not to move.

'Perhaps if it had only happened at home, I'd have managed better,' he went on, sounding more like himself. 'But we were at the same prep school and he carried it on there. Made the rest of them join in until it felt as though the whole world had permission to wipe its feet on me.'

'The prep school, the boarding prep school you were sent to when you were eight years old?' Trish said, trying not to let out any of her old outrage at the savage custom of the old British upper classes. She could hear her accent slipping back into the one she'd used at her own state school.

'Mmm.' The unarticulated sound suggested agreement.

For a moment she couldn't think for fury on his behalf. Once, years ago, he'd mentioned in passing the difficulty of being a short, fat, bespectacled, clever chess-player in a school of sports freaks, but he'd never mentioned this extra, unbearable cruelty. She felt him move, push himself further up the pillows, as though he couldn't manage the rest of the story lying down.

'I don't need you to feel sorry for me, Trish. In fact it's

the last thing I want, which is probably why I've never told you.'

'But—'

'I need you to know me as the man I am now, not the miserable boy I was. We're two different beings. It doesn't affect me any more. It's only relevant because it's what makes me respect Jay so much for fighting back. OK?'

But it does still affect you, she thought, looking back at some of the trickier moments of their past together.

Questions banged about in her brain, butting up against his warning that he wouldn't say any more.

Only if you know everything can you be safe, she thought, and make everyone around you safe.

But there were other ways to find out and she cared too much about him to make him go any further tonight, so she kissed his chin and asked if he wanted a cup of tea, late though it was.

Chapter 11

Angie sat in court, listening to Robert Anstey re-examining the scientific expert, as he gave evidence about the weather conditions in the week before the explosion.

She could have told them about the weather herself. After all, she wasn't going to forget that week. It had been beastly: cold and wet and horrible. No wonder Trish Maguire hadn't bothered to turn up for this morning's session. Questions like these would be much too boring for a woman so pleased with herself. And so successful. And so glossy.

'How, in your opinion, Doctor Jonas,' Anstey said, sounding as detached and uncaring as a robot, 'would the weather conditions have affected the activated charcoal in the tank's filter system?'

'In itself the weather wouldn't have had any effect. Charcoal like this heats up during the day and cools at night. With temperatures such as these tanks experienced before the explosion, there is no chance they could have spontaneously heated to the point of ignition.'

'And so how can you explain what happened?'

'The only possibility is some kind of blockage of the air inlet valves.'

The judge looked as bored and irritated as Angie felt. They'd been here so often before.

'How long would such a blockage have had to be in place before it caused the fire that led to the explosion?' asked Robert Anstey.

The expert, a weaselly little man with tiny glasses and bad skin, looked at the judge:

'My assessment, given the relative temperature of the days and nights preceding the explosion, is about seventy-two hours.' He smiled, a nasty little smirk, in Angie's direction. 'I cannot be specific to the minute, My Lord.'

'Thank you, Doctor Jonas,' said Robert, sitting down.

Angie got to her feet, wishing she'd bought more than one suit. It was beginning to feel painfully tight around the waistband after all the carbohydrates she'd been eating. And the jacket was too short to disguise the fact that she'd undone the top of the zip. As Marty had promised during the party, members of FADE filled the spectators' seats behind her. At least they wouldn't mind that she was bursting out of her skirt, or mock her for it. Suddenly gratitude gushed through her and she turned to the expert like a conqueror.

'Doctor Jonas, are you seriously telling this court that a man who had successfully monitored the filters on these tanks for three years, during heat waves and blizzards, would have failed to spot a blockage for seventy-two hours? That's three whole days and nights.'

'Mrs Fortwell,' said the judge, leaning towards her and looking over his half-moon spectacles. 'Please remember you have already cross-examined this witness. You do not get a second chance. In any case, you may not ask a witness to speculate about facts of which he can know nothing.'

Hearing a stifled giggle from one of the lawyers, Angie felt a child's blush making her cheeks boil. The conqueror-feeling oozed away. She tried to get it back, bowed a little, and said: 'I am grateful for Your Lordship's reminder.'

The judge nodded in return, then told Doctor Jonas he could go. Angie heard the doors behind her open and someone walk in and move into one of the benches. Was it Adam? She'd been so relieved this morning to see no sign of him in court that the thought of facing him when she turned round made her feel absolutely stony.

Trish looked at the map with the five differently coloured routes she'd plotted from the blogs Hal had found and the others she'd traced herself. There were dotted lines here and there, where she'd had to guess, but enough of the routes were firm to make it seem worth the exercise. The orange line was Peter's, the purple Adam's, the pink James and Clare's, the yellow Chris and Sal's, and the green Ron's. They all intersected at different points within a day's walk of the Fortwells' farm on different dates in the week before the explosion.

With Antony's advice and Bates's orders to ignore the possibility of sabotage at the tanks, she shouldn't have been doing this, but Robert was more than capable of conducting the day's session in court. She had proved to him, her clerk and anyone else who might be interested that she hadn't hesitated to pick up the case at no notice; now she could take a day away to try to find the answers she wanted without sacrificing anything. It was fairer to do it herself than make Hal steal more time from his pupil-master's tasks.

*

Forty miles away, in a village on the far side of Chelmsford, a harassed woman was trying to make her 3-year-old daughter and her friend's son get in the back of the car. She'd been late collecting them from their morning nursery and they were playing up to punish her. Minnie, the baby, was already strapped into her seat and screaming. Charlotte and Jake were messing about with damp sticks they'd picked out of the gutter.

'Pah!' shouted Jake, jamming one end into Charlotte's chest. 'Gotcha!'

Charlotte grabbed the stick in one plump powerful fist and wrenched it away from him, before whacking him on the side of his head, dancing out of reach and chanting: 'Silly boy. Silly boy. Silly boy.'

Jake promptly burst into tears. Charlotte's mother, Ellie, whose head already felt as though it had three drills powering through it, grabbed her daughter and almost flung her into the high back seat of the Grand Cherokee Jeep her husband insisted she drive to keep them all safe.

'Sit there and do up your seat belt,' she shouted. 'And don't touch Minnie.'

Charlotte promptly started to grizzle. Ellie slammed the door on her and went to fetch Jake, who was hiding his shame behind the nearest tree.

'Come on out, Jake,' Ellie said, moderating her voice. You shouldn't yell at your own children, of course, but everyone did. Other people's were different. You had to be kinder, however you felt about wimpy little boys who couldn't stand up to your daughter. 'We have to get back so we can have lunch and be ready when your mummy comes to pick you up. Come along, Jake.'

'Don't want to.' But he emerged from behind the tree, knuckling his eyes and dragging his expensive shoes in the mud.

At last Ellie persuaded him back to the car and wiped the worst of the sticky mud off his shoes with a pile of leaves. Charlotte was playing peek-a-boo with her little sister, both as happy as they could be.

Be pleased, Ellie told herself, while she absorbed the knowledge that they'd never be so cooperative if she'd actually asked them to play together. She helped Jake into the car and did up his seat belt for him, before heaving herself into the driving seat. She took extra care to check the traffic before leaving the parking space because this was the kind of mood that caused accidents. A shabby dark-blue lorry was a bit too close for safety, so she waited until he'd passed, then pulled out behind him.

He took her turning at the roundabout, which was a nuisance. She had only eight miles to drive, but stuck behind something as big as this could mean all kinds of hold-ups. And he wouldn't keep a steady speed. For some reason he kept accelerating then reining back, almost as though he was trying to wind her up.

The road was narrow and twisty here, so maybe he just didn't know it well and slowed down to take each bend with extra care, but the changes were jerkier than she'd have expected for something as simple as that. She kept finding her front bumper only inches from his back wheels. And then the bastard went and stopped dead. She jammed her foot on the brake and managed to stop in time, with her hand on the horn.

You shouldn't use your horn as a rebuke, she remembered

from the Highway Code. But how else were you supposed to tell people to stop playing silly buggers and let you get the children home?

Ellie thought of the shepherd's pie she'd put in the oven before she set out. It would soon be dried out and inedible. The lorry hadn't moved, although its engine was running again, and puffing out smelly exhaust that was blowing in through her ventilators. It shouldn't have been on the road at all in this condition.

She put her hand on the horn again and gave the lorry driver an even louder blast. But the noise made Minnie start whimpering, so Ellie had to turn round to console her.

By the time all three children were quiet, the lorry had moved a good fifty yards ahead, which at least meant Ellie could put her foot down for a little while. She got up to thirty before she caught up. Then the lorry driver braked sharply once more, making her swear.

'What's that man *doing*?' Jake asked.

There was a damp popping sound, which meant Charlotte had taken her thumb out of her mouth. 'What man?'

'I don't know, Jake,' Ellie said, reaching for her mobile. 'But he's driving really stupidly.'

There was a phone number at the bottom of all the advertising stuff on the double doors at the back of the lorry and above the diamond-shaped orange HazChem signs. Flicking her eyes between the road ahead and the numbers on her phone, Ellie rang it, silently rehearsing her complaint as she waited for an answer. The baby's wails rose to an earsplitting shriek.

'Charlotte's hitting Minnie,' Jake said in an interested voice.

Ellie glanced back, to see Charlotte's thumbs bearing

down on the baby's eyes. She dropped the phone and flung back one hand to grab her elder daughter's arm and pull her away.

'Leave her alone, Charlotte. For once in your life, leave your sister alone.'

'Stop!' shouted Jake, just as the jeep hit the back of the lorry with a noise like the end of the world.

Ellie felt a sickening wrench in the arm that was stretched out behind her and her neck cracked as her head whipped back and forth. She could see the lorry driver's door opening. It was his sodding fault for messing about so if he tried to pin the blame on her, she'd fight back.

But it would be easier if she wasn't actually attached to the back doors of his vehicle. She put the car into reverse and moved back a couple of feet or so, before hauling up the handbrake and switching off her engine. With her hand on the key, she saw the lorry's dark-blue double doors swing open. Inside, were rows and rows of large, rusting oil drums. Most were standing, but a few were lying on their sides. As Ellie watched in horror, one rolled forwards and hovered on the edge of the lorry. She reached for the key and turned on the ignition, pumping her accelerator, but she couldn't get the Jeep moving before the drum fell, crashing down on to bonnet. The bung flew out and a thick, oily greenish sludge oozed out.

The drum bounced down on to the road, spraying its filthy contents as it went, but all Ellie could see was the Jeep's paint, lifting and blistering into great wet bubbles under the sludge. Then she smelled it, coming in through the ventilators as the exhaust had done. But this was sharply acrid. Choking. Dangerous.

She had to get the children out before the stench triggered

asthma attacks. Or worse. The lorry driver was coming towards her yelling something, but her ears weren't working. His mouth moved and it was easy to see some of the words were 'bitch' and 'stupid cow'. But she couldn't hear. The children were making a noise too, shouting more words that meant nothing.

It took her whole weight to get the driver's door open and she felt as though she was moving like a snail, but she did eventually reach the baby's door and fumbled to get it unlatched. There was no point telling the others to move yet because the child locks meant they couldn't open their door from the inside.

At last, the latch gave way and the door opened. But then there were the buckles of Minnie's straps to deal with, and Ellie's fingers felt like unbending iron bars.

'Undo your seat belts,' she shouted to the others, who were both crying. At last she had the baby's straps free and could grab her hot little body. Ellie's ears started to work again and Minnie's screams bit into her brain. She could hear the driver too, and none of what he said was an insult any more. Her brain was still sluggish, but slowly she made out what he wanted her to do.

'Give her to me and get out of this and get your shoes off.' The terror in his hoarse voice was as bad as anything except the smell. 'Don't touch your feet. Get away to the far bank and kick off your shoes. Don't touch them with your hands or feet. Just kick them off. Quick as you can. Come on now. It's important.'

As the weight of her child was pulled away, Ellie fled to the far side of the car. He was shouting at her now, the same words in the same order all over again. But she had to get the children out first. She pulled open the door.

'Mummy, your feet,' Charlotte said, whimpering. 'Your feet, Mummy, your feet.'

Ellie looked down.

Her shoes were melting in the stinking green ooze that covered them. And so was her skin. She began to feel again and everything the driver said made sense.

This time the screams were hers.

The driver knew he couldn't vomit. He had to hold himself together until the ambulance came. There wasn't anyone else to keep these children away from the chemical filth that had spilled out of his lorry.

As soon as the ambulance crew had taken over here, he was going to phone his fucking boss and ask why the fuck he'd not only landed him with this load of toxic crap but also sent him out in a death trap of a vehicle with spongy brakes and a criminally dodgy clutch. And then he was going to the cops.

CWWM, he thought, staring at the letters stencilled on one of the drums. What the fuck's CWWM? Is it going to kill this poor woman? And what's breathing it in done to *me*?

The judge rose for lunch and Angie had to turn round. The late arrival had been Adam. Now he was glaring at her from behind his unfashionably huge spectacles and looking exactly like her own younger self. His hair was chopped off like hers, too, and much the same washed-out brown hers had been before the coarse grey streaks had appeared.

She made herself smile and saw a minute reflection of the movement in his lips.

'Greg,' she said. 'My son is here again. D'you and I need to talk over lunch or can I eat with him?'

'Why don't we all eat together?' His beard rose up around his face like vegetation around a nestling rodent as he smiled, and his eyes looked more lopsided than ever.

'We've still got an awful lot of catching up to do, Adam and I; it might be better if we . . .' She let her voice tail away and didn't wait for Greg's agreement. Instead, she walked briskly towards Adam and kissed him without, she hoped, showing any sign of reluctance. Fran was standing a couple of rows behind him, looking friendly, which made smiling easier.

'D'you feel like a bit of lunch in the coffee shop?' she said to Adam.

'Why not?'

Only once they were sitting with sandwiches in front of them did she ask why he'd run out on her yesterday.

'It was all getting a bit heavy. I needed time to think. Didn't the waiter give you my message?'

'Message? No. All I found when I got back to the table was a wad of money, far too big for the bill.' She reached into her bag and took out three twenty-pound notes. 'Here's your change. Oh, go on! Take it. I don't need tipping, you know.'

'Sorry,' he said, neatly folding the money into his wallet. 'I didn't mean to insult you.'

'While we're on the subject of why, Adam, can you tell me why you never answered any of the letters I sent to you at the university after that awful day?'

He shrugged, then ate a large mouthful of sandwich to give himself an excuse for silent chewing. Angie did the same and watched him swallow.

'Too angry,' he said at last. A large crumb settled on his lower lip and he brushed it away with an impatience she could recognise. She tried to put herself in his position.

'With me?' she said at last.

'I told you: I hated the way you let him bully you *and* pretended you liked being his victim. I could've ki—' He coloured.

She thought of the Land Rover powering towards her, with the farmyard's mud spraying up from its tyres.

'You could have killed me?' she suggested, trying to sound as though she was making a joke of some kind and not remembering the way he'd aimed the Land Rover at her. 'If you were so convinced *I* was the victim, why weren't you angry with your father?'

'Are you mad? *Of course* I was angry with him. On really bad days, I used to fantasise about all the things I'd like to do to him.'

Angie flinched, like a dog that's been beaten once too often. Adam was still talking:

'I knew I could never change him. Whatever I said, he'd go on putting you in the same position as Schlep, making you work all day for him and then have to wait on his pleasure before you were even allowed to eat.'

'That's *not* what it was like,' she said, but still Adam wasn't listening.

'But I could have helped you if you'd only been prepared to admit how much you hated him.'

'I *didn't* hate him.'

John was dead. He had weathered the loss of his only son, just as he had weathered every other cruelty the Fates had thrown at him. Nothing Angie said or did now could alter one iota of the unhappiness he'd suffered, but she still had to make Adam see the truth.

'I loved him, Adam. Of course he could be a difficult sod

when he was worn out or stressed. Everyone can be. Even you. But I *never* stopped loving him. You have to accept that.'

'So, you're still in denial. And I've wasted my time coming here,' Adam said, his bitterness rasping her feelings like a grater. 'You know where I am, so you can get me if you ever decide you want us to have an honest relationship. I'm off.'

He left three-quarters of his sandwich, pushed back his chair with a horrible squawk of its legs on the hard floor, and stalked away. Angie's vision blurred. All the other lunchers, from distinguished lawyers to hard-pressed litigants, swam around her in a multicoloured liquid mess.

A warm hand on her back, and an even warmer voice asking how she was, told her Fran had seen everything and come to offer comfort. Angie leaned sideways until her sore head met the softness of Fran's body. Her arm tightened into a hug and she stroked Angie's hair.

'It'll be all right. He'll come back. You need to be strong now. You've come so far, you mustn't lose heart. We're nearly there, and the judge likes you. I'm sure you'll get the judgment you deserve and big enough damages to rebuild a proper life for yourself.'

Oh, God! Why did I ever let it start? Angie thought, straightening up again. Why did I let my vile temper drive me to it? Why didn't I wait for the official reports like everybody told me? Why didn't I accept that generous cheque instead of tearing it up and throwing it back? Will I ever learn not to let the anger send me over the edge?

David walked back from the gym with the rest of his class, hoping he'd find Jay in school with one of his highly coloured excuses for being so late and missing a whole morning. But he wasn't there. David stuffed his smelly gym clothes in his locker and headed off for lunch. Pity it was Wednesday, which was liver day. He hated liver, more than anything else the school cooked. Sometimes he even thought of being a vegetarian so he wouldn't have to eat it. Then he remembered all of George's best recipes and knew he couldn't.

Someone rammed his arm round David's neck in a high tackle and he leaned as heavily as he could so they got shoved against the wall. Pulling himself away, he looked and saw Sam, who was really his best friend, but who couldn't stick Jay.

'Where's your spotty little underclass toerag today then?' Sam said, putting on a voice like his dad's.

'Shut up, you fucking twat,' David said. 'He's OK. He's just not here now.'

They swaggered into the refectory together, two of the tallest boys in their year, and gritted their teeth over the dried-up slabs of liver. At least they were allowed ketchup with it, which made it just possible to swallow.

'Disgusting!' Sam said. 'You got time for chess?'

'David!' His form monitor's voice was even louder than usual.

'What?'

'The head wants to see you now. Don't wait for pudding. OK?'

Sam's heavy face, with nearly as many spots as Jay's, broke into a smile. '*You*! You never do anything wrong. What's he want with you?'

'Fuck knows. Warm up the chess board and I'll find you Sam.'

Mr Black's secretary wasn't at her desk; no one was there, so David hovered for a bit, then knocked on the door.

'Come in,' said Mr Black and David pushed open the heavy brown wooden door. 'Ah, there you are, David, good. Come and sit down.'

There were two other people already there, a bloke in jeans and a black leather jacket and a woman in police uniform. They were still on their feet, so David ignored the chair.

'This is David Maguire. David, these are DS Brown and WPC Jenkinson. They'd like to ask you a few questions.'

'What about?'

'Jay,' said Mr Black.

'Just a minute, sir,' said the bloke in the leather jacket. 'We can handle this. David, when did you last see Jay Smith?'

'What's he done?'

'Just answer the question.'

'Are you arresting me?'

The head and both the police officers laughed. It didn't sound real. David pulled himself as straight as he could and was glad to see he was taller than the WPC.

'Because if you're not, I don't have to say anything. And I'm not saying anything without my sister being here.'

'Sister? What's she got to do with it?'

Mr Black intervened, quick and smooth, like a chocolate fountain. 'A much older half-sister, she's a barrister – a QC in fact. I've already left a message on her mobile, David, but she hasn't answered so I'm assuming she's in court again.'

'I don't think we need worry her, David,' said the police bloke, sounding all sugary now. 'You're not in any trouble that I know of.'

'Nor me,' said Mr Black.

'I just need to know when you last saw Jay Smith. Is there a problem about telling me?'

'No,' David said, trying to be polite. 'But as a matter of principle it's important to remember that police powers are limited in this country and it is the responsibility of British subjects to make sure they abide by those limits.'

'Phew,' said the bloke, pretending to be impressed. 'That sounds as though you learned it by heart. Did your sister teach you?'

'She says it sometimes. Actually the last time I heard it was when she was talking to my godmother. She's Detective Chief Inspector Caroline Lyalt.'

The bloke's thick black eyebrows wiggled and he looked seriously pissed off. Which was better than the smarminess.

'You are well connected, aren't you? I'm sure the DCI would advise you to answer the question, and I haven't much time to go on playing games. We've got important things to do. When did you last see your friend Jay Smith?'

'If Trish's in court, then I need to discuss this with George before I talk to you.'

The plain clothes officer rolled his eyes upwards as though he was dealing with a special-needs specimen.

'His sister's partner, a solicitor,' said Mr Black. 'Have you got his number, David?'

'Course.' David pulled his phone out of his inside pocket and rang George. His calls were being diverted. David rang the switchboard at Henton Maltravers and said who he was and what he wanted.

'Sorry, David,' said Charlie, the receptionist. 'He's out at a client's. Can I take a message?'

'Just ask him to call me on my mobile,' he said before

turning to the officers. 'Until one of them's here, I don't want to say anything.'

There was an angry-sounding sigh from the man, but the WPC said quietly: 'How would it be if we got in touch with DCI Lyalt to see what she thinks you should do?'

David shrugged, then nodded. The WPC went outside and they waited, not saying anything, for nearly five minutes. Then she came back and handed her phone to him. He put it to his ear in a gingerly kind of way, as though it might explode, and said, 'Hello?'

'David?' said a familiar voice.

'Caro?'

'Yes, it's me. It's all right to talk to the two officers. They've told me about your friend Jay. I'll leave a message for Trish in chambers so she knows what's going on, but try to tell them everything you know about Jay and where he could be. He may need rescuing. OK? See you soon. Bye now.'

'I didn't realise Jay was lost,' he said as he handed back the woman's phone. 'Sorry. We did our homework together in George's office after school yesterday, then he took us to Pizza Express, then he got a cab and we dropped Jay at his estate and George and I went on back home to Trish's.'

'That's better,' said the bloke, while the WPC smiled and made notes. 'Now all we need is George's name and address and some idea of the time when you dropped Jay at the estate.'

David provided the information too quickly for the WPC, so he had to say it again more slowly, adding: 'I think it was about nine o'clock, but I didn't look at my watch or anything so I can't be sure.'

'And do you know, David, which entrance to the estate Jay was going to use?'

'Where we always dropped him: at the Westgate arch, you know, where there's the green-and-white map of the estate and concrete lumps on the path to stop cars going through.'

He knew he'd said too much when he saw the WPC's face go cold and stiff.

'What's happened to Jay?' he said for about the fifth time.

The head said he really thought the officers ought to say. But they didn't. Instead the bloke asked him if Jay had ever said anything about his mother.

'Never,' David said, which wasn't quite true. 'What's *she* done?'

'You must tell him,' the head said. 'He and his family have been very good to Jay Smith.'

'OK. Last night Jay's mother was found with very bad injuries near the Westgate entrance to the estate, and no one has seen Jay since.'

The liver churned around in David's gut like clothes in the washing machine.

Fran understood that Angie needed to walk alone after lunch and she didn't ask any of the questions Greg would have, only reminded her the judge wanted everyone back in court by half past two.

Wanting to breathe, Angie crossed over the Strand and cut down Milford Lane, heading for the Embankment and the view down the Thames. It wasn't like being in the country, but at least you could see out in both directions. And sometimes you could get a faceful of fresh breeze that didn't smell of dust or other people or petrol.

Adam's voice echoed in her head: 'On really bad days, I used to fantasise about all the things I'd like to do to him.'

Adam's temper was even worse than her own. She'd always known that, but she'd never thought about it in the context of the tanks until he'd reappeared in her life. Now she couldn't think of anything else.

Looking back to the night of the explosion, she saw again the silvery-blue landscape and the frosty edge where the trees met the sky, and the whitish lumps of the sleeping sheep. And in front of it all, like a figure crossing the screen in a cinema, she saw Adam, muffled up against the cold, with a mask over his face like a pantomime villain, heading for the tanks with a bunch of wadding in his hand.

Was it possible? Had he hated his father so much that he could have stuffed something into the vents of the tanks, knowing that would make them explode? Had his furious misguided championship of her made him try to destroy the farm he thought was ruining her life?

The more she'd listened to this morning's witness, the less she'd been able to hang on to any faint belief that the tanks could have blown up by chance or because of some negligence of CWWM's.

Bong, bong, bong, bong. The quarter chimes of a vast clock somewhere close behind her made her move. Whatever the truth, she couldn't see that she had any option but to get back into court now and fight on as though she still believed in her case.

Could she do it? Could she challenge the rest of Maguire's witnesses if they made as much sense as Doctor Jonas? Could she still make the passionate final speech she and Greg and Fran had spent so long preparing with all this suspicion in her head?

Streams of people were walking towards her, dividing like water around her. It felt as if only she were going north, fighting against a wave that would drown her if she let down her guard for one second.

Good training, she told herself. You've always been stubborn. Stick with it. The trial can't last much longer and you never need tell anyone about Adam. So long as you never talk, ever, you'll be safe. And so will he.

But what if the judge awarded the kind of damages Greg and Fran expected? Could she take them now? And if she didn't, how could she explain it to everyone at FADE?

And how could she look at Adam and not let him see what she suspected?

She'd come to a halt, waiting at the crossing even though the traffic had stopped for her. She saw Trish Maguire, without her wig or gown, pausing on the steps of the court opposite with her phone held to her ear. A sharp hoot made Angie look to her right, where a taxi driver was angrily gesturing her to get a move on. She stepped on to the crossing and hurried over.

As she got closer to Trish, Angie saw her face contorted and distinctly heard her say: 'Oh, God! No!'

Trish flipped her phone shut, longing to abandon everything to do with CWWM so she could rush to the school and find out where Jay was and whether he'd half-killed his mother. She knew exactly how David would be feeling now and she had to help.

The phone in her pocket buzzed again. She looked at the clock above her head. There were only six minutes before she had to be in court. But if there was news she had to know what it was.

'Hello?' she said into the phone, just as someone knocked into her. She realised she'd come to a standstill and glanced round to apologise to the impatient stranger, who flounced onwards without a word.

'Hi,' said a South London voice down the phone. 'It's Shelby Deedes here, Jay's social worker. I wanted to talk. We still haven't found him, and I've looked in all the likeliest places. But there's one bit of good news: his mother isn't doing as badly as they thought at first. She's in Dowting's Hospital, in the orthopaedic ward because of her broken bones. Serious but stable is how they're calling it at the moment.'

Trish tried to blank out the worst of the pictures that had been in her mind since she'd first heard the news.

'Thanks, Shelby. I'd like to talk to you about it all later, but I have to go into court now. May I phone round about five o'clock in case there's anything new?'

'Sure. Leave a message if I can't answer, and I'll get back to you.'

There was no sign of Adam in the public benches. Angie moved to her own place at the front, glancing at the lawyers' empty bench beside her. Should she ask Trish Maguire whether CWWM would still be prepared to settle? She'd hate doing it, but it would keep Adam safe. How on earth could she ever justify it to Fran and Greg?

'You OK?' Greg whispered as she sat down beside him.

'What?'

'You're pale and shaking, Ange. What's happened?'

She dredged up a memory of how to smile. 'Indigestion. I was talking so much, I ate too fast.'

He laughed and patted her. 'Well, try not to throw up this

afternoon. We're so nearly there, Ange. Stick with it. Another few days and it'll all be over. You've done brilliantly. I always knew you would.'

She thought of the night when she'd escaped to the pub and Ben Givens had rounded her up like a stray. He'd lectured her then about how much she owed Fran and Greg. He'd been right. There *was* no honourable way out.

Chapter 12

Robert was a couple of yards ahead when Trish phoned Shelby. The journey back to chambers could take as much as eight minutes if you walked slowly, and you could get through a lot of questions in that time.

'Hi,' she said as soon as Shelby answered. 'Can you tell me exactly what happened to Jay's mother?'

'She'd picked up her benefit just as the Post Office was closing. I can't think why she left it so late because normally she'd have been there first thing. On her way back to the estate she loaded up with a dozen cans of White Star at the offie.'

'White Star?'

There was a laugh down the phone. 'You do live a sheltered life, don't you? It's cider; the strongest there is. One can equals four units of alcohol. So ten cans is more than any woman should drink in two weeks. Rosie Smith was well into her fourth, sitting in a warm corner by the central heating vents at the foot of the first tower block inside Westgate.'

Trish had no difficulty picturing the scene or feeling the humiliation of drinking in the open. She said as much.

'Rosie's long past feeling humiliated,' Shelby said. 'She

drinks outside because she knows Darren will always take any alcohol he sees and make her watch as he pours it down the drain.'

'Where was he when she was attacked?'

'Well alibi'd by Kimberley, and—'

'She'd lie for him, though, wouldn't she?' Trish said. 'Don't you think he's a much more likely suspect than Jay?'

'I know you're prejudiced against him.' Shelby's voice was as cold and sharp as an ice pick, 'But you must accept the truth: he didn't do it. Kimberley's not his only alibi. One of the neighbours – a woman of thirty-two, so old enough to know better than to lie about something like this – dropped in to borrow a cup of sugar and stayed to chat.'

'Is she reliable?' Trish was slowing down as she neared Plough Court, still wanting to know a lot more. Did anyone really borrow a cup of sugar? Wasn't that just a soap-opera way of getting characters to introduce each other to the audience?

'There's no reason not to believe her,' Shelby said. 'She's OK. And Darren's never been violent to his mum. Ever. In spite of all the provocation. Like I said, you don't know him.'

Nor do you, Trish thought, wanting to make her take Darren's violence seriously.

If only Shelby had seen Jay on the day he'd come to the flat with blood pouring from the wounds on his face! But she hadn't. By the time Jeremy Black had persuaded her to pick him up from school, the damage had begun to scab over and didn't look nearly so bad.

'Did you look to see whether there were any marks on Darren's knuckles?' Trish said into the phone.

'The attack wasn't done with hands.' Shelby's voice was

different now, not quite placatory but kinder. 'She was kicked, all over her head and body. If whoever did it had been wearing boots, or even hard shoes, she'd be dead; but it looks as though he was in trainers. The police haven't found any in the flat with any signs of blood. But Kimberley noticed that a pair of Jay's are missing. I've got to go.'

'Me too,' Trish said. 'If you get any news of Jay, will you tell me?'

'Sure.'

Trish flipped her phone shut as she caught sight of Robert, re-emerged from chambers and beckoning furiously.

'Come on. Hurry up. Hal's got some news for you.'

'What?' Trish said as she reached him, stowing her phone in her pocket.

'He's been on the track of Chris and Sally Bowles from the Northumbrian walkers' blogs, checking out the address they gave in the Fortwells' visitors' book. There's no such place. Which suggests they could've been using fake names, too.'

'So it *is* them,' Trish said, already running upstairs. When she reached Robert's room, Hal looked up from his computer. His freckly face was more eager than she'd ever seen it.

'Did he tell you, Trish?'

'He did. Terrific news. Now we've got to track them down and find out exactly what they did while they were at the Fortwells' farm seventy-two hours before the tanks went up in smoke. It would be an incredible coincidence to find such a shifty couple there at exactly the right time if they weren't involved.'

'What I thought we could do,' Hal said with his fingers still on the keyboard, 'is get in touch with all the bloggers we can, that's all the ones who also signed people's visitors' books and left either email or snailmail addresses, and find out what they can remember of these two and perhaps provide us with physical descriptions. Lots have put pix on their blogs, but there aren't any captioned "Chris and Sal" unfortunately.'

'Good thought,' Trish said, even more pleased with him.

'Don't forget,' Robert said from behind them both, 'you're my pupil and, unlike Trish, I've got four big cases in the pipeline. I need you to work on them.'

Some of the brightness in Hal's eyes dimmed, as did Trish's growing affection for Robert.

'I won't go anywhere; I'll only email, and that won't take long,' Hal said. 'I'll do it in my own time.'

'Anything you can do by email would be great,' she said with a nod to Robert, 'but don't compromise the rest of your work. I'll talk to Hoffman and see if he can persuade the client to have investigators put back on the case.' She paused in the doorway and looked back.

'Thank you, Hal. You've been terrific. We will get to the bottom of it now.'

His eyes sparkled.

In her own room, she looked round at the heaps of papers and books all over her desk. In the old days before she'd taken silk, she would have had a pupil too and he – or she – could have tidied up this mess. Ignoring it, she phoned Hoffman's number and told him she needed him to talk to their client again.

'Can't at the moment. He's on his way to Kazakhstan.'

'Why? More trouble?'

'Yes. CWWM have a thoroughly satisfactory tank farm

there that's been doing good business ever since independence, and they've been trying to expand into most of the neighbouring states. One new site across the border is halfway to development but the local authorities have just rescinded their planning permission.'

'Can they do that when it's already being built?'

Trish wished she could believe Greg Waverly capable of organising something like this. Even though she was now certain his shambolic persona was an invention, she couldn't see him managing large-scale bribery of local politicians thousands of miles away.

'Not by any normal standards, no,' Fred said down the phone. 'But life is still pretty Wild West in some of the old Soviet states. It's particularly irritating for Bates because CWWM went through a ghastly time sorting out what sweeteners they could legally provide from this end and, in effect, paying through the nose for the planning permission they did get.'

'When will he be back?'

'Who knows? He's always been remarkably hands-on. Likes to do all the trickiest stuff himself. He told me he was going on an open ticket because he had no idea how long it would take. He's got his development director with him. They'll be checking in with head office at intervals, so I could get a message to him if your request is urgent.'

'It'll keep. Thanks.'

The phone rang again. Picking it up, she gave her name and Antony replied, sounding faint and quivery:

'Trish . . . I need to see you.'

'I have to get home. David needs help.'

'Is his life in danger?'

'Of course not,' she said sharply, far more sharply than

she usually spoke to anyone, let alone a hospital patient. 'Sorry. I didn't mean to be so arsy. What's the problem, Antony?'

'I need you, Trish. Please come.' Still his voice had the unnatural shakiness. He put down the phone before she could ask any more.

She took a taxi to save time and ran into his bay in the big ward, dreading what she might find.

'You look better,' he said in his normal voice, not looking at all fragile.

He was smiling up at her from his hospital pillows, more relaxed than at any time since they'd eaten their partridge together in Covent Garden. He had better colour in his face, too.

'Like you,' she said, full of suspicion. 'So what was all that desperation about?'

'I've been slowly dying of boredom for days. I was desperate, Trish.'

Words roiled in her brain. She understood exactly what George had meant when he'd talked about accepting what other people did to him while silently fantasising about violence. At some level, a private voice told her, she could cheerfully have taken Antony by his cage, pulled him to the floor, and banged his head until he screamed for mercy.

The rest of the bay was quiet, with all the other patients either dozing or reading under their dim lights. She was the only visitor tonight. There didn't seem to be any nurses anywhere in the ward. How they could they leave so many vulnerable patients unprotected like this? Anyone could do anything to them and get away without being seen.

'Trish? What's up?'

She used all the self-discipline she'd learned over the years and managed not to snap out a brisk description of the real anxiety David must be facing at this moment. Instead she turned to the alcohol-gel dispenser and rubbed the stuff all over her hands to zap any lurking bacteria.

'I'm sorry you're stuck in here, bored and probably in pain,' she said at last, 'but I've got a tough case to defend and a serious situation to deal with at home. I do *not* have the time or energy to play games with you.'

'Trish, I—'

'I thought something terrible had happened, even that you were dying. I . . . Oh, *fuck* it!'

'Trish, I'm sorry.' Antony held out a hand, which she ignored. 'What's happening at home? George? Or David?'

'David. I told you on the phone.'

'I didn't realise it was that important,' he said, sounding almost ashamed. 'But now I've got you here can't you forgive me and sit down for a while? Waiting an extra ten minutes couldn't do David much harm.'

He was right, and she loathed behaving like a hysterical virago, so she did sit and tried to smile as she laboured to make conversation.

'Have they said when they'll let you out of that contraption, Antony?'

'Not too long now. They're pleased with my progress. The possibility of clots has more or less died down to nothing and my bones are knitting.'

'You've been lucky.'

'You're telling me. The cases I see brought in here every day make me shudder. There's a woman in the bay at the end who was kicked practically to death yesterday.'

Jay's mother, Trish thought instantly, remembering what

Shelby had said about Rosie Smith being sent to the orthopaedic ward here. Maybe this wasn't such a wasted detour.

'D'you know anything about her?'

'Not a lot. The police were round this morning, enlivening things considerably. We were all agog,' Antony said, cheering up at the sight of her interest.

'Has she had any visitors?'

'A scrawny young man in a hooded top and a much younger girl came today. But I don't suppose they got much joy. She's a drunk as well as having head injuries, and isn't making sense yet. They don't think she'll be able to identify her attacker.'

'You know a lot about her for someone who's never bothered much about what other people think or feel,' Trish said, smiling more naturally.

'Boredom can make a man interested in almost anything,' he said. 'I've reverted to a kind of pre-literate, country-bumpkin curiosity in anything out of the ordinary. I even chat to the chaplain when he comes round. Did you bring me anything today?'

'Like what?'

'Grapes, drink, chocolates, anything. I've gone all childish as well as pre-literate. I need treats and tribute to keep me happy.'

'I'll bring you a nice cuddly toy next time I come,' she said and heard his most sardonic laugh. He really was mending in every possible way.

'But in default of that, a progress report on the case wouldn't come amiss.'

She gave him a quick account of the latest developments and her growing conviction that there had been sabotage at the Fortwells' farm, and that Greg Waverly had to be involved in it somewhere.

'I thought everyone had told you to ignore third-party intervention, and concentrate on mitigating the damages our client faces.'

'Yes, but—'

'Trish, it matters that you do what we agreed.' Now he was serious and in charge again. 'No one's expecting you to beat Angie Fortwell, but the way you conduct this case will have far-reaching effects on your reputation.'

'Doesn't nailing the saboteurs matter more? What if they go on to do it again? What if more people die because no one could be bothered to find out what really happened when John Fortwell was killed?'

He laughed. 'You're beginning to sound like the nightmare pupil I used to go out of my way to avoid when you first came to 1 Plough Court.'

'Nightmare?' she repeated, momentarily distracted from the benzene tanks as well as Jay and his mother, and David.

'You were white-faced and gangly, with a terrible haircut and ghastly clothes; and so chippy you couldn't hear the few compliments that came your way.' He laughed again. 'Wherever you went, you exuded hate and fury. No one could get near you.'

She tried to marry his vision of the past with her own: wearing charity-shop clothes because they were all she could afford, doing her best in court while often sick with terror, determined to fight for her first few clients and build a career for herself that would earn enough in brief fees to leave a little change after she'd paid her basic living expenses. For a long time making money had seemed to be the only way she'd ever find any kind of safety.

'It was touch and go around the time of your sabbatical,' Antony said, no longer looking at her. 'You know, whether you were going to be invited to look for other chambers. But we could all see by the time you came back that you'd sorted something out with yourself. So you got to stay.'

'I'll be back,' she said, not looking in his direction. She needed time to absorb the implications of what he was telling her. 'There's something I have to do.'

Leaving his bedside, she found her way to the bay in which the new arrival lay asleep.

The clipboard at the foot of her bed confirmed the patient was Rosie Smith and gave a date of birth that would make her thirty-six. Even asleep, she looked more like fifty. Maybe it was her injuries, but Trish didn't think so. The wrinkled bagginess of her skin had a long-term look about it.

The cheapest kind of garage-forecourt flowers sprawled in too big a vase on her locker, but there were no cards or books. A familiar squeak made Trish turn to face a curious nurse, the first she'd seen this evening.

'Are you family?' she said in an Australian accent.

'No. I heard about her from the man I was visiting at the other end of the ward, and—'

'Sightseeing?' The nurse, whose name tag announced her as Sheila Jackson, inserted her uniformed body between Trish and the bed. 'I think you should leave. Now.'

No stranger had spoken so dismissively to Trish for a long time, but she was so glad to see evidence of some patient-protection that she walked meekly away to say goodbye to Antony.

'You will come back, won't you?' he said. 'When you've sorted David and he doesn't need you so much?'

'You know I will.'

She walked out of the hospital and headed for the Jubilee Walkway beside the river, registering the full glory of the Thames's north bank. Extravagantly lit buildings of every period were shining above their reflections in the black water of the Thames, but she couldn't stop to gaze at them tonight. David was waiting.

There were no smells of cooking at the flat and no sounds, but there was light leaking out from under the front door and around the edges of the blinds that covered the huge windows. She unlocked the door, calling his name.

'Hi.' His face was whiter than she'd ever seen it and his hair stood up on end, as though he'd been electrocuted.

'Where's George?'

'Driving round, looking for Jay.' He rubbed a filthy hand across his eyes. 'I wanted to go with him, but he said one of us ought to wait here in case Jay came. We couldn't risk leaving him outside by the bins – or make him run somewhere else.'

To Trish's eyes, it looked as though David wanted to say something quite different. She unwound her scarf and undid the buttons on her heavy overcoat, draping both over one of the black sofas.

'Have you heard anything from him?' she asked casually, with her back to David. 'Phone or text or email? Anything.'

'No,' he said in a kind of whisper that worried her. She turned. 'Honestly, Trish, I haven't a clue where he is.'

'It's OK, David. I believe you. Try not to worry too much: he's as old as you and even more street wise; I'm sure he'll be OK.'

'But d'you think he did it? D'you think he kicked his mother like that and nearly killed her?'

She took a moment to sort through her ideas. With David in this state, she couldn't produce either mindless comfort or anything that would sound unfairly critical of his friend.

'I don't know. I hope not. But I believe it is true he once attacked her before.'

He shook his head. His face was a mask of obstinate refusal. 'No. He burned her clothes, but he never hurt *her*.'

'Are you sure? If he set fire to her clothes – which is what I've heard too – then they'd both have been extraordinarily lucky if she weren't burned too.'

'She was in the kitchen and he burned the clothes in her wardrobe,' David said, looking at her as though she was a monster of injustice and cruelty. 'And he was only seven then, and she was flat out drunk on the kitchen floor and he and Kimberley hadn't had any food for two days and there wasn't any money for them to get any.'

'"Set fire to her clothes,"' Trish quoted. 'Of course. I'm sorry, David. I misunderstood. Did he tell you about it?'

'Yeah. He doesn't often say things about her. But he did tell me that. Trish?'

'Yes?'

'When the police asked if he had told me anything about her, I said he hadn't.'

He looked so anxious she forgot he was fourteen and stroked his hair, as she'd done in their earliest days together. 'So long as he didn't tell you anything about what's happened now, that's fine. Don't worry about it. It sounds as though you handled the whole police thing like a pro, like a lawyer. I'm really proud of you, but it must have been pretty upsetting.'

His anxiety broke up in a smile, not his best but still convincing.

'Now,' she said, much cheered, 'did George feed you before he went off?'

David shook his head. 'I wasn't hungry.'

'That's really worrying,' Trish said lightly, before setting off for the kitchen. She couldn't help looking back for his reaction and felt her guts clench as he provided another smile, this time less successfully. 'I'm going to have something. It won't help Jay or his mother if we starve ourselves. What about another omelette? You could manage that: they don't take much chewing.'

'OK.'

'Great. Come and help me and we can talk. I'm sorry you couldn't get me on the phone when you needed me today.'

She waited for an answer, but he didn't produce one. This was going to take some time and a great deal of care. Being interviewed by the police must have been bad enough, but worrying about whether Jay had half-killed his mother was worse.

George came back just as they were clearing their plates and she was facing the fact that David was not going to talk about anything that mattered. George's expression was nearly as troubling. Trish hated the depths of anger and fear she could see in it. She got up from the table and put her arms around him, taking care to smile at the unresponsive David over his shoulder.

'No sign of Jay?' she said, as George absent-mindedly patted her head. She might have been a pet dog.

'No. I drove all round the streets around the estate and went to all the shelters and refuges my criminal-law colleagues told me about, but no one admitted to seeing him. The police had been to most of them, too, so it's possible the inhabitants weren't talking in case I was one of them. I . . . Oh, hi, David; I didn't see you. How're you doing?'

'Not too good. I've texted him and phoned, but there's no one there. And I don't even know if his mother's still alive.' David's voice seized up, but this latest fear was more than Trish had got out of him.

She was sure that in his mind he was back in the streets on the night his own mother had been murdered. He'd followed the escape instructions she'd given him as soon as he was old enough to understand, and he'd run through the dark to this flat and the half-sister he'd never met. He'd been eight at the time.

'She's definitely still alive,' Trish said, looking first towards him and then at George. 'I was at the hospital tonight and I found her bed. She's regained consciousness, although she slips back at intervals. She was asleep when I was there. And quite safe.' So long as no one who's afraid she might identify him realises how few staff there are and has another go at her, she added to herself.

'George,' she said casually, trying to make the evening as normal as possible, 'I'll do you some eggs. And, David, I don't suppose you've done your homework yet so you'd better get on with it.'

'I can't work *now*.'

'The only way to deal with real scary worry is work. Concentrate and you'll—'

'Feel as though I'm alone in Piccadilly Circus,' he said, mocking her with a sharp edge that was new. 'I know. Work, work, work: it's your answer to everything.'

'David—'

'It's OK. I'll keep out of your way.'

'*David*!'

This time he didn't answer and when he shut the door of his bedroom behind him there was more than a suggestion of a slam. Trish thought about following him, but George held her back.

'Let him go. He's facing a lot right now. Don't try to make him be polite about it.'

'I wasn't. I wanted to help.'

'You can't.' George seized the open bottle of wine and slopped some into her glass before taking a deep swallow from his own. 'You can't mend everything that's broken. You've got to learn that; and so has David.'

'You were trying tonight,' she said mildly, going into the kitchen to crack three large eggs into a bowl. She took down a clean pan and melted a large knob of butter in it, hardly noticing the enjoyable sizzle as it turned nut-brown at the edges. Tipping in the beaten eggs, swirling the pan to spread them through the butter, was automatic. All her mind was on George's struggle.

'I was only trying to save Jay from getting into worse trouble.'

'I know. D'you think it could've been him?' She slid a spatula under the semi-cooked egg to let the liquid stuff run underneath to set in the pan's heat. 'Who attacked his mother, I mean.'

She turned off the gas, shaved four ultra-thin slices of Parmesan off the block with a potato peeler, laid them on the smooth mass of pale-yellow egg, flipped it over and let it slide on to the waiting plate. There was some fresh chervil in a jar on the windowsill, so she pulled off a couple of sprigs for a garnish.

'God knows,' George said. 'I wouldn't have thought so. But it did happen a few yards from where we dropped him, and I've no idea precisely what time it was; something around nine. Which is more or less when she was found.'

He sank his head in his hands, ignoring the omelette cooling in front of him.

'I keep asking myself why I didn't leave David in the taxi and at least see Jay to his front door.'

'Now who's taking on responsibilities he shouldn't?' Trish said gently.

She poured more wine into his glass and pushed it towards him. 'You've never escorted him to the flat before. Why should you have done anything different last night? You didn't know his drunken mother might be waiting just inside the estate, offering yet more provocation.'

'True. But he's had such a raw deal I feel responsible for him.'

'I know.'

George fell asleep at last, one hand still gripping Trish's wrist. She lay, wakeful and worried, hoping to ease the cramping pain in her back without disturbing him and trying to think how to help Jay.

Much as she liked him when she could stop worrying about the effect he had on David, she thought Jay could be capable of attacking his mother. And if he hadn't done it, why had he run away?

George snorted suddenly and his grip on her wrist tightened, then relaxed completely. Moving with fanatical care, she eased herself away. He didn't move again and his breathing sank to a regular rhythm of suck and puff.

That sounds remarkably smutty, Trish told herself, hoping to feel better. It didn't work.

She knew she wouldn't sleep for a while so she slid out from under the duvet, grabbed her dressing gown and padded downstairs, knotting the tie around her waist as she went.

There was no line of light under David's door tonight, and no sound, which suggested he'd managed his feelings well enough to fall asleep. She moved silently on to the kitchen and made herself a cup of camomile tea. Said to be a soporific, it always tasted to her like wet hay, but the suggestion might work to slow her overactive brain.

Lying on one of the black sofas, with her chilly feet under a red cushion, she sipped the boiling brew and enjoyed the quiet and space around her. She'd never want to go back to living entirely alone, but there was pleasure to be had now with both the others asleep and no huge feet or hungry half-buried emotions for her to worry about.

Sounds came from all around her, little clicks and pops from the cooling logs in the great fireplace and creaks from floorboards adjusting to the change in temperature. It was as though the old building was settling itself for the night. Faint buzzing noises from the traffic a hundred yards away on the bridge were almost pleasant. A twanging slap from a wind-driven cable somewhere close by was followed by soft footsteps on the iron staircase.

Fully awake again, Trish leaned sideways to place her hot mug on the floor without making any sound of her own. The footsteps stopped, as though their owner was listening. She waited. On they came again, soft and very slightly squeaky, as though made by rubber. Trainers?

They stopped again. A faint whirr followed, then a familiar metallic shriek as the flap of the letterbox was pushed inwards. There wasn't much light in the room so the opening rectangle looked bright from the streetlamps. Trish peered towards it but saw nothing useful.

'David!' The whisper was hoarse, urgent. 'David! David!'

Trish was off the sofa in a second and running to the door. She didn't want David waking to this.

'It's me, Trish,' she said. 'I'm unlocking the door, Jay. Just hang on.'

Terrified he would run away, she fumbled for the keys, almost dropping them and catching one fingernail agonisingly in the key ring. The nail bent right back but didn't break. She couldn't give it any attention now.

'It's OK, Jay. I'll get the door unlocked in a second. Hang on. Hang on, Jay.'

At last she got the key into the deadlock and turned it. George must have been oiling the wards because they slipped noiselessly round. Pulling open the door, she dreaded the sight of an empty step, but Jay was there, shivering in his crumpled school uniform with David's trainers clasped to his chest.

He slipped by her without another sound and waited, juddering with cold, while she closed the door again. His tie was pulled down below the open neck of his shirt, and he was very dirty.

'Come over to the fire,' she said quietly. 'There's still some warmth in it and I'll put on another log. There's a rug too, and I can make some tea. Are you hungry?'

'Yeah.' He was looking round the room, trying to see through the murk as though she might have hidden enemies there ready to jump him. Both arms were hugging the trainers. He seemed much younger than the tough dangerous teenager she'd first seen.

The fire was soon blazing again and he crouched in front

of it. So far he hadn't met her gaze once. And he didn't put down the trainers.

'Cooking anything will take too long,' she said. 'Is bread and cheese and a mug of tea all right?'

'Yeah. Great.' He half turned his head, as though he wanted to look at her, then went back to staring at the flames. 'Thanks.'

Wow, she thought, recognising the first expression of gratitude she'd ever heard from him. Now what do I do? If he admits he did kick his mother into a coma I'll have to hand him over. But if he denies it, do I hide him, turn him in, find him a criminal lawyer or what?

The kettle was still hot so it took no time to make the tea and load a tray with a full mug, as well as bread, butter, cheese and chutney. An afterthought made her stop and go back to add sugar bowl and teaspoons. She carried the tray round the central block that held the fireplace and laid it on the floor beside Jay.

'Help yourself,' she said, waiting for the moment when he would put down the shoes.

He tucked them under his left arm and used his right hand to add three heaped teaspoons of sugar to the mug and stir so roughly that tea slopped over the edge. Then he hacked off a chunk of cheddar, not bothering with bread or butter, and crammed it in his mouth.

'Chew it slowly,' Trish said. 'Or you'll give yourself indigestion. When did you last have anything to eat?'

'Pizza Express,' he said through the mouthful of cheese. 'With George 'n' David.'

'That's twenty-four hours ago. Where did you sleep last night?'

He looked over his shoulder. His eyebrows were so low over his eyes she couldn't see into them.

'Out,' he said and picked up the mug of tea.

He must have burned his mouth because he nearly dropped the mug. She waited while he downed another lump of cheese. It would have weighed nearly a hundred grams, she thought.

'Trish?'

'Yes?'

'Why were the police at my flat?'

She waited again, knowing that what she said now, and how she said it, could change their relationship for ever, and David's too.

'Your mother's in hospital.'

'What?' He looked astonished.

'She was attacked, kicked.' Trish watched him carefully, trying to find something that would tell her whether he was faking. 'A passer-by found her lying unconscious and called the police. They got an ambulance, which took her to Dowting's Hospital. She's alive and doing OK, but it'll be a while before she's able to come home.'

'Was she pissed?'

'I think so.'

'Who done it?' He glanced at her for a second, but only out of the corner of his eyes, so she couldn't tell what he was thinking. He definitely looked shifty.

'They don't know.' Trish paused, then added slowly: 'They're trying to talk to every member of your family and everyone in the estate who might have seen something. They will need to talk to you as well.'

He was very still. She hoped it was the fire's heat and the

burning mouthful of tea that had stopped his shivering, not extra unbearable fear.

'Shall I cut you some bread?'

There was a long pause before he said: ''f you want.'

She sliced it thickly and added butter. 'D'you like chutney?'

Another long pause gave her the time to understand George's determination to feed her in moments of stress.

'I dunno.'

'OK. I'll just put the cheese on.' That, too, she sliced thickly and laid it out, cutting the slice in two before retreating to her sofa.

The camomile tea was no better for being cool, but she drank it anyway.

'They'll want to know when you last saw her, I expect,' she said casually, as though it didn't matter. 'And what kind of state she was in then.'

He hadn't touched the bread, but he did drink some more tea.

'In the morning before school. She was sober then and angry,' he said, staring into the fire and sounding tired and surprisingly adult. 'And stinking too. Like she always is before she gets her benefit, when she can't buy no more White Star. Darren was shouting at her to bring the money straight home and she was shouting back and Kimberley was hiding in her room.'

'What did you do?'

'Went to school.' He picked up the bread and took a bite. When he'd finished chewing, he went on: 'Then I tried to come back here with David to work, but he said we couldn't without you or George, so we went to George's office; then we went to Pizza Express.' He stalled.

'And George took you back to the estate in a taxi, didn't he?' Trish offered, knowing she was leading her witness in a way that would never be allowed in court.

'Yeah. Right.'

'Then what?'

'I went home. I was walking up the stairs when I heard things.'

'What things?' Trish asked when the silence had gone on too long.

'People talking. I could tell they was police. So I went round the other end of the block and looked along the balcony and saw them. All clustered round the door of my flat, talking to Darren. So I legged it.'

'Why, Jay?'

'Only sense, innit? They ask you things about people. And whatever you say they don't believe you and they twist it. 's better not to let them ask you anything.'

'I don't understand. What kind of things do they ask? And about which people. Your mother?'

You're not in court, Trish, she reminded herself. This boy is not a witness.

He was blushing, which troubled her, and peering all around the room, his eyes moving so fast in their sockets he looked panicky.

'Jay?' she said as gently as she could. 'What things?'

He stared at the floor and hugged the trainers more tightly.

'How did you manage to rescue the trainers?' she asked lightly when it was clear he wasn't going to answer. 'You can't have had them with you in Pizza Express. And where's your school bag?'

He hunched his shoulders and gave all his attention to

the bread and cheese. Trish watched his back and waited.

'Jay?' she said again, trying not to sound aggressive but determined to get at the answers somehow.

'I waited,' he said. His voice was tight with strain. 'Till I saw Darren taking Kimberley to school 'smorning. There was no one else about, so I let myself in to the flat and took my trainers and legged it again.'

'But why?'

He looked at her as though she was mad. ''Cos they're the ones David give me. I couldn't leave them for fucking Darren.'

'Right. I see,' she said, remembering why she so often liked him so much. 'And the schoolbag?'

'It's by your bins, under the iron staircase. I hid it there last night after I run.'

'I'd better rescue it,' she said. 'The binmen come tomorrow and we don't want them taking it by mistake.'

'C'n I go to the toilet?'

'Of course. I should have said. And have a hot shower, if you like. Use my bathroom, but be as quiet as you can because George is asleep. Go up the spiral stairs and it's the first door on the left. There are lots of clean towels in the airing cupboard.'

She was as quiet as she could be on the stairs outside the flat and took enough time at street level to stand under a streetlamp and peer at the bag. There were no signs of blood that she could see. But a CSI or a lab technician would undoubtedly do better if they ever got hold of it.

When she took it back into the flat, Jay was crouching beside the fire again, drinking his tea. The trainers were neatly lined up by his side. He heard her and tensed, then picked them up again and tucked them under his arm. She carefully double locked the door.

'C'n I stay here then?'

'Tonight? Yes, of course. We will have to talk about what's best to do next, but you should get some proper rest now. I haven't got a spare room so d'you think you'll be OK on one of the sofas if I get some rugs and a pair of David's pyjamas?'

He turned then and looked fully at her. She saw his face and hair were still wet, as though he hadn't dared take time to dry before he put his clothes back on.

'You sure?'

'I'm sure, Jay.'

He glared at her, as though daring her to retract, then nodded. She'd passed a test. He carried the trainers to the end of the sofa, then went back for his mug.

'I'll get some more rugs,' Trish said, not knowing whether she'd done the right thing but certain she'd taken the only possible course. No one with any humanity could have sent this vulnerable boy back into the physical cold of the streets, or to the worse cold of a police station cell.

When she came back with the rugs, he was huddled in his underclothes, clutching a cushion and looking even more defenceless. He gabbled something so fast it took her a full minute to disentangle the sounds and work out what he'd said:

'I thought the police was going to ask me about George.'

'George?' she repeated. 'Why would they want to talk to you about him?'

'Because Darren's always going, you know, George is a kiddy-fiddler and that's why he keeps bringing me in the car.'

Trish felt like someone clinging to a frail tree in a hurricane as the full force of rage hit her.

Jay was looking terrified, so she smiled and watched his expression ease. She was so touched by his battle to protect George that she wanted to take him in her arms and hug him as he'd never been hugged in his life. She couldn't, of course, so instead she unfolded the rugs and spread them over him, tucking the top one securely under the sofa's solid cushions.

'You shouldn't have put yourself at so much risk,' she said, tidying his strange fringe. 'George is big enough and old enough to protect himself against silly allegations like that. He'd hate to think of you spending all night in the cold so you didn't have to answer questions about him.'

'You're wrong, Trish.' Not even the most passionate defence counsel could have sounded more serious. 'You don't know what the cops are like. They can do you even if you haven't done it. The more you say you never, the more they say you have. That's why I won't talk to them, why I run away.'

'It was very generous of you, but next time you mustn't. You must phone one of us instead and we'll help. Don't worry about it now. Good night. Sleep well.'

'Night.'

Upstairs, with George asleep beside her, she realised that Jay's explanation of his flight had completely distracted her from the questions about his mother. He'd never answered any of them.

What if, running from Darren, he'd passed his mother and seen how drunk she was just when he needed her to protect him? Who could blame him if he'd hit out?

*

Trish must have slept eventually because she woke to the smell of grilling bacon and the sound of running water. Why hadn't George woken her? On cue, her alarm clock beeped at her and the news came on.

'Hi,' he said, returning with his towel in its usual toga style. 'You must have been very quiet with your midnight feasts. I had no idea we had an extra inhabitant this morning until I smelled the bacon David was cooking him.'

'When was that?'

'About half an hour ago. I thought I'd leave you to get whatever sleep you could. What time did he get here?'

'Two-ish, I think.'

'So you must be knackered. Will you be all right in court this morning?'

'I'll have to be.' She rubbed her sticky eyes and tried to make her brain work. 'I'll feel better when I've had a shower. I was thinking last night, George: do Pizza Express bills have the time on them, as well as the date? A lot of places do.'

'Possibly,' he said, 'but I think I threw it out.'

'You? You never throw away receipts. You're an even more obsessive checker of your credit card statements than I am.'

'I paid in cash.'

'I bet you stuffed the receipt into your pocket. Even if you didn't, we could presumably get it from the restaurant. They must keep records longer than this.'

George unwound his towel and rubbed the remaining water from his legs.

'Trouble is, Trish, that would be fine if the times mean Jay couldn't have attacked his mother.'

She reached out a hand to him, glad he'd known instantly what she was thinking.

'But if they show he could've had time to do it,' he went on, 'he'll be stuffed. If the police want to check with Pizza Express, that's their business. I wouldn't even try to stop them. But I won't do it for them.'

She swung her legs out from under the duvet and sat on the edge of the bed.

'He told me why he ran away.'

George came towards her and laid one damp finger between her eyebrows.

'Don't frown, darling. What did he say?'

She told him and watched the expressions fly across his face like scudding clouds. There was a rage as deep as her own, there was compassion, and there was a terrible sadness. Then the sadness was overtaken by decision.

'I can rejig things at work this morning so I can sort this out,' he said. 'I'll take the boys to school, talk to the head for Jay, and then go with him to the police. If they still think he could have had anything to do with the attack on his mother, I'll make sure they provide him with a decent legal aid solicitor, who'll stop him incriminating himself.'

She let the frown ease and briefly held his hand to her cheek.

'But we can't condone—'

'We're not condoning anything.' George smiled. 'But we don't have to deliver him up to trouble. Think, Trish. We both know what he's had to put up with from that woman. If he did it – *if* – it was only after years of provocation, and the most desperate kind of unassuaged need.'

'We don't, in fact, know anything about her at all.'

'She's a drunk.' George had rarely sounded so unforgiving. 'Whether it's a disease or a matter of choice, her fault or not, it's buggered up her children's lives.'

Trish started to speak, but he didn't give her time.

'You can't sit there thinking about it with nothing on all day. You're due in court. Get on with it before the wicked witch turns you to stone.'

She gave him the laugh he deserved for trying to cheer her up and ran to wash her hair.

Chapter 13

Callie MacDonald woke early on her sixth birthday. She never liked staying in bed if she didn't have to, and today she had her dad's words from last night ringing in her head: 'You never know what the tide will bring a wee girl on her birthday. If she's good.'

She dressed as quietly as she knew how and heaved the heavy great storm lantern off its ledge in the front porch, switching it on as she unlocked the door.

Outside it was still dark, but the stars had gone, so it wouldn't be long till morning. She knew the way down to the beach as well as she knew her own bedroom, and the storm lantern gave enough light to show up any holes in the path.

Some days Callie didn't even hear the wind and the sea because they were always there, but now they sounded extra loud, pulling her on to see what the tide had brought her for her birthday.

Her feet crunched on the pebbles and the wind felt very cold, sliding up under her sleeves and down her neck. But it was worth it.

She waved the hard white beam of light all around, but she couldn't see anything. For a minute she thought her dad had lied. Then she knew. She was too early. The tide hadn't turned yet. She hunkered down to wait, shivering.

At last the sound of the waves changed and the feel of the air. Soon it would come, her surprise from the sea. She turned on the lamp again, her strong thin fingers managing the heavy switch easily.

There *was* something, dead ahead and coming up the beach, pausing with each wave that stopped as if it were teasing her, then coming on again. Only ten minutes later it was high up on the shingle, a big rusty tin, nearly as big as she was. There was some old writing on it, where the rust hadn't gone. The letters were so faded and worn they were hard to read, but she could see a big C and M. It must be hers, with the birthday present hidden inside.

She tried to open the screw top. But she couldn't. Even though her fingers were really strong, she couldn't do it. There'd be sharp stones, though, all over the beach, which might help her get inside the tin. She spent a long time looking for the best: one like a triangle with a sharp point; and another bigger and rounder to use like a hammer.

Bashing the pointy one down on the tin, she made a few dunts, but no more than that. She needed help, but she didn't want to leave her birthday present for anyone else to steal. Tugging it further up the beach was too hard. Even when she stood with her back to it and her feet pressing into the pebbles, she couldn't push it.

So she tried again and again, banging with the big stone to push the point down into the rustiest, bentest bit of the tin.

At last the pointed stone made a tiny hole. She bent down to see if she could peer inside, but the smell was awful. It made her choke. And something was bubbling out of the wee hole. She'd got some on her nose. Her skin felt all burning like the time she'd put her finger in the toffee while it was boiling in the pan.

MacDonalds don't cry, so she tried not to. But it was awful hard. She tried to wipe the stuff off her nose and her hand started to hurt too. And the smell was worse and worse. She was coughing so much she didn't hear anyone come, but she felt his hand, grabbing the back of her jersey.

'Hold your breath,' said her dad as he ran towards the sea with her dangling from his hand.

A minute later, he was holding her face down in the freezing water, sloshing it over her head and her hands.

'What did you think you were doing, lass? Messing about with filth like that?'

'It was my present,' she said, gasping as soon as he lifted her up. 'You said it would come with the tide.'

'Oh, Callie! You could've . . . We must get your poor wee face to the doctor, before—'

'Before what?'

He laughed, but he didn't sound at all like he usually did when he was happy. 'Before he goes off on his rounds, lass.'

Angie hung over the lavatory, waiting for the next paroxysm. Through the pain and the whirling in her eyes and the iron band across her gut and the disgusting sensations in her nose and throat, she thought: I hate being sick.

A damp cloth was pressed to her forehead and a strong hand stroked her back.

'You'll be OK, love,' Fran said. 'This can't last much longer. There isn't anything else to bring up.'

Saliva filled Angie's mouth and she knew she was for it again.

'Go,' she said, just before the worst happened.

Fran stayed, holding her head, through the whole horrible episode.

'I think that's it,' Angie said when she could speak again. She wiped her mouth on a bunch of loo paper and reached for the handle on the cistern to flush away the evidence. 'Sorry.'

'Come back to bed and lie down.'

'I can't. There isn't time. We'll be late as it is.'

'You can't go to court like this. Up you come.' She helped Angie to stand. 'You've no colour in your face and you're as floppy as cooked spaghetti. You need to rest. It must have been something you ate.'

'It can't be. You two are safe. We had exactly the same food yesterday.'

'Then it could be an infection – or a migraine. I used to get them and I was always sick. Better afterwards in fact. Does your head hurt?'

Angie tried to nod, then wished she hadn't because it felt as though her brain might burst out through her skull. She put a hand out to touch the wall to remind her how to balance.

'I have to go to court.'

'No, you don't. We'll get an adjournment. It's no problem. People get ill all the time. There are ways of dealing with it, even in that shithole in the Strand.' Fran laughed, with a gurgling sound that was too soft to jar against Angie's headache. 'Come on. Back into bed. I'll make you some mint tea, which should settle your stomach. And if you're no better this evening, the doctor said he'd come out to have a look at you.'

'I didn't know you'd phoned. What—?'

'It seemed like a good idea. He said so long as your temperature doesn't get much higher or you develop a rash, we don't have to worry about anything like meningitis. But he wants you lying down and me close at hand in case you suddenly feel worse. So we'll send Greg to court with a message for the judge – that's better than just phoning – and I'll look after you here.'

Angie felt too ill to say anything more. She closed her eyes and tried to find some comfort in the coolness of the pillow beneath her neck. Fran said something else about mint tea and left.

It isn't a migraine, or meningitis, Angie thought once she was alone and it was safe to let the idea form: it's Adam and the tanks. I can't stand up in court, waiting for someone to mention his name and pretend I've never . . .

On her way to chambers, Trish felt as though she had a hangover. It was years since she'd drunk too much, but the burning eyeballs, queasy stomach and aching head that were the result of lack of sleep seemed horribly familiar. The squeak of the door into chambers made her wince and the cheery sounds of the clerks' room were nearly as bad.

She closed her own door and leaned against it, enjoying the quiet, the familiarity, the privateness of her space. There was a push against her back as someone tried to open the door, then knocked. Moving away, she called out, 'Come in. It's not locked.'

Hal pushed his way in, making far more noise than necessary, yelling: 'I've got them. I've got them, Trish. Come and look.'

'Got who?' she said, staring at his broad, freckly face.

'Chris and Sally Bowles.'

'Whom, Trish. Whom.' Robert's voice sounded from outside in the corridor. He put his head round the door. 'Didn't they teach you anything at your bog-standard comprehensive?'

'If you can forget your public-school superiority for a second,' she said as she got to her feet, 'you can come and join the party. Hal thinks he's found our saboteurs. How did you do it, Hal?'

'Peterthewalk. I emailed to ask if he had any pix of the people in his blog and he sent me these. Look!' He pointed to his computer, which showed a pretty young woman in a cagoule standing against a blurry green landscape. There was a man beside her, but he was so much taller than she that the picture had cut him off at the neck.

'Did he give you anything else?' Trish said, peering at the screen, greedy for facts. 'Like real names or a working address?'

'No because he thinks they're really called Chris and Sally Bowles. I Googled those, incidentally, but there's nothing except the link to the blog.' He was beginning to sound less triumphant. 'I thought the pix might help on their own.'

'I'm sure they will,' Trish said with automatic reassurance. But she wanted a lot more.

'Unlikely.' Robert's drawl was so full of self-satisfaction that she wanted to hit him. She sent a sympathetic smile to Hal, who looked like a deflated beach ball.

'Why?' she said, turning back to see Robert pointing halfway down the screen.

'These two are climbers, not walkers,' he said. 'Your blogger's stringing you along. I doubt if this was even taken in Northumberland. The Cairngorms, maybe. But nowhere flatter.'

'How could you possibly know?' Trish couldn't bear Hal's disappointment. 'The background's far too vague to tell you where it was shot.'

Robert's finger rested on what looked like a smallish cloth lump hanging from the woman's belt.

'That's a chalk bag. Walkers don't have them.' He was extravagantly pleased with himself. 'This photograph was taken on a climbing trip.'

'What's a chalk bag?' Hal had found his voice again, but it sounded petulant and quite unlike him.

'When one's scared,' Robert said kindly, 'as one often is on a climb, one's palms sweat. So, one keeps hold of the rock with one hand and stuffs the other into one's chalk bag and takes a handful of the stuff. Chalk makes one's grip on the rock safer, you see.'

Trish did see. But she wasn't giving up.

'I can understand that a rambler who'd never climbed wouldn't have a chalk bag. But don't you think a climber might simply have forgotten the one clipped to her belt when she went walking?'

She scoured her mind for some technical terms to make Robert stop sneering at her as though she was the worst kind of ignoramus.

'After all, she hasn't any carabiners or pitons, has she? And I can't see a single rope.'

'So?' His sneer had taken on a mulish air. He'd never liked being challenged by anyone but least of all her. 'The rest of the kit could be on the ground, out of the camera's range.'

'Suppose you're right and she is a mountaineer, you could find out what her real name is, couldn't you?'

'I doubt it, Trish. I've already told you I don't climb any more.'

'Couldn't you phone a friend?'

'Great idea,' Hal said, then quailed at the look Robert sent him.

'But almost certainly not worth it. I'm still not convinced these two have anything to do with any sabotage, even if there actually was any.' Robert paused for a moment, then added, as though from a distant throne: 'No climber would consider blowing up—'

'Does mountaineering of itself ensure honesty?' Trish heard a suppressed laugh from Hal.

'Actually, I should have thought with all the self-discipline and courage it needs, it would.' Robert's tone suggested he was serious. 'But it's more to do with care for the natural envir—'

The phone on his desk rang, and he abandoned his explanation. Trish asked Hal if she could see Peterthewalk's email.

'Yes?' Robert said into the phone. 'Ah, Steve.' There was a pause. 'What a bore! OK. Thanks. Yes, I'll tell her.'

Trish was standing behind Hal, reading the email over his shoulder.

'Angie Fortwell's ill,' Robert said, making her look up. 'Too ill to come to court, so we're adjourned.'

'Oh, sod it!' she said. 'When we're so nearly there. How long for?'

'Months, unfortunately. The RCJ have told Steve they'll be slotting in an urgent fast-track case because Angie's doctor can't say how quickly she'll be well again, and they won't have time in the lists to give us any more days until the end of next term.'

Trish wanted to swear again. It always took ages to get yourself back into a tricky case after a long gap. You had to reread most of the documents and distil everything that had happened into a form of words that would remind the judge not only of the evidence but also the personalities and likely honesty of everyone involved.

Antony would be on his feet again by the end of next term, so he might even take the case back. Trish felt herself bristling at the very idea. Having come this far, she wanted to be in at the end.

'And Steve wants to talk to you, so you'd better hurry up,' Robert added, with another patronising expression twisting his perfect features.

When she'd first encountered him in chambers, she'd thought he looked like a romantic hero from some slushy 1940s film. Now she thought he was much more like one of John Buchan's villains, whose good looks and perfect grooming signal their wicked intentions from their first appearance on the page. The stories were George's comfort books, and Trish had learned from them that a great and honest man should always be a little shabby or at least rumpled.

Refreshed by the thought, she went back to her own room to phone her clerk and hear him say he had the sniff of another brief for her and she wasn't to leave before he'd confirmed it.

'Thanks, Steve,' she said.

When she'd finished with him, she rang George's mobile to leave a message telling him about the adjournment and asking how his session with Jay and the police had gone. At least she'd have time now to sort out her family and perhaps help Jay with his.

I could even look for Sally and Chris Bowles, she thought as she put the receiver back on its cradle, and find out exactly what they were doing within yards of the Fortwells' tanks at the crucial time, and whether Greg Waverly had any hand in paying them to do it.

That would teach sodding Robert.

The phone rang.

'Trish Maguire.'

'Hi, it's me,' George said. 'Thanks for your message. It went OK with the police. Jay was clear enough about where he was yesterday and last night, and convincing enough in his ignorance of the attack on his mother. And they've checked with Pizza Express and we didn't leave until after they think the attack happened.'

'Thank God for that.'

'But he wouldn't tell them why he fled at the sight of the uniformed cops on his doorstep.' George hesitated, then sounded worried as he added: 'I didn't think it was my place to do it if he didn't want to.'

'You're probably right,' Trish said when she'd had a moment to think through the consequences. 'You never know where that kind of announcement can take an over-excitable cop with targets to meet.'

'Anyway, Jay's back in school now. There's no question of any kind of charge, and the police are still doing some local house-to-house, so they may get an eyewitness. Which should confirm his innocence.'

'Fingers crossed.'

'In the meantime, I've got an enormous favour to ask, Trish.'

'Go ahead. I owe you plenty after the last couple of weeks.'

'It's my mother. She's just phoned about some plumber, who's cocked up the work he was doing but won't reduce his bill and has told her he'll be round at half past twelve to collect a cheque. Or else.'

'Oh, poor woman.' Trish had had plenty of experience with emergency plumbers, making leaks worse and leaving a terrible mess behind them.

'I know.' George sounded surprisingly impatient. 'I tried to phone him to remonstrate, but he's not answering. So I told her to make him ring me the minute he arrives. She got quite hysterical and said any right-thinking son would drive down to be with her and sort it out himself. But I can't possibly go today. She slammed the phone down on me and hangs up now every time she hears my voice.'

'I can understand. That kind of thing is scary enough for anyone, but when you're in your late seventies . . . d'you want me to go down there and sort him out for her?'

'Good God no. It's ninety miles each way. I just hoped you'd ring her for me and get her to see reason.'

'I can certainly try.'

'You're a star, Trish. Thanks. You'll do it far better than I could. She listens to you.'

Trish laughed. 'Only because she and I have no history. I'll email to let you know how I get on.'

'Great. See you later.'

Having fetched herself a double espresso, Trish came back to her desk and picked up the phone.

She had always got on reasonably well with Selina Henton, but they'd never become intimate. Accustomed to her own mother's bottomless wells of warmth and emotional openness, Trish had found Selina's chilly stiff-upper-lippery offputting. Maybe this would be an opportunity to get to know her better.

'Hello?' Selina said with extreme caution when she picked up Trish's call. 'Who is that?'

'It's me. Trish. I was phoning to see if I could help with your plumber.'

'You are kind. George has just told me to pull myself together and stop being so silly. But you have no idea what the plumber's like. He—' Selina's voice hesitated. There was even a suspicion of a sob before she added in a rush, 'he's started threatening me now, Trish. And he's huge and young, and I'm alone here, and I'm . . . I'm—' She couldn't bring herself to say it.

'You're frightened.' Trish didn't make it a question. There was no need.

She looked out towards the Embankment. She couldn't actually see the road from here, but the traffic sounds were relatively light for once.

'Look, why don't I come and sort him out for you?'

'Oh, Trish, I couldn't ask you—'

'You're not, and I've got an unexpectedly free day. It shouldn't take me too long. Hang on, Selina, and if he gets to you before I do, just tell him I'm on my way. OK?'

'I don't know what to say, except thank you. I'll see you in a couple of hours or so.'

Trish sent a quick explanatory email to George, collected her belongings and set off across the bridge to the lock-up where she kept her Audi. There were many times when she'd thought it absurd to pay so much to keep a car she rarely drove. But today wasn't one of them. Selina lived near the Suffolk coast, which might be only ninety miles from London but took much longer than any other journey of the same length.

As Trish bleeped up the locks of her soft-topped Audi, she

tried to decide whether to head out of London through the City or Docklands.

Whichever way you chose, it was always wrong and you'd be clogged in jams. Then, inevitably, you'd meet someone who told you how amazingly little traffic there'd been on the other route.

Still, it felt surprisingly good to be behind the wheel again, picking her way through the tangled streets of the City. At least here in the car she was in charge. She switched on the radio and smiled as Mozart's clarinet concerto swelled into the empty spaces all around her.

Today the gods of road management were generous, and she was through the City, out of the suburbs and speeding on to the motorway in record time, which meant she arrived at Selina's house in a reasonable mood.

The place looked as good as ever in the autumn sunshine: a long, low farmhouse of red brick, which had mellowed over the four centuries since it had been built. Set in a comfortably contoured landscape of green hills and old trees, it had a grace about it that came, Trish had always thought, from the honesty of its construction and lack of showiness. There had been no design involved; it had simply been built of the available materials to shelter people who worked the land and felled the trees and nurtured their animals.

The garden wasn't quite as manicured as it had been when Trish had first seen it, as though Selina's energy for hard physical work had waned since her husband's death, but its lines were as elegant as ever. And there were enough evergreens and shrubs with interestingly coloured or patterned bark to stop it looking bleak now most of the flowers were over.

Trish locked the car and made her way round to the back,

where the kitchen door was always left open. In spite of everything she and George had said over the years, his mother insisted that life in the country was still safe and she wasn't going to yield to their scaremongering with bolts and alarms.

'Selina?' Trish called. 'Are you there?'

She emerged from the drawing room, as immaculate as ever, with her white hair drawn back in a velvet scrunchie and her tall figure dressed in the familar straight tweed skirt and cashmere twin set.

'It's sweet of you to come,' Selina said, offering a softly powdered cheek for Trish to kiss. 'But George shouldn't take advantage of you. Just because he thinks his work is so much more important than anything else; even yours.'

'It's all a question of whose clients' needs are more urgent on any one day,' Trish said without aggression.

There was no point trying to make Selina understand George's standing in his profession. To her, he would always be the small boy in grey-flannel shorts with scabby knees and bottle-bottom glasses.

'D'you want to show me what the plumber did before he gets here?' Trish went on. 'Where are the leaks?'

The problem wasn't complicated and the plumber himself turned out to be reasonably amenable, so Trish had the whole thing settled within half an hour.

'I just don't like being taken for a silly old fool,' Selina said when he'd gone. 'I was sure he was cheating me.'

'He told me he's worked for you for a long time. And apparently he comes out at all hours when you need him. I'd have thought that alone would have told you it was safe to trust him.'

Selina snorted. The sound was extraordinary coming from a woman who had always presented such a dignified front to the world.

'Now,' she said, smiling again and straightening her back, 'you've had no lunch, Trish. You can't possibly drive back without anything. I have some smoked salmon in the fridge and a nice brown loaf. Come along and sit down.'

Watching Selina manoeuvre her arthritic fingers around the knives and food, Trish lost the last of her impatience. This woman had managed the transformation from pampered wife of a powerful man to woman-on-her-own with real courage.

It couldn't be easy to find yourself widowed in your seventies when you'd gone straight from your father's house to your husband's. You'd have to learn to deal with solitude as well as all the practicalities of house maintenance, tax and bills you'd never tackled, just at the time when your body was starting to punish you with slowness and pain, and your mind with a whole new set of fears and forgetfulness. Her own have-it-all-generation might complain about being permanently exhausted, but they'd had too much experience ever to face a challenge like Selina's.

'There,' she said, laying out her prettiest plates and putting a white dish of smoked salmon in front of Trish. 'Help yourself. And give me your news. How are you?'

'I'm fine, although we've been having a rather dramatic time recently with David's latest school friend. He's a magnet for trouble, and his family is so fractured and hopeless they can't help. Poor George even had to go to the police with him today.'

'No wonder there wasn't any time left to come here and

help me. Why is he taking so much trouble for a criminal youth?'

'They get on surprisingly well. In fact,' Trish said, seizing the opportunity, 'George confides in Jay. It wasn't until I heard them talking one day that I knew Henry even existed, let alone how badly—'

'Please stop there, Trish. I really don't want to know what George told some unsavoury child about his brother.' Selina's voice was icy and her face looked as though she'd had far too much Botox.

'I don't understand. What—?'

'It was all over a long time ago, but it was extraordinarily painful at the time, and I don't wish to think about it.'

'It's not over for George.' Trish ate a corner of brown bread, then looked up at the other woman, whose eyes were like grey pebbles in her rigid face. 'I want to help him, and I can't unless I know what happened. What did Henry do to him?'

'*Henry*?' Selina's protest was unnaturally loud, almost raucous. 'Henry wasn't the problem. That was George, who insisted on trumpeting his every success and rubbing his brother's nose in his less satisfactory academic record.'

Trish frowned, trying to understand, but Selina was still talking.

'We should have sent them to different schools to give Henry a free run, but my husband wanted them both to go where he had been, so there we were.' She blinked and Trish saw astonishing tears hovering on the edge of her eyelids.

'Was Henry your favourite?' she asked more gently than she felt. How could any mother have so misunderstood what she saw?

'I love and loved both my sons equally.' Selina had quickly dried her eyes, and her back was even more upright than usual. 'Henry just needed more help and protection. Life has always been so easy for George.'

That's all you know, Trish thought, as Selina smoothed back her impeccable silver hair, looking as beautiful as ever. Beautiful and as emotionally blind as the day her younger son first battled with his brother's jealousy.

'Could you maybe give me a phone number for Henry?' Trish said. 'I'd like to try to broker some kind of peace, let George—'

'Please don't interfere. I know you mean well, but it's been beyond mending for decades. Leave it alone.'

Later, driving back to London, Trish wondered whether to talk to George about different ways of looking at his past.

'Hating anyone is such a waste of time,' she said aloud, checking her mirror before overtaking an enormous car transporter. 'And energy.'

Safely past the transporter, she turned on the radio and found herself listening to the local BBC news.

'Mrs Eleanor Lawrence, who was injured when her four-wheel drive crashed into a lorry carrying caustic sludge to a waste-treatment plant, has now had both feet amputated above the ankle. The hospital say she is in a stable condition and they believe they have stopped the damage spreading through her body.

'The driver and the company that own the lorry are cooperating fully with the police and accident investigators. They have expressed their sincere regret for Mrs Lawrence's injuries and relief that all three children who were travelling with her remain in good health. But they say their driver saw her in his rear-view mirror using her mobile phone, which was not hands-free, and turning to talk to her children moments before she crashed into the back of his lorry. Her husband, on the other hand, says that his wife was so worried by the lorry driver's erratic behaviour she was phoning to alert his company and get help.'

This cannot be coincidence, Trish thought. Someone *is* sabotaging the safe disposal of toxic waste. And not caring who gets hurt in the process. This is John Fortwell all over again. Whether it's Greg Waverly or not, whoever's doing it has got to be stopped.

Chapter 14

Back in London in mid afternoon, aching with sympathy for the unknown woman who'd been so excruciatingly injured, Trish returned her car to its expensive but secure space under the old railway arches and took the familiar route across the bridge to chambers.

Apart from the now leafless trees, the only natural thing she could see was the Thames, mud-brown and moving sluggishly between the great masonry bulwarks of Bazalgette's embankments. She breathed in dust and exhaust fumes and wondered why she felt so much happier with them than the clean Suffolk air and its ravishing landscape.

Only a few people strolled along the pavements as she crossed the road and walked through the grey stone arch into the Temple. She heard her name called and looked to her right to see Sarah Fortescue, a solicitor who had often briefed her while she was still a junior. Sarah was waving from one of the benches in the garden.

Trish waved back and was about to carry on to chambers when she remembered her need for new work. Then she noticed the man sitting on the bench beside Sarah and walked quickly across the crisp grass.

Sarah stood up, smiling, and Trish leaned forwards,

presenting first her right cheek, then her left, for the kind of professionals' kissing ritual that was as stylised as any dominance display in the animal kingdom.

'How *are* you?' Sarah said. 'It's been ages.'

'I know. There's always so much stuff going on that none of us has enough time for anything except work. How's everything with you?'

'Absolutely fine.' Sarah turned suddenly, as though belatedly remembering her companion.

Ben Givens rose to his feet slowly enough to look reluctant. Trish had recognised him at once and she could see her knew her too, but there wasn't even the faintest hint of a polite smile on his square face. She noticed the scars of ancient acne on his broad cheeks.

'Trish, d'you know Ben Givens?' Sarah said. 'Ben, this is Trish Maguire.'

'I know your name, of course, but I'm not sure we've ever met,' she said, holding out her hand and pretending she didn't hate every single thing about him.

'No, I don't think we have.' He shook her hand briefly, dropping it as soon as he decently could.

She didn't mind that. His palm had been clammy, which seemed odd in such an apparently confident man. She thought of Robert's explanation of the chalk bag and the fear that made climbers' hands sweat.

'Although your name came up somewhere recently,' she added, putting her hand up to her forehead as though its pressure on her skull could help her think. 'Only I can't remember in what context.'

'Never mind,' Sarah said briskly, looking from one to the other. 'You'll remember in due course. One always does.'

'Usually in the middle of the night,' Trish agreed, laughing.

'And you're bound to run into each other. In a world as small as ours, I'm surprised this is your first meeting.'

Ben Givens hadn't said anything, apart from the graceless greeting. Trish heard some angry dogs scrapping on the far side of the hedge, followed by a human shriek and some sharp protest. It didn't stop the dogs. She decided to see what would happen if she goaded him.

'But then my mind's all over the place at the moment,' she said. 'I was just driving back from Suffolk and listening to the local news: some poor unfortunate woman has had both feet amputated after they were covered with toxic gunk when she crashed into the back of a chemical-waste lorry and its contents burst out.'

She was watching Givens carefully. He looked as though he might be sick. Good.

'You'd never believe anyone could be so vilely irresponsible, would you?' she went on, pushing and pushing, and wondering whether his hands would feel even wetter now. 'Crippling someone because they couldn't be bothered to provide properly secure containers for their dangerous chemicals. It's despicable.'

Sarah was murmuring some generic kind of sympathetic outrage. But Givens turned his back on Trish.

'Sarah, I must go,' he said with a rasp in his voice. 'There's a call I'm expecting in chambers. My clerk'll never forgive me if I'm late. Good to see you.'

'Of course,' Trish said clearly, 'the toxic spill might not have been the company's fault. It could have been the result of some kind of sabotage.'

Givens stopped and turned back to look at her again. For

a second he didn't even breathe. Only his eyes moved, blazing out of a face that still looked yellow with nausea. Had she gone too far?

'I'd be careful flinging around irresponsible accusations like that, if I were you,' he said.

'Of course!' Trish smiled as though someone had given her a magnificent present. 'You do defamation, don't you? Now I remember. Someone was telling me only the other day about that completely astounding sum you won for GlobWasMan. Well done, you.'

His lips clamped together and whitened as the blood was forced out of them. The expression in his hot-looking eyes offered a tougher warning than anything he could have said. After a moment he stalked away.

Sarah looked after him with astonishment; Trish, with acute interest.

'What's up with him?' she asked. 'Was it something I said?'

'I've no idea, Trish. We were just settling in to an important post-mortem about a con with a big client. There was no talk of phone calls then. Weird. I'm sorry about that.'

'Not to worry. What about some coffee? I could do with it after my journey.' Trish mentally crossed her fingers. Clearly Sarah knew Givens quite well. She could be very useful.

'I'd better not. There's a mountain of work waiting for me. If I can't have my post-mortem, I'd better get on with it.' Sarah smiled again, a lot more naturally than Givens had. 'But I'll be in touch with you – and with your clerk, of course.'

'I look forward to it. See you then.'

*

Trish's shoes clacked against the stone stairs of 1 Plough Court. Steve nodded as she walked past the open door of the clerks' room, but he didn't call her in to tell her any more about the new brief.

One of the other silks, who was checking his pigeon hole, turned to ask whether she'd seen Antony recently. She passed on the news of his physical recovery and encouraging signs of intense boredom.

In her own room, she dumped her bag on the windowsill and stood looking out at the black branches of the plane trees. They made intricate patterns against the grey-white sky, changing with each new gust of wind. Winter was definitely on its way. Her mind wove in and out of ideas that were almost as intricate and quite as changeable.

At last she abandoned the view. Until there was some reaction from Givens – or Greg Waverly – there was no more she could do. The morning's newspaper was lying on her desk, with the business section still unread. But she ought to send George a reassuring email about Selina and the plumber first.

Pushing away her laptop when the message had gone through, Trish scoured the financial news, trying to be interested in petroleum futures and fluctuations in the short-term money markets. An interview with a psychopathic-sounding tycoon was more alluring, but the diary beckoned. The style was nearly always witty in a mildly malicious way, and the stories usually showed more human interest than everything in the rest of the section put together.

Today the diary paragraphs were duller than sometimes, but her eye was caught by a reference to GlobWasMan. She wasn't surprised. You could go months, years even, never noticing a name or an idea, then have it brought to your attention once and subsequently find yourself tripping over references to it wherever you went.

> Family reasons is a wonderful catch-all excuse for anyone moving out of one job and into another, much less prominent one. It covers sacking, redundancy, and losing the will to live with boredom. In the case of Carl Bianchini, Company Secretary of GlobWasMan, it appears to be real. Our sympathies to his wife in her illness but also to his erstwhile colleagues, who must be struggling without him as they go for an IPO on AIM at last.

This was certainly an odd time for such a crucial figure to leave any company. Even if the company secretary's wife was ill, surely he could have hung on for a month or so until the shares had been sold in the Alternative Investment Market. Anyone who owned a slice of the business would reap a big profit then. Even if this bloke didn't, he could expect a pretty big bonus. Why would anyone willingly forgo that kind of money?

Or was this sabotage, too, but of a financial rather than a physical kind?

Somewhere Trish had the GlobWasMan Pathfinder prospectus Fred Hoffman had suggested she read. So far she hadn't even opened it. Shuffling through her papers, she eventually found the thick brown envelope tucked under a heap of old briefs in one of the drawers.

She was impressed by the lavishness of the glossy brochure. GlobWasMan – or their backers – must have spent a fortune in their attempt to persuade institutions and individuals to buy the shares they were offering. The manifesto at the front began:

> With increasing regulation in all developed countries, the disposal of hazardous waste will become more and more difficult, but the need can only grow.
>
> GlobWasMan has unrivalled expertise in all areas of medical and chemical waste, heavy metals, hi-tech equipment and white goods. We have a better safety record than any of our competitors. We are also in negotiation for sites and planning permission all over the world to allow for the planned expansion. Profits will be in the region of . . .

Blah, blah, blah, Trish thought, uninterested in any of the sums. The overconfident tone would have put her off investing, even if she hadn't renounced equities after listening to too much hopeless advice in the past.

There was no mention of last year's successful libel case anywhere in the prospectus, of course, and no reference to Givens. Turning the pages for something about the decamping Carl Bianchini, she found a double-page spread devoted to photographs and biographical details of all the directors and officers.

The chairman, Ken Shankley, the managing director, Leo Cray, and the finance director, Jed Shaw, were still only in their late twenties, which surprised her. They'd worked together before, setting up one of the fountain of small Internet companies that had sprung up just after the millennium. Unlike most of their rivals, these three, only a year or two out of university, had sold their business just in time and emerged with a fortune, some of which they had invested in buying the tiny chemical-waste company they'd now built into a considerable force.

Bianchini looked quite a bit older, and it didn't sound as though he had been part of their inner circle or had any stake in the original company. Interestingly, though, he was also described as the head of the legal department, which meant he must have worked with Givens over the libel trial.

Had they cooked up this plot as soon as the jury's record-breaking verdict was announced? Or had Givens waited until the initial public offering was launched before trying to suborn Bianchini and so wreck it?

Most heads of legal departments had trained as solicitors. If Bianchini were one of them, he shouldn't be too hard to find. A few keystrokes on her laptop brought up the Law Society's website, but there was no reference to him. Surprised and rather annoyed, Trish checked with the latest legal directory in her bookshelves, and there he was.

When she telephoned the Law Society for an explanation, she was told he had voluntarily taken himself off the roll and they had no other information to give out.

'That must have been pretty quick,' Trish said. 'When did it happen? And why?'

'I don't know,' said the voice at the other end of the phone. 'We have details of solicitors who've been struck off, but not the ones who choose to go.'

'Thanks,' Trish said.

Her next call was to Fred Hoffman, who sounded preoccupied but as friendly as usual.

'Pity about Angie's illness screwing up our timetable, isn't it?' he said. 'What can I do for you, Trish?'

'I'm going against all the client's orders and pursuing sabotage, now there's time to spare. You see, I don't think he's the only victim. Someone's going after GlobWasMan, too, and trying to scupper their IPO. If we find out more, we may be able to get some proof of what they've been doing to our client.'

'Trish!' Fred's voice was vigorous with protest. But she was not giving up now.

'It has to be worthwhile, Fred. Come on. Do you know anything about a onetime solicitor called Carl Bianchini who worked for GlobWasMan?'

'Can't say I do.'

'Could you ask around? See if anyone knows him?'

'Should I be encouraging you in speculation directly contrary to the client's wishes? Indeed contrary to his orders?'

She thought she heard a hint of the familiar good nature somewhere in his growly voice and decided to trust it.

'I take it that's a rhetorical question. Do your best for me, Fred.'

'Don't I always? Got to go. Good bye.'

She hadn't paid much attention to any of Don Bates's disasters except the explosion at the Fortwells' farm, but he had talked about environmental protesters in the States.

Could they be linked to Greg Waverly and Givens? Even though corruption of planning officials in one of the old Soviet states wasn't likely to be within their scope, environmental protest in America might well be. FADE looked too homespun to have transatlantic reach, but maybe that was just the way Greg wanted them to be seen. After all, Trish had never been convinced by his unkempt beard and grubby jeans, his sandals and shuffly manner.

She was reaching for the phone as her mind suggested the ever more devastating forms of eco-terrorism they might try next. She flicked through her address book with the other hand as she looked for Anna Grayling, the friend whose intervention had stopped her joining Antony on the crossing the day he was knocked down.

Her call was answered after only one ring and she had to listen to the usual quick-fire sputter of news. As soon as Anna's rattling voice stopped for a second, Trish said:

'Didn't you tell me you were working on an environmental film, Anna?'

'Of course. Why?'

'Great. You're just the woman I need then. Have you ever come across this organisation FADE that's backing the litigant in person in my current case?'

'I've heard of them.' There wasn't much colour in Anna's voice, certainly no discernible excitement or reserve. 'Why?'

'I just wondered how the rest of the environmental community sees them.'

'As a joke.' Anna's noisy voice softened in a warm laugh. 'They're a tinpot amateur group. There was a flurry of interest a while back when they first got involved with your opponent, but it's died down now.'

'You don't happen to know how they're funded, do you?'

'Haven't a clue. With these little mushroomy groups that spring up and then disappear, it's usually a one-off legacy or conscience-salving donation from a rich individual.'

'Like Ben Givens?' Trish suggested hopefully.

'Who? Never heard of him. But if he's got money for environmental good causes put him in touch with me. We're running short of funding for the film.'

'He's a barrister. You'll find him in the phone book.'

'Great. I'll get on to him asap. Got to go now. See you soon, Trish. Oh, how's your friend? He didn't—'

'Die? No, he didn't.' Trish hadn't meant to sound sharp, so she added: 'Thanks for asking. Bye now.'

Her mobile bleeped as a text came through. She read it and smiled at George's eccentric style. He'd learned some techniques from David, then made them all his own:

> Tx a billn, dling ma + plumb = hell 4 me u trans4m my lfe cul8er tk gd

Angie looked down at her big mug of Fair Trade tea because she couldn't bear to face Fran and Greg.

'I've got to go home. You've both been far too kind to me already, way beyond what was needed for the case. Now we're not going to be able to finish it for months, I can't hang around, battening on you, getting in your way.'

'You could never be in the way,' Fran said, the warmth in her voice making Angie feel even more guilty.

'You are kind. And I'm sorry. But I have to go. It doesn't mean I'm not grateful for—'

'Don't worry, Ange. We won't let you off the leash for long,' Greg said in a voice that was colder and harder than anything except the stone floor of the Low Topps kitchen.

'Greg!' Fran sounded shocked.

He smiled through the beard and quickly changed his tone, warming up his voice and softening the edges of the words. 'And we *will* need you. Not just for your own case. You're part of our lives now.'

Angie rubbed both hands over her face, hating the dryness of her skin and trying not to feel so suffocated that she did something stupid. She longed for the clean emptiness of the north and for Polly's undemanding company, which never drove her into losing her wicked temper.

'He's right. We'll be starting a new campaign soon,' Fran said. 'You could help us with that.'

'You could indeed.' Greg's smile was turning into a grimace that pulled his whole face out of shape and made the beard wobble.

How Angie hated it now! She had to get away. But she'd better show interest. 'What campaign?'

'There's been a horrible spill of some of CWWM's chemical waste after a traffic accident on a country road in Essex. A woman's had to have her feet cut off because they were so badly damaged by the caustic sludge.'

Angie's heart jolted. She put both hands to her chest, as though that could ward off any suggestion that she owed this new victim something. She didn't have any strength or emotion to spare for anyone else.

'*And* a child's been hurt up on the west coast of Scotland,' Greg went on, drilling at her like a torturer. 'CWWM again, of course. They're losing so much money, they're having to cut corners as they dump their muck all over the world. They don't care who they hurt. Just as they didn't care when they killed John with their lethal tanks, Ange. We've got to stop them. And you've got to help us.'

She hardly heard him. Chemistry, she was thinking. Adam moved from English literature to chemistry. He'd know as much about toxic sludge as about explosions. Is he afraid I've guessed what he did at the farm and might tell the police? Has he hurt these new people, too, to throw off my suspicion? A woman and a child . . . What the hell do I do now?

'And there are likely to be lots more CWWM disasters coming to light.' Greg was looking revoltingly happy. She felt ill again.

'Now we've started to look for them, I mean,' he added hastily.

She turned away. All she could think of was Adam's face. Greg's voice buzzed on and on, until she had to pay attention. He was repeating her name urgently.

She looked at him, licking her dry lips, trying to get the pictures of Adam out of her head. Fishing for the right words out of the stew of her mind, she decided honesty was her only hope, partial honesty anyway:

'I owe you both more than I can ever repay. And I'll do whatever I can to help you with any campaign once my case is over. But I must get back home now. I need time out.'

Her hair needed cutting. Long as it was, it made her whole face itch; she pushed it away, tucking some behind her ears. The strands felt very coarse, quite unlike Fran's gleaming tresses.

'I'm losing touch with who I am and why I ever started this legal action. I need . . . I need to get home and be there again, and remember John, and—'

'Breathe contaminated air and drink contaminated water?' Fran's big hand was stroking Angie's back as so often before. But that made Angie itch too. Fran's kindness was coming to feel almost as threatening as Greg's demands. 'It's dangerous, Angie.'

'I know.' Angie was just managing to hold in her temper. 'But I have to do it.'

'Where will you live? At the farm? Isn't that a bit—?'

She shook her head. 'Not immediately. I've arranged—'

Breaking off to send a rueful glance she hoped they'd take as an apology, she coughed, then added: 'I've arranged to stay with Polly Green, who lives about six miles away. She's my oldest friend – oldest, in both senses of the word – and needs help, even this late in the season, so it'll suit us both.'

'Until the case starts up again,' Greg said. 'You will be back in good time for that.'

It was not a question.

'Ange?'

'Of course I will.' Her reluctance was so powerful she found it hard to get the words out. 'How could I not after everything the two of you've done for me?'

Robert was almost swaggering as he invaded Trish's room at half past four that afternoon and dumped two batches of computer printout on her desk.

'What are these?'

'Contact details for your supposed saboteurs.'

'What?' She grabbed them.

The first was a prospectus for a climbing school in Swanage called the Fleming-Stuart Academy; the second a blurb for some 'Victorian walks' in London. She looked up at him.

'I don't understand.'

'One of my climbing mates did recognise your so-called Bowles woman with the chalk bag. Her real name's Maryan Fleming and the headless man with her is probably her boyfriend Barry Stuart.'

'My God! You've really found them.'

'They used to run this climbing business but it collapsed under a wall of debt, and now they've split up,' Robert went on, not acknowledging her comment. 'Barry Stuart is climbing in New Zealand and the girl is dragging tourists around Victoria and Albert's landmarks in Kensington.'

'That's great. Thank you, Robert.'

'But I don't believe they're saboteurs, and I'm not taking any responsibility for anything you do with this information. You do understand that, don't you, Trish?'

She got up and walked round her desk so that she could reach up to pat his cheek.

'Absolutely, you old hand-washer. On my head be it. I'm still grateful.'

Her phone was ringing. Robert pointed to it in a lordly way and left the room. She picked up the receiver.

'Trish?' Fred Hoffman here. 'I've got some info on your Bianchini bloke.'

'This is turning out to be a much better day than I'd expected,' she said, tucking the receiver between her ear and her shoulder so that she could pick up a pen to take notes while he talked. 'Why did he leave GlobWasMan just when he could have made a fortune in the IPO?'

'The general consensus is that he must have had a kind of road-to-Damascus moment and done it out of conscience.'

Like the story about Givens himself, Trish thought. I don't believe it of either of them.

'What my main source says is . . . Hang on a minute,' Fred said. 'I wrote it down so you could have it verbatim. Good. Here we are. Ready?'

'Absolutely.'

'"Not nearly as exotic as his name, Bianchini has always been an earnest, nerdy, do-gooding sort of bloke. Outsider. Didn't join in at Law College. No drinking. Used to lecture us about eating the wrong food, drinking, taking drugs, that sort of thing. Spent time charity volunteering. We all thought he was sad."'

There was a short pause, before Fred added: 'Got all that, Trish? In the slang of those times, I believe "sad" means weedy and pathetic rather than unhappy.'

'I think you're right. Thanks, Fred. That's helpful.'

'He's now working for a charity called Start Again, set up by a couple of doctors to help young offenders – like their own recidivist patients – go straight when they come out of prison.'

Trish thanked him again before she cut the connection, silently cheering. Bianchini's choice of good works could have been tailor-made to give her cover for the questions she had to ask.

Her call to the charity's switchboard was quickly answered by a human being instead of a recorded voice offering multiple choices at the press of a button. Trish was so surprised she nearly dropped the receiver. She asked for Carl Bianchini and was put straight through.

'Oh, hi,' she said. 'You don't know me, but I'm at the Bar. My name's Trish Maguire. I was hoping to ask your advice about an adolescent at risk of reoffending. Is there any chance we could meet?'

'Goodness. Hello. I know your name, of course,' he said in an unexpectedly quiet voice, which sound jittery with nerves. 'But I'm not really your man, you know. I've only just started here full time and I have nothing to do with the clients or their families. I could put you through to one of the others, who might be able to help. How old is the boy?'

'I really would prefer to talk to *you*,' Trish said. 'As fellow lawyers we'll use the same language. If I could only explain my dilemma face to face, I think you'll see why I need you.'

Her overactive conscience was already beating her up for using Jay like this, but it wasn't pure exploitation: she really did want to know what kind of professional help might be available for him beyond Shelby's well-meaning but compromised efforts.

'Maybe I could buy you a drink one evening,' she said.

'I wish I could accept.' His voice did sound wistful. 'But my wife's not been well and I always have to go straight home at five-thirty.'

'Lunch, then?' she said. 'Something simple that won't take up too much of your time. Where are your offices?'

'King's Cross.'

'OK. There are pubs up there, aren't there? But they can be noisy. What about the café at the British Library?'

There was a pause. 'Why not? Tomorrow? I always lunch at twelve-forty to avoid the queues.'

'I'll meet you there. I'll be wearing a dark brownish-red jacket.'

'And I'll be in brown cords and a black V-neck sweater because I've no meetings tomorrow.'

'Great.'

She grabbed the Pathfinder again, looking for his photograph. The small rectangle couldn't tell her much except that he had a plumpish face and dark eyes. His hair was receding, he was probably in his late thirties, and he wore heavy-rimmed glasses. For the photograph he'd been dressed in a formal dark suit, plain shirt and discreetly patterned tie. He looked honest, but that, like the kindness of anyone's voice, meant nothing.

Hal's peculiarly heavy tread sounded in the passage

outside her room, which made her check her watch, then reach for her bag and coat. This was the day she'd been going to take back the domestic responsibility from George, yet here she was still at her desk well after five. She ran down the stone stairs, almost tripping at one moment, and was home in a record fifteen minutes, wondering what she'd find and begging the Fates to keep Jay calm and happy for once.

The boys had beaten her back, but they were already hard at work and absolutely quiet when she pushed open the front door. Her banging heart slowed. David looked up and smiled, but Jay didn't acknowledge her in any way. She tapped her chest then pointed towards the kitchen. David nodded.

Opening the fridge door and flinching in the blast of cold air, she wondered what to cook for them. It had to be something substantial enough to satisfy their ever-growing appetite, and be reheatable if George did make it to the flat later on. Nothing in the fridge appealed to her. There wasn't time to roast the leg of lamb and they'd had too many omelettes recently. But there were plenty of potatoes, and a good big chunk of Parmesan, as well as nearly half a small truckle of Cheddar from some special cheesemonger found by George. She shot a look at the vegetable basket to see a pile of onions.

Cheese, onion, and potato pie, she thought as she turned on the oven, filled the kettle, and then reached for the peeler. It wasn't too unhealthy, and it should make even the hungriest of boys feel full.

Her eyes grew as wet and painful as usual while she sliced six large onions. Sniffing in a way that would have shocked Selina, she turned her face to wipe her eyes on her shoulder.

Almost at once she felt George's hands around her waist and leaned back against him, grateful for the sense of solid safety he could always give her.

'What a good thing I made it out of the office sooner than I expected,' he said into her ear, brushing the skin with his lips. 'D'you want me to take over?'

'I'm nearly there. But you could make the cheese sauce if you wanted.' She waved her knife at the vegetables. 'For our old standby pie.'

'Sure,' he said, not moving. 'In a minute. This feels great.' He kissed her hair.

'I loved your text.'

'Good. You did a fantastic job. My mother phoned and is nearly as besotted with you as I am.' He tightened his arms and kissed her again. 'I ought to be taking you out for the grandest possible dinner tonight, not making you cook.'

She finished chopping with the warmth of him pressed against her back. She wanted to say something about the pleasure of it, how this simplicity did more for her than any multi-rosetted restaurant. But putting her feelings into words might make them sound fake, and she trusted him enough now to be pretty sure he would know what she wasn't saying.

At last he unplastered himself from her back and set about making the sauce with his usual economy of movement and effort. Although the kitchen was tiny compared with the rest of the flat, a galley only six feet wide, they managed to work around each other, only touching on purpose.

When the pie was safely in the oven, George filled a couple of wine glasses from a newly opened bottle of Californian Pinot Noir and suggested they take them upstairs so their chat wouldn't disturb the boys' work.

In Trish's bedroom, propped up on piles of the softest pillows, they sipped the light fruity wine and swapped news.

'Have you ever come across Carl Bianchini?' Trish asked, putting down her glass. 'A solicitor in his thirties.'

'Can't say I have. Why? Or can't you say?'

'Better not. For the moment anyway.' She squeezed his hand. He used his free one to smooth the hair away from her forehead, letting one large finger rest on the space between her eyebrows.

'Don't frown. It can't be that bad, whatever it is.'

She laughed. 'It isn't. I still forget sometimes and crunch up my forehead without meaning anything by it.'

He kissed her, then pulled back so sharply she was worried.

'My mama thinks you're too thin, although she approves of the way you do your hair now, and . . .'

Trish laughed.

'. . . and she's afraid I can't be treating you right. I think she was a bit embarrassed that I made you go all that way for something so trivial.'

'She doesn't ask for much, and it was easy today.' Was this the moment to embark on a conversation about Henry? 'George—'

A shout from downstairs interrupted them.

'Trish? When's supper? We're starving.'

'So what's new?' she murmured, before raising her voice to suggest that the boys should lay the table. Swinging her long legs off the bed, she added more quietly: 'I suppose we'd better go down. Are you staying tonight, or is Fulham calling? You've hardly had any time there at all since Jay first came here.'

He grabbed her hand, holding her back. She looked down at his face and read the answer in his expression.

'Good,' she said, wondering as so often before when they'd rationalise their eccentric arrangement and actually live together in the way ordinary people did.

Chapter 15

When Angie's train eventually limped into the station 300 miles from London, it was twenty-five minutes late. Polly, like the good friend she'd always been, was waiting patiently under the wooden canopy that provided the only shelter on the small wind-blown platform. She was wearing her habitual uniform of brown corduroy trousers, washed into softness over many years, gum boots and ancient green Barbour.

Angie hauled her suitcase down on to the platform, balanced it then turned to kiss Polly. After all Fran's habitual stroking and hugging, she'd forgotten that up here you didn't fling yourself into an old friend's arms just because you were pleased to see them.

'It's been bad, hasn't it?' Polly said, which came to much the same as a passionate embrace.

'Fairly awful, yes. It's good to be back. I'm sorry you've had to wait so long.'

'Come on.'

Even the rattling, battered old Land Rover was a welcome change. Polly drove as she always did, as though both the machine and the road were hostile, to be tamed only by those prepared to ignore their challenges and fight to the last drop of blood. Angie was amazed the engine and gears had lasted this long. She felt her teeth banging against each other and was glad they had only eight miles to go.

After the wild ride, the silence of the ancient stone farmhouse was a relief. Bill greeted her with a barely noticeable nod, then a gesture that offered to carry her case upstairs. Angie, twenty years younger if less fit these days, couldn't have let him. In any case, she wanted a moment or two to herself. Polly told her which room had been made ready and said supper would be on the table in ten minutes.

'Mutton stew,' she said as Angie returned to the kitchen, carrying the two bottles of wine she'd brought from London. 'That's kind. Put them on the dresser, will you? They'll be good at Christmas, won't they, Bill?'

Her husband grunted amiably enough and rubbed both knarled hands through his sparse white hair.

Angie, who'd hoped for a decent drink tonight, reluctantly did as she was told. The stew was good and they ate in companionable silence. Bill's eyelids were already looking heavy as he finished his plateful and they closed completely a moment after he'd put down his cutlery.

'See,' Polly said quietly.

Her own round red face showed all the marks of exhaustion in deep brown crescents under her eyes, dragged lips and deep lines across her forehead and around her mouth.

'It's all too much for him now. So if you really can look after the house and the food and the visitors, I can help a bit outside.'

'Of course. Will I wake him if I clear now?'

'Nothing will wake him now, but you don't have to work on your first night.'

'Yes, I do.' Angie looked straight at her. 'I'd like to tell you how much this means, Polly, but if I do I'll cry, so I'd better leave it to your imagination. Is that all right?'

A softening in Polly's weathered face told Angie she'd done the right thing, and without another word, she carried the dirty dishes to the sink and turned on the taps.

'Did you see Adam while you were in the south?' Polly asked from behind her nearly ten minutes later.

Angie stilled, with her hands in the sudsy water. 'I did. But how did you know?'

'He lives down there, doesn't he? Near Brighton?'

'Yes, but . . . How d'you know? When did you last see him?'

There was a pause, then Polly said in an unconvincingly casual tone: 'It must have been eighteen months ago. Not long before the explosion, anyway. He came wanting to make peace.'

'Peace with you?'

'Don't be daft. With you and John. I would have told you except he begged me not to say anything on the night he came back here and said he hadn't been able to make himself knock on your door.'

'Came *back* here?' Angie repeated, feeling like a witless parrot. 'D'you mean he stayed with you?'

'Yes. He booked himself in by phone and arrived like any other walker.'

Angie leaned against the hard cold edge of the ceramic sink, knowing she had to ask the next question and terrified of the answer.

'When was it, Polly?' she whispered eventually. 'I mean exactly.'

'I can't remember the actual date, but it'll be in the visitors' book. As I said, it wasn't long before John died.'

There was a silence, broken only by Bill's snores. 'I've been sad ever since that they didn't talk. A man shouldn't die thinking he's lost his only son when he hasn't.'

The tears Angie had been so keen to avoid were slipping down her cheeks, making her need to sniff. Fran would have been full of strokings and murmurs of comfort and clean handkerchieves and special herbal remedies for distress. Polly's sympathy was expressed in silence and by keeping her back to Angie while she got herself under control.

Wind rattled the windowpanes and boomed in the chimney. Bill's snores built up towards a shattering climax, then stopped.

'Wha . . . What's going on?' His voice was thickened and hoarse.

'You woke yourself up,' Polly said. Angie could hear that she was smiling from the way her voice lilted just a little. It was full of affection. 'Just in time for a cup of tea before bed.'

'I'll make it,' Angie said, shaking the greasy water off her hands and wondering how she was ever going to walk back into court to fight for damages from Clean World Waste Management now.

'There's a hand-delivered letter for you.' Steve's voice caught Trish as she passed the clerks' room on Friday morning.

Still feeling sleek and sorted from last night, she stopped and took four steps backwards to look through the open door.

'In your pigeonhole.'

'But no brief yet?' she said. Seeing him smile, she braced herself for a sententious quotation from his latest hero.

'"Our patience will achieve more than our force."'

'Oh, very good! Burke again, I take it?'

'Naturally.'

'I sometimes wonder how you ever sleep with all this learning by heart you make yourself do, Steve. See you later.' She scooped her letters from the pigeonhole and took them to open in private.

The handwritten letter proved to be from Jeremy Black, once more sent tactfully to chambers so that the sight of it wouldn't worry David.

Dear Trish,

I thought you should know the general feeling at the governors' meeting last night was that we should accept your generous offer to fund half of Jay Smith's school fees for the next four years. We have not yet said anything to him because we still haven't seen enough evidence of sustained good behaviour, but we have all been impressed with the increasing quality of his homework. The latest essay, written the night before the unfortunate incident involving his mother, has real quality about it.

So much improved was it, in style, content and general thoughtfulness that his history teacher was worried that David might have had a hand in it, but comparison of the two pieces of work has shown no similarities at all. We are as grateful to you and David as Jay's family must be.

I should, of course, be glad if you would keep this development to yourself until we can be sure that Jay can keep up the improvement.

With best wishes,

Jeremy Black

Trish refolded the single sheet and tucked it into her handbag. There had been many times since she'd made the offer when she'd regretted it, but the principle still stood. Offering Jay a chance of escaping his miserable background and then ripping it away would have been cruelly unfair.

Walking into the British Library's courtyard twenty minutes later on her way to meet Carl Bianchini, Trish took a moment to look around. This was her first visit. After all the grim press reports she'd read as she grew up about the great building's construction and ugliness, she hadn't expected anything like this airy space with its monumental Paolozzi bronze and spindly trees, or the satisfying proportions of the unusual red-brick terraced building ahead of her.

There was a helpful map just inside the door and she had no trouble finding the café, but she couldn't see anyone who looked like her quarry. She was reaching for a salad from the counter when she heard a tentative voice saying her name. Looking round, she recognised Bianchini at once from the Pathfinder photograph.

She could see exactly why his Law College friends had described him as 'sad'. There was something old-fashioned about his spectacles and the way he'd brushed back his dry, receding hair. His eyes held a defeated look, too, as though he were readying himself to endure the next practical joke in a long and brutal series.

Trish ignored her tray in order to shake hands. Selecting their food and then arguing politely about who would pay for it helped build the first bridge between them. She won the argument easily.

'So, how is it you think I can help you?' he asked when they were sitting opposite each other.

She told him about Jay and what she hoped to make Blackfriars School do for him, seeing Bianchini nod at intervals, as though the story fitted with what he already knew of troubled, dangerous boys. Then out of nowhere came a confession that surprised her as much as him.

'And I so hate the thought of what he goes through at home,' she said, 'that I've been wondering whether I ought to offer to foster him as well. What do you think?'

'Why on earth should you?' Bianchini's impatience shocked her into letting out more of the ideas she'd been ignoring.

'Because I've interfered,' she said, facing some of them at last. 'And made him trust us. How can I go on sending him back to his ghastly brother and useless mother?'

He took a moment to consider, forking bean salad into his mouth. When he'd swallowed, he said:

'There aren't many people who'd even help pay for a decent education. There's no reason why you should worry . . .' He paused. 'No, that's not what I mean: everyone should worry. But you're not responsible for his home life. Quite frankly you'd be mad to take him in.'

Trish nodded. She knew that. But it didn't help.

'Have you any idea of the *risk*?' he went on in spite of her agreement.

'Yes.'

'With a background like his, he's always going have issues, always be challenging. With a job as demanding as yours, you couldn't begin to give him what he needs.'

Trish ignored the remains of her salad. She couldn't eat with all this going on. The café was filling up as the time edged towards one o'clock. There'd soon be far too many eavesdroppers to make any of her other questions safe.

'Isn't the mind weird?' she said, moving towards them fast. 'I thought I was perfectly happy with what I've been doing for Jay. Now I find my subconscious telling me it's not nearly enough. I suppose you must have been through the same sort of thing.'

'What d'you mean?'

'According to the papers you gave up a lot of money to work in the charity sector. There must have been a pretty good reason.'

Bianchini's smile died away to nothing, and his forehead corrugated in a frown even more intense than any of hers.

'There was. I told you on the phone: my wife's ill. We have two children. I had to have more time at home.'

'I'm sorry. Is it serious?'

'She has some form of ME. Completely debilitating. I couldn't go on working in a job that demands 24/7 commitment. That's all. There's no mystery about it.'

Now she understood his air of waiting for another blow. She'd seen it before in carers who spent their lives fighting their own resentments as hard as the hatred they received in return for the care they gave.

'I'm sorry,' she repeated, meaning it.

'Thanks.'

'But in the circumstances it must have been very hard to leave just before your company went public.' Trish watched his changing expressions and almost gave in. This was no Ben Givens, ready to respond to a difficult question with a threat. This was a man who looked as if the next practical joke had now been played on him.

'I mean, you must have been in line for a considerable profit,' she said, driving on only because she had no choice. 'Or do you have options you can still exercise?'

He drained his water glass and looked around for an excuse to leave. She began to eat again, as slowly as she dared, assuming he wouldn't go while she was actually chewing.

He didn't say anything, but he didn't move either. When she risked another glance, she saw him jiggling in his chair as though longing to leave but kept there by something even more important.

'I suppose I've been more than usually interested in the GlobWasMan IPO,' she said, 'because I remember hearing about the libel case last year, when Ben Givens did so incredibly well for you.'

'Nothing to do with me, any longer. I have *nothing* to do with anyone in that company,' he said with enough passion to make himself sound a little tougher and her to feel less like a bully.

'Then there was a diary item about you only yesterday,' she added, 'suggesting that someone – you or one of the directors – had ulterior motives for your departure.'

Suspicion made his dark eyes harden. She thought she'd better add a distraction.

'What was Givens like to work with? I've always thought he sounded very tough.'

Consulting his watch, Bianchini muttered something about having to get going. Time to gamble, Trish thought.

'You look to me like a man who wants to talk,' she said in her cosiest voice.

'I can't think what gave you that impression. I want nothing less.' He no longer looked at all defenceless. 'I must get back to work. Thank you for lunch. I'll talk to my colleagues about your protégé. If any of them come up with anything, I'll be in touch. Assuming you really are looking for help for him.'

'I really am. Here's my mobile number,' she said, scribbling it on a paper napkin. Rather to her surprise, he took it.

Back in chambers, she stood in her usual place at the window, thinking through her suspicions as she watched the branches criss-crossing and tangling, before the wind freed them again. She couldn't approach Greg Waverly because of her role in Angie's case, and Ben Givens had made it clear she'd get nothing but threats from him, so she'd have to try the people she was sure they'd used as their tools.

She found Hal's digest of Peterthewalk's blog and then the prospectuses for the defunct climbing school and the Victorian walks in Kensington and reread them.

Ten minutes later she put her head round the clerks' room door to make sure Steve wasn't about to give her news of the forthcoming brief, then left chambers for the tube.

Chapter 16

Trish stood with her back to the great red oval of the Albert Hall, which she'd always rather liked, and looked straight at Queen Victoria's chief monument to her dead husband, which she'd always loathed. Ugly, with its wildly over-ornamented pinnacles and gaudy mosaics, and completely out of place in its garden setting, the memorial was surrounded by massive stone statues representing four continents.

Crossing the road at the traffic lights, Trish saw the group she wanted almost at once. Maryan Fleming, also known as Sally Bowles, was standing in the shadow cast by the figures of Asia and looking tiny in comparison. One step below her, their upturned faces gazing more admiringly at her than at any of the statues, were her customers.

Trish waited until the lecture was over and the last of the tourists had torn himself away. By then Maryan was sorting the tips she'd been given, pouring the change into a purse, which looked surprisingly like the betraying chalk bag in Peterthewalk's photograph, and straightening the ten and twenty pound notes. It seemed like a good haul.

'Hi,' Trish said.

Maryan glanced up, then felt in the pocket of her jacket.

She pulled out a slim packet of leaflets and handed one to Trish.

'There won't be another walk here till next week,' she said, with an apologetic smile. Her voice was very sweet, and quite unthreatening. 'But there are lots of others; one every day somewhere in London.'

'Thank you. But that's not what I wanted. I wondered if you had a moment to talk about a different kind of walk.'

The gentle face, fringed with shaggy blonde hair, looked surprised, but not at all worried.

'In Northumberland?' Trish said. 'When you were with Barry Stuart on the edge of the national park there in April last year. Do you remember?'

Maryan stuffed the leaflets back into her pocket. 'Why would I? We did lots of walking in those days.'

Trish smiled widely to make herself look reassuring and said casually:

'It was the time you and Barry were paid to block the vents of the chemical-waste tanks. I should've thought that would be pretty memorable. Unless you did that kind of thing often.'

'Of course not.'

'But you did do it that once, didn't you?'

Maryan looked as though she might cry.

'I've got timed and dated photographs that put the two of you in the right place on the day the tanks were blocked,' Trish went on as though there was no doubt about anything she said. 'So there's not much point pretending. And I'm not after you in any case. All I want to know is who paid you to do it.'

'But I don't *know* who they were.' Maryan looked and sounded convincingly helpless. 'Barry never told me.'

Trish wanted to swear. Having tracked down one of the saboteurs it would be excruciating to find that she knew nothing useful. Had Barry taken her along as cover? Or as someone to blame if they were spotted hanging around the tanks? Unless she'd changed since then it seemed unlikely he'd have wanted her for anything more active.

'I didn't know anything about it. Honestly,' Maryan said, blinking the tears away. 'He said he was going up north on his own, that he needed space to think things through. But I didn't believe him. I thought he was seeing someone. So I said I was going too, whatever he said. In the end he said I could if I wanted, but if I couldn't keep up he wasn't going to wait for me.'

'When did he tell you why he was really there?'

'Only at the last minute, when he saw I wouldn't let him leave me behind in the b&b like he wanted that day.'

'Did he say why he was doing it?'

'Only that there were people who didn't think it right that dangerous waste was being stored up there so near the national park.' Now Maryan was staring at the tops of the trees and letting her eyes move only in the direction of the clouds of birds that wheeled around the bare branches.

'Did you agree?'

'Of course not,' Maryan said in a little-girl voice. 'I said we couldn't. It'd be wrong. Then he told me how much they were paying him and how bad things really were with the bank, and how we'd lose the climbing school if we didn't get more money from somewhere. And so . . . And so—'

'And so you agreed.'

'I had to. But I wish I hadn't.'

'I'm sure,' Trish said, thinking of the appalling consequences and wondering why Maryan hadn't denied all knowledge of the plan. 'But why, in particular?'

'Because we lost the school anyway, and everything else went wrong as well. And it wasn't even necessary. There'd been something wrong with the tanks all along.'

'What d'you mean?'

'Didn't you read about it in the papers? They were really dangerous. Quite soon after we were there, they blew up. We needn't have ever gone anywhere near them. I wish we hadn't.'

Could she really not have made the connection between the blocking of the vents and the explosion? Looking at her charming face, Trish didn't see a lot of intelligence, but even so she was doubtful. And the little-girl voice was definitely assumed. She'd sounded perfectly normal when they'd started to talk.

'Where's Barry now?' Trish asked.

'We split up. The money he got from the tanks wasn't enough to save the school.' Maryan wiped away the tears with both hands, but they went on oozing out of her eyes. 'So we shut it down. We tried to go on together for a bit after, but he got so restless. And the people he'd been to for loans and stuff were harassing him, threatening him that if he didn't pay up they'd . . . they'd . . . you know.'

'Break his legs?'

Maryan shuddered. 'Something like that. So he said we had to get away.'

She'd found a handkerchief at last and mopped her face more effectively, and blew her nose.

'Why New Zealand?'

'I don't know.' Maryan sniffed. 'He hadn't told me he was keen to go there or ever bothered to ask if *I* wanted to, so I said I wouldn't. And he said, OK, was he bothered? I was just a millstone round his neck. And if I wanted to stay and take my chance with Ken Shankley that was OK by him. Which was stupid because I never fancied Ken at all. I mean, I always liked him. But I never fancied him.'

Trish heard a whirring sound and someone shouted 'Look out' just as a heavy weight hit her in the small of the back. Shock stopped her breathing. Then came sharp pain.

A sensation of small warm hands clinging to her legs banished most of the shock. She twisted round to see a child of about nine, wearing enormous roller blades, jeans and a crash helmet, howling at her feet. She couldn't tell from above whether it was a boy or girl. An adult woman came running up, panting.

'Sorry,' she said casually in the kind of voice Robert used when he wanted to be annoying, then bent down to the child. 'Barbie, I told you to be careful. You're lucky you didn't fall right down the steps and break something.'

Trish waited for a more fervent apology, a question about whether she was hurt, or a suggestion from the woman that her child might say something to excuse what had happened. Nothing came. The pair of them moved away.

'Well, I think that's outrageous,' Maryan said, sounding less sorry for herself and considerably older. 'Her kid really hurt you. I could see. People are *so* irresponsible! You need to sit down. There's a bench there. Can you manage? Take my arm.'

Trish, whose back was genuinely aching, accepted her help.

'Who's Ken Shankley?' she said as they settled on the bench.

'A climber. One of our best customers at the school. First he used to come on his own, then he started bringing colleagues from GlobWasMan for what he called corporate-bonding weekends.'

'GlobWasMan?'

'Yes. They came three or four times.'

'Did they ever bring a lawyer with them? A man called Ben Givens?'

Maryan sat, stroking her cheek with her right hand, round and round. Then she took it away and nodded decisively.

'A tall man with greying hair, a bit curly? Rather arrogant?'

'That's right, and old acne scars.'

'Yeah, it was him. He came once and he couldn't climb for toffee.' She laughed.

'What's so funny?'

'He hated Ken for being so much better at it than him, and Ken teased him. Barry joined in, which is why I thought Barry liked Ken. That's why I was nice to him. But it was never any more than that.'

'So why did Barry think you wanted to stay in England for him?'

'I don't know. And it doesn't matter now. I've drawn a line. Forgotten it all.' Maryan looked uncomfortably at her watch. 'Are you OK now?'

'I'm fine.'

'Great. Because I've got another party of tourists arriving in Chelsea and twenty minutes to get there. They'll get lost if I'm not there.'

'You carry on. I'll rest a little longer,' Trish said, still not sure whether Maryan was a brainless innocent or a highly efficient actor with a scapegoat conveniently out of reach.

Still, the leaflet she'd given Trish had two phone numbers, as well as postal and email addresses. She'd be easy to find again.

David sat in the dark cinema, next to Jay, waiting till the ads were over and the film could begin. With luck that would fill up his mind and stop him worrying about what Jay was going to do next. He'd already mucked about with the overflowing rubbish bin in the foyer and threatened to tip it up.

The ads were flashing and noisy, trying to sell them jeans and cars and drinks, and Jay was fidgeting and muttering. Some of his breathy swearing was as bad as it had been on the night of the Scrabble drama. But at least he wasn't screaming and yelling tonight.

He was being like this because David had insisted on getting tickets for *Henry V* instead of Kathryn Bigelow's *Near Dark* in Screen Two, which Jay wanted to see because it was full of vampires and cowboys and lots of blood. At first when David had handed over the ticket, Jay had said it didn't matter a fuck which screen it was for because there was hardly anyone about and they could just move from One to Two once the films had started and no one would notice.

'George gave us the money for *Henry V* because of school,' David had said all over again, knowing he sounded like a girl. 'So that's what we've got to see.'

'He won't ever know if we don't.'

'He would,' David had said with conviction.

George could always tell what you'd been doing when you tried to lie. Anyway, David didn't want to see any horror film. He wanted to see *Henry V*.

It was always easier to deal with set books if you'd got pictures in your head and seeing a film or some telly was the easiest way of getting them. And he liked the speeches, although he'd never admit it to anyone: 'He that outlives this day, and comes safe home . . . will yearly on the vigil feast his neighbours, and say . . .'

It was partly the bit about coming safe home, David had decided as the woman with the torch showed them to their seats. And partly the thought of the yearly feast and the remembering and the courage needed for dealing with all those wounds and scars.

He liked the quiet bit before the battle, too, with the soldier Michael Williams telling the king the truth about 'all those legs and arms and heads, chopped off in battle'. He silently recited it in his mind again now while he waited for the ads to finish.

Flick. Flick. Flick.

The sound forced David to look at Jay again. All he saw were flashes in the dark. Then he understood: Jay had a cigarette lighter.

David sat on his hands. It would only cause trouble if he tried to grab the lighter or say anything.

Flick. Flick. Flick. In spite of the flashes no one was looking at them. Jay was right: there were hardly any people here.

David turned, twisting his neck so he could look across the empty seats towards the place where the woman with the torch had been standing when they came in. There was no sign of her or her light now.

A disgusting smell stuffed itself up his nostrils. Jay was holding the lighter to the back of the seat.

'Fuck! It won't light.'

'Of course not, you fucking twat,' David said, trying to sound like they all did at school so it wouldn't set off one of Jay's worst rages. 'It's fireproofed.'

Jay turned to him with the lighter's flame bigger than ever flickering up over his face, making him look like a gargoyle.

David didn't say anything else as he thought about grabbing the lighter after all. Jay let it go out and bent double to scuffle about in his schoolbag. David held his breath, wondering what was coming next.

The ads had finished and there was the old-fashioned black screen now, saying the film had been passed for exhibition to everyone. Then came the music. George had told him to listen out for the sound of a thousand arrows fizzing out of the longbows.

Jay straightened up in his seat at last and sat fiddling with something in his lap. Then he started flicking the lighter again. Concentrating on the screen, David hoped Jay would stop if he didn't show any fear. The actors looked weird: wooden and made up like clowns. A smell of real burning caught in his throat and made him cough. In the silence afterwards, something crackled, and bigger flames lit up the space in front of Jay.

Trish went home in good time to oversee the boys' prep and cook, only to find no sign of them in the flat. Instead, there was George sitting on one of the black sofas with Shelby Deedes, who looked very comfortable with her short legs crossed, a mug of tea in her hand and a plate of biscuits conveniently close beside her. They weren't talking, but both stared at Trish as she took off her coat. Their expressions were self-conscious enough to suggest they'd only just stopped discussing her.

'Hi,' she said, trying not to feel that something important was being negotiated behind her back. 'No boys?'

'No,' George said. 'They went off to the flicks to see the six o'clock showing of the old Laurence Olivier *Henry V*. It seemed a surprisingly tame and educational choice.'

Shelby flinched visibly.

'What's wrong with that?' Trish asked too aggressively. She moderated her voice. 'It's one of their set books.'

'Nothing's wrong, if that's what they *are* watching,' Shelby said. 'But the local cinema's also showing a 1980s arthouse horror film called *Near Dark*. Are you sure they're not going for that?'

'Does it really matter? They're fourteen,' Trish said. 'There can't be many films worse than their beastly computer games.'

'Jay is very susceptible at the moment,' Shelby said, pursing her lips with a particularly prissy air. 'Horror or violence on the big screen should definitely be avoided.'

'I think it will be,' George said comfortably before Trish could make a remark about Shelby's refusal to take Darren's actual violence half as seriously as this. 'David swore they'd see *Henry V*, and he's like his sister. They always keep their promises.'

Trish blew him a kiss.

'Anyway, moving on,' he said, acknowledging her gesture with a secret smile, 'Shelby just missed them, so I thought we'd have tea to make up for her wasted journey. Jay hadn't told me he'd arranged to meet her here or I'd never have let them go to the cinema at all.'

'I can imagine. How irritating for you, Shelby,' Trish said, trying to feel friendly. 'But good in one way because I wanted to run something by you.'

'Oh yes?' She sounded not just doubtful but actively hostile.

Trish bit her tongue to keep her own dislike in check. Then she smiled.

'Jeremy Black may have told you that I've volunteered to pay half of Jay's fees at Blackfriars, but I've been wondering since whether it might be better to find a boarding school for him. It would be a lot more expensive, of course, but it could be worth it to get Jay away from Darren for three-quarters of the year.'

And it wouldn't be half as difficult as having him living here, she added to herself, then went on aloud: 'What do you think, Shelby?'

'Sounds ideal to me,' George said with even more warmth. 'Just what Jay needs. I'll happily chip in the extra.'

Shelby wrinkled up her nose as though trying to get rid of a pungent stink.

'Not a good idea,' she said.

Trish was about to protest when George extracted himself from the depths of the sofa.

'Tea, Trish?' His warning voice told her he thought she was about to be unhelpfully provocative.

'Thanks,' she said, smiling up at him and trying to show she knew they needed to keep Shelby reasonably sweet for Jay's sake. 'That'd be great.'

She and Shelby watched George's backview as he disappeared into the kitchen.

'Boarding school would be divisive, Trish,' Shelby said, recrossing her short legs so that her right foot stuck out. She was wearing diamond-patterned tights, which made her legs look even fatter. 'I mean, why should Jay have so much, when the other two will never get a chance like that?'

'Isn't it better that one is saved than none at all?'

'Not at the cost of the others.' Shelby paused, uncrossed her legs, then offered a small placatory smile. 'You see, there's hope for the family now they've got the man who attacked Rosie.'

'Have they? I hadn't heard. Thank God for that. Who is he?'

'A rough sleeper, who seems to have passed Rosie, seen her cans of White Star and tried to get them off her. Rosie fought back, which is why the beating was so bad.'

'So, once more Jay was innocent when half the world was sure he was guilty.' Trish looked at the other woman, hoping to see some signs of shame on her very pink face. There weren't any. 'He *is* worth helping, you know.'

'Rosie'll be dried out by the time she's released from hospital,' Shelby went on, as though she hadn't heard Trish's comments or didn't think them worth discussion. 'We're arranging some family therapy so she can learn to interact safely with her kids when she gets home. If Jay's taken away now and given all these extra advantages, the whole dynamic will be changed, and that could screw everything up for the other three.'

Trish wanted to push it, but George came back with her tea before she'd thought of a safe form of words.

'You must be so busy, Shelby,' he said, handing the mug to Trish. 'We shouldn't keep you. I'll ask Jay to give you a ring as soon as the boys get back.'

'Thanks, George. I'd appreciate it.' She picked up a sacklike bag and stuffed a notebook into it. 'Goodbye.'

'I'll see to your car. Back in a moment, Trish.'

She hoped he'd take the opportunity to dent some of Shelby's prejudices against Jay. When he came back he was looking preoccupied. Trish sipped some tea while he flumped down beside her on the sofa.

'She's not such a bad woman,' he said. 'Although she was expecting to see Jay, she actually came to tell me I've been officially cleared. Which was good of her. She didn't have to do it.'

'Cleared? What on earth d'you mean? Cleared of what?'

George kissed her. 'You'd forgotten, too, hadn't you? Apparently Darren didn't stop at telling Jay I was a paedophile; he told Shelby too.'

'That's ridiculous. Surely she didn't take it seriously.'

'She had to look into it. Come on, Trish, with all your experience in the family courts, you know what's done to children. Any allegation like this has to be investigated.'

He was right. But it was different when it affected your own family.

'You haven't actually been interviewed by the police, have you?' she said, appalled at the idea that she might not have noticed something so important going on in front of her.

'Nope. Shelby's too experienced to take anything Darren says at face value. When she asked for evidence, Darren talked about the trainers and the iPod and the Play Station – about which, of course, she already knew. So she was more or less sure there was nothing in it, but just to be safe she had Jay physically examined by a doctor.'

'Poor boy,' Trish said. That kind of physical examination could seem like an outrageous intrusion to anyone; to a damaged adolescent like Jay it might be unbearable. 'As though he hasn't had enough to put up with!'

'Precisely. But there's nothing we can do about it now. So, what would you like for supper? Shall I do the lamb? There's time to roast it before the boys get back.'

'Why not? Who's that now?' Trish said, as the iron staircase clanged outside her front door. A key crunching in the lock told them both. Trish snatched a look at her watch: it was far too early for the film to have finished.

David skidded in and came to an abrupt stop as he saw both of them staring at him.

'What?' he said with an aggression that was new.

'What's happened?' Trish said, still wanting to protect Jay, still trying not to blame him for the way David was changing.

He shrugged and turned away, dragging off his jacket.

'David!' George said in a voice that made Trish flinch.

'Something's happened,' she said, much more gently. 'Can't you tell me what it is?'

David stood where he was, shaking his head. His chin jutted as it had when he was much younger and she'd tried to make him do something he hated, like handing over his favourite clothes for cleaning or washing his hair.

'Is it Jay?' Trish said. David didn't move, so she said: 'Where is he?'

'At the cinema.'

'What did he do?'

He turned his head a little towards her and looked out from under his fringe.

'Why d'you think he did anything?'

'Because you look so worried. Did you fight? Did he—?'

'He had a cigarette lighter,' David said, looking at the floor and picking his nose. Now was not the time to tell him to use a handkerchief.

Trish thought of all the arson cases in which appalling damage had been done by boys of Jay's age. Was this a reaction to whatever Shelby's doctor had said or done to him?

'He was trying to set fire to the seats in front,' David went on, 'but they wouldn't light.'

'No,' George said in a reassuring voice, obviously trying to cool the emotional temperature. He smiled at both of them. 'Too much fireproofing, I imagine.'

David's pale skin was flushing. In spite of the colour, he looked more like his usual cooperative self. 'That's what I said too, so it's my fault.'

'What is?' Trish asked, feeling as though they were all standing on the very edge of a cliff. 'What happened when they wouldn't light, David?'

'I tried to concentrate on the film, so I didn't see what Jay was doing. Not really. But he took off his socks and filled them with bits of paper torn out of the books in his schoolbag, then he draped them over the seat in front and flicked the lighter on again. I was still there when the first bits of paper started to crackle and smell. The flames were getting bigger when I left.'

'Did you tell someone?' George was keeping his voice impressively calm.

Trish searched David's face and clothes for burn marks. There were none. Would Jay have been so lucky?

David nodded. George and Trish both breathed again.

'I said if he didn't stop I would. And he didn't stop. So I told the person in the ticket booth, who was the only one I could find. Then I came back here. I didn't want to get him in trouble, but . . .' His voice faded and he had another go at excavating his nose.

'You were quite right.' Trish remembered a fire at a private cinema in north London some years ago. A lot of people had died.

'Try not to worry too much,' she said. 'Jay was probably only testing you, trying to find out how far—'

'Why do you always have to talk about everything?' he shouted. 'It's fucking boring!'

He stormed off to his room and slammed the door behind him.

'*Shit*!' Trish said. She looked up at George. 'I should have handled that better.'

'Yes,' he said, putting an arm around her shoulders. 'Although you were right. Maybe not lamb tonight. I don't suppose we'll be seeing Jay and you won't want a great huge lot of meat after that. I'll go and turn off the oven, then I'll phone the cinema and find out what's happening.'

Chapter 17

Angie spent Saturday morning cleaning. The more she did, the more she understood how tired Polly had become, and how poor her eyesight must be. At first sight nothing in the house had looked too bad, but with every wipe of wet cloth or duster, more dirt had been revealed. Each time Angie moved a piece of furniture she saw curls of dust floating above years' worth of grime and dead insects. There were hard black mouse turds too. But no sign of rats, which was something on an isolated farm.

When Polly came in for lunch, ahead of Bill, she was limping and one hand was clamped to the small of her back. Angie, who had her own aches, could see how much Polly hurt from the careful way she was breathing. But when she caught sight of the table, already laid, with cold mutton and hot vegetables, as well as a newly defrosted loaf and a hunk of cheese, she smiled.

'What luxury! Thank you, Angie. Bill will be here in a moment.'

'You look all in.' Angie pulled out a chair for her. 'Sit. D'you want some tea? Or just water?'

'Tea would be great. But why haven't you laid a place for yourself? You're not going to pretend to be a servant, are you?' Polly rubbed her eyes, then put back her glasses, blinking. 'That would be silly.'

'I thought, if it was all right with you, I might make a sandwich and go over to Low Topps. I need to see—'

'How the caretaker shepherd's been managing? Of course you do. D'you want to take the Land Rover? I don't think Bill will need it today, but we'd better check first.'

Angie looked away. 'I thought I might walk actually.' She waited for Polly's protest about the unnecessary time it would take and the amount of work that still needed doing in the house.

When she didn't speak, Angie had to face her again. What she saw in Polly's expression almost made her gasp: all the compassion there'd been in Trish Maguire's before she turned into a vengeful harpy.

'In Adam's footsteps?' Polly said. 'It won't help, you know, pet.'

Angie grabbed hold of the chair in front of her. She felt as though the floor was unsafe. How much did Polly suspect? Adam had been staying here only days before the explosion that killed his father. It wouldn't take a genius to make the connection. Or did she actually know something?

Had Adam confessed and sworn her to secrecy about this, too, perhaps making her believe all he'd wanted was to blow up the tanks and that killing his father had been a terrible accident? Polly had never been one to talk if talk wasn't necessary. She could well have decided that reporting Adam to the police wouldn't bring John back to life and would double Angie's grief.

Was this why Polly was looking at her with so much pity?

'They're unknowable, our children,' she said now with a gentleness that made Angie's eyes water. 'They think we need protecting from knowledge that wouldn't hurt a fly; and yet they can do and say things so cruel it feels as if they've ripped the skin from our backs. By all means walk to Low Topps, pet, but don't expect it to help you see into Adam's mind. It won't.'

Angie only nodded. She couldn't say anything. Polly nodded as though she had.

'If you're too tired to walk back, phone me. One of us will come and pick you up in the Land Rover.'

'Thank you. You're—' Hearing Bill's footsteps, Angie left the kitchen by the internal door to avoid any more explanations. Only when the sound of his chair legs scraping along the stone floor told her he was safely at the table did she get her boots and set off.

It was the perfect day for a walk: bright and cold. With her hands in the softly lined pockets of her old Barbour and a scarf around her neck, just covering her mouth, she strode out. Some of the aches eased at once. Using muscles for walking was quite different from stretching and compressing them as you scrubbed and swept. Low Topps was six miles away; it shouldn't take too long. And walking might help clear her mind of some unbearable thoughts.

Two and a half hours later, she stood on the last hill above her farm. The retired shepherd she was paying to keep an eye on the animals had obviously done as he'd promised. They were dotted about the fields, as they'd always been, peacefully eating. They were no more now than grass-cutting machines and living subjects of experiments in the adverse effects of benzene-poisoning, but they had to be kept from straying and mixing with other flocks; flocks that had yet to be contaminated.

The little lough looked perfect inside the ugly five-foot chain-link fence the health-and-safety people had erected. There was hardly any wind today, so the surface of the water was like polished silver again in the middle of the soft green land. But the fish had died and so had some of the wild duck. No animal could drink from it without risk.

Off to the right was the jagged wreck of the tanks, surrounded by the dead cypress trees, the broken concrete walls, and the blackened earth all around. Angie thought the whole site looked like a broken tooth in a rotting gum. Orange, diamond-shaped HazChem signs were posted along the temporary fences here too.

Had Adam stood like this, when everything was still clean and alive, to hatch his plan? Or was the story Polly had offered actually true: had he come to make peace and failed to find enough courage?

Maguire and her witnesses had been so convincing in the evidence they'd given that Angie now knew all this devastation had to have been caused by a blockage in the breathing vent of one of the tanks. But she still clung to the hope that it could have been an accident, that something might have been blown into the vent by a freak wind.

She sank down until she was squatting, all her body weight resting on her calves and heels.

The trouble was she couldn't remember any freak winds around that time. And she still found it hard to believe that John could have ignored a visible blockage for seventy-two hours. The only explanation for his leaving something in the vent would be if it had been stuffed so far inside he couldn't actually see it. And the only way that could have happened was by human agency.

You could walk down from here to the tanks in a straight line and never be seen from the house. If John had been checking the tank enclosure when saboteurs approached, he would have seen them. But if he'd had been at his normal job, his real job of sheep-farming, the intruders could have spent hours uninterrupted while they fiddled about with the tanks.

Of course, whoever they were, they would have had to break into the locked enclosure. Or maybe climb the concrete walls.

Angie tried to forget that Adam had always been an agile tree climber. When she couldn't, she told herself the smooth concrete walls of the enclosure would have presented real problems to anyone without a ladder.

So maybe he'd brought bolt cutters with him, or a crowbar and smashed his way in.

Had it been a broken padlock and swinging gate that had attracted John's attention in the end, so that he'd gone to investigate just at the moment when the overheated charcoal burst into flame and triggered the explosion? Or had he felt the heat from outside the enclosure and rushed to find out what was wrong?

No one would ever know because the fire had destroyed the gate.

Angie wasn't crying now. Sympathy from a woman like Polly might make her do that. This kind of horror was far too much for tears.

Her heart jolted – once, twice – as though offering her the chance to stop it completely.

Trish and George cooked the lamb on Sunday, after a tense twenty-four hours she never wanted to repeat.

When George phoned the cinema manager on Friday to find out what had happened with Jay, the man was furious. His staff had found no evidence of any fire-raising, or any sign of a 14-year-old boy on his own in either of the two sections of the cinema. He told George to warn his 'son' that if he ever played a trick like that again the police would be called and he would be barred from the place.

None of them slept well. On Saturday Trish sent the others off for their usual training hour in the swimming pool and later felt passionately grateful for David's interest in chess and Scrabble, and for George's tolerance of both. They played one or other game for most of the day. There was no sign of Jay, no phone call and no response to any of David's texts. At eight on Sunday morning David bounced into her room to ask if his old friend Sam could come for a traditional Sunday lunch and life began again.

George was carving the roast lamb now. As Trish spooned redcurrant jelly on to her plate, she watched David shedding all the emotional armour he'd had to acquire for dealing with Jay. At one moment she thought: yes, *you're* the boy I knew before this term started; I've missed you.

After lunch, she waved the two boys off on some private expedition of their own, without the slightest anxiety about what they might do. She and George cleared up together, neither talking much. It was as though there were too many things to say and too little action they could take until they knew more about what had happened to Jay. Trish had phoned Shelby to warn her about the cinema episode, but she'd had to leave a message and there'd been no return call yet.

'Has it crossed your mind, Trish,' George said as he scoured the last crusty lumps from the roasting tin, 'that

David might have invented the fire-raising as an excuse for dumping Jay?'

'No.' She reached for a cloth to wipe the worktop.

'He's been getting more and more difficult, and it wouldn't be surprising if David—'

'But this isn't his style, George. He's never lied about anything except being "fine" when he obviously isn't.' Trish put down the cloth and stood with her back against the worktop.

George swilled detergent foam off the roasting tin and leaned over to kiss her cheek.

'Don't look so worried,' he said. 'One way or another we'll get it sorted.'

'I hope you're right.'

'So why don't we allow ourselves to revel in having the flat to ourselves for once?' He balanced the roasting tin on the rack and dried his hands.

She felt the tension in her face crack, letting all the muscles soften. 'Good idea.'

'Are you working this afternoon, or do you feel like a—' He broke off, to push a few stray strands of her hair off her face. 'A healthful snooze?'

She kissed him, glad of the opportunity to bury her fears. 'A healthful snooze sounds wonderful.'

He put an arm around her waist and swung her out of the kitchen. They climbed the spiral staircase to her bedroom, dredging up silly jokes and catch phrases from their earliest days together and trying to forget all their responsibilities until the light went and David came home. They managed well enough, but Trish couldn't quite stop listening for the knock on the door that would signal Jay's return to their lives.

*

She phoned Carl Bianchini again as soon as she reached chambers on Monday morning to tell him she'd met Maryan Fleming and wanted to know whether he'd been on any of the corporate-bonding sessions at the climbing school when he worked with GlobWasMan.

'My other phone's ringing,' he said. 'I have to go.'

She waited, while ideas trickled through her mind like sand in an hourglass. To her surprise he hadn't cut the connection. She could hear the traffic beyond the trees on the Embankment and Steve's voice as he ranted at someone at the far end of the corridor. On the open phone line, she heard only soft breathing, until at last it was overtaken by a question.

'Have you really got a troubled teenage protégé called Jay Smith?'

'Absolutely,' she said, encouraged. The harshness, the long silence and now this suspicious question told her he had some secrets. But if he didn't want to hand them over, why was he hanging on? Could he possibly be afraid of eavesdroppers?

'And there's lots more I want to ask you about him,' she added quickly. 'Perhaps I shouldn't be doing it on the phone. Would you prefer it if we met somewhere face to face again?'

Another long pause.

'That might be a good idea,' he said at last. 'But I'm not sure . . . Yes, I know: I have to be near Trafalgar Square this afternoon. I could meet you by Landseer's lions at one-thirty.'

Bizarre, she thought, but why not?

'I'll be there.' She clicked off the phone as Steve put his head round her door to tell her the new brief would be in her pigeonhole within the week and that Sarah Fortescue had phoned him to open negotiations for a very large banking case. Trish leaned back in her chair, stretching all her limbs in relief.

Three hours later, she left chambers to walk up to the Strand and on to Trafalgar Square, enjoying the crispness of the air on her cheeks as much as the sunlight dancing over the pinnacles of the buildings and the shiny bodywork of the expensive cars.

There was no sign of Carl Bianchini anywhere near Landseer's lions, so she sat on the white stone parapet of one of the fountains, closed her eyes and tipped up her face to the sun. There was still some warmth in it. She felt as though her skin was becoming more elastic under its care and her mind let go of all kinds of minor stresses.

As she allowed herself to relax, a mental guard she'd raised began to drop too. The sensation of comfort dribbled away.

For the first time she thought of the link between children like Jay – clever, worthwhile but unhappy, frustrated and therefore explosively dangerous children – and the kind of toxic waste stored by companies like CWWM and GlobWasMan. Twenty-first-century society created both in frightening quantities and there weren't nearly enough facilities to keep them safe.

She closed her eyes again, groping for her old defences and for the few blissful moments of relaxation she'd felt under the sun's warmth.

'Trish? Anyone in there? Trish.' The familiar quiet voice made her open her eyes again, but all she could see was a dark figure against a dazzle of light.

'Carl,' she said, blinking and moving so she could get a better view. Today he was wearing a suit again, but his hair was as dry and untidy as ever and he looked even more worried. 'Thank you for coming.'

'I had to be near here anyway.' He lowered himself to the stone parapet beside her, but he didn't say anything else.

After a while, Trish said: 'Why are you so quiet? I thought you were going to come clean at last.'

'Come clean?' He sounded outraged. 'About what?'

'About how you got embroiled with Greg Waverly and Ben Givens in their campaign against the chemical-waste industry.'

'What on earth are you talking about?'

'And why the three of you picked the benzene tanks at Low Topps Farm for Maryan Fleming and Barry Stuart to blow up.'

'You're mad,' Binachini said. 'I don't know what you're talking about. And I've never wanted to blow anything up.'

He forced himself to his feet and walked hurriedly away from the fountain, only to stop, turn on his heel and come back. He opened his mouth, then shut it again and took off his spectacles and tucked them in his breast pocket so he could rub his eyes. They looked so red he'd clearly been at them before. At last he sat down again, with his hands clamped to the white stone either side of him. His muscles were so tight, Trish almost expected to hear them humming.

'If you didn't come to tell me the truth, well away from listening ears, why did you agree to meet?' she said more kindly.

'I had to stop you blabbing those names over the phone. Haven't you any idea what you're risking?'

'No. Tell me.'

'Who the hell are you? And who are you working for? I know you do have a protégé called Jay Smith because I did some checking after we spoke this morning. But why d'you think I might give you information about Fleming and Stuart?' He waited for a nanosecond, then added unconvincingly: 'Whoever they are.'

'Carl, why are you so hostile?' Trish said.

'Can you really not know?' He stared at her with a kind of dread that told her how much of his aggression was driven by fear; not just wariness but real physical gut-churning fear. 'Are you fiddling with this completely blind?'

'I must be,' she said, briefly touching one of his rigid hands. He whipped it away.

'Because I haven't a clue about what's making you so scared,' she went on. '*Haven't* you been working with Ben Givens and Greg Waverly?'

He raised one hand to cover his eyes. She waited.

'This is lunacy,' he said at last. 'I've had no contact with Givens since the libel case. And I have never heard of Greg Waverly.'

'But you must have heard of Maryan Fleming and Barry Stuart,' Trish said. 'Because they organised the corporate-bonding weekends for GlobWasMan at their climbing school in Swanage.'

'Oh, Christ!' he muttered.

'Carl, you have to explain. Otherwise I'm going to do unintended damage as I trample around. If you don't know about the connection between Givens and Greg Waverly, what's the significance of Fleming and Stuart in your life?'

'All I can say is that I came across those two names in the accounts at GlobWasMan.'

'So what? They should be there. As I said, they provided corporate-bonding weekends.'

'Except they didn't,' he said. Now he sounded exhausted, as though he'd run out of defences.

Again she had to wait. This time the silence stretched on and on. The muscles around his mouth were jumping as though he was clenching and unclenching his jaw. Come on, she thought, come *on*.

The wind got up suddenly and blew the fountain's spray towards them. Trish could feel it on the back of her head. Carl straightened up, took a pristine handkerchief from his pocket and took off his spectacles to wipe the lenses. Once they were dry again, he spent another minute or so fastidiously wiping his face and then his hands.

'The dates didn't work,' he said at last. 'Not for the most recent weekend anyway, and probably not for some of the earlier ones either. No one was available to go. Never would have been. So the money was paid out for some other reason, just disguised as payment for another directors' climbing weekend.'

Trish felt as though she were watching a film of shattering glass run backwards so that the mess of flying debris was miraculously sucked back together again to show the full, unbroken pane.

She knew what the payment must have been for. And she thought she knew who had been threatening Barry when he'd asked for more money. And what he'd meant when he'd told Maryan she could take her chance with Ken Shankley if she didn't flee to New Zealand.

'What did you think the money was for?' Trish tried to sound mildly interested and not at all suspicious.

He was biting his lips so hard she expected to see blood at any minute.

'It wasn't the only odd payment.' You'd have thought the words hurt his mouth from the way they twisted up his face. 'Once I'd found it, I started to look for more. You see I shouldn't ever have known anything about it because I didn't deal with the nitty-gritty of the accounts; I only saw this entry because there was a struggling temp in the department one day and I was the only person around in the office to answer her question about which code to give the invoice. I had to make a search to find out and that's when I started to see the anomalies in the books.'

'Why did they worry you so much?'

He frowned, as though he couldn't believe anyone could be so obtuse, then whispered: 'Money-laundering.'

'What?' Trish felt her jaw slacken as she stared at him.

'It had to be. And it explained everything. All the oddities and strange remarks and weird threats.'

'You mean you think GlobWasMan isn't just cleaning up chemical waste but dirty money, too,' she said, needing to be sure of what he was telling her.

'Exactly. And dirty money means organised crime. Drugs. People-smuggling. The kind of men who kill anyone who might get in the way of their profits. I got out as soon as I could. And I reported them to the Fraud Squad. I had to; otherwise I risked a prison sentence, too, and what would have happened to my family then?' He shivered.

'What is it, Carl? What happened?'

'When I told Ken Shankley, the chairman, that I had to resign because of my wife, he looked at me without saying anything. That's when I knew he knew I knew.' Bianchini swallowed hard, as though he had something huge and painful in his throat that had to be choked down. 'Then he went, "You know what'll happen to her if you talk, don't you?"'

Trish couldn't bear to leave him in this much agony.

'Carl,' she said. 'Look at me.'

After a while he did, and she said with great deliberation:

'You're letting your nightmares overcome your judgement. The sums you found in the accounts must have been too small to be of any interest to a money-laundering gang of violent organised criminals. Their profits are vast, far too big to be hidden in a business the size of GlobWasMan.'

He shook his head. 'You don't understand.'

'Yes, I do. For instance, how much was the payment to Fleming and Stuart?'

'Only five grand. But that's how money-laundering works: dozens, hundreds, thousands of small transactions that all look innnocent.'

Five thousand pounds, she thought. John Fortwell was killed for the price of a second-hand car.

'I must go.' She stood up.

He grabbed her wrist with both hands, clutching at her. Even if there'd been nothing else, that gesture would have shown her how near the edge he was, how eaten up with irrational anxiety.

'You won't use my name, will you? Nowhere? Never?'

'I never will, Carl.'

She left him and walked quickly towards the south-eastern corner of the square. Watching the traffic move at a sluggish crawl around the lower edge of the square as she waited for the lights to change, she thought of Angie Fortwell's hatred that first day in court.

Being able to tell her the truth about what Maryan Fleming and Barry Stuart had done, and why, and for whom, might assuage some of it.

Her phone rang.

'Trish Maguire.'

'Trish, it's me.' Antony's voice was reassuringly vigorous. 'I need you. Now. I know you can't have any work to do because Steve's phoned to say you're adjourned. And you can't be itching to help David again because he must be in school. Please.'

'Oh, all right. I'm in Trafalgar Square. I could be with you in about ten minutes.'

He might even be useful, she thought, so long as he didn't rant at her for taking such an unorthodox line with her work.

Visitors were milling about in the hospital foyer, waiting for the end of the post-lunch quiet period up in the wards. Trish had forgotten about it. But she wasn't going to waste any more time.

Hurrying figures in white coats passed by with stethoscopes flying. Bored children ran about, screeching, while their parents looked on in tired resignation and elderly visitors with outrage. Trish made for the lifts.

The brushed steel doors opened and a crowd of nurses rushed out. Trish took their place, barely noticing the other five or six people who followed her, and pressed the button for the tenth floor.

The first thing she saw as she emerged was Jay's familiar figure slumped on one of the orange plastic chairs outside the entrance to the two main orthopaedic wards.

Today he was wearing torn jeans and a round-necked grey T-shirt that did nothing to make his screwed-up blob of a face and aggressively ugly haircut look less threatening. She'd taken two steps back before she realised what she was doing and stopped herself.

He looked so vulnerable. And so unhappy.

There was a messy bunch of evergreen branches and three wilting roses in a neatly folded cornet of newspaper on the chair beside Jay. The mixture of the bedraggled flowers and the tidiness of their holder reminded her of everything she liked about him and everything George and David admired. Her sneaking wish to get him out of their lives seemed cruel.

He was looking vacantly at the far wall and kicking one clean trainer against the chair leg in a disturbing, rhythmical way that made her think of news footage of damaged children in third-world orphanages.

'Jay?' she said at last, leaning down a little towards him so that he would hear her quiet voice. 'Are you on your way to see your mother?'

He looked up and smiled like a newly woken baby sensing a feed, as though there'd been no estrangement, no attempted arson. He stopped kicking and sat straight. He wasn't nearly as tall as David, but as he stretched she remembered he was fourteen: no longer a child; barely even a boy. Others of his age were already fathers. Could the damage he'd suffered for so long be mended or was it already too late? At what age *should* you lose the get-out-of-jail-free card?

'Hi, Trish. Yeah. But I can't go in till the cops've finished with her. What are you doing?'

'I'm visiting a friend. How's your mother?'

'Still too bad to come home. Her skull's broken, as well as her ribs.'

'I'm sorry. And I'm sorry I didn't see you on Friday as I'd expected,' she said, determined to get to the bottom of the cinema episode. 'The day you and David went to see *Henry V*'.

He looked up at her from under his lids as the old sullen expression settled over his features, blotting out the intelligence.

'Why?'

'Jay, what happened then? I know David couldn't have made up that story about you setting fire to your socks, whatever the cinema manager said when George rang him up to check.'

He said nothing.

'D'you think David's got a good enough imagination to think up something like that?'

Jay met her eyes. A faint smile brought back hints of awareness to his expression.

'I don't either,' she said.

'I wasn't going to admit it though, was I? Stupid, innit? When they come looking for me I took my bag and hid in the toilets, then I went back and saw the rest of the film.' He swung his legs again, whacking the heel of his trainer against the chair leg. The noise or the vibration must have appealed to him because he did it again, and again. His face returned to vacancy.

She would have a lot to say to him if David wanted him back, but until she knew that, there was no point even trying. She left him and went to find Antony.

He was sitting in his chair beside the bed, wearing an ordinary neck collar now instead of the cage and fully dressed in dark corduroy trousers, a checked shirt and a heavy cashmere cardigan that was knitted in a complicated cable pattern. She'd never seen him in such informal clothes, but they were as much of an improvement as the neck collar. His blond hair seemed thinner than usual and his face was netted with new lines, but he no longer looked like a victim.

'Hey! Congratulations, Antony.' She bent to kiss his cheek. 'Does it still hurt?'

'Not too bad, but they're getting a bit mean with painkillers these days. The physio's helping, though. I'm due out tomorrow. Liz is coming to pick me up at ten-thirty, after the consultant's ward round.'

'Fantastic news.'

'So tell me what you've been up to.'

She filled him in on everything that had been happening and most of her suspicions about the case, distracted at one moment by the bustling departure of two uniformed police officers.

'They've been interviewing the assault victim,' Antony said. 'They're the third lot today.'

'Why so many?'

'They want her to ID their suspect from photographs because she's too ill to go to the nick. First time, she wasn't making much sense; second time, she started yelling and swearing at them. This last round has been quieter.' He grinned. 'I was reduced to offering my services, via the prettiest of the nurses, during the shouting. But the answer came back that she didn't need no interfering brief telling her what to do.'

'She had no idea what she was turning down, had she? The great Antony Shelley, offering pro-bono help to a woman who—' She broke off.

'There's no polite way to describe her, according to what I've heard. Never mind her now. Tell me what you've been up to.'

Trish went back to work, glad to hear his qualified approval of her unorthodox search for the people who'd paid Maryan Fleming's boyfriend to sabotage the tanks. Minutes later, a hoarse screaming voice ripped through the air behind her:

'Get out of my sight, you filthy little stinking waste-of-space.'

Trish couldn't help looking round, although there was nothing to see.

'It's only the drunk,' Antony said. 'At it again. I thought the cops had gone.'

'Hang on a minute,' Trish said.

Her heels slipped on the polished vinyl floor as she hurried to the far end of the ward. There, in the last bay, she saw Jay, clinging to the bars at the bottom of his mother's bed. His chin was quivering with the intensity of his silence and his back was stretched even tighter than Carl Bianchini's had been. Through his thin T-shirt, his spine looked like a piece of high-tensile steel wire. There was aggression in every aspect of his figure. But it was his mother who was pouring out the invective.

'Can I help?' Trish asked, cutting through the diatribe with a quietness that made the other woman strain to hear her.

'Fuck off, you interfering middle-class cunt.'

'You OK, Jay?' Trish said, turning towards him without responding to the insult.

'She wants me to go and buy her some cans of White

Star and I said I won't and that's why she's like this.'

Trish saw the improvised bouquet on the floor, spilling out of its carefully folded newspaper holder.

'Fucking little waste-of-space, coming here bringing me weeds and sticks. Get out of my sight and don't come back. I never want to see you again. If it wasn't for you I wouldn't never of needed to drink.'

Longing to put an arm around his shoulders, Trish couldn't think how to help. Shelby's optimism for the family's chances seemed wildly unrealistic.

'Go on. The pair of you. Fuck off.' The woman's voice was a scream now. Nurses were converging on them from all over the ward, and the patient in the next bed was cringing against her pillow as though she expected a physical battering at any moment.

'Come on, Jay,' Trish said, still not getting within touching distance.

His hands were white around the bedstead, as though the clenching had driven all the blood back up into his wrists, which was hardly possible. He drew in a huge breath and Trish waited for some gross outburst. In the end he just let it out in a shuddering sigh, unclamped his hands, and whirled away. She caught up with him near the nurses' station.

'Withdrawal makes everyone aggressive,' she said, trying to make it less hard for him. 'Your mother didn't mean any of that.'

He stopped and kicked the laminated panel beneath the desk. Then he looked at Trish. There was no contempt now, or rage; just weariness.

'Yeah, she did. It's what she thinks; what she always says. She's scared of Darren and she likes Kimberley. But she hates me.' He looked away again. 'Fucking bitch.'

'Don't, Jay. It won't help. Look, I don't want to be tiresome, but shouldn't you be in school now?'

The look he gave her could have scorched paper.

Chapter 18

Don Bates, the managing director of CWWM, arrived in his solicitors' meeting room straight off an overnight plane. Even so, his vigour was undimmed. Only the slightest clenching in the corners of his eyes and a barely distinguishable yellow tinge to his skin told Trish he was even tired.

One of Fred Hoffman's trainees was standing by a tray, pouring coffee and handing milk and sugar. There were biscuits too. Fred took one and chewed noisily, but the others ignored them.

'So, Ms Maguire. Fred tells me you've got some news,' said Bates, just as the trainee took herself out of the room.

Fred retreated to the far end of the long table, where he settled into an armchair and watched the other two.

'The adjournment of the case has given me some time to step back, think, and do a little research,' Trish said, seeing the light catch in his eyes as he looked from Bates to her and back again. 'I've discovered who sabotaged the tanks, and who—'

'Hold it.' Bates's bark made even Fred look quite scared. 'Didn't I tell you not to go there?'

Trish smiled with a slow confident widening of her lips.

She was tough enough to stand up to Bates, but she didn't want to challenge him so obviously he'd have to rev himself up into a real rage.

'"Don't waste time" was what you said. Having an unexpected slug of uncommitted hours because of the adjournment, I knew I wouldn't be. Look, I think you've been the victim – worldwide – of a systematic campaign by a small waste company called GlobWasMan.'

'Don't be ridiculous.'

'They're about to list on AIM, and—'

'We all know that.'

'With the intention, I suspect,' she went on with a doggedness she hoped would eventually get through to him, 'of raising enough money to mount a takeover of CWWM.'

She paused to allow him to make another protest if he wanted, but he seemed speechless with disbelief. Fred leaned across the table to reach for more biscuits, almost flattening himself like a snooker player. No wonder his suits always looked so crumpled.

'Obviously the amount they'd need would be much less if they could reduce your share price,' Trish said. 'And the easiest way to do that would be to make your operations look dangerously careless.'

'Where did you get this . . . this fantasy? I don't mean to be rude, Ms Maguire, but really! Those clowns at GlobWasMan are a bunch of overgrown schoolboys, who have no interest in me or my company.'

She thought about the Pathfinder prospectus and the manifesto printed at the beginning of it, which she'd now reread several times. If she couldn't persuade Don Bates any other way, she'd take him through it line by line, pointing out all the claims to unprecedented safety measures and being way ahead of any of their competitors in the preservation of the environment.

'How do you know what they want?'

'I know all about them. Listen,' Bates said, jabbing a finger at her. 'They got their first taste of money in the dotcom boom. There were four of them then and they sold themselves to a bunch of naive investors, who believed anyone young enough and slick enough could make a killing out of the Internet. Then they bailed out just in time to keep their own profits and laugh at the losers as the company disappeared like an ice cube in a heatwave.'

'Shows a certain amount of acumen when you think of everyone who lost their shirts at the time,' Trish said and saw the ghost of agreement in Fred's expression. She wondered who the fourth dotcommer was, and why he – or she – had not joined GlobWasMan.

'Pathetic lemmings,' Bates said as though he could never make a misjudgement like that.

'You seem to know a lot about them,' she added with a disarming smile. 'Were you one of their original backers?'

'God no! I stick to what I understand. It's the only secure basis for investment. One of them applied for a job with us after they sold out. I heard all about it at his interview.'

'I thought you said they made a killing,' Fred said from the far end of the table. 'Why was he applying for jobs?'

'They hadn't made nearly as much as they pretended, and they knew they'd have to go on working. A couple of them set up as freelance techies, but there wasn't a lot of call for that around the time of the crash. Most companies were fighting shy of the Internet just then. But we needed someone to design our new systems. When we advertised Ken applied.'

'Ken Shankley?' Trish said.

'That's right. He didn't do a bad job and while he was with us he saw how profitable the business could be. When we turned down the idea of taking over GlobWasMan, because its sites were in such a poor state and too small really for us to bother with, he thought he'd have a crack at it himself, raising the money from the few other people who'd bailed out of the Internet boom in time.'

'Did he ask you for help?'

'Nope. Cocky little sod that he was, he thought he could do it all himself. I warned him though.' Bates laughed. '"Watch the hubris," I said. "Take a bit more advice this time and you may build up a useful little business that will last." Did he listen? Did he hell!'

Ah, Trish thought. So here's the personal element. Ken Shankley wasn't just grabbing a commercial opportunity when he decided to wreck your share price; he saw a chance to humble you too. Irresistible, I should think.

'To give the boy his due, after a year or two he eventually saw the point of my warning,' Bates said. 'He got in some experts, chemists, lawyers and so on, and he's built up a reasonable company now. But it's still tiny. And your ideas of world domination are completely bonkers. He's going to sell out and move on to the next growth area as soon as he can.'

'I'm not so sure. And there are—'

'Listen to me, Ms Maguire. And listen well. I know what I'm talking about here, and it's a world that's entirely new to you, however good you may be in court. Ken and his friends are planning to do exactly what they did with Goforthebrains.com. They've spent tens of thousands on their glossy Pathfinder in order to snare another bunch of overhopeful investors. I've seen it, and it sticks out a mile. Watch. And learn.'

No, *you* watch, she thought, as always loathing this kind of contemptuous dismissal. She might have come to the dangerous-waste business late, but human motives and behaviour were her core subjects, and they didn't change with the place in which you found them.

'You should know these overgrown schoolboys of yours paid £5K to a couple who did not provide the service for which they were ostensibly charging, and who were within five minutes' walk of the Fortwells' tanks exactly seventy-two hours before the explosion. Which is the time specified by our expert for the blocking of the vents. D'you really think that's a coincidence?'

'If they'd put something in there, Fortwell would've seen it and picked it out.' Bates looked as though he was fighting to keep his irritation under control. 'It's what we paid him for, and he was a conscientious bugger.'

'He may have been once. But, as we've shown in court, he'd been slapdash and dilatory in many different situations in the months leading up to his death.'

Trish waited for some acknowledgement but it didn't come. Fred was staring at the table so that he didn't have to react. She told herself not to let them get to her and bared her teeth at Bates in what she hoped would be a reasonably convincing smile.

'OK, so forget the tanks for the moment. Was it by any chance *your* drums of waste that were involved in the crash in Suffolk, when a woman had to have both feet amputated?'

His face told her all she needed to know, but he surprised her by saying:

'Are you going to hit me with the girl on the Scottish beach next?'

'I don't know anything about a Scottish beach,' Trish said. 'What happened there?'

He shrugged. 'Another inexplicable accident with some of our worst waste. I must say, in the context of these spillages, it would be convenient if you were right about those clowns at GlobWasMan. How d'you expect to prove it?'

'I doubt if there's enough hard evidence left anywhere for real proof. But more than enough of the circumstantial sort to persuade Angie Fortwell to withdraw her claim. May I try?'

'Fred? What do you think?'

'Makes sense to me, Don. Whether Trish is right about GlobWasMan or not, she can present a convincing argument. And Angie was looking as though she hated being in court the last time I saw her. She might jump at an offer to settle now.'

Bates stood up and marched to the far end of the room, helped himself to another cup of coffee, which he then dumped on the table and ignored. Obviously a man who preferred to make decisions on his feet, Trish decided. Even the slight signs of tiredness had gone from his eyes and skin. He looked powerful and ready to take on the world.

'OK. Let's do it.'

'Would you want to be there at the settlement meeting?' Fred asked, which made Trish frown all over again.

She couldn't think of anything less helpful than having a client like this in a delicate negotiation with someone as emotional and unpractised as Angie Fortwell.

'No. Better she and I don't meet.' Bates looked at Trish from under his eyelashes, almost like a flirting girl, which disconcerted her. 'I might not be able to keep my temper after the grief she's given me. And I don't suppose you'll be able to get my costs back.'

'Probably not. She hasn't any money. But at least you won't be stung for damages.'

'True.' Bates picked up his heavy overcoat, swung it around his shoulders and said he had a lunch to go to. He didn't wait to shake hands. But he stopped at the doorway and turned his head back to look at Fred.

'What do we do then? If there is anything in this story, the police should be told and get those clowns closed down before they do any more harm.'

'We can lay information, yes.' Fred made another note.

'Get it done fast, then,' Bates said and left without another word.

Trish and Fred were left to slump in their chairs and agree that he was just about the most exhausting man either of them had ever met. Fred then said he would phone her clerk as soon as he'd been able to set up the meeting with Angie, and Trish walked the short distance back to the Temple.

She was so absorbed in trying to decide whether Don Bates's humiliation of Ken Shankley was enough to explain what he'd been trying to do or whether there were yet more layers of conspiracy to find that she almost walked into Steve, who was hanging about in the corridor.

'What's happened? You look like hell,' she said, stepping back and registering the greyish tinge of his skin and the way it seemed to hang more loosely than usual under his narrow chin.

'It's Mr Shelley. He's had an embolism.'

'*What*? But I saw him only yesterday.' Trish felt as

though someone had hit her in the face. 'He was fine. Ready to go home. Is he—?'

'He's going to be all right, they think. But it's set him back, probably by weeks. I don't know when we'll see him here in chambers again.'

Angie emptied the last bucket of water down the scullery sink. It was clean enough to show her that she had, at last, scoured all the dirt from all the floors in Polly's house. She'd scrub the sink itself now. Once that was done, there was nothing but making the beds and, given they had duvets instead of blankets, it would take little more than five minutes.

She hadn't expected to want more. Loathing housework and cooking as she had in the bad years at Low Topps, it seemed perverse to go looking for extra tasks now. But she didn't want time to think.

Some days she was sure she ought to go down to Brighton and face Adam and ask outright whether he was responsible for killing his father and mutilating the woman in Essex whom Greg had mentioned. And the child in Scotland.

Then there were other days when all she wanted to do was hide from Adam for ever. If she knew for certain he was guilty, she wouldn't be able to ignore it. If she told anyone else, the police would get involved and she'd find herself back in court, giving evidence against her own son. She could just imagine the awful Trish Maguire haranguing her as she stood in the witness box.

'Are you really trying to persuade His Lordship that your son did not intend to cause fatal harm to you and your husband, and the land itself, when he blocked the vents of your chemical tanks? Can you deny that if he knew enough to do it, he knew what effect it would have? Have you not testified to his post-graduate degrees in chemistry? Are you trying to suggest he didn't know precisely what effect the benzene would have on your land and streams?'

She saw Maguire's beaky face in her nightmares now and when she woke in the mornings. There were times when she felt as though the woman was sucking truth out of her even at this distance of hundreds of miles. She tried to keep Adam right out of her mind to avoid doing anything that might make anyone else suspect. But she was sure Polly knew.

Polly still wouldn't talk, but ever since the first evening when she'd told Angie that Adam had stayed here, there'd been odd looks and even more wordless sympathy than simple widowhood and a failing claim for damages should arouse.

The terrors and regrets had built up in Angie's mind until she felt as though she had to let them out somehow if they weren't to burst her skull apart.

'Are you ill, pet?' Polly's voice shocked her and she turned so fast she sprayed scouring powder all over the draining board.

'No. No. I'm fine. You surprised me; that's all. Sorry. I'll clear this up. And I'm late with lunch. I don't know what I was thinking. I—'

'Shhh.' Polly's voice was as soft as it could be with a dead ewe's lamb. 'Shhh now. It doesn't matter about lunch. But you were keening. What is it that's troubling you so?'

Angie put her hand over her face and then cursed as she felt the biting sharpness of the scouring powder in her eyes. That helped, distracting them both, as she first washed her hands, then rinsed out her eyes with cold, fresh water. Any tears she might have been shedding got mixed up with the water, so they didn't count.

'Come and sit down.'

'I can't, Polly. Bill will be here any minute now, needing food. I hadn't realised it was so late.'

'We can have cheese and apples. Come and sit down and stop being so silly.'

Angie backed away from Polly's criticism. Her whole face felt cold.

'Good,' said Polly, apparently not noticing the withdrawal. 'Now, tell me what this is about. You've not been sleeping and you're not happy. I need to know what the problem is.'

'It's John,' she said, looking away and hoping that would be enough to stop the questions. In the old days it would have been. 'I can't stop thinking about him.'

'I know what mourning is like and it's not this. This is anger. Fear too. What's eating you, Angie? At first I thought it was the damage to Low Topps, or the cancer-risk, or the pollution, but it's none of those. I think it's a person. Are you trying to run away from someone by hiding up here with us?'

'Polly, I can't—' She put her head in her hands.

'Don't you trust me, child?'

I haven't been a child for nearly forty years, she thought as a way of fending off the sad question, and you can't be much more than twelve or fifteen years older than me, in spite of your wild white hair. When we first came to live up here, *I* was the one with all the knowledge and the drive to find out how you could get at all the European money you needed. You wouldn't have called me 'child' then. And you couldn't have managed if it hadn't been for the grants we organised for you.

'Angie!' This time there was urgency in Polly's voice, as well as sadness.

'It isn't you,' she said, remembering her gratitude and her need, and hating the way the ever-threatening rage could make her resent even Polly. 'I'd trust you with my life. But I can't talk about this. I have to—'

The phone rang, a harshly unfamiliar sound in this quiet place. Polly would never leave it to ring unanswered. To her, such a summons meant either someone wanting to spend much-needed money by booking in for bed and breakfast, or that there was an urgent problem to which only she could provide a solution. She pushed herself up from the table and walked with obvious pain to the phone on the dresser.

Angie began to lay the table as quietly as she could. It wasn't possible to avoid listening to Polly's anxious voice.

'Yes. Yes, she's here. Would you like to speak to her?'

Bracing herself, Angie put down the plates she was holding. 'Is it Adam?'

Polly shook her head and held out the receiver. 'A man called Greg.'

Angie took it from her, and tried to think herself back into London and the case as it had been before Adam.

'Greg? What's the news?'

'They want to settle, Ange. I've had Hoffman, the solicitor, on the phone this morning. He wants to arrange a meeting with Maguire and you and me to discuss a settlement.'

'But we've already told them we won't,' she said, sounding as dazed as she felt.

'I know. Which must mean they've found some information or a witness or something that tells them they can't win, so they're ready to offer more than last time. Ange, you've had your chance to tell the judge and the world what they did, so you've done the main thing you wanted. Why not let them pay you off now? We can make sure it's a proper sum, and we can refuse any confidentiality agreements because they're obviously desperate to make an end of it now. That way we can make an enormous public splash with the way they've caved in and admitted their part in killing John.' He broke off, realising that she hadn't said anything for some time. 'Ange! Ange, are you still there?'

'Yes, I'm here. Are you sure it isn't that they've found something that proves *we* can't win?'

'Don't you think they'd wallow in that and string us along until they could make fools of us in court?'

'Would they?' She felt more uncertain than ever.

'Of course. You must see it makes sense, Ange.'

'What would I have to do?'

'Come south again. They want to meet as soon as possible and have suggested either Thursday at 4 p.m. or Friday at 9 a.m. You can make one or other, can't you?'

'I don't know. I suppose . . . Hang on a minute.' She put her hand over the receiver and looked at Polly: 'There aren't any walkers coming before the weekend, are there?'

'No. Not even at the weekend. The next lot are due on Monday.'

'So, would you mind if I went to London again for a meeting on Thursday?'

'If it helps you, Angie, you must go as soon as you want.'

'OK. I'll come.'

'Great. Take an early train on Thursday so we can swot up all the facts we need to really rub their noses in it. Fran'll be pleased. She's been missing you.'

Angie put down the phone, trying to remember how much money she had left. 'Polly, may I ring to book a taxi for the train?'

'I'll take you. Now, there's Bill coming. Lunch. Go and get the cheese from the larder.'

Chapter 19

Trish couldn't find any website for Goforthebrains.com. The Internet wasn't that out-of-date. But her search did turn up a reference to the company in an old financial report illustrated with photographs of some of the main players in the dotcom boom. There were the few real winners, whose businesses had survived and prospered, and there were the rest, including the Goforthebrains.com four. Unfortunately the caption didn't give their names, only that of the company.

She sent an email to Fred asking him to get hold of their details.

Too impatient to do nothing while she waited, she stared at the photograph of the last member of the team, the one who didn't appear in the Pathfinder prospectus for GlobWasMan. He had very short hair, which did nothing to improve a long face with a lantern jaw, oddly set eyes and an ugly nose. He certainly had not transmogrified into Ben Givens. But he could have grown a wild and woolly beard and be Greg Waverly.

The photograph was only eight years old but a young man could change a lot in that time. Trish copied it and moved it to a temporary file on her desktop. Then she scanned in one of the photographs of Greg from the report submitted by Fred Hoffman's enquiry agents.

With the two pictures side by side, she still couldn't be certain they were of the same man, although the setting of the eyes looked similar, as did the large noses with their bulbous nostrils. But the wild hair and woolly beard in the more recent photograph were a dreadful distraction. Trish struggled with the photo-editing software that had come bundled with the computer when she bought it. In the end, she had to send for Hal, who was young enough to find computers as easy to understand as his own body.

He had the beard and most of the hair off Greg's face in no time, then he hovered the cursor over the younger face and dragged it over the older.

'That's it,' Trish said with satisfaction making her feel wrapped in success. 'They *are* the same man.'

'So d'you think he's been working for GlobWasMan all along?'

'Actually I don't. The failed organic food business Fred's investigators found must have been genuine. Bankruptcy's a matter of public record. But once Greg had gone bust the clowns at GlobWasMan must have realised he'd be open to offers to infiltrate FADE for money.'

'They're great ones for that, aren't they?' said Hal, scratching his head. 'D'you think they're all in it? All three of the others, I mean?'

'Haven't a clue,' Trish said. She pointed to the photograph of Ken Shankley. 'But I'd put my money on him as the leader of the plot. He's the one who threatened poor Carl Bianchini, and he headed up the dotcom company as well as GlobWasMan. Fancies himself, too, if you read the blurb in the Pathfinder. I think he's the type who doesn't see why he shouldn't have anything he wants and will think more and more creatively until he gets it. And screw anyone who gets in his way.'

The phone in Trish's pocket bleeped. A text was coming through. She pulled out the phone and saw that David wanted to talk to her before the end of his lunch break.

'I must deal with this, Hal. Thanks. I couldn't have done it without you.'

He blushed a little and found it hard to get out of her room, first backing and then turning round, and at last giving a cross between a salute and a wave from the doorway.

'Hi,' she said when David answered her call. 'I got your text. What's happened?'

'Jay got an A+.' His voice was shrill with triumph. Trish lurched between delight in his enjoyment of someone else's success and gloom at the discovery that Jay was still so important to him.

'That's absolutely brilliant,' she said trying to sound as generous herself. 'I'm really pleased. What did he get it for?'

'*Henry V*. We had essays to do on the responsibilities of the king and what it must have felt like. And he got an A+.' There was a strange sound down the phone, a grunt or a laugh; perhaps even a sigh. 'He must've stayed in the cinema on Friday after all, whatever that manager said to George. Maybe he hid when they were searching.'

'He must have. It's a pity you had to miss the film. How did you do with the essay?'

This time the sound was unmistakably a laugh. 'Oh, I got an A+ too. It was only me and Jay out of the whole year. So we can celebrate tonight. Will you be home in time to see him?'

'That's fantastic. Well done,' she said, trying to keep her voice enthusiastic.

'*Will* you be home in time?'

'I'll try.'

'Great. Got to go. See you later.'

She put the phone back in her pocket, as pleasure in his excitement fought with her reluctance to have Jay as a fixture in the flat any longer. There had been many times when she'd been brought up short by David's guts in tackling what had happened to him, so she shouldn't have been surprised at the way he was hanging on to the friendship. She felt even more ashamed of her own self-protective instincts, but she couldn't shift them.

What everyone needed now was for Rosie Smith to beat her demons, stop drinking, find a way to admire Jay, look after him properly, and free him to let himself use his talents. It didn't seem likely, so he'd go on needing a safety net.

Was four years such a long time? Trish asked herself. The boys would be going to university then. Couldn't she hold her family together – with him in it – for forty-eight more months?

At the moment she couldn't think of a good enough reason to say no.

She rang George to pass on the news, adding that she didn't know how long her settlement negotiations were likely to take and whether she'd be back in time to cook.

'No problem,' he said. 'I haven't got any meetings this afternoon. I can guarantee to be back to welcome them, *and* whip up something suitably glutinous for supper. My other phone's going. See you later.'

Thank God for George, Trish thought, as she pushed domestic details to the back of her mind once more and collected her notes for the encounter with Angie Fortwell.

Chapter 20

Angie's suit didn't feel at all tight as she emerged from the train to find Greg waiting for her.

'Did you have some lunch, Ange? I don't want you fainting in the middle of the meeting.'

No greeting, she thought, or an enquiry about how I am. He's just making sure his property is well fuelled and functioning. Sod him.

'Did you, Ange?'

'Yes. Sandwiches. As soon as I caught the train. What about you?'

He smiled. As his beard moved, she realised she hadn't needed to ask. All the evidence was there.

'I see you did. Whiskers, Greg,' she said, parroting Fran's tactful warning.

He put up a hand, brushed it against the beard, then examined the result. For a second she thought he was blushing.

'Too many tomatoes,' he said. 'They get everywhere.'

Tomatoes? She didn't want to engage in this particular conversation, but the evidence looked too purple for that. More like plums.

'Let's go,' she said aloud.

A few minutes later, they were sitting side by side in a half-empty tube. One or two elderly women with shopping bags avoided eye contact with a few aimless-looking young people, but they were nothing like the angry, shuffling crowds of the rush hour, who had made her journeys to court such an ordeal.

'I had a word with Ben Givens,' Greg said, having got over his embarrassment. 'You know, the barrister I introduced you to at our party.'

'I remember,' she said, thinking, and I remember the way you sent him to drag me back from my one moment of freedom. What did you think I was going to do then? Who did you think I was going to talk to? And what possible damage could I have done?

'When I told him about this summons,' Greg said, totally unaware of her resentment, 'he was sure the only reason must be that Maguire's come up against a flaw in her case. He hasn't worked out what it is yet, but he thinks we should pretend we know. That way we'll look confident enough to get the maximum out of them.'

Angie stared at her reflection in the black window opposite, bisected by the dirty cables strung along the tunnel's wall outside. Her browny-grey hair was tidy but lank and her eyes looked huge and hurt. Like a dying cow's, she thought without any humour at all.

Should she mention Adam? Warn Greg about what Maguire must have found? Or would it be better to lie and protest when the information came out, and pretend the idea of Adam's involvement had never once crossed her mind? Could she do it convincingly? If not, it would be better to confess now.

'Here we are,' he said. 'Brace up, Ange. You look as if you

expect them to walk over you. You've got to be tougher. Else everything we've done will be wasted. Come on!'

She hardened her shoulders and felt pain all down her spine. 'I'll do my best.'

'Great.' He put a big hand on one of her rigid shoulders, but he wasn't nearly as comfortable with touching as Fran, so it just felt awkward: heavy and unpleasant. She wished Fran could've come with them. But Greg hadn't let her.

At least the solicitor's offices weren't as chillingly formal as the courts. Angie left it to him to tell the receptionist who they were and take the lead on the way into the meeting room.

The air inside felt cold, but in the stuffy kind of way you'd never get in the country. The walls were icy blue and the oval conference table was a kind of blond Scandinavian wood, polished like a skating rink. The far side of it was full of people. They looked only vaguely familiar and were all staring at her as though she was a freak who might suddenly take off all her clothes or start throwing things.

Fred Hoffman stood up, and the movement helped make Angie's brain work. She began to recognise the rest. Today Trish Maguire was wearing an unbelievably well-cut jacket of some silky stuff that looked as if it had been made from fibres spun from a rich red stone like carnelian.

The word triggered a memory from a novel read long ago: someone saying 'carnelian heals anger'. If only! Angie knew she was letting her mind ramble only so she wouldn't have to acknowledge the renewed compassion in Maguire's face. But it was so hard to miss Angie had to look away.

Greg met Angie's gaze and beamed smugly. Presumably he thought he was exuding confidence. His beard and bright red lips revolted her even though he'd picked off all the bits and pieces of food caught in the whiskers. Now her mind was latched on to stories read from the past, she couldn't help seeing how the combination made him look like the giant in Adam's favourite collection of nursery rhymes. The one he'd especially liked went 'Fee, fi, fo, fum, I smell the blood of an English man.' An early sign of his interest in killing?

John. Adam. John. Adam. The names were like tennis balls being batted to and fro in her brain while the others were all talking, saying trivial things about how nice to see each other again. Angie felt detached, as though she were floating outside her body. The head that wasn't where she was even talked, like the others, and said all sorts of polite stuff. Then they all stopped and sat down and everyone looked at Trish Maguire. Angie looked down at her, too, from the place where she was floating above the rest.

'It's hard to know how to say this,' Maguire began, smiling from one to the next.

Angie gripped her hands under the table, which brought her back into herself. Greg's beam got even wider. She wanted to yell out a warning, but it was much too late now. Instead she stared straight at Maguire, fighting the pity that looked stickier and stickier with every movement.

'As we showed in court,' Maguire said in the so-ordinary voice that gave no clue to her ruthlessness or power, 'the explosion at the tank farm can only have happened because something was lodged in the vents, blocking the inflow of air. I have now come to understand that it was done deliberately.'

Adam. Adam. Adam. He was once our baby. John was there when he was born. John cradled him when he was still covered in my blood, before they'd even weighed and wiped him. Later on, he played with Adam, taught him, comforted him, spooned in the food. Loved him. No wonder Maguire looks so sorry for me. How much exactly does she know?

'By this couple.' Maguire offered them a photograph of a woman standing beside a man with no head.

Oh, stop it, Angie, she told herself. Of course he has a head. It's just out of the picture.

'Who on earth is she?' said Greg with quite unnecessary aggression.

Trish pushed the printed version of Peterthewalk's photograph of Maryan Fleming and the unidentifiable Barry Stuart nearer to Angie, who looked blind and stupid, which she clearly wasn't.

'Don't you recognise her, Mrs Fortwell?'

'I—' She wouldn't say any more, even though her lips moved.

There hadn't been much colour in her thin, lined face when she'd arrived, but what there had been was gone now. Beside her Greg sat, with the suspicion hardening in his eyes, making him look less squishy-minded, almost as threatening as Ben Givens.

'Of course she wasn't working alone,' Trish went on, smiling at them both. 'There's the man with her, obviously, and—'

'I've never seen her in my life before.' This time Angie's voice was more vigorous, almost challenging, the kind of voice you use when you have something to hide.

'Actually,' Trish said. 'I think you'll find you have. She stayed with you, bed-and-breakfasting, three days before the explosion.'

Angie hunched one shoulder. 'I can't be expected to

remember all the walkers who come to Low Topps. There've been hundreds over the years.'

'I'm sure, but, believe me, she is in your visitors' book – admittedly under a false name. She's told me that her boyfriend was paid to sabotage your tanks.'

'They were never *our* tanks.' Angie looked as though she was explaining something obvious to a fool. 'That's the whole point of all that pre-trial stuff you missed, when we still had Antony Shelley to deal with: they were CWWM's tanks, on what was technically – and actually – their land. Only leased from us.'

'I'm sorry. The tanks beside your land, I should have said.' Trish smiled, in spite of her curiosity about Angie's changing emotions. 'This woman had been told her boyfriend's action would shut down the tank farm. That was all. She's not very bright and she still has no idea it caused the explosion or killed your husband. She believed they were saving a beautiful piece of the north from wicked capitalist exploiters.'

Angie's fingers were twisting round and round each other. Her face was the colour of uncooked pastry and she was biting her upper lip as she stared at the photograph of Maryan Fleming. When she relaxed her jaw, Trish could see the mark of a bruise already spreading above her thin lip. At last she looked up. When she spoke, her voice was tighter even than it had been on the first day in court.

'Have you got a photograph of her boyfriend with his head showing?'

Trish shook her head. 'This is our only one. He called himself Chris Bowles then, but his real name is Barry Stuart. He sounds quite a bit more intelligent, or at least more aware, than she is, and he's fled to New Zealand. The police over there are looking for him now.'

Angie moved but Trish was distracted by Greg, who leaned right across the table, glaring at her, as though he thought he could intimidate her.

'This is a fairy tale. Do you expect anyone to believe it? Have you any evidence they were paid?'

'They got five thousand pounds from one of your old friends from Goforthebrains.com.'

'Don't be ridiculous,' Greg said with so much contempt in his voice that Trish wanted to tell him how much she would enjoy his eventual arrest.

'Oh come on, Mr Waverly,' she said instead. 'You know as well as I do that Ken Shankley paid them, just as he paid you to infiltrate FADE so you could take advantage of Frances Showring and make her urge Mrs Fortwell to bring the case against CWWM.'

'What?' Angie said, looking from one of them to the other.

Trish kept staring at Greg as she went on: 'And there's plenty more, isn't there? There were the people who stole some of CWWM's most dangerous waste and sent it out on the smallest roads in Essex in a truck with wrecked clutch, brakes and back-door locks.'

His face tightened into an expression she couldn't read. Was it surprise that he'd been found out? Or rage? Or genuine disgust at the consequences of his friends' antics? How much had he known?

'That crash led to a woman's feet being amputated. And Mrs Fortwell's husband died,' Trish added to push him, hoping for some honesty at last. 'You never factored in the human cost, did you, Mr Waverly? Just as you never got your sums right in the old days of Goforthebrains.com or your organic food business. It's no wonder you keep failing. Over and over again.'

Trish heard a sotto-voce protest from Robert, but she ignored it while she watched realisation dawning in Angie's eyes.

'Greg, you talked about a woman in Essex with her feet cut off,' Angie said, with horror deepening her voice. 'You knew about it, didn't you? And there was something about a child in Scotland, too. What the hell's going on?'

He pulled a piece of paper out of his pocket and scribbled on the back of it. Trish watched Angie read it and scowl.

'Come on. *What* haven't you been telling me?' she said, crunching the bit of paper into a ball.

'Nothing.' He smiled, but it was a sickly version of his usual beam. 'Ms Maguire's talking right over my head.'

'If that's so,' Trish said, smiling back, 'I'll put it very simply. Your old friends, who are now running GlobWasMan, decided to increase their share of the market in the disposal of hazardous chemical waste. They knew they'd have to get rid of their chief rival, CWWM, and so they've been working to bring down the company in every possible way. Making you encourage Mrs Fortwell to mount her claim was only one of their ideas. And to ensure it worked, they paid Benjamin Givens, the barrister, to give you secret legal help, didn't they?'

Angie looked as though she were examining a field full of diseased livestock, searching for signs of new damage, or corpses. Eventually she stared straight at Greg.

'This explains a lot.' Her voice had all the repelling intent of barbed wire.

'No, it doesn't.' Greg swung round in his seat so that he

was talking to her alone. 'Ben helped us because he was so ashamed of having taken money to act for a chemical waste company in the past. He wanted to make amends by ensuring you won your case and got compensation for the farm and for John's death. Which is what Fran and I wanted too. You mustn't believe this . . . this evil story.'

Greg hitched himself even closer to Angie so that his beard was almost touching her ear.

'Ange!'

She pulled away, actually moving her chair, and Trish knew she'd get everything she wanted now.

David smelled the toffee sauce George had made to go with the caramel pancakes and ice cream and hoped Trish would be home soon. It was his favourite pudding and he was ravenous.

He and Jay had had a toasted sandwich each as soon as they got in, but George was being amazingly mean and not letting them have a second one. He wanted them to have enough appetite for the braised steak that was also smelling pretty good, and then for the pancakes. David knew he and Jay could eat four sandwiches each and still have room.

He sneaked a look at his watch. It was only half past six. Trish might not be back for hours yet. He sighed.

'Concentrate, David. Jay's way ahead of us both,' said George, who was keeping the Scrabble score, as usual.

David looked at the seven tiles in his rack, then back at the board. He could see two places where he could get at least twenty-five points, which was more or less the minimum he allowed himself these days. In the old days, when he'd still been a child, he'd been happy with as little as ten. Now that would be a humiliatingly small score, so it was good he had two opportunities for more than double. But both Jay and George could still block him.

Jay mouthed 'Yes!', then leaned forwards to add 'que' to 'to' to make 'toque', a word George had used the last time they played and which happened to wipe out one of David's two chances. Then Jay stood up and said he had to go to the toilet.

Knowing George's views on what words you were supposed to use and when, David hoped he wasn't going to correct Jay. It was always a mistake, because it made him angry, but the grown-ups did it a lot of the time without even noticing the effect they were having. Although sometimes they grinned as if they thought they were giving him a present with it. Luckily tonight George didn't even blink. Instead he looked at the letters Jay had just put down and said:

'You are a nasty little toerag, you know. I had my eye on that triple.'

Jay laughed, an ordinary cheerful OK kind of laugh, and walked off towards the bathroom attached to David's bedroom.

'Now, what on earth am I going to do?' George said, leaning on one elbow. 'You two are getting too damned good for my liking. I'm not sure how much longer I can go on risking my supremacy like this.'

'It's the natural order of things, I'm afraid.' David was quoting something George had said to Trish only a few days ago.

'You may be challenging my supremacy, old boy,' George said, looking up at him with a warning kind of smile, 'but I'm damned if I'll let you get all pompous on me. Well done, by the way, for getting such a great mark for the English essay. I'm really proud of you. So's Trish.'

David pushed his right hand through his hair, which was suddenly itching. George hardly ever praised him like this and he didn't really know what to say. A joke would be best, but he couldn't think of one. George wasn't looking at him, so maybe he didn't have to say anything. If it had been Trish, he would've had to; she was a great one for talking about stuff.

'What's up, David?' George said after a while.

'Nothing. Why?'

'You're all strung up and anxious. What's the problem?'

'Nothing,' he said, wondering why there wasn't much noise from his bathroom. Jay usually crashed about wherever he went. And George had at last managed to persuade him to flush the loo each time he used it.

'Incidentally,' George said, smiling, 'I ordered a DVD of Olivier's *Henry V* for you last Saturday so you could watch it in peace, but it's taking rather a long time to arrive.'

David stared down at the busy Scrabble board, thinking about how he liked knowing George was here, ready to help whenever it was needed but not getting in the way when it wasn't.

'Of course you may not want to bother with it now you've written the essay,' George added.

'No,' David said, looking up at him. 'I *do* want to see it.'

'Great. Now stop distracting me and let me get to grips with this board.'

David sat back, watching him and hoping he'd miss the one excellent blocking opportunity that was left. George always took for ever to make his move. David's fingers inched towards his i-Pod, which was lying on the floor just beside him, but George usually got irritated if you didn't give your full attention to whatever you were supposed to be doing with him.

Just before impatience made him want to screech 'Hurry up for fuck's sake', George put three tiles on the board, taking the other possible triple. Then he looked round.

'What d'you think Jay's up to?' he said. 'Hasn't he been rather a long time in the bog?'

'No idea.'

'I'll go and make sure there's nothing wrong,' said George, 'while you see what you can do to claw back my enormous lead.'

David nodded. Between them they'd left him with only a pathetic nineteen for a score, so he jumbled up his letters looking for a different word to leap out at him. George had taught him ages ago, when they first started to play together, that if you looked long enough you could nearly always find something better than your first attempt.

He turned round the score sheet and saw he was thirty points behind Jay and eight behind George. What he needed now was to get all his letters out in one go and so win an extra fifty. That might be enough to keep him ahead till the end of the game.

Without George to disapprove, he plugged in his i-Pod so the music could help him think, then stared down at the board till his face started to ache. He rubbed his hands over it, but that didn't help. He couldn't see any existing word he could extend. And his letters weren't going to make any single word on their own, even if he could find somewhere to put it. He blinked in case that helped him see better.

A heavy thud reached him through the beat of the music. He pulled out one earpiece to listen. There was nothing more, except the clock in the kitchen, ticking even louder than usual. He looked up. If he leaned back he could just see the clockface. It was nearly ten to seven. What could be taking so long? Jay must have been in the bathroom at least fifteen minutes now, and he never stayed that long, even when he was having a crap. David was getting to his feet when his bedroom door opened and Jay rushed out clutching his shirt in a bundle against his bare chest. There were drops of water all over him.

Seeing David, he pulled the door shut. 'I was sick. He's cleaning up. I've got to go.'

He was already past the fireplace and on his way to the front door.

'Wait,' David said. 'You need a towel. And if you've been sick, you ought to have—'

'Gotta go.' Jay wrenched open the door and hurled himself out, pulling it back behind him with another almighty bang.

David thought about going to help George, then decided not to. He'd only get in the way and there was nothing like someone else's sick to make you want to upchuck yourself.

The clock kept ticking. It was the only noise, except for the crackling of the wood in the fireplace. George was being amazingly quiet too. And he hadn't come out to get any cloths or bleach or anything from the kitchen. David stood up again, then slumped back into the sofa. It was silly to think something could be wrong. Why would it be?

The clock went on. The ticks were like being hit with a hammer. He couldn't go on waiting. He walked extra quietly, as though there was something in his bedroom that mustn't know he was coming, which was silly, so he made himself crash open the door like he usually would have.

George was lying on the floor with blood pouring out of a slash in his arm, making his sleeve look dark brown instead of grey. His face was grainy and white, like washing powder, and he was breathing as if he had something stuffed up his nose. David plumped on his knees, reaching for his phone. Then he saw it: his old clasp knife sticking out of George's chest in a direct line from the arm slash.

David's fingers slipped as he tried to press in the number for Trish's phone. But he made himself do it. He only got her voicemail. So he rang her clerk on the chambers number. Steve said she was out at a meeting. There wasn't time to wait and leave a message, so David clicked off, then forced 999 into the phone.

They took ages too and they wanted his name and address and phone number, then asked which emergency service he wanted. He shouted at them that George was stabbed and bleeding. Then they had all sorts of more questions to ask and he answered them as best he could. George was looking worse and worse and more blood was leaking out round the knife all the time.

They wouldn't let David go. He said he had to phone Caro. So they wanted to know who she was. He clicked off and phoned her. While he was waiting for her to answer, he looked around his room and saw all his stuff had been chucked about all over the floor and the bed. His computer screen was hanging off the desk from its cables, and all the drawers were open.

'David? Hi.' Caro's voice made things in his head slow down a bit. 'How are you?'

His eyes felt scratchy and wet, as if he was going to cry. But he couldn't do that. His voice wouldn't work. Caro said his name again. He pushed his throat muscles together inside and at last he managed to make a noise, but it was only a kind of gasp. Then he got some words out:

'Jay's stabbed George. He's on the floor. I don't know what to do. I can't get Trish. It's my fault. I took too long coming in. I don't know what—'

'Hold on, David.' He could hear more in her voice now. It wasn't panic but it wasn't soothing either. He needed her here, not telling him what to do down the phone. 'Listen. Are you listening, David?'

'Yes.'

'The first thing is to get an ambulance. I want you to—'

'I've done that. They're on their way. And the police.'

'Good. Well done. That's the most important thing. Where's Jay? Is he still with you?'

'No. He ran off. Before I knew what he'd done. Or I would have stopped him; tried to stop him.'

'We'll deal with that later. Is George still breathing?'

'Yeah. And bleeding. Not conscious.'

'Right. Can you hear the ambulance yet?'

He strained, but all he could hear was the kitchen clock, beating out the time while George was bleeding to death.

'Not yet.'

'OK. It shouldn't be too long. Did you pull out the knife?'

'No. I saw on telly that makes the bleeding worse, but I—'

'Well done! You've done everything exactly right so far, David. Now, what—?'

He stopped listening as he caught the sound in the distance: a swooping kind of wheep-beep, wheep-beep.

'They're coming. The ambulance.'

'Good. Then I want you to ring off now, find out where they're taking George and ring me back. OK? I'll be waiting for your call. Then I'll ring Trish, so you don't have to worry about that. Then I'll come and get you.'

'I'm going with him in the ambulance. I've got to.'

'Fine. But call me as soon as you know where you're going. And don't forget to lock up. It's easy to stop doing ordinary things with something bad like this.'

There was a great banging on the front door. He ran to open it and grabbed the first green-suited man who came through.

'It's this way. Come on. Quick. He's dying.'

Angie was rehearsing in her mind the words she would pick to ask Greg for the truth at last while she straightened out the note on which he'd written: 'Don't accuse me here. Save it for later and calm down. Otherwise we'll get nothing.'

Tempted to throw it back at him, she turned the paper over and saw it was a restaurant bill for one person, covering lobster soup and a fillet steak at a huge price. She checked the date. It was today's.

So the purplish scraps in his beard hadn't been plum after all, let alone tomato as he'd claimed, but steak. He wasn't even an honest vegetarian. The bastard! The faking bastard!

She looked up ready to give him back the invoice and show him just what she thought of his lies when the receptionist who'd shown them into the room came back and whispered into Maguire's ear.

All the colour drained out of her face. Angie was on her feet, forgetting Greg and the fact that she'd ever hated this woman.

'What is it?'

Maguire looked at her in a daze she recognised.

'George,' she said. 'My partner . . . he's been stabbed. They think he's . . . I'm sorry, I have to go. Robert, will you take over?'

Now she'll know what it feels like, Angie thought, not listening to the sidekick saying he thought they'd finished anyway. She wanted to say something kinder to Maguire but knew she mustn't hold her up now. She could always write.

The receptionist had gone on to talk to Robert Anstey. He looked across the shining table at Greg.

'Apparently the police are waiting for you outside, Mr Waverly,' he said. 'They're keen to talk. I'll take you to meet them.'

So it *is* true, Angie thought, as all the old terrifying magma rose in her brain.

Her hands clenched as she fought down the words she wanted to fling at him. Looking into his misaligned brown eyes in search of something to explain what he'd done, some capacity for evil, she found nothing but selfishness and surprise. Had he really thought they'd get away with it?

His eyes fell and he shuffled away beside the impeccably dressed barrister who was acting as his jailer. He hadn't even got the balls to apologise for the terrible human cost of what he'd done for his greedy friends.

Chapter 21

George had thin tubes plugged in all over him, and a wider, corrugated one like an albino elephant's trunk over his mouth. His eyes were closed and his skin was greyish-yellow. His bed was surrounded by humming whirring machines, and the sheets were neatly folded down around his waist. Green patches were stuck to his chest, with some of the tubes sprouting out of them. And there was a long dressing covering his right arm between the elbow and the shoulder.

There were other people in the Intensive Care Unit, sitting by the beds of more half-dead patients, who were breathing through machines, while nurses worked quietly at the bank of desks in the centre. One of them got up and walked to the bed at the far end of the unit. She made no noise as she went. At the bedside, she checked on the patient and made a note on his chart. She came towards Trish, who realised she was staring only when the woman smiled at her.

'Try to talk to him,' she said with a gentleness that didn't hide the criticism. 'It's what he needs now. We think he can hear and it would help if you could stimulate his brain. Try.'

'But it's so quiet in here,' Trish whispered. 'I don't want to disturb—'

'You won't. So long as you don't shout, you won't hurt the others. And it's worth touching him too. Any sensory stimulus could help now.' She moved away, as though to give Trish privacy. But there were no curtains. The staff needed to see everything that happened to all their patients.

'Caro's taken David home,' she said laboriously to George's unresponsive face. She laid her hand on his, taking care to avoid the drip's needle, which had been inserted into one of the veins. 'He did so well to get you here. I feel awful that it was so long before I knew what had happened. And when I saw him, rigid and white-faced, holding on to all his feelings until it was safe to hand over the responsibility, I could see how he blamed himself.'

She licked her lips. This wasn't coming out right.

'He did really well,' she said again. 'I think you can feel very proud of his resourcefulness and calm under pressure. He made his report to me like a pro, giving the facts and none of the feelings, telling me what the doctors had said to him. Caro was standing behind him as he did it, both hands on his shoulders. And when he'd finished telling me everything, he just sagged back against her, as though all his muscles had given up the effort of holding his bones together.'

That wasn't right either. She couldn't remember any anatomy. Did muscles hold the body together? Or was that tendons? Or skin? That was the biggest organ of the body, she remembered from a quiz night at David's school. Weird to think of skin as an organ. This wasn't helping George.

Try again, Trish. Think of something to say, anything. They can make him breathe artificially and feed him through these tubes and deal with the body's wastes, but they can't make his brain keep working. You have to do that.

She felt the first tears leak hotly on to her skin. The shock and the need to keep David going and show him how well he'd done and make sure Caro could keep him safe while she did this, had kept her from feeling anything else. Now, she looked at George and felt it all.

There was so much she could have said if she'd been sure he would hear it. And that no one else would. She wanted to tell him about all the things she wished she'd never said in their ten years together, to apologise for all the times she'd misunderstood what he was doing and been angry with him, and for all the times she'd let him down, or not been there when he needed solace, all the clumsiness and irritability and insensitivity.

He looked diminished. Even his hair had lost its spring and the endearing wildness he'd fought so hard to control.

She should have phoned Selina to tell her what had happened. But that would have to wait. As would the decision about whether to alert the unknown Henry. If George were dying, his brother would surely want the chance to come and make his peace.

That's for later, Trish reminded herself. She was supposed to be talking to George, not shuffling through her own thoughts. It was never usually this difficult to talk; there was always something she wanted to tell him, or ask.

'The meeting I was in when David tried to get me,' she said, pulling the information out from behind her terror, 'was about settling the CWWM case. You don't know about that yet. But we found the people who caused the explosion. When I told Angie about the sabotage, she first looked stricken; then when I told her who the saboteurs were and who'd paid them, she was transfigured. I didn't think of it at the time; now I'm wondering if she thought it could've been her son who did it.'

This was stream-of-consciousness stuff. Trish hadn't formulated the idea about Adam Fortwell; it had come out of nowhere. It was as though her mind was making links and connections everywhere to weave a kind of safety net between her fears and reality.

'Anyway, whether it was that or not, she's agreed to withdraw the claim. It's rough on Don Bates that he won't get any of his costs back, but it does mean he avoids having to pay damages. Which, given Rylands v. Fletcher, is more than he could've expected at the beginning.'

This is so boring, she thought. How can I expect to spur George's brain into wanting to go on living with this sort of work stuff? Maybe I should talk about Henry. No, because he didn't want to remember, didn't want to be back in his 8-year-old self, fighting for survival. His brain and body need everything they've got to fight this battle, not remember the old one. Better just tell him the truth.

'George. I need you. David needs you.' She felt the trail of tears all the way to her chin and wiped the back of her hand under it to catch them. 'Antony said to me the other day that taking the sabbatical ten years ago made me human; it wasn't the sabbatical. It was meeting you. I know things weren't always easy for you either. I was spiky too.

'There were times when I felt you were bullying me; then others when I thought you hated me, when I couldn't understand why you kept coming to the flat when everything I did seemed to torment you, and I tried never to do today the thing you'd hated yesterday, but the thing always changed.

'I tried to be what you wanted; it was ages before I

realised you wanted me, the real me, not the me who would fit into the pattern you seemed to be telling me was the only one you could bear. It wasn't till I stopped lopping off bits of myself to fit what I thought you wanted that everything started to work. We wasted so much time making each other unhappy; but it's been so good these last few years. Don't run out on me now.'

The words dried up. Unlike her tears. She couldn't see anything now except the wet fog between her and the world. A hand touched her.

'Sorry. Mustn't stop talking.' She swallowed hard and began again, trying to be tougher, more optimistic. 'So, what I thought we'd do when you're convalescing is rent a house somewhere quiet and gorgeous. Maybe by the sea in England; maybe somewhere warmer. We always talked about seeing Sicily. Maybe we should get somewhere there. It sounds—'

The hand gripped more tightly. She turned. It was the nurse.

'We've got to change his drip,' she said. 'And then we're going to close the ward for the night. You ought to go home and get something to eat. I know we told you to talk, but it won't help him if you exhaust yourself. Can you stand?'

Of course I can, Trish thought, then found herself staggering. Pins and needles made her legs useless. The nurse put a strong hand under her elbow until she was steady again.

Trish walked stiffly away. She knew she couldn't eat, but if they needed the ward emptied of visitors, she'd do her part. She'd do whatever it took to help George hang on.

When she reached the alcohol-gel dispenser near the doors, she pumped out an extra-big pool and rubbed it over and between each finger, under her rings, around her cuticles; everywhere bacteria might lurk.

'Trish,' said a voice she knew.

'Antony?' She looked away from her fingers and saw him sitting in a wheelchair near the double doors. There was heavy shadow in his corner, but she'd have known him anywhere.

'I heard what had happened to George and came down.'

'But you had an embolism. You're—'

'Not dying this time either.' He laughed a little, with a strange, tense teetering sound unlike anything she'd heard ever from him. 'They caught it before it did anything too awful to my brain or heart. But I'm not supposed to walk yet. They agreed to get a porter to bring me down here to see if I could help George.'

'No one can help, except the medical staff. And time.'

'And you. You were talking as though only your voice could hold him here.'

'That's what they said I had to do.' But it may not be enough.

She couldn't articulate the last bit; it mattered too much.

Antony held out his hand, but she didn't want anyone to touch her now, so she stayed where she was.

'Trish, I'm—' He wiped his hand over his forehead, as though he was sweating with tension. Or fear. 'I never realised you loved him that much.'

She looked at him, determined not to let out any more tears. Making a huge effort, she said:

'I did.'

Chapter 22

Adam hadn't wanted her to come to his lab, so Angie was waiting for him outside the Pavilion. She'd never been to Brighton before and had assumed its chief landmark would be an enormous, glittering palace, but it wasn't. Set in grass on a kind of traffic island, it was surprisingly low built and painted a pale mud colour like a particularly dreary kind of mushroom. It didn't help that the thick grey sky was dripping the nastiest sort of drizzle over everything or that she'd had another terrible night.

Greg had been arrested, along with Ken Shankley and the young woman in Trish Maguire's photograph. Angie'd phoned Fran to try to explain why she was never coming back to the flat. And Fran had wanted to know all sorts of things Angie couldn't tell her. She just didn't know enough. Then she'd found the cheapest possible hotel in the grottiest bit of Earls Court and phoned Adam to set up this meeting.

Shivering in the rain now, she hoped he wasn't going to be much later. She hadn't brought an umbrella, and the drizzle might feel soft but it was still wet. As she shrugged her shoulders to try to shift the ache, she rubbed both hands up under her hair and felt the wetness run all over them.

'Angie!'

She whirled round and saw her son, dressed in jeans and a full-length mac with a beautiful blue scarf draped around his neck. He was carrying an enormous golfing umbrella.

'Come on under here. You're soaked. You're mad, you know! Why didn't you go in?'

'I'm not sure,' she said, looking round at the open door to the Pavilion. 'I thought . . . Oh, I don't know: penance maybe. Can we have some breakfast?'

'Haven't you had any? What is this?'

And so she told him, standing there in front of him, with the rain pouring down over her face, who had killed his father and why.

He frowned at her, puzzled, trying to understand, then shook his head. 'Why did you have to come to tell me all this? Why not write?'

'Because I couldn't be sure you'd open the letter,' she said. 'And you needed to know. And because . . . because—'

At last he saw it. 'Because you thought it might have been me?'

Her head drooped. She couldn't go on looking at him. She shook all over, freezing cold, not sure whether to admit it or excuse herself or leave him to think whatever he needed. 'I'm so so sorry. I should've known better. I—'

She felt his hand cupping her elbow.

'Come on, Mum. We need to get you out of this wet and eating something hot.'

Half an hour later, with a huge mugful of strong tea inside her and half a plateful of bacon, eggs and sausages, she watched him take off his spectacles and polish them. She'd talked herself right out and felt limp but purged.

'I still don't understand why you never told him how

much you hated life on the farm,' Adam said. 'I've kind of grasped why you thought it would be disloyal to tell me, but why not share it with him?'

'Because there wasn't anything he could do about it. We'd poured everything into the bloody place; we had no money, except what was tied up in it. We'd been trying to sell for years, but never had any offers that came anywhere near what we needed – or had spent. I had to make the best of it. Do everything I could to avoid heaping my . . . my misery on to him.'

'But *why*? He was a grown-up. He could've taken it. You were only there because of him. He should have been told.'

She picked up a piece of cold sausage in her fingers, then dropped it again and wiped her hand on her napkin.

'This is what I could never get you to understand,' she said, meeting his angry gaze with difficulty. 'We were only there because of me. Because I'd lost my temper with the bank.'

'I don't understand.' He didn't look as though he cared either, turning to call over his shoulder to the waiter for more tea.

Angie clasped her right shoulder and rotated the joint. It didn't help, leaving her to think she might hurt like this for ever.

'You were fourteen months old,' she said, looking past his adult features to the squidgy pink baby she'd had to hand over every morning before crushing herself into the tube to get to the bank. 'I'd been back at work since six weeks after you were born, leaving you with the nanny. Every day, I had to pretend I wasn't a mother. It was the only way you could make it in the City then. Perhaps it still is; I don't know. I hated doing it, but it seemed important.'

'More than me?' he asked in a detached voice, as though it didn't really matter.

'Of course not,' she said with a snap. 'Which is why you had the best nanny we could find; she was so good in fact that you much preferred her ministrations to mine.'

'I don't remember that.'

'Good. Anyway, we came to bonus time at the bank. Even though I'd done just as well as the men on the team, put in the same hours, stayed just as late when all I wanted to do was be at home with you, made as much money, they gave me only 10 per cent of what the nearest equivalent man got.' She paused, bringing the memories into focus. 'Donald Mackenzie-Bates-Stuart. Arrogant, pompous as his triple-barrelled surname, and not nearly as hardworking as he pretended. But he said the right things, and went to the football games, and went drinking with anyone useful higher up the ladder so they knew he was one of them. Whereas all I wanted was to get back to you. They thought I had babysick on my mind if not my suits and that made me an alien.'

'What happened?'

'When I heard about his bonus, I lost it and screamed and yelled about their stinking chauvinist monstrous behaviour. I can see their terrified faces now, as they backed away from me.'

'You mean you were really screaming?' A smile she hadn't seen for years was lighting up Adam's face. 'Literally?'

'Yes. And picking up files and flinging them around the office.' She smiled back, well into the present again. The past definitely seemed like a foreign country. 'They sent for John, poor John, who was already leading a team and doing brilliantly. He was as embarrassed as you can imagine, but he didn't let it stop him. He ignored the lot of them, put his arms round me, kissed my head and said: "Hello, Angie-darling. Let's get you out of here."'

The waiter brought two more mugs of tea, which made a helpful distraction.

'He got doctors and lawyers involved, and negotiated a big payoff for me. We talked about what we should do and decided to look for a farm to buy. At first it was wonderful: we were happy; the place was gorgeous; you thrived in a way you never had in London.'

She paused, thinking of it and how she'd felt and how John had looked as though the lifting of the burden of her distress had liberated him to be the man he should always have been, the man she'd had glimpses of on some of those long happy drives.

'I thought we were in heaven.'

Adam looked as though he was going to protest, so she hurried on with the rest of it.

'Then it began to go wrong. We discovered how little we knew. You grew up to understand and hate the isolation. We began to lose money. The work got harder. We got older. It was like a battle, every day. We fought the weather and the sheep diseases and the mad constricting laws, and failed. And in the end John died because we were there, because he'd left his own successful career for me.'

'Or because your hysteria gave him a safe exit,' Adam said with a dryness she'd never heard from him. 'Come on, Mum. Don't look so blank. Did it never occur to you? You're not stupid. You must have thought of it.'

'Thought of what?'

'No man who likes his job is ever going to do anything as final as resign just because his wife can't hack it.'

Angie stared at him.

'*Think.*'

'You're wrong, Adam. You never understood his generosity or his grit or—'

'Or his need to be top dog all the time.'

Wanting to protest, she couldn't make the words come, as though something in her knew what he meant and wouldn't let her pretend any longer.

'I know what life in those City jobs is like,' he went on, leaning forwards in his determination to make her accept what he was saying. 'You're at the mercy of everyone: the man above you, your uppity subordinates, your angry needy clients, the regulators, the press. He must have absolutely hated every moment of it, but, being the man he was, he couldn't admit it. Your crack-up gave him the way out he needed.'

With a tremendous mental effort, the equivalent of heaving four immense hay bales on to the tractor in one go, Angie forced herself to see the story from Adam's perspective.

'And you,' he added, 'being the martyr I always said you were, blamed yourself.'

'I don't know . . . How can you—?'

'You never discussed it, did you? You never asked him why he did what he did after you lost your temper in the bonus row?'

She shook her head, beyond speech now.

'Think what a difference it could've made if you had. To all of us.'

The waiter was behind the little bar, making espresso for someone amid a cloud of steam as Angie struggled with herself, and her past, and her son. Her nails were digging into the palms of her hands and her teeth were clamped on a chunk of the inside of her cheek.

'What?' he said, with an aggression that made it all harder to say what needed to be said at last.

'Adam, say you're right ... although it doesn't make any difference to the past now ... but say you're right: is it too late?'

'For us?' The beginnings of another smile softened the muscles around his eyes. 'Who knows? We can only try. And see.'

Trish came back from the lavatory to find a man who looked like George's ghost standing at the foot of his bed, staring at his unresponsive face. At the sound of her step he looked round.

'Trish? You must be Trish.'

'I am.'

'I got your email.'

'Henry.' It wasn't a question. She knew he couldn't be anyone else. She'd found his tables-selling website and clicked on the contact button to send a message telling him what had happened.

'Yes. I'm not sure why I came, what you think I can do. Why did you send for me?'

'I didn't. I thought you should know what had happened to George in case you wanted to come. I thought seeing him might help you to for—' At the look in his eyes, she stopped.

'Forgive him?' he said.

She noticed his broad stubby scarred hands were gripping the rail at the end of the bed as tightly as Jay's had when he'd been staring at his mother.

Trish looked from Henry's face to George's. This wasn't a time for tact. There might not be any time.

'No. I thought it might help you to forgive yourself. That's always harder.'

He turned his face away, as though the sight of her was unbearable.

'Isn't that why hiding inside one's rage and hate is so much easier?' she said, needing him to see what he'd been doing.

'I don't know. Does it matter now? Look at him: it's too late for either of us. I'd better go.' He found a smile from somewhere and looked even more like a thinner, rubbed-out version of George. 'Thank you for trying.'

Trish knew what she wanted to say but she wasn't sure she'd get the words out before she started crying again. Gripping her own hands together, she tried and failed. He looked at her with something that might have been kindness and walked away.

Epilogue

'And Ken Shankley has now been charged,' Trish said to George's unresponsive face nearly a week after Henry had gone home. She'd given up expecting to see him again. 'Which is more than any of us expected. I don't know whether they'll ever get a conviction, but there will be a trial.'

She paused to look at George's face. But there were still no signs of awareness.

'They're still trying to find Barry Stuart, but he seems to have disappeared. New Zealand may have been a decoy destination. But he probably doesn't matter all that much because Greg Waverly is apparently singing like a canary now. Angie Fortwell will see justice of a kind. And so will Don Bates of CWWM.'

David was sitting on the opposite side of the bed. He was looking a bit better, but the terror and guilt of the last week had marked him, perhaps for ever. Trish caught his eye and smiled. His lips twitched slightly in response, which was progress.

There was some progress with George too. He had been promoted from the Intensive Care Unit to the High Dependency Ward once he'd started to breathe on his own again. According to one of the nurses, this meant the doctors no longer thought he would die.

Henry hadn't come back, but Selina was often here. She couldn't make herself talk into the vacuum of George's unconsciousness, but she did come every other day.

'Other things are going right for Angie too. Don Bates has persuaded his board to rent large chunks of her land,' Trish went on, trying to sound cheerfully conversational and not as though she was having to force herself to talk. Her throat felt as though she had swallowed a tube of sandpaper. 'She's written me a kind letter, asking about you, and filling me in on all the news. Apparently CWWM are developing a new organic way of decontaminating polluted ground, but it needs extensive testing before it can be marketed. Low Topps Farm turns out to be the ideal place. Which is a kind of irony when you think about it.'

She paused and looked at George's face, then up at David's.

'Did something move?' she asked. David shook his head, his eyes still like black pools of despair. 'I'm sorry to be boring on about the case, but they say it'll help him come back if we talk; and it's hard to think of things to say, except what we've been doing and I've run out of home stuff.'

'I know.' David's eyes closed briefly. 'I've told him all about school and rowing club, which is just the same as your work; and what I'm going to cook for him when he comes home; and . . . all that kind of thing.'

Trish waited. David seemed to be hovering on the brink of something else.

'And how sorry I am,' he whispered, as though the words burned his mouth as they came out and if he said them quietly it might mitigate the pain. 'If I hadn't made friends with Jay and made you let me bring him home all the time, it wouldn't have happened; if I hadn't introduced Jay to Scrabble, it wouldn't have happened; if I hadn't taken so long—'

'Hush, David. None of that's true. You did not cause this. It is not your fault.'

His lips set in stubborn parallel lines she recognised from the mirror.

'George isn't going to die. Not now.' She tried to smile, although her eyes were betraying her again and leaking yet more sticky, demeaning tears. 'And if we go on talking we'll bring him back properly. We *will*, David.'

He got up abruptly and moved to the far end of the ward, then out through the heavy swing doors. Trish turned back to the bed, fighting the irrational fear that her switch of attention might have caused a relapse.

'And you know, I have a feeling Don Bates might know more about her than he let on. They're the same sort of age and in some ways the same type. But I don't suppose I'll ever be in a position to ask.'

She looked across at the far wall of the ward, where charts and warnings about hygiene were pinned up in orderly rows. It was odd to be talking like this without getting any reaction. In court, she'd often had to make speeches as long as any of these sessions with George, but that was different. When opposing counsel didn't interrupt with objections or points of law, she'd have the judge nodding every so often and making notes. She always knew in court that she was being heard, even when she was sure she wouldn't get the result she wanted. Here, only the passing nurses, who didn't care, knew what she was saying.

And she had no idea whether she'd get the right result.

'I've been wondering, you know, George,' she added before she noticed the change of subject, 'whether it's wrong to try to make your life as near perfect as it can be just for you and your family and forget the webs connecting you to the rest of the world. I can't work out whether you ought to share, even if you know newcomers may be so damaged and dangerous they'll ruin it for themselves as well as you. What do you think?'

There was no reply, of course. She looked around the ward and saw no one else listening to her either, so there was no reason not to articulate her current obsessions about the way she'd let Jay into their lives and failed to listen to the selfish fears that had turned out to be so reasonable.

In her peripheral vision Trish saw another visitor appear and pull a chair up beside the equally silent inhabitant of a bed on the opposite side of the ward. She looked more carefully and saw it was a woman, heavily veiled and wearing flowing robes.

Time to change the subject again. But to what? All the most urgent words in her mind were unsayable. She couldn't mention Jay by name in George's hearing, or say how Caro was keeping them up to date with news of the police's handling of his case. He was in secure accommodation again so at least he couldn't attack anyone else, but it would be many months before he came to trial. The precise charges he'd face would depend on what happened to George now.

Trish gripped the edges of her seat, holding in everything she mustn't even let herself think in case it all sounded in her voice. She tried to think of Jay as he'd been when he'd run from the police in case they were going to use him to accuse George of unspeakable crimes, and again the day he'd come to the flat after Darren had beaten him up, and again how he'd looked as he'd waited to visit his mother, sitting beside the pathetic bouquet he'd collected for her. Trish thought if she could fasten on the vulnerability and not the violence, the generosity and not the fatal resentment, she might find a way to stop hating him.

She opened her mouth to spout one more tedious narrative then stopped herself, sure that something was different about George's face. The skin looked less slack and his colour was better. She looked over her shoulder for a nurse, and a short brisk Irish woman came to find out what she needed.

'Something's happening.'

The nurse took a few moments to check, then said kindly but without excitement: 'Facial muscles often twitch, in a kind of mini-spasm. I expect that's what you saw. But we'll keep an eye on him. You're doing a great job. Ah, here's your son again. He's brought you a drink.'

Trish loathed the wishy-washy hospital coffee David offered her, but she took it with murmured thanks to cover his tacit apology as much as the tall cardboard cup. He went back to his seat.

'I've been thinking Sicily might be tricky for your convalescence and wondered about the States, the west coast, maybe. Brilliant doctors, fantastic weather, glorious beaches. What about it?'

There was a definite movement in George's face and his right hand clenched suddenly. Trish and David looked at each other across the white cotton bedclothes. She put the tall cardboard cup on the bedside locker and stood by the bed, stroking his forehead.

'George! George!' She let her voice rise from the level at which it couldn't disturb any of the other patients. The veiled woman looked round. Understanding what was happening, she bowed her head in a graceful gesture of encouragement. 'George? It's Trish. And David's here too. George!'

At last his heavy eyelids opened, then closed again. Something squeezed in her chest, almost stopping her own breathing. Then his eyes opened once more. His head moved very slightly towards her.

'Trish?'

'Yes, George, it's me.' She fitted one of her hands into his, thumb against thumb.

'Accident,' he said. His voice was hoarse, and using it seemed to hurt him.

'Not exactly,' she said gently, still holding on to his hand. 'But you're on the mend now. You're in hospital and everything's going to be all right.'

'No.' The painful voice croaked again. He licked his lips, tasting them, almost like someone experimenting with a new prosthesis. 'Accident. The boy didn't mean to do it.'

Trish and David looked at each other.

'Messing about with David's stuff. Had the old knife open. Said his name. Cross. Like you said, arrogant. Probably shouted. Gave him a shock. Grabbed his shoulder too. Must have thought I was going to hit him. Whirled round. Slit my arm. Then it went in here. So easy.' He was patting his front now, as though he expected to find the knife still sticking out. 'Didn't mean it. Not his fault.'

David buried his head in the blankets and howled out his relief. George's free hand fumbled for his head. Trish watched him stroke the untidy rough black hair. Then he looked back at her and his lips moved. No sound emerged. Her lip-reading wasn't good enough to guess what he wanted.

'What, George? What is it?'

'Don't go away.'

She felt like following David's example. Instead she tightened her grip on George's hand.

'I'm not going anywhere.'